A STIRRING TALE OF AN AGE
WHEN FAITH AND MAGIC FOUGHT FOR A WORLD

In the earliest days of Christianity, the old magics still had power, and the world was ruled by pagan gods. The young leaders of the Church were driven by their faith to supplant the old ways with the light of God's holy word. THE LAST RAINBOW is a spellbinding saga of that half-forgotten age of Celtic twilight, when the ancient world and the new faith that would transform it coexisted for a brief moment in the ruins of a mighty empire.

A powerful tale of passion and devotion, it is the story of two young lovers—one who would become a saint and the other who would lead her people to a miraculous destiny—who found a power greater than either could have imagined that transcended both their worlds.

Praise for Parke Godwin's FIRELORD . . .

"With its superb prose and sweeping imagination, FIRELORD brings to life a realer King Arthur than we have ever seen before."
—*Chicago Sun Times*

. . . And for BELOVED EXILE:

"A BLOCKBUSTER . . . I'm incredibly impressed. This just might be the most vivid novel I have read for many years."
—Marion Zimmer Bradley

"A compelling character study; Guenevere fascinates the reader in every phase of Godwin's supple, sensual yarn."
—*Publishers Weekly*

"A fine novel, a delightful reading experience. I recommend it highly."
—Morgan Llywelyn,
author of *Lion of Ireland*

"Essential for readers of both fantasy and historical fiction."
—*Library Journal*

also by Parke Godwin

Beloved Exile

Darker Places

Firelord

The Fire When It Comes

A Memory of Lions

(with Marvin Kaye)
A Cold Blue Light

The Masters of Solitude

Wintermind

THE LAST RAINBOW
A Bantam Book / July 1985

Epigraph quotation from In the Steps of St. Patrick *by Brian De Breffny.* © *1982 by Thames and Hudson Ltd. Published by Thames and Hudson and reprinted by permission.*

Book design by Nicola Mazzella.

Library of Congress Cataloging in Publication Data

Godwin, Parke.
  The last rainbow.

  I. Title.
PS3557.0316L3   1985   813'.54   84-91010
ISBN 0-553-34142-1 (pbk.)

Published simultaneously in the United States and Canada

Bantam Books are published by Bantam Books, Inc. Its trademark, consisting of the words ''Bantam Books'' and the portrayal of a rooster, is Registered in the United States Patent and Trademark Office and in other countries. Marca Registrada. Bantam Books, Inc., 666 Fifth Avenue, New York, New York 10103.

PRINTED IN THE UNITED STATES OF AMERICA

FG 0 9 8 7 6 5 4 3 2 1

The
Last
Rainbow

Parke Godwin

BANTAM BOOKS
TORONTO · NEW YORK · LONDON · SYDNEY · AUCKLAND

I did not proceed to Ireland of my own accord until I was almost giving up, but through this I was corrected by the Lord, and he prepared me so that today I should be what was once far from me, in order that I should have the care of—or rather, I should be concerned for—the salvation of others, when at that time, still, I was only concerned for myself.

—Magonus Succatus Patricius (Saint Patrick)

I
Dorelei

E arth Mother and her husband Lugh Sun got along very well but argued now and then as men and women will because they are different. Once when they were very angry, Lugh Sun deserted Mother to show her how helpless she was without him. But Mother was stubborn. Even covered with ice she refused to surrender.

"See here," she demanded, fixing Lugh with her mooneye, "many of my animals have died for lack of your warmth. My first children, my Prydn, shiver in caves. Stop this foolishness and come back where you belong."

"When you admit I am the master," said Lugh. "What are you without me? Dark and cold."

"What are you without me?" Mother asked. "Nothing to shine on. No children to love you."

So they were both right and for once both had the sense to keep quiet about it and Lugh shone on the earth once more. The ice melted and Mother's children, the Prydn, followed the herds north as they grazed the new grass, until they came to a place so fair Mother drove her seas across the lowlands to make it an island for Prydn.

3

Other men came later and gave the island queer names like Albion or Britannia, but the Prydn with their long memories knew it was theirs and would always be.

From time to time Mother and Lugh still bickered and each said things harsh as they were true.

"You are careless," Mother accused. "At least once a year you wander off just like a man and leave us cold, and we have to beg you to come back."

"That shows how much you know about it," Lugh answered. "There are places where I shine all the time, where it's never cold and always green."

"Then where is such a place?" the Prydn demanded, growing restless as children will when they have to wait for anything. "What is it like? We have never seen it."

"Can you see the mole on your own back?" Lugh replied. "Earth is larger than you know. It is there."

The children always remembered that. The place their father made for them must be wider than they knew, with a secret place for Prydn alone to find when they needed it. They called it Tir-Nan-Og, the land of the young, because no one grew old there and the grass was always green. A part of earth to be sure, but beyond what they knew.

This they remembered from the first days, from the time of the ice. This was told by Mabh herself, the greatest queen the Prydn ever knew. Tallfolk feared all Prydn, but they went in awe of Gern-y-fhain Mabh and still used her name to frighten bad boys.

So it must be true.

The moor was silvered with Mother's eye-moon light as Owl glided low over the stone circle on Cnoch-nan-ainneal and down the hill-side beyond. Her hunting eye caught the mound of sheepskins—saw it move, saw the small dark-haired creature rise and gaze up at the moon. Too large for food. More curious than hungry, Owl flew closer.

The girl was very small as Owl knew humans, not much larger than a child, and yet full grown. She confused Owl with her disproportion, yet there she was, naked, glossy hair tumbling over her shoulders and back, staring up at moon-eye.

Owl was not the brightest of Mother's children; what served as her memory was concerned with food and her young. Dimly she remembered that there were once many more like the small girl, as many as the bigger ones in the lowland villages where food was easier found. But now they were few, always moving along the hilltops with their flocks from which Owl *might* snatch a new-dropped lamb to feast on, if she

4

were very lucky and very fast. These were the small folk of the hills, moving from one earth house to another, setting their rath poles over the crannog tops and covering the skins with turf so that they looked like part of the hill itself. And dangerous: their small bronze arrows flew faster and truer than others.

Owl veered close, saw the girl's dark head lift to follow her gliding path, then flew on, thinking of field mice to eat. These small humans were not as skillful at getting as the bigger ones; little wonder there were so few of them now. Look at her there, staring up at Mother in the open where any food she hunted could see her first.

"Fool!" jeered Owl as the girl looked up and their eyes met for an instant. "Foo-foo-fooool . . ."

"Faerie."

Dorelei tasted the sound, the tallfolk word for herself and Cru. Hard to say, hard to understand, like everything about tallfolk.

"Faerie. Feh-uh-ree."

Cruaddan snuggled closer under the sheepskin robe. "What?"

Dorelei ran her tongue over Cru's moist lips, teasing him. It delighted her when they'd just loved each other to taste and smell herself on him. "Be us. Tallfolk word for us."

". . . um." Being a man, love tired Cru more quickly. He was already floating down the soft darkness toward sleep.

Well, not all tallfolk, Dorelei corrected herself. The Atecotti of the northern pastures never used such a word, but they were almost as old in the land as Prydn. No, it was a southern word, a Briton-word, first heard this spring when they came south near the Wall, the long rampart that divided Briton-men from Venicone Picts. Dorelei didn't divide them; they were all tallfolk.

More serious, the grass here was no better than at Skirsa, as they'd hoped. Sheep could manage anywhere, but their few cattle had to be butchered or traded. There was always better graze in the valleys, but Venicones kept them out. It was always so. The scrubby hilltops belonged to her people. The lush valleys were taken by the users of Blackbar-iron.

She was gern of a new fhain and the first daughter of a gern. Her people were few but they looked to her to lead as her mother, Gawse, had. That frightened Dorelei sometimes, although she knew it shouldn't. She was sixteen, long past time to be grown up with child-wealth of her own. But Gawse's fhain was already too large for the sparse living north at Skirsa, so before this last Bel-tein, Dorelei was summoned to her mother.

"Take Neniane second daughter and Guenloie and thy husbands and so much of our flock and herd. Do thee graze south."

From the sacred treasures of the fhain, Gawse took a heavy gold torc set with ruby and emerald. She placed it about her daughter's neck. "First daughter be now Gern-y-fhain."

Dorelei's heart came up into her mouth; done quick as that. On a day when she expected no more than her usual tasks and loving Cru—a gern, queen of her own people. The torc lay heavy on her breastbone.

Fhain should be four generations in one rath. Hers was only two and the second barely in the world. Second daughter Neniane's sickly child might not last the summer, surely not the winter, did she not take more strength from her food. Nine in all, counting the bairn. Well, they were young and healthy, and new fhains must start somewhere. But it was frightening. Dorelei felt the fear in the cold weight of the torc. She was Gern-y-fhain: all descent would now be traced through her, all disputes settled, all decisions concerning their welfare would come from her. It was as if the torc held a growing-magic, pulling her too swiftly toward maturity, making her see in a new light the boys and girls she'd played with only a season ago. Seven separate minds she must know as her own hand for weakness and strength, and none of them was that strong.

Her sister Neniane was changed even since last year's Bel-tein fire. Once a playmate, she worried all the time now about the sick child who was not even named yet, so sure they were it would die. Her husbands, Artcois and Bredei, were still new in their own manhood, delighted with the child and not terribly concerned who fathered it, which was only proper. One couldn't make them worry for long about anything, still careless children themselves. Dorelei never noticed until now, but it was stone truth: none of them were very grown up and wouldn't last unless they were. Gawse couldn't take them back. It would be the deepest shame a first daughter could bring on herself to run back home after receiving the torc.

Then there was Guenloie, fourteen, cousin to herself and Neniane, and a coil beyond understanding. Her father was pure Prydn, her mother a changeling girl of the Taixali tallfolk, cradle-taken in a year when there was no child-wealth in the crannog. The child grew taller and much lighter-hued than Prydn, with hair so red they feared Lugh Sun might be jealous. She became all fhain in her heart and took a good husband. Guenloie was the only child of five to live beyond her first year. She was fairer than Dorelei and betrayed her mixed blood in the reddish-brown tresses that fell down her back in waves rather than straight. Outside blood could strengthen fhain, but Guenloie

6

was drawn to outside ways as well and sometimes acted as if her Taixali ancestors made her better than the rest. That could be dangerous. Tallfolk feelings toward Prydn were always a two-edged blade. You never knew when they would turn and drive you out. They feared Prydn magic and yet sought its aid. Relations between them were always wary. Wise Gawse said it was natural.

"A's taken from us the best grass and water. How should a feel when we look down from the hill on their thievery?"

Thief: that was another Briton-word. Fhain never stole from each other and nothing taken from tallfolk could be called stealing, so there was no need in Prydn for such a word. But tallfolk were best kept at a distance, especially the young men, who might take the wrong meaning from Guenloie's too-eager friendliness and her scant clothing. Dorelei never had to think on that until this summer. Prydn women wore short kilts or fringed skirts that left their legs bare, and usually the open sheepskin vest that allowed them to nurse children as they rode. Dorelei thought nothing of it until they started trading with the Venicones and saw how the young men looked at Guenloie's pretty bare breasts bursting through the loose vest. Dorelei sensed the disapproval in the Venicone women and, without knowing why except that she was gern and must think of such things, became queerly conscious of her own body and a shapeless danger. She fastened her vest with its seldom-used gold brooch and told Guenloie to do the same.

"Why?" Guenloie wondered. "Be not cold."

One day Guenloie lagged behind in a village, speaking to the loitering young men. Dorelei sent Drust and Malgon ahead while she waited on the hillside, thinking what she must say as her cousin ran out the stockade gate and up the hill toward her. Dorelei made her face stiff as Gawse's when she was reproving a mistake.

"Guenloie, thee shames thy husbands."

"How?"

"Tallfolk men have no respect for thee. Do not understand thy ways or dress. Do think thee whore."

Her cousin's smile was completely innocent. "Whore?"

Dorelei wondered if she used the word correctly, having never heard it until this summer among Venicones. "Be woman who cares not who beds her."

Guenloie was honestly bewildered by the idea. "But have husbands."

"Do thee remember it. What did a say to thee?"

"Who?"

"Those men."

7

"Oh—when did come again a would show where did byre a's kine."

"Nae doubt. And thee could lie on the straw to see how soft a was. What else?"

"And where did buy my gold armlet. As if gold could be bought." Guenloie laughed, touching the thick gold wire twining up her supple brown arm. "Did say the truth. Gift from Rainbow."

That again. Tallfolk were always surprised at the gold Prydn wore but never traded. It did come from Rainbow somehow, but none of them remembered how or when.

"Guenloie, speak less with a's men. A will spit on thee. Think of Drust and Malgon."

That teasing smile again that men would always misread. "Do know what to do, Gern-y-fhain." And Guenloie skipped away after her husbands.

Drust and Malgon were steadier than Artcois or Bredei, but then they had to be, dealing with a wife always between two fires, never one thing or the other. Dorelei never had to lecture them on behavior or responsibility, although Drust second husband was a bit jealous and possessive of Guenloie and the most injured when she smiled at the village men

Artcois and Bredei had to be told all the time of their responsibilities for the flocks. They'd be contrite and nod: yes, they'd be more careful on watch—and next day the sheep would be wandering and Neniane would screech and box their ears in sheer vexation.

Cruaddan was eighteen and the oldest, finding it necessary to grow up fast as Dorelei. It sobered the mischief out of them some of the time, but Cru was a good provider. When ponies begged to be night-borrowed, Cru was there to liberate them. Hawk flew wide of their flocks when Cru was near. There was a time two Bel-teins past when Hawk was hungrier than careful, and a new lamb wobbled away from its mother on untried legs. Hawk was a black blur against the sky, stooping out of nowhere to sink his talons in the lamb's soft back. The lamb bleated its terror as Hawk labored to rise with it—then there he was, rising away from the ground, gaining speed and height with every stroke of powerful wings, and Dorelei screaming Cru! Cru! Cru! jumping up and down in helpless fury.

Then Hawk lurched sideways and hung like a picture-bird drawn in the earth with the arrow through him before he fell like a stone. The lamb broke two of its frail legs in the fall and had to be butchered, a wasteful luxury. Mutton was to eat. Lambs were to grow and increase. The most succulent portion went to Cru, the wool to wrap the newest child-wealth in Gawse's fhain. Tendons were dried for cord, the head roasted for a delicacy, porridge boiled in the stomach, fat stored in a pouch. Nothing of a sheep was ever wasted but its bad temper.

Cru wore Hawk's pinion feathers in his hair and made a necklace of the claws, and always after that, Hawk was careful of Cru's bow.

The night was not really cold. Dorelei looked down at Cru sleeping and pulled the sheepskin blanket from his naked body. In sunlight Cru was dark bronze, darker in moonlight, shoulders very broad for his short stature like all Prydn men. They were cousins, and neither could remember a time when the other wasn't there, playing in the warm crannog or trudging the hills behind the ponies. They fought and explored together. Dorelei was there when Cru's fhain scars were cut into his cheeks without a sound from him, and he held her in turn so that the painful knife could not make her cry out. They rode reckless over the hills on the nights of fire festival and knew without words that life was good and theirs the best of all.

Then came a season when their play turned feverish, when they could not touch each other enough. The playing kindled a fire, pawing turned to clawing, and it was taken for granted that Dorelei would have Cru for first husband. She loved his body that fit so perfectly to hers, the spirit of him that joined with hers like halves of a stone with no rift at all. Side by side, peering at their reflection in still water, they seemed much alike, but it was not until this spring—a day of much learning and marvel—when they stood before a tallfolk woman's bronze mirror, wide-eyed at their true selves. They were alike as two blackberries: the same glossy black hair, fine and straight, high-bridged noses with mere slits for nostrils, the same gray eyes set above their fhain-scarred cheeks in a manner different from tallfolk. Cru was perhaps a finger-width taller. Except for the breadth of his shoulders and Dorelei's breasts, they could be small twin brothers. The woman even remarked at it.

"Faerie girl, is he your brother?"

"Husband."

"Husband? Och—peas in a pod."

The mirror delighted Dorelei. It was like seeing a whole new self. She wanted to see more, to know the self of her that others saw, like Lugh spying the mole on her back. Then Guenloie crowded in, eager to inspect her own image, and didn't look to her husbands for comparison but to the fair-skinned women of the house, preening when they noticed her waved hair.

"Mother be Taixali," she told them proudly.

On the day of the mirror, Dorelei resolved that if Guenloie ever brought trouble to fhain because of her too-free ways or let herself be taken by a tallfolk man, she could stay among them or go off with her husbands. Fhain would not have her back.

She took another hurtful surprise that day when she heard the fat wives of the house whispering about them.

"Don't they smell, dirty little things."

"And so ugly."

Ugly, she and Cru? They were the most beautiful of all Mother's children, made in the first days when Mother herself was young as Dorelei and bursting to create.

"Cru, how be we ugly?"

"Remember the Lughnassadh tale," he soothed her. "A's but jealous."

He was a comfort and a steady warmth, her Cru.

These summer nights Dorelei and Cru liked to take their sleeping robes away from the rath where they could hear the night sounds around them as they loved, starting out snug between the heavy fleeces, throwing them aside as their hunger rose and they went deliciously mad with each other. Then, sated, the night would chill their sweat and they'd cover again, only to start all over, stroking and licking each other's flesh until the sheepskin went flying once more along with their spirits. But though they loved enough for the whole fhain, no child-wealth came of it.

"Do try too much," Neniane counseled. "Wait until thy blood's come and gone. Rest and try again."

But they couldn't wait any more than a river could pause or Lugh turn back in the sky. Cru had the fire of Herne in him, she had Mother's own need to be filled. Their bodies and spirits were so matched, one hungered with the other's need.

Cru rolled over, face up. Dorelei brushed the hair aside where it tangled over his cheek and kissed the two V-shaped fhain marks. She eased down on her back beside Cru, staring full into Mother's eye.

What dost want of me? Be too young for Gern-y-fhain, not wise like Gawse.

Yet now she must be wise. She must learn more about tallfolk to be ware of them. They were strange. Sometimes Prydn were allowed in the villages, sometimes no closer than the stockade gates, the village traders wearing Blackbar magic about their necks as protection, knowing as well as Dorelei's folk that the iron would always be a wall between them. For tens of generations her people had feared the magic of Blackbar that they couldn't make or master. She didn't know why it was potent against them, but Gawse never questioned it or her mother before her, so Dorelei never touched, named, or even looked at iron if she could help it. Only in rare moments like this, awake beside sleeping Cru, did she sometimes ponder on it. What was in the Blackbar magic to make it so potent against her people?

Whatever, tallfolk knew and used it. They would never allow Dorelei near their children, but they would travel a full day to find a Prydn midwife whose birth-magic they knew far better than their own and for good reason. Prydn women bore their children in far less comfort than Picts or Britons and knew the best ways to bring them easily and keep them alive. If one of their own lived past its first year, it would grow stronger than others, supple and tough as willow from running the hills. Many were born on the move. Tallfolk never understood the moving.

"Why do you always wander?" a Venicone asked Cru only weeks past. "Why not stay in one place?"

"Herds move."

"Pen them up as we do."

"Why?"

"Do we not own the land?"

Own? Pen? Tallfolk always used such words. Dorelei couldn't fathom their thinking except for the greed. Small wonder they fought all the time. They'd forgotten Mother and her way. A poor lot. Mother must have made them on a bad day toward the end when she was tired of it all. How do children pen off parts of a mother? That was like Salmon fhain saying Dorelei's left arm was Neniane's, the other Guenloie's. How could that be when earth was a living thing, Lugh moved, and the herds drifted as they always had since Mabh followed the reindeer? They moved as birds who were born on the wing, their whole lives pressed to the breast of the wind and taking suck from it.

And yet a hard truth stayed with Dorelei. There was only one sickly infant in the rath, and she had none in her. The grass was not good here, nor was it better for them anywhere she could remember. If they were Mother's first children, why did they grow fewer and weaker while tallfolk lived fat in the glens? Why did outsiders seek Prydn magic in important matters like birth or illness and then hate and fear them for having it to give?

Gawse must have pondered these things. That was what took the lightness from her step and made her brood in the crannog of winter nights. While Dorelei rolled in her sleeping robe, Gawse thought of tomorrow. Now it was her turn. She could already feel the weight that bowed Gawse's shoulders and turned down the corners of her mouth, a weight on the soul.

Where is tomorrow for us?

She wouldn't think of that now. Lughnassadh was coming, the

day when their sun father marked them apart from tallfolk. Dorelei would tell the story to fhain as Gawse did each year. Neniane's infant daughter was too young to understand, but the others would expect it. They would feast and drink barley beer, but after Lughnassadh the mist on the moor would grow colder each day, the sun lose its warmth, and forgetful Lugh be that much more distant from them until it was time to crowd the flocks and ponies into the crannog against one more lean winter.

She turned to push herself against Cru, half hoping he'd wake and talk to her, but he only sighed and burrowed deeper into sleep. It would be light soon. Already Dorelei could smell the rain on the east wind. She couldn't sleep with so much troubling her. Perhaps if she went alone into the circle now and talked to Mother, there might be wisdom. The hill above her, Cnoch-nan-ainneal, was the oldest circle known to Prydn. It was said Mabh's own people dragged the stones into place. She could start her own fhain in no stronger place. Dorelei wrapped the wool kilt about her hips, clasping it with the bronze brooch. She slipped into her vest, bent to pull the robe over Cru, then padded barefoot up the dew-wet slope toward the circle of great stones.

On summer nights the heath never grew really dark, just a silvered gray. Dorelei could see every part of the hill, every light and shadow on the stones above her.

Then the gray and silver moved.

Dorelei froze to a stone herself. Only her eyes moved, following the shape that flowed in and out of shadow.

Wolf.

Dorelei waited. It moved again. Only one. Not hunting. Wolf never hunted alone. Like Prydn they lived beyond the tallfolk fires and spent much time singing to Mother. Tallfolk feared Wolf's song without understanding that Wolf sang much the same as men did, for the pleasure. Hungry wolves were a threat, but in deep summer with food plentiful, Wolf was just another child wandering the moor for the whim of it.

The gray wolf sat near one of the stones. She growled deep in her throat when Dorelei slipped into the circle but did not crouch or retreat. Dorelei moved upwind of the wolf bitch and squatted on her haunches, arms dangling from her knees. The wolf growled again, a tentative warning.

"Be still," Dorelei assured her.

Wolf lifted her muzzle to try the new scent and its many facets—grass, sheep, man, but none of the fear smell that came from humans when she was close. That confused Wolf. Fear and threat always went together. The growl softened to a questioning whine.

Dorelei grinned at her. "Dost talk to Mother?"

What mother?

Wolf clearly didn't know what she meant. Foolish bitch, be nae better than dog.

There were fewer wolves now. Men hunted them out of their lairs, remembering a time when they themselves huddled in protective circles of fire and Wolf waited patiently in the dark beyond for the fire to burn down, though it never did. Men grew bigger and Wolf smaller—

Like thee.

—And now Wolf was dying out of the land.

Like thee, said Wolf.

"Be still. Dost nae remember Mother?"

Wolf's tongue lolled out. She laughed at Dorelei in the moonlight.

Remember what? There is hunting and mating and cubs, and now your fear smell rising. You will die out.

"And what of thee? Could not even bargain with men to live by their fire like common curs. Must always live outside."

Like thee. Will come a time when Prydn-Faerie is only a name to frighten their pups as mine is: Wolf will eat you. Faerie will steal you. Thee's nigh hunted out, Dorelei.

Wolf flowed up off her haunches and stalked to Dorelei, sniffing at her knees and between her legs.

"Take care, woman. Do have my knife."

Be hard as tallfolk knives? They are ten times greedier than I. In their ten-times heat they forge harder knives.

Blackbar magic was bad luck even to mention, but Dorelei crossed her fingers against it. "My knife be made from bronze in good stone mold."

Flint broke flesh. Bronze broke flint. Iron will break bronze.

Dorelei felt an urge to cuff her. "Mother will not let us be broken."

Broken and forgot.

"No."

Wolf leered at her. What place has thy name on it? Cannot live on the wind and leave a trail.

"Rainbow does."

Where dost point thee, Dorelei?

Wolf tasted morning in the air. Time to return to her own pups, who were whelped with more sense than this silly woman would ever have. She flirted her tail at Dorelei and loped away down the hillside.

13

Rainbow *must* point somewhere; unthinkable that the most beautiful of earth signs should have no significance. There was a meaning, Dorelei was sure. When she looked at Rainbow, a memory stirred deep in her, rising a little in response to her effort to recall before it sank again.

Where dost point thee?

Dorelei rose and stood among the dark stones of the circle. "Mother, speak to me."

Not the proper address or respect. She should stand in the right place and scatter the white stones, but this once in her need, woman to woman, Mother might forgive her.

"Mother, speak to me. Be Wolf right? Would let us be forgot?"

But the reassuring strength that always filled her with Mother's voice did not come. *What mother?* Dorelei shivered at the treacherous thought. It was not Mother's eye at all but only a light in the sky with no more love for her than the eye of a fish might hold. Dorelei reached to cup the mooneye and wash her hand in its light. It vanished in dull cloud, eluding her.

"Do not turn from us."

No hint of Mother anywhere on the moor, only the east wind and the first drops of rain. Never before had Dorelei felt so utterly alone, so abandoned, the stomach-sick moment before falling. The rain pelted her upturned face; she backed a step, whimpering. The night was no longer soft, the stones not old friends but strange giants glaring at her with no more pity than Hawk gave the lamb. In a moment they would begin to rock back and forth, tearing themselves out of the ground to bump heavily in at her, leaning over her, crushing her under their weight into the earth that was never friend but only cold dirt—

Cru!

Mother turned from her, the world was cold and dead. Dorelei fled from the circle and down the hill to the only safety left. The rain was falling harder when she dove under the fleece robes, writhing against Cru for comfort.

Sleepily he brushed her away. "Wet."

"Oh, Cru . . ."

She wanted to tell him about Wolf and the drab taste of her thoughts, the emptiness where there was always comfort before. She wanted to know Wolf was foolish, that Mother did hear them. But how strong would Cru feel in turn if Gern-y-fhain herself was lost to magic? She felt bleak with the truth of it. She dare not tell Cru or any of them even when the fear was crushing her spirit. Dorelei squeezed against Cru and set her teeth to his shoulder. He woke foggily. There

14

was still sleep in him and the robes were warm against the rain. He didn't see her tears or the rain that washed them away in secret. In a little while Dorelei slept herself as a mercy, but she dreamed of Wolf.

When Dorelei raised her head out of the robes the early sun slanted on the stone circle. Far to the west the rain still lowered over the hills, but the east was clear and blue.

And there was a rainbow.

Wolf lied. Mother had not turned from them. The rainbow trail arced across the morning sky, and Dorelei wanted to cry again for relief at its clear beauty. She thought of the old song, the few words of it she remembered.

Be not where but only when—

None of them, not even Gawse's old mother, could remember the rest.

Cru yawned and stretched. "Must go back to rath."

Dorelei bent to kiss him. His mouth smiled under hers.

"Did make child-wealth last night?"

"Perhaps. Cru . . . ?"

He sat up, pushing the long silky hair back from his face. To the northwest, around the side of the hill, a few of their sheep straggled away from the flock, nibbling at the wet grass.

"Cru, dost remember Rainbow song?"

Cru's mind was on food, but he allowed part of it to her question, remembering no more than Dorelei. There once was such a song in the old fhains.

" 'Be not where . . .' "

" 'But only when.' Be more words than that."

"Not in my head." Cru cupped the breasts of the rainbow-rapt Dorelei from behind and nipped at her neck.

"Dost nae remember the tale?"

"Of what?"

"Rainbow, fool."

"Nae."

"Was a sign," Dorelei said.

"Of what?"

"Do nae *know*."

Neither of them could remember the story. It was long ago. They had no concept of time like house-dwelling Venicones or Britons, but counted from seasons and fire-festivals, and it seemed tens of seasons past, when they were little more than infants, that Cru might have heard something of it. He was barely walking then and Dorelei still slung from Gawse's shoulder.

15

"Came a woman from some other fhain," Cru struggled to recollect. "Were in western pastures then and tallfolk there, Brigantes and Roman men. Gern told the story to them."

Cru remembered only that the woman spoke of Rainbow and wore more gold and silver than any gern in his young memory. Even the Romans wondered at it.

But then their herd dog, Rof, barked from a shoulder of the hill. Artcois hallooed after, holding up cheese and milk and reminding Dorelei and Cru that they were hungry.

Some fire festivals were shared with tallfolk, but not Lughnassadh, since it meant different things to them. To Venicones and Votadini, it was a harvest fire, a lamentation for the death of old Barley Woman and celebration of new Barley Maid. In old times a person was chosen as Barley King for the year and scythed with the harvest at the end of it. Prydn once sacrificed for the same reasons, for the prosperity of the herds, usually a prisoner or stolen child. Old days were crueler. With children so precious now, such a thing would be foolish.

Now it was all pretend, although the devotion and the serious meaning remained. From their hilltops fhain could see the harvesters working furiously through the narrowing stands of barley. None wanted to be the last to finish. On the last day the remaining workers were closely watched until only one man or woman remained with a sheaf uncut. Then, with much ceremony, the village head or the wise woman would lead the ritual mourning for Barley Woman who gave birth to Barley Maid even in her death. The cailleach doll made from the last sheaf would bear in its center a smaller image of the Maid, and mourning would turn to celebration. The last laggard harvester took a fun drubbing from the rest of the village, and dire predictions for the next year were cast for him. If a man, he would be childless. A woman would remain barren or unmarried at all. There was feasting then and much making of child-wealth, as was fitting. As man sowed wealth in woman, hay and cabbage and other crops could now be sown in the ground. All their magic had to do with crops and staying in one place.

Prydn remembered the reindeer. The herds moved in the oldest dance of earth. Fhain's festival was one of movement. In the summer Lugh rode close to earth, his feelings for Mother at their warmest. It was this marriage Prydn celebrated. The men brushed down their shaggy ponies, decked the saddles with heather, and rode in a procession to the foot of Cnoch-nan-ainneal. Dorelei, Neniane, and Guenloie waited there, circlets of vervain, ragwort, and pimpernel in their hair. As Cru pranced his pony toward her, Dorelei shot her hands high in the air.

"Have seen Raven. Lugh be with us!"

Raven was one of the forms Lugh took in flesh, and to see him on this day was a sign that he favored Salmon fhain. Cru leaned from the saddle and caught Dorelei, who hopped up nimbly behind him. Neniane rode with Bredei, Guenloie with Malgon, Artcois and Drust bringing up the rear. They paraded in solemn pomp three full circles about Cnoch-nan-ainneal.

There was work to do preparing the Lughnassadh feast. There would be oats and ground pork cooked in a sheep's stomach with aromatic basil and garlic to make the pleasured tongue beg for more, barley soup thickened with mushrooms and all the week's leftovers, and a measure of mead traded from the Venicones, plus a honeycomb paid to Guenloie for a charm against the suspected evil eye of a neighboring ancient. Fhain had great fun with that.

"Will work as well as not," Guenloie reasoned.

And the centerpiece of their repast! A lamb who looked unhappy in its Venicone captivity until Cru night-borrowed the fortunate lostling, its tender meat flavored with mint and wild garlic. This night fhain would feast until their stomachs popped ·

At dusk, like eyes opening all over the land, one could see the Lugh fires kindled in one tallfolk village after another, inside the stockades or beside the fields. From a special dry corner of the crannog, unburned remnants of last year's fire, a gift from Gawse, were brought out and used to kindle the flame and replenished with aromatic clumps of dried peat. From the new fire torches were lit by Neniane and passed up to the mounted fhain.

Torch aloft, Dorelei gazed across the few miles to the closest fire-lit village and felt the fierce, ancient pride swell her chest. "We are the Prydn," she whispered to the distant light. "You are not so old in the land as us."

She swooped her torch in a fiery circle. "Be the people of the hill!"

The torches wheeled against the darkening sky. "Yah!"

"First children!"

"Yah!"

"Will carry Lugh's light."

Six torches strung out behind her, Dorelei rode a route along the hilltops. As her sure-footed pony plunged up and over the ridges, she knew no lowlanders would venture within a mile of them this night; they called this procession a Faerie rade, and deep in their beliefs was the certainty that this time could bring the worst luck

17

one could imagine, like blighted crops or dead children. Some Venicones would not even look up at the moving lights, and every person and threshold bore iron as protection. In these southern parts where the crown-shaven priests of the Christ-man had passed, some believed that these were the false lights of Lucifer, sower of confusion and harm. No matter how one believed, Faerie were best avoided when they rode at night.

Dusk deepened to dark and stars as they rode. Mother's eye rose and opened to approve their worship, and Dorelei's heart felt warm as they approached the rocky outcrop that marked the entrance to their rath. Neniane stood waiting with the bairn in her arms, shaggy Rof capering about among the ponies.

"Feast! Come feast," she called to them as they dismounted. "All's prepared." But Dorelei sensed a forcing in the welcome and knew her sister's heart was not in it. While the men led the ponies to their byre, she placed her own flower crown on Neniane's head and kissed her.

"The bairn?"

Neniane's serious dark-kitten face bent to the wrapped child. "Still fevered."

Dorelei placed the backs of her fingers against the tiny brow: far too hot. In spite of potent magic, the child's preserved birth string greased and laid near the fire, in spite of lavender tea and beech-fungus poultice, the bairn still grew weaker.

"Should never have left Gawse," Neniane mourned.

"Hush. Be home now. Will brew more tea for it."

Neniane's daughter was given more hot lavender and wrapped in lamb's wool to sweat the fever out of her. The flushed infant barely moved. Dorelei felt hopeless. She had no real zest for the feast but dared not show it. More and more this summer she was coming to realize that much of the strength and courage of a gern lay in the masking of troubles from her people while they nourished on her spirit.

The order of seating at a meal was a statement of position within fhain. Everyone had a certain place. Only children were allowed to roam about or partake of any dish at random. As gern, Dorelei sat on a flat stone in the highest place, Cruaddan on her right hand, Neniane on her left. Then to Neniane's left and Cru's right came Artcois as first and Bredei as second husband. Then Guenloie, Malgon, and Drust in the same order.

Dorelei dipped from the soup and cut a portion of meat; Neniane followed, and then they talked and laughed freely, deferring only to Dorelei when she spoke as gern. For this reason, as Gawse had, she chose her times carefully for gern-speaking and listened more than she spoke. It lent her needed gravity and set her somewhat apart like her mother.

The men's talk turned to the Wall. It fascinated them even more than the high stone brochs of the north, a solid stone wall fifteen feet high and stretched the width of the land from sea to sea with castles every mile and camps in support. All things Roman were a source of wonder and more than a little fear. Everything they built was to last, all square and counted and uniform, cities, armies, even men. Squares seemed awkward to fhain, whose idea of perfect unity was circular. The Romans had been in Britain forever; yet now, suddenly—

"A's gone," said Cru.

Drust couldn't believe that. "Nae!"

"Did hear from Venicones."

"Gone where?"

Well, as Cru gathered from villagers, there were wars oversea and all the soldiers went to fight in them and none were left but Briton-men. Rome claimed all the earth south of the Wall, which meant nothing to fhain. Their journey south this spring was the longest any of them could remember. Anything greater had no meaning. And when was this leaving?

Cru searched for a measure. "Oh, tens of seasons past. But Wall be guarded yet."

" 'Gainst Venicones?"

"And us," said Cru.

That sat strangely with Malgon. " 'Gainst Prydn? What be in Briton-land we would want?"

The notion was comic; Artcois spluttered through his soup. "Can picture it: tens and tens of Briton-men a-shiver on the Wall while Dorelei and Cruaddan lead fhain flying against them."

Cru swept his arm in a great arc. "Forward!"

"Forward! Yah!"

Neniane lashed out suddenly. "Be still!" They all heard the thin-worn desperation behind her temper. "Bairn can nae eat. Can nae have a little rest at least?"

Artcois subsided. "Be only joke, wife."

"Thee's always joking. Thee's a fool."

"Why?" Guenloie wondered. "May not even laugh at feast?"

Neniane turned away in disgust. "Be those who can do little else."

"Second daughter be right," Dorelei settled it. "Bairn needs rest. Do not wake her."

They quieted in concern and respect. Neniane was worried and not enjoying the feast even though Dorelei saved the tenderest cuts of lamb for her.

"But did hear there be good graze south of Wall," Guenloie nodded. "An could use't."

"And thee's worse than fool," Neniane lashed out at her. "With thy mooning after tallfolk men and boasting thee's one of them."

"Nae true," said loyal Malgon.

Guenloie bristled. "Mother be Taixali."

"And proud to be fhain," Dorelei reminded her. It wasn't wise for Guenloie to hold such thoughts, much less voice them. Her husbands were pained by it, especially Drust who was achingly in love with her. Dorelei was suddenly sick of them all. "Neniane, hold thy temper. Do all care for bairn. Guenloie spoke only of graze."

"Which is *good* in Briton-land," Guenloie glowered.

"Not for us." Cru spat out a piece of gristle. "Lugh promised us Tir-Nan-Og."

"When?" Neniane asked. It was a hopeless, disbelieving sound. "Where?"

"In the west," Bredei said. "At world's edge."

"Or even farther," Artcois amended.

Neniane glared at her husbands like a brace of idiots. "What be farther than world's edge?"

"Thee knows the story," Dorelei said. "Can see the mole on thy own back?"

Family bickering subsided as the richness of the feast thickened and warmed their blood. When all were mellow with mead and only nibbling at honeycomb, when talk had fallen to a torpid murmur, one or two of them glanced expectantly at Dorelei. She sat cross-legged on the stone, back straight, hands on her knees, and spoke the ritual words as gern, praying she had her mother's stern command or at least a hint of it.

"Was in the first days."

Dutifully, fhain sat back to listen, although Dorelei knew there was none of Gawse's husky, low authority in her voice. Nevertheless, she told the story as her mother did, even with the remembered inflections that she practiced in secret. Gawse did it so easily; her voice had the weight of distant thunder across the sky even when it sank to a whisper.

The Lughnassadh story was mainly for children, that they remember their honored place among the offspring of earth and sky. Neniane took up her child and brought her to the fire.

"Gern-y-fhain, tell my first daughter of Mother and Lugh."

"Was a time when all men were nigh beautiful as Prydn," Dorelei began.

But Mother and Lugh gave so much of food and wealth that many grew larger and sleeker. They could look down on the heads of the first children, and so looked down on their hearts as well. In their pride, tallfolk forgot their kinship with Prydn and the animals, and even the generosity of their parents.

"Was in the long summer before Lugh grew angry and went away. Before the ice came. Was in the first days of his love for Mother. A were like fhain then." Dorelei smiled at her folk. "Young and strong and loving all the time."

But the younger children grew too proud for even Mother's patience and she admonished Lugh. "See how haughty they grow. They need a lesson."

Lugh knew Mother was right. Tallfolk were so proud they no longer spoke the language of their kin even though Lugh commanded it.

"Speak to your brothers. Thee knows I go as raven on earth. What is my song then? What does the wolf say?"

But in their arrogance and greed, in making new words for new things, they had forgotten the first language. Only the Prydn remembered and were able to speak to Mother and their brothers.

"What is that to us," the tallfolk jeered. "They're stupid and backward, these first children. We are the humans. They are not our brothers."

Well, what father or mother could tolerate such arrogance?

"So be it," Mother said in judgment.

"So be it," said Lugh to seal her command. "You are no longer my children. Do you go out and make your own way. Only these first small ones will we call our own."

And that was the whole of it. The proud ones went off in a huff, and to mark the division, Mother kissed the Prydn on each cheek to leave her sign, and Lugh saw to it that their black hair and beautiful dark skin did not lighten, as with some of the ignorant ones. This honor was passed from generation to generation among Prydn in the fhain marks they wore with pride. Oh, there *were* some crafty tallfolk who tried to pass as Prydn when things went bad for them, dyeing or scarring their skin as the Picts still did.

"And were some who cut the foreskins of their men," Dorelei confided darkly, "and others even the pleasure-buds of women."

Guenloie squirmed her legs together at the distressing thought. "Ooo ..."

"But could nae fool our parents. Did know a's own. And real as

21

the fhain marks on our cheek is Tir-Nan-Og, the land of the young where a will lead Prydn in a time after tomorrow. Was promised."

"Yah!" Cru hissed in approval.

Dorelei took up her mead bowl and drank, pleased that she'd told the tale almost as well as her mother. The story of Mabh, now, was usually told at Brigid-feast, but she guessed it wouldn't hurt to hear it this night. Perhaps Neniane would tell it. All through the feast her sister had been withdrawn and joyless.

"Neniane second daughter, will thee tell fhain how Mabh led her people to this land?"

Neniane's head was bent over the swaddled child. Dorelei touched her arm. "Sister?"

From Neniane came only a low, falling whine. "A's gone. My bairn is gone. Mother does turn from us."

She rocked back and forth as the bowls were lowered, food dropped from all hands. One by one Artcois and Bredei took the dead child from her and looked to see, as if only then would it be true. Then they added their deeper voices to Neniane's keening. Dorelei wanted to flee as the sound of it darkened around her and tore at her courage. Just now it was too much for her: all this way south just to find poor grass, hostile tallfolk, and dead children. Were she alone she'd run home to Gawse this night, whatever the shame.

The fhain swayed back and forth around the fire in the mourning that began as feast. Neniane's cries rose above the others. She tore at her hair and stumbled out of the rath into the darkness of the hill. With a glance at Cru, Dorelei followed. Neniane stared up at the moon riding over a bank of cloud

"A turns from us, Dorelei."

"Nae, dost not."

"Must go home."

"Cannot, thee knows it. Be home now."

"No. Would not have died at home," Neniane denied, hoarse with crying. "Gawse be strong. A's strong magic."

"And sister has not? Be nothing for us north. Would be shamed."

"Want my baby!" Neniane wailed. "Want to go home. Mother turns from us. Be nothing here but death." She wilted on the ground, beating her fists against the turf. Dorelei cradled her close as if Neniane were the sick child, wiping the tears from the small face, crooning to her. "Will take the bairn to the circle afore barrowing. Will to speak to Mother about this."

"Will need more than speaking," Neniane whimpered.

"Nae, strong words. Do need better fortune for fhain."

"A will not h-hear, sister—"

"Hush, hush. Did see thy husbands' sorrow? Would make it heavier?"

"What of mine?"

"Will go in the circle."

"Will go *home*."

"No, no." Dorelei rocked her back and forth. "Sister will care for you. Thee has good husbands. On Bel-teins after tomorrow, our flocks will cross Gawse's trail, and thee will have child-wealth anew to show her. Will ride with one child on the saddle and another running behind as we did, and Gawse will know her seed was strong enough to grow where tallfolk could not."

"Was mine," Neniane whimpered against Dorelei's breast. "Was out of me, a piece of me. So little. Artcois thought 'twas his but Bredei made it . . . oh, must nae tell that, sister."

"Nae."

"Was a good mother, never left her alone."

"Be still . . . hush."

Their words blurred to mere soft sounds, the cry for comfort, the comfort given, blended with the keening from the rath in a single bleak voice that cried the loss of future in the midst of now, for the flesh of tomorrow cut from them. The chill sound like a bleeding lifted on the night air and sang to the wind that carried it from the hill to the valley beyond. The feast-drunken Venicones, lying with their own women, heard the loss of life in the act of getting it, and were goaded to fiercer need without knowing why. The hill was far, the wind an unreliable messenger. It spread the mourning wail thin on its wings, not quite like wolves nor yet quite human as it reached their ears and those of their fathers for hundreds of generations, so that it even had a name now. The bravest of them would not go outside his iron-bolted door while the *bean sidhe* cried from the ancient stones on the hill.

They could not give up now. At least Cru realized that, but Cru was older and steadier than the rest. Dorelei depended on his strength more than she ever admitted. A Gern-y-fhain with a weak husband was a woman with only one arm, and Dorelei's mind struggled with a problem that touched them all. If Mother and Lugh had forgotten them, where could she take fhain? Dorelei wondered if Gawse ever felt so confused and alone, having to be strength itself when she felt lost and frightened as Neniane.

Men were no more helpful in death than in birth. A word to Cru and he kept them enormously concentrated on the stone molds, making new arrowheads and gathering white moonstones for the coming night. Neniane couldn't bear to look at her dead daughter, and Guenloie was watching the flocks. Dorelei alone prepared the child for barrowing. It should be interred right away, but she'd come to a decision. When the fhain had voiced their proper grief, Dorelei told them what she planned.

"Will take the bairn and show it to Mother in the circle of stones. And the grass and oats."

Neniane assented listlessly. Dorelei felt her helpless fury and that of the others. That day the wheeling birds learned quickly to fly wide of Cru's angry bow. Tod-Lowery, the fox, narrowly escaped with his hide when Bredei sank an arrow inches from his swift-running paws.

Drust made a paste of clay and reddish macha for Dorelei to work with. The dead child was painted with the mixture and each eye sealed with white clay. Dorelei placed the body on her gern stone, took up a bronze hammer, and broke the large bone of each limb with one sharp blow, which must be done to release the spirit. Then she wrapped the child in its lambskin and carried it out to Neniane.

"Go in the circle with thy husbands. Uncover it to Lugh. Our parents must be concerned with this."

Dorelei fasted all that day as Gawse would. No more than water had passed her lips since the child died. When the moon rose, she led the rest of fhain up Cnoch-nan-ainneal to the circle. Neniane had placed the child before the large eastern stone where Lugh rose on Midsummer morning. With her people behind her, Dorelei cupped her hands to take the stones from Bredei. He'd washed and rubbed each carefully so that they shone white as moonlight itself.

"Mother. Lugh. Prydn would speak with thee."

Dorelei scattered the pebbles with smooth motions of her arms. The ritual offering done, she spoke the mind of fhain. All of them heard the firmer tone in her words. Gern-y-fhain did not say "please" now, but "listen!" Their need called for it.

"Mother and Lugh: fhain keeps thy festivals and wears thy mark, given in the first days. Do follow the herds as Mabh's people followed the reindeer. Do use no Blackbar, turn to no parents but thee.

"Why, then, in the plain sight of thy eye, do Prydn grow weaker? Our child-wealth dies, we get only the leavings from tallfolk who have long since turned from thee. A put names to us that are not ours, and fences to keep us out. A tell lies about us and yet grow fat in the land while Prydn starve and die like Neniane's child. Prydn would not turn from thee...."

Dorelei felt her people tense behind her as she uttered the

words. She'd thought it out all day, her mind clear from fasting. Above all else, they must survive. Bargains had two sides. Earth and sky could not expect worship without a like return. It was not disobedience, merely the desperation she saw growing in Neniane and the rest of them. Without some hope and a strong Gern-y-fhain, they would drift away from her.

"Mother and Lugh: can see our wants. Send them to us." *Or we will turn away.* Dorelei dare not say it, but what did earth or Gawse or any of them expect of her? They needed a miracle.

"Thee has promised us Tir-Nan-Og in the west. Show it to us. Give us a sign. Thy children put their hands out to thee, hungry. We must have Tir-Nan-Og now." Dorelei took a breath and swallowed and made the plunge. "Or will make new magic without thee."

Out and said; she felt her shoulders hunch as if Mother might open and swallow her on the spot. Cru's head turned slightly; she knew his thoughts: she was bargaining and threatening, uttering words on the edge of blasphemy, but fhain was dying before it could begin. What else could she do?

"Go back to the rath," Dorelei bade her folk. "Will watch with Cru tonight and barrow't when the sun rises."

Still Neniane lingered by the small bundle. Dorelei knelt by her. "Take my promise, sister. Tir-Nan-Og will be found. Will be like hound rooting after fox, will tear Mother's secret places apart to find it. Fhain will prosper and thee bear again."

She embraced Neniane, hoping to squeeze a firmness of faith into both of them. A disturbing thought had been growing in her mind, something not so much said by Gawse as what her mother had *been*— absolutely unwavering in her faith and her holding to the correct way, as if the faith were more important than the fact. She still had no assurance she was right, except that Gawse's fhain lived and hers withered. She had to show strength before her people and hoped Mother understood the need for strong words.

"Artcois, Bredei—take second daughter to the rath."

Standing silent by the dead child and the other objects carefully placed beside it, Cru and Dorelei watched the line of ponies wend down the dark hillside. Cru brought his new cloak from the rath to keep them warm on the vigil, which must last until sunrise. The cloak was huge and thick, traded to Cru by a Venicone farmer in return for the mending of harness. It was too large even for most tallfolk and once belonged to a man of the yellow-haired Angles from oversea.

"Was a giant," Cru marveled, shaking out the oceanic folds. The farmer said the Angle was so big he needed two days to stand in the same place. When Cru tried it on, it flowed down and over the ground in waves so that he looked like a corn shock with a man's head on top. He could wear it riding, but its best use was for sleeping, he and Dorelei engulfed in its thick folds. For tonight's vigil it was perfect to warm them both, their small heads cowled together within the wide hood. The great dark cloak made them look like part of the stone they rested against.

"Did speak harshly to Mother," Cru said.

"Cru?" Dorelei's voice was small and tentative inside the hood. "If Tir-Nan-Og be in the west . . ."

"Was nae told so?"

"Where?"

"Who can say? Beyond world edge."

"Could Prydn go there? Find a curragh to sail beyond world edge like Lugh?"

It was not one of his wife's strange questions, like Where do the clouds go? or What holds the world up? Dorelei wanted an answer. "Well, now . . ." Cru tried to picture such a craft but honestly considered it beyond even Mabh's formidable powers. "Who could build such?"

Dorelei didn't know, but they must go somewhere, find quickly those ends and rewards promised them, or all go into the barrow with Neniane's child. The shape of wolf-truth and world-truth was plain as that.

Cru's arm emerged from the cloak, pointing down the valley. "See."

In the gloom where the Venicone village would be, a torch was lit, tiny in the distance, but as they watched another and another spark flared up until Cru counted ten of them. The lights milled about for a few moments, then formed two straight lines close together and began to move. The lights passed out the stockade gate and kept moving. Most strange: tallfolk never left their stockade after dark.

"Where do a go?" Dorelei wondered.

In a few moments they knew: not going but coming.

"Here," said Cru.

His name was Magonus Succatus Patricius, and it had been remarked of him, to his secret pleasure, that he was obsessed with God. In later years he would sign himself Patrick to all the Christian world. In later centuries miracles as preposterous as his present youthful self-esteem would be solemnly ascribed to him and devoutly believed. In his twenty-eighth year, like many men who grow slowly to the simplicity of greatness, he was quite unfinished and thoroughly insufferable. Patricius admitted this in moments of candor, but it disturbed him to think that men who professed a devotion like his own, men of the Church, found him abrasive. Later in life, Patricius often chuckled over the obvious answer. Not his holiness but his holy naïveté and brash assumption of absolute right. Among wise and worldlier men, a little youth goes a long way.

Patricius' father was a decurion of Clannaventa on the north-western coast just south of Solway. Since the rank was hereditary, Patricius might have looked forward to a secure and uneventful career preparing the town's tax schedules, maintaining the baths, and arranging public entertainments. The legions left when he was a child; the Britain in which he grew to young manhood was a part of Rome only in hopeful spirit. Most men were sure the legions would return; meanwhile, the engine of administration churned on in Roman form if not efficiency.

In his early youth Patricius could not be called either pagan or Christian. More accurately he thought very little about it. Rome had given him a secure land to grow in, unchanging and tolerant, sheathed in the Pax Romana. His father, Calpurnius, was a Christian, and his grandfather Potitus a priest of the growing new faith. Like most educated citizens of the Empire, they took sophisticated delight in the verses of Martial, were vaguely disturbed by the attacks on the rich by young British monks—not wrongheaded attacks, but tending to shake the established order of things—and in matters of faith inclined to the reasonable humanism of Pelagius rather than Augustine. Pelagius was, after all, British and patrician, postulating a reasonable God who would not create men intrinsically incapable of their own salvation.

Augustine was a hotheaded African, and no matter how impassioned his arguments on the necessity of Grace and the very few destined to receive it, there was about him the vulgar taint of the fanatic. He decried as sloth what civilized men took for granted, eschewed good manners in debate, and launched his attack on Pelagius from the vicinity of the gutter. Augustine's human failings, like those of any rigid reformer, perfectly complemented his purposes. He lumped all his opponents, political and religious, into one composite enemy and called him Evil. The Enemy. He knew no compromise.

More than one catalyst in history has been slighted by his contemporaries as a bad-mannered boor whom one could not comfortably invite to dinner. If Augustine was shortsighted, the Pelagians were equally myopic. They failed to see that the temper of coming times was Augustine's, or that their own was fading. Rome had proved less than eternal; its power and grandeur shrank and faded even as they watched. Men saw this world ending and yearned for the security of one truly enduring. The old days of tranquil meditation wherein a philosopher might construct an ethical dialogue between the trained human mind and the intents of God were quite gone. The world men knew had turned to quicksand. The Chi-Rho symbol of Christ was no longer to be debated but battened on for sheer survival.

At sixteen none of this bothered Patricius overmuch. When he thought of it at all, he made comfortable obeisance to Christ and just as blithely dropped a pinch of incense on the altar of Mercury, and went whistling out of the chapel to bask in the last rays of the long Roman sunset. But for Patricius, night came suddenly.

The mouth of the River Esk was always tempting to Irish pirates. One day they appeared suddenly at his father's villa, pouring through the gates, the doors, the rooms. His mother and father were mercifully absent. Patricius happened to be alone in the courtyard. Along with a few able-bodied young slaves, he was chained, thrown into a curragh, and rowed for a short, lurching journey to the pirate vessel at Esk mouth and dumped on the hard deck. For Calpurnius' slaves it was only a harsher degree of the servitude they'd known all their lives. For Patricius it was the end of his world. Alienated, his whole being an open wound of hunger, pain, and fear, his newborn faith was not surprising to anyone but himself.

He was sold at Slemish in the north of Ireland to a lord called Miliuc maccu Bain, who styled himself King of Dal Araidhe, when in fact he ruled from his ringed hillfort little more than a minor Roman magistrate. It was a primitive country with more kings than sheep, it seemed to Patricius, who was set to herd them. Cities and towns were unknown. For six years, Patricius lived mostly under the open sky.

The cold, damp, solitary life of a shepherd rubbed the Roman out of Patricius and exposed the bedrock Brigante youth who needed something—anything—to keep his guttering spirit alive. His world in small, he clutched at a personal God for present comfort and deemed the comfort an absolute. Shivering on an icy mountainside, he wasted no time in defining his newfound God beyond protection and warmth, but prayed because he needed to, believed in order to survive in a slave's life where nothing short of iron belief would see him through one more day.

When he escaped finally with other runaway slaves and made his way into Gaul, he was an aggressive believer in the Christ who sustained him in the lions' den and totally intolerant of any dissent. The Augustinians preached the need for God's Grace; he had received that Grace and would not question it. They preached imminent judgment; he would be cleansed and ready if it came that day, that minute. He had never thought deeply about God or anything else and deluded himself that he was now doing so. In mellowed years Patricius saw that the salvation he clung to then was no more than a surrogate nipple. He sucked at the Church like a breast or a baby-thumb, without defining it.

When he and his companions were captured by Franks and shortly ransomed by Christians, his course was set. He found his way to Auxerre and went to the old bishop, Amathor, to be admitted into holy orders.

The years of slavery scrubbed from Patricius' soul any sophistry that might have clung to it. He would be a priest as his grandfather Potitus. What a worldly man would call his self-conceit, Patricius knew for destiny. He studied diligently under Amathor while scorning the bishop's liberal views.

"There are no disbelievers in the cold," Patricius said. To his own credit, Amathor had enough tolerance for himself and one fire-minded young man. When his social friends in Auxerre made fun of the terribly serious young acolyte, Amathor only responded with a knowing smile.

"This one is tough. This one will last. Give him time."

Patricius heard with a flush of righteous vindication that Augustine was favored over Pelagius at Rome. When Amathor died and was succeeded in the diocese of Auxerre by a rigorous Augustinian, Germanus, the young priest knew he'd come into his own. Germanus had no use for playing with words or the easygoing Pelagianism that pervaded the British Church and was spreading its seductive poison even to Gaul. Man's pride-ridden error that his own intelligence and natural inclination to good would save him, Germanus thrust aside with rough contempt, preaching that only those chosen by God would receive Grace, and that blessed company was much smaller in number than the complacent heretics would dare to guess. Germanus routed out and challenged the Pelagian heresy wherever he found it. When he sailed for Britain to beard them on their very doorstep, Father Patricius followed in his wake like Peter after Christ on the shore, to be a fisher of men.

Germanus was much more popular with the British commoners than the educated followers of Pelagius. Like Caesar, he came and conquered. His appeal was emotional and direct, a strong man in severe garb, plainly speaking his beliefs and supporting them with Scripture. He caused a stir and flutter, announced his victory, and left Britain again.

After Germanus' departure, Patricius was something of a man without a star. For all the triumph, he could see no marked difference in his countrymen, not even his parents, with whom he now had nothing in common spiritually. It was not enough to preach, then; one also had to proselytize. The true men of God were not in the established centers of faith. Potitus had been thus, comfortably preaching to the converted. His father still dozed through the Mass and the sermons along with the other well-fed decurions and tradesmen of Clannaventa. Not for him: Patricius' panting zeal remembered the caustic purity of Germanus and viewed with the eye of unforgiving youth those Britons whom he now saw as a people gelded of honor or pride, begging Rome to return because they were unable to fend for themselves, yet, like contrary children, wanting their own way in the bargain. Where was the glory in such a congregation of sheep? He would go where men were still benighted but vital, fallow but ripe for his seed. To Ireland.

This called for a tedious round of protocol. Certain prelates must be seen; he must have a sponsor. Patricius grated as harshly on clerics as he did on the laity. The bishop of Camulodunum listened politely and referred Patricius west to the prelate of Caerleon, who neatly deflected him with tactful letters of introduction to Bishop Meganius at Eburacum.

Thus, blind luck and God's intervention being perhaps two names for the same effect, Patricius came on a summer evening to the man who could shape his life for the best while it was still malleable.

Like Patricius, Cai meqq Owain was the son of a decurion and styled himself Caius Meganius to the clergy at home and abroad, with whom he was in continual touch. A mellow and worldly man well past fifty, Meganius knew to the core the spirit and needs of his people and those of the Church that had consecrated him bishop of Eburacum. If the needs were often at odds with the spirit, so were those in any marriage. The faith would endure, as would the people of his diocese, both strong enough to tolerate a few differences.

"Surely you will take a little more wine, my lord."

Smiling at Prince Marchudd, Meganius barely lifted his hand to the hovering servant, and the prince's silver goblet was refilled. Meganius savored both his wine and that exquisite moment when the heat of the afternoon was softened but not quite gone from the day. The sun was well below the courtyard wall, light still sparkled on the water of the fountain, and the mournful falling cry of the peacocks punctuated the tranquil afternoon.

Prince Marchudd's fingers drummed on the arm of his chair: a restless man, Meganius thought, quite aptly named before he changed the appellation. He was christened Rhys, which means "rapid" or "rushing," and only on his accession to the throne of the Parisii and Brigantes did he style himself Marchudd or "horse lord." Some clergy saw this as a lapse of faith. Meganius knew it was entirely political, helping Marchudd and his consort to identify with the unbaptized among their tributary chieftains, especially the remote Brigantes. The royal house of Eburacum, like the Church, would do or be whatever it needed to survive.

Marchudd shifted in his chair, obviously more comfortable in movement than repose. A small, darting, intelligent man, he was more at ease in British trousers and tunic than the purple-striped gown and toga his visit prompted him to wear. The toga trapped his left hand, holding it in place, quite an annoyance since he was left-handed, and forced him to wear the gold armlet of the Parisii and Brigantes on his right arm, where it always felt awkward.

"On this matter of the Coritani," he said in clipped tones, "if they want a war, they've got one. I've relinquished the claims on their northern lands, but I'll have their respect. The cattle raids will cease, by God. Those people are worse than Faerie for thieving and I've told their nuncios as much."

"How do you think it will come out?" Meganius plied in real concern.

"In all candor?"

"And all confidence."

"I think in a year or two I'm going to be at war—och! Let's talk of pleasanter things." Marchudd's balding pate jerked impatiently. "My new son."

"Ah, yes. How does he?"

"Lusty as a bull, hungry all the time."

"A proper princeling."

"We'd have him baptized tomorrow if you will officiate."

"Of course. What will you name him?"

"We thought of Constantius, but the princess thinks something old-fashioned might be better, so we'll name him Cador."

"Excellent." The bishop bobbed his head judiciously. He raised his goblet to the notion. "May he be chosen prince in his time and grow wise as his father."

As a matter of fact, Meganius' wish was answered with an embarrassment of riches. Marchudd was an able administrator. Cador grew into one whom even Ambrosius noted as a wizard at playing both ends against the middle, and he sired Guenevere, who was much of the political genius ascribed to Arthur.

Meganius was distracted for a moment; his gatekeeper had just admitted a stranger, a young priest who stood waiting inside the portal, noting with obvious disapproval the bas-relief of Janus carved into the gate arch. The gatekeeper relayed his whispered message to the servant in attendance on Meganius and his guest, who then hurried to the bishop's elbow.

"Who is it, Corus?"

"A Father Patricius, your grace. He says you have had letters from Caerleon of his coming."

"Oh, yes," Meganius verified without enthusiasm. Then to Marchudd: "The young Augustinian, my lord. One of Germanus' lion-killers."

"Well." Prince Marchudd rose, eager to be away and to waiting business as always. "I'll leave you to receive him. I can't abide that sort."

"Perhaps he's still green enough to be salvaged. Besides, I think you know his father. Send him to me, Corus."

Marchudd looked blank. "His father?"

"The decurion Calpurnius of Clannaventa."

"Oh, of course."

"Shall I present him?"

"If you wish, but then I must be off. People to see ..." the prince-magistrate trailed off vaguely. "Yes, he does favor Calpurnius somewhat. Spent some time as a slave among the Irish, didn't he?"

"Six years."

Marchudd whistled softly in compassion. "Ought to take that off purgatory for the lad."

"From what I've heard of Father Patricius, I don't think he'd permit it."

As the young priest strode energetically across the atrium, Meganius couldn't see where Irish captivity had done him much harm. Patricius had a rugged, unpriestly gait. He bobbed his head to the prince and dropped to one dutiful knee to kiss the bishop's offered ring.

"Thank you for receiving me, your grace."

"My blessing, Father Patricius. Prince Marchudd, allow me to present Magonus Succatus, the son of Calpurnius."

"Father."

"Honored, my lord," Patricius said in a brusque tone that signified a deal less than that.

A comely enough young fellow, Meganius decided: in his mid- or latter twenties, reddish hair shaven across the crown, eyes large and inconsistently brown in the round face, the fair skin permanently darkened from years of living in the open. Where many British priests allowed themselves light linen in warm weather, Patricius was severe in coarse dark woolen canonicals, the studiedly plain garb Germanus wore when he refuted the Pelagians in debate.

32

Yet, somehow, Meganius sensed the severity of Patricius to be something laid on and not inherent, like an actor striving too hard for effect in a role. He'd paused a moment coming across the courtyard to stroke one of the house dogs and note with pleasure the lush spread of a peacock's tail. Underneath the zeal, Meganius suspected a sensual and perhaps very sensitive man.

"Until tomorrow, your grace." Prince Marchudd turned to go.

"My anticipated pleasure, my lord."

Bishop and priest inclined their heads as Marchudd hurried away, wrestling with his toga.

"So that is Marchudd Rhys, prince of Parisii and Brigantes." Patricius dropped it like an accusation. "Why does he style himself in the pagan manner when he is baptized?"

The bishop waved him gracefully to the vacated chair. "Sit down, Father. Some wine?"

"No. Thank you."

"Well—I will in any case." His goblet hardly needed refilling, but Meganius felt a need to turn aside the rigid intensity of the young man. "You and I are priests with one allegiance, Father. The prince has many to deal with, not all of whom have seen the light of God."

"Germanus noted that. And deplored it."

"And rightly, perhaps, but Germanus is in Auxerre. You, Father Patricius, might at least attempt the patience of the Church that ordained you and give our prince a year or two to convert them." Meganius raised his goblet. "Long life—which hardly needs my invocation by the sturdy look of you, Sochet."

"No one has called me that since I left home. Your grace is a Brigante?"

"Born and bred. Cai meqq Owain. I thought I recognized the accent. We northerners have a prickly sound that doesn't fade."

"With your leave, I would speak of my mission."

Mentally Meganius riffled through the letters from Caerleon. "Yes ... Ireland?"

"Will you sponsor me?"

As a bishop, Meganius was of necessity a diplomat. "Well, I will certainly consider it. Ireland surely needs a mission. Meanwhile—"

"It is my calling." The young priest thrust forward in the chair, serious and intent. "Frozen and burned into me through six years. And in a vision at Auxerre, I heard Irish voices calling me back to preach to them."

"Yes ... so said the bishop of Caerleon. Admirable." And an annoyance. Meganius saw some malice on Caerleon's part for sending this bristling avatar to him; they were hardly personal friends. Meganius felt his irritation rising. The priest's rudely direct glance might be unsettling to some. Patricius gave the impression that he was weighing one's every word—one's soul—against the feather of his truth and finding you light in the balance. Strength was there but that pitiless youth as well.

"You doubt my calling, your grace?" *You dare?*

"No, no." Meganius found his usual courtesy an effort. There is nothing more rancorous to an older man at peace with an imperfect world than a young one reminding him of unsullied verities, especially when the young one may be essentially right. Canonical volunteers for Ireland did not crowd the western ports. "My boy, if I sponsor you and Auxerre sends you a consecrated pallium, you will be bishop of Ireland."

And while he was not yet an experienced parish priest, no more than a year in Germanus' charismatic wake, no doubt Patricius saw himself in Meganius' robes with the pliant Irish kneeling to kiss the diocesan ring. Meganius saw them boiling him alive for his callow arrogance. Pagan or not, the Irish kings and their shamans were men of experience, apalling as much of it could be. Reason, wisdom, and maturity might round off their sharp edges, but not this ponderously self-important young man. Meganius trusted his stomach in the measure of a man, and his stomach had hope for Patricius as a priest and a man who might in time wield the shepherd's crook as a guide, not a weapon. But not this week.

"We will talk of it over dinner. And perhaps you will say Mass tomorrow in my stead. I must officiate at the baptism of Marchudd's son."

Patricius relaxed a little. "I will say Mass for your grace. But as to dinner, I am vowed to fasting three days out of the week and can eat no meat."

"Oh, what a pity. My cook's done up a wine-drowned chicken."

"Oh, that's my favorite!"

Meganius' stomach was justified; for an instant a healthy, hungry young man glowed out of the brown eyes before the ascetic reined him back. "But . . . my vows."

"Permit me to grant you an indulgence for this evening."

"Well . . ."

"You would please me to accept it."

Patricius' smile was broad and unreserved now. "Your grace is kind."

For his own part, Patricius tried not to like Meganius, not because he didn't want to but rather feeling he shouldn't. An avowed

Pelagian and suspiciously tolerant, Meganius was just the sort of prelate Germanus inveighed against. Patricius would accept the indulgence and enjoy his chicken—a little, no more—and add several paternosters to his devotions before bed. He would hear the confessions the busy bishop urged on him for the morrow and quite eagerly take the day's Masses, since the well-to-do of Eburacum would attend at least one. There would be the wealthier merchants and perhaps even one or two of the royal family. Patricius' eye gleamed with frosty zeal. *Dyw!* Would they not hear a Mass! And the *sermon* ...

And the sermon. Suffice to say, any flesh left unflayed on the body spiritual of Britain by Germanus was colorfully flagellated by Patricius in his sermon. He glared down from the pulpit on the genuinely alarmed citizens of Eburacum—doubtless as the angel once surveyed Gomorrah, with an angel's suffusing and peculiarly merciless innocence—as he reminded them of how Jerome and Augustine fought for years to defeat the presumption of "your corpulent, corrupted hog of a darling, Pelagius."

And those who confessed to Patricius, accustomed to reasonable penances for reasonable sins, found themselves hanging by a shred over the fiery pit and under penances of an Anchorite severity. Meganius heard it from the breathless royal scribe who had it, brief and blistering, from the princess: who *was* this rabid sin-catcher? They were of a tolerant tradition; they ruled with Christ and the older gods in sensible conjunction, did they not? This hellfire preaching would *cease*, did the bishop understand?

Meganius understood and winced and went back to saying Mass himself. He took Patricius aside, still avuncular but sterner. "They must be led to faith, Patricius, not flogged to it."

The young priest flushed under the warning. "It does not matter. My mission is not here among the complacent but in Ireland."

"That again? Permit me to note that you will go to Ireland when and if I send you, Sochet."

But Patricius had heard the reaction of the royal house and was in fine defensive fettle. "Permit me to note, your grace, it seems an injustice."

"Oh? How, Sochet?"

Patricius' uncomfortably direct glance turned aside in some deference. "Your grace is a Pelagian."

"Which is to say I place some value on human common sense in attaining heaven."

"And that is the human error!" Patricius exploded. "Man cannot reason with God. 'I am that I am.' Man is *nothing* without God. He must

35

submit totally to achieve Grace. Ireland his virgin pasture. I will teach the truth with no heretical error."

"No doubt. And God help the Irish. They take their religion quite seriously. But let me remind you further of the abysmal failure of earlier missions there, which surprises me less than it does plebeian bigots like Augustine. It's not enough to speak their language. Their wise men, pagan though they may be, will look into your heart and quickly read you for the ill-writ, half-finished page you are. No, don't interrupt me. To be ignorant of Christ is not to be ignorant of men. They'd know you for an arrogant pup, Sochet. You wouldn't last a month. No. I will not send you to Ireland, not yet."

Caius Meganius was anything but a severe man. The dressing down he gave the younger priest upset him perhaps more than Patricius, who could shrug it off with the resilience of his righteousness. The priest avoided his bishop for several days—to brood further, Meganius suspected. He was agreeably surprised when Father Patricius accepted his invitation to dinner, evidently with new matter on his mind. They were finished with the cold oysters before Patricius broached his subject. Apparently the young man had not only thought on the bishop's words, he'd profited by them. His humility, ordinarily that of an actor projecting it from a stage, seemed genuine now.

"I prayed for guidance. I asked where and how and when I was to be used if my calling is real. It's not enough to teach or preach, not enough to wear an anointed sword. One must use it, strike with it. And yet . . ."

Meganius allowed the priest his own time and tether. "Yes?"

On his dining couch Patricius made a vague gesture, cleaning his fingers in a bowl of rose water. "I asked myself: is it only my arrogance, this mission to Ireland? I feel like—like a mosaic, each tile a truth adding to a whole if I could arrange them right. Your grace has put doubts in my mind, and now . . ."

"Not into the mind of the priest, only the man," Meganius cautioned gently. "Do you know clearly why you took orders, Father Patricius? Did you feel drawn back to Ireland then?"

Patricius took up his wine and swallowed a little, contemplating the goblet. Not the priest but the man answered the question. "There was my vision. I called it that. It was early in the morning after a night of poor sleep. I can't honestly say I wasn't dreaming."

So he was not without the ability to question his own motives, Meganius thought. "There's so much dissent in the Church now, one forgets what it all rests on. Put aside the war for now. I am interested now only in the heart of Magon Sochet, a Brigante like myself. What does *he* want to do for God? What does he want from God? I don't think you'd be honestly content pattering after luminaries like Jerome. You're not much of a Roman and hardly a Greek for subtlety."

"Lord no!" Patricius laughed heartily at the idea, and his expression lost its tight self-containment. "I'm a plain man. I like plain people."

"And open skies. And animals."

"Yes. Just that I can't think of myself as anything but a priest, not since I was seventeen."

"I see."

"Do you? Much of it's for myself, I admit that. The Church tells me the why of all things. I want to *know* why. Sometimes I think it's myself I'm trying to save," Patricius finished unhappily.

As I did at your brutal age; Meganius smiled inwardly.

"I want to find the Grace I preach, else I'm no more than a scribe babbling his master's word. I want to find where it is, dig for it, hold it in my hand, define it. Hold it up and say, 'Here! Here is ultimate truth!' "

Meganius sighed over his wine. The men who would be drunk on God: a heady wine, and Patricius already an addict. The inconsistency troubled the bishop. If Patricius were truly another Jerome— narrow, abrasive, forever unresolved himself between the Scylla of flesh and Charybdis of faith—nothing would help now or later. But there was a disconcerting humanity to this young man under the carapace of Germanus' laid-on rigidity, a healthy clay Meganius felt wary of molding hastily in the wrong shape. For all that, purpose was seeding in his mind.

"There is a mission to which I will sponsor you. Not Ireland, not yet, but north across the Wall among the Picts. There have been priests there; the Venicones have some knowledge of Christ. If you can establish a mission among them, then we might speak of Ireland."

The young man's headlong passion for godhead concerned Meganius enough to address a large portion of his private prayer to the problem that night.

"Did I do wisely in sending him north? Was it guidance, or am I simply an old man impatient or fearful of younger strength? Stagnant water jealous of the fresh spring? My God, my God, this Patricius needs Your special care. He would go over a cliff for You. Have I shoved him to the edge? He will never be the zealot he wants to be."

The Pictish mission was not Patricius' dream but a league toward it. He had the character and perseverance to accept it with a glimmer of humility if not full enthusiasm. When he set out for Corstopitum during the Kalends of July, Meganius' personal relief was not unalloyed with scruple. He'd purged his own headache by giving it to the Picts.

*   *   *

After six years among the Irish, the Venicones were not a cultural shock to Patricius, although he found them startling enough. Some of them were tattooed over much of their body from the neck down and lived naked to display it, their faces dyed or tattooed to the point of nightmare. The warriors stiffened their hair into bleached quills with birdlime. They lived in colorful sloth, each household of brothers with as many communal wives as they could maintain and fearing very little that went in daylight. With sundown, however, their hearts quailed. They barred the doors with iron and lived under siege of the evil dark until the sun rose again.

Curiosity opened gates to Patricius. Shamans of the Christ were still a novelty to the southern Picts, and he was welcome to preach to them if he didn't mind doing it over dinner or in the fields or while the village elder was pronouncing a sentence of death on someone for any one of a dozen sanguinary reasons. Patricius found it hard at first translating the profundities of Latin into their tongue. It was not that different from his native Cumbric but far less altered since their ancestors brought it from Gaul. The Venicones applauded his message of salvation. They were less impressed with his notions of virtue, especially at the riotous feast of Lughnassadh, when Patricius preached of Paul the Apostle and the basic tenets of Christian marriage. He stood close to the door of the smoky longhouse and called on the village elder, Vaco, to relinquish four of his five wives, tragically ignorant of what he demanded.

Picts might fear Faerie as reincarnated spirits of the dead, but they shared one age-old custom with them, from king to village head: descent through the female line, brothers sharing wives in common. To Patricius the custom was as legally vague as it was sinful. He knew and cared nothing for the reasons behind it. Each wife brought into a family linked it specifically within a social pyramid. Women were carefully chosen and not lightly discarded. This Briton's teaching was not only radical but dangerous. He exhorted men to celibacy and women to virginity with marriage as a poor alternative, as if a new generation would grow of itself like grass on the heath.

"I do not like this Christ-man," Vaco counseled with his two brothers, glancing at the knot of wives equally puzzled by what they understood of the sermon. "He does not teach but that he demands."

The younger brother snorted. "He thinks he is better than us because he speaks and dresses like a Roman."

"And we know them," Vaco commented sourly. "It is in my mind to send him away."

"He is not of importance. There is not one mark of honor on his body. Kill him," the second brother urged. "Quietly. Say his god took him in sleep."

That sat poorly with the elder, who did not earn his position for impulsiveness. "This god of his, this Jesu Christ, is powerful not only in Britain but across all the world to the city of the Romans themselves."

"Is not Lugh then as strong?" the younger argued. "Is it that we have ever had a better harvest or so many wives with child? We do well keeping the way we know."

"Aye, kill him," the second brother urged again, wiping greasy hands on his brilliantly tattooed chest.

"That is a thought. We might do that." Elder Vaco gave his attention to the mead pot to allow himself a moment's reflection. The priest's teachings were subversive and downright arrogant. Nevertheless, they were close enough to trade with Roman camp towns on the Wall or raid when it suited them, and the idea of profit was to lose as little as possible when you didn't have to. Nothing would be gained by killing the priest or flouting their own gods.

"There is that way which is in the middle," he told his brothers. "We'll cripple him and leave him on the hill. If Faerie or wolves kill him, his god was not strong enough. If he lives and returns, we will know that even Lugh is not stronger. Then ... we will see. Meanwhile, we lose no favor with Lugh."

The brothers mulled this and nodded soberly. Their brother chief was a wise man who ever held first the good of his people.

"Crack his bones and take him to the hill of the fires."

It hardly need be said that Picts were a shrewd people, older than Britons in the land and serpentine in bargaining even with the gods. By virtue of this prudence, Patricius was allowed his life and two broken legs—but, for the time, no converts.

He thought he was going to die when they dragged him to the stone and threw him on it, sure of it when the elder approached with the hammer. They were going to dash his brains out. He closed his eyes against the weak mortal fear and tried to whisper as much of a contrition as he could before the blow fell.

He shrieked when the hammer first struck his ankle, fainted at the second. When he could think again, he was jolting on a rough litter through the darkness flanked by torches. His head was lower than his feet; they were toiling him uphill. The pain in his ankles throbbed steadily.

Now the men stopped in the darkness. Patricius saw the new fear in their faces limned by the torchlight. He was too far gone in pain and shock to be frightened himself. He tried to pray again, but his numbed mind couldn't frame the words. Looming dim beyond the torches, he saw the ring of great stones and caught the sibilant drift of the men's timorous hesitation.

"Well, come on! We have to put him *in* the circle."

"Nae, I will not go in there, not tonight."

"Is it coward that you are?"

"That I am not, but Faerie's abroad this night."

"Fool! It is a special need that this is, and a moment's work. Come on."

"The stones moved. I saw them move."

"Come on!"

For all his determination to follow orders, the leader did not tarry within the ring of haunted stones. His men huddled close together, glancing fearfully over their shoulders every few moments while two of them hauled Patricius off the litter and dumped him on the ground. He cried out when his ankles hit the earth. Then the light dimmed and the torches receded with the hurrying bearers, jittering with their haste.

The great circle of stones towered around him as the moon sank in the west. His fear drained away into exhaustion and shuddering. The throbbing in his legs settled to a deep, dull pain. Patricius felt gingerly at the swelling ankles. Broken for sure—fractured, more likely. The bones did not seem wrenched out of place, but he couldn't be sure. If he lived long enough, if he could find someone who'd care enough to set them, he might survive. Small chance; they'd have to find him, he could barely crawl. He finished his contrition, crossed himself, and tried to keep warm by curling his misery into a ball. The moon went down, and gradually the light brightened in the east. Patricius woke from shallow sleep to cold morning and terrible thirst, nauseous and light-headed when he tried to sit up.

Cold sweat prickled his forehead. After a few moments the nausea passed. His lower legs were swollen twice their size, with huge blue-black bruises edged with yellow. Part of the pain came from his sandal straps cutting into the swollen flesh. With considerable pain, Patricius loosened the thongs and eased them off. It took all the strength and will he had left. He lay back on one elbow, panting with the exertion, and only then noticed the small bundle close to one of the stones. Something wrapped in lambswool with several smaller objects by it, including a bowl.

Food.

Yes, of course, the same way he wrapped his own rations when out all night with Miliucc's flocks.

"Sweet Lord, I thank you."

His voice sounded ragged and weak as he dragged himself toward the bundle. Whatever shepherd had left the food would come again and find him. Not Venicones; this was obviously a place they feared, but no place on earth was hidden from God or His arm. Patricius felt some of his courage returning. They thought they could finish *him* with broken legs and a night in the cold? He'd spent more cold nights on Irish mountains than there were stones, and each night in the Hand of God. He would pay for the food and pray for the shepherd when he came.

Queer objects: the bowl contained only a handful of oats. Beside it lay a sheaf of grass carefully tied with a strand of flax. Chewing the oats, Patricius unwrapped the bundle. The food turned to ash in his mouth.

The swarthy infant lay amid the fleecy folds, the clay discs great staring white eyes in the small face. Each of its limbs had been broken like his. Already the small toothless mouth tightened in the rictus of death, as if the child itself mocked his hopes.

"Savages . . . animals."

The child had been left dead or nearly so. No one would come. Besides the Venicone village he could see only hills and unbroken moor. Crawl as he might, in two days or even one he'd be too weak to move. The wolves and ravens would find him long before that.

He heard the sudden rustling and turned his head.

One of them had found him already.

The raven perched like disinterested Fate on a stone across the circle. Two more wheeled in the morning sky.

Patricius dragged the little bundle closer to him. A poor end to his mission, but the child was already gone. He would follow shortly. He must pray for them both, even though the infant was probably unbaptized. He mumbled through dry lips, felt the weak tears of self-pity welling up. "And yet I fear the hour of —*oh!*"

He was jerked over onto his back, felt the cold blade at his throat. The scarred faces peering down at him were detached and expressionless as the raven. They looked like twins, two small, fierce children. Quickly the boy cut the thong that held the iron Chi-Rho medallion at Patricius' breast and hurled it beyond the circle.

When he realized they were more curious than predatory, he managed to speak. "The child is dead," he croaked, hoping they understood. He nodded weakly at the boy's bronze knife. "No need of that. I'll die soon anyway. Do you . . . have some water?"

He had to ask again. The girl said something to her companion, pointing to Patricius' legs. Then she scurried behind one of the stones and brought back a clay jar. She pointed to the wounds again, excited. She seemed overjoyed at his injuries.

"Drink," she said.

Sweet Jesus! Not water but good, strong mead. He swallowed greedily. "Thank you."

The girl touched the thick, gold torc around her brown neck. Able to think more clearly now, Patricius noted the incongruity of the opulent torc against the rest of her scant, ragged costume. The fine-worked gold was rich enough by itself; the emeralds and rubies inset made it worth a prince's ransom.

She spoke again, something about . . . being sent by the raven? Mother? Her dialect was akin to the Venicone but even more archaic, with some words he understood not at all, especially with her queer, aspirated manner of speech. When he could only sign his lack of understanding, she touched the torc and said it again.

"Be Dorelei. Dor-a-lay. Gern-y-fhain."

The boy jabbed his knife at Patricius. "Thee's Briton-man?"

"I am Fa . . . Father Patricius."

The boy cocked his head at the queer sound. "Pad . . . ?"

"Patricius."

They had difficulty until he repeated it again, each syllable distinct. Then the girl flashed a sudden smile of comprehension, small white teeth startling against the brown face and even darker lips.

"Padrec, Cru. *Padrec.*"

Although she came to love him dearly, that was the best Dorelei could ever do with such an ungainly name. He was Padrec.

42

II

Gift from Raven

Tey were already weighted with the death of Neniane's child. This new thought of Dorelei's was odd and dangerous, that Padrec was sent by their Parents to aid them. They saw only a crippled stranger, and tallfolk at that. They didn't question Gern-y-fhain, who appeared a rock of certainty. It must be so, she said: how often did Venicones venture to the hill of fires in the daylight, let alone the dark? And see where the bones of his legs were broken as they broke those of the dead child to let the spirit out. So the living spirit of Padrec was now at the service of fhain.

Well—it could be true, but not even staunch Cruaddan was convinced at first. "Be sure, Dorelei?"

She only gazed down at him from the height of her infallibility and touched her gold torc. "Did speak as Gern. A's sent to us. Gift from Lugh-Raven."

Once the rest accepted this much, that Dorelei herself believed it, they took good care of Padrec, shared unstintingly, and drowned him in comfrey tea to heal his bones. Padrec missed his Chi-Rho; they might have left him that, but when they prudently removed his tinderbox as well, he realized it was not the symbol but the iron itself they feared.

"Worst evil of all," Drust warned darkly while Dorelei whispered magic over the tinderbox to dispel any lingering evil before it was abandoned a goodish way down the hill.

They splinted his legs with meticulous care and made sure he had soft fleeces to rest on. Hardly a laconic lot, they talked to him all the time—talked *at* him, rather; Padrec had difficulty at first catching the queer fall of their dialect. Under the Roman veneer, the Brigante of him took it as axiom that Faerie were less than human. His ear, sifting its knowledge of various dialects, knew otherwise. If alien, they spoke an argot he analyzed as more Gael than Brythonic, older than both and akin to that of remote villages in Gaul. Some words were completely foreign, more aspiration than sound. They reminded him of the old Atecotti man from the barren country of the brochs in the far north who'd been one of his father's slaves.

"You are Atecotti?" he asked Dorelei.

She knew the name, apparently, and with gestures and few words told him Atecotti were honorable folk, oldest in Mabh's island next to hers. Then she touched her own breast.

"Prydn. Pruh-din."

"Faerie?"

She only shrugged, squatting beside him with her wrists dangling over her knees. That was his word, if he wished to use it. Prydn was an older name from before Britain was an island. "Most oldest."

Her stunted size confused Padrec at first, no larger than a child of twelve. The smallness was deceptive. Dorelei was a full-grown young woman in exquisite miniature. She would be ancient at fifty, if she lived that long, but her slight body would remain tough and supple throughout the brief, rigorous life of her kind.

They were not that far from the village that cast him out to die, yet no men came any nearer Cnoch-nan-ainneal than they could help. Not that it mattered. Soon enough fhain would be moving to new pasture before settling into crannog for the winter. To a certain extent they hibernated like bears.

When his legs were well on the mend they carried Padrec out of the rath to enjoy the last of summer. He breathed deep of the fresh air after the heavy atmosphere of the rath. It was no longer offensive to him, an effluvium of food, dog, human skin and sweat, sheep-odors, the oil of raw fleece, all blended into a pungent musk. But the view from the hillside was breathtaking at early morning, the heath and its swaths of color—red, yellow, blue, and lavender against the azure of the sky and its always stately procession of many-mooded clouds. Sky was important to fhain. Sky was male, Lugh's domain, and changed moods as their Father did, so that from the hillside, Padrec could see many different moods at once, much as in Ireland. The beauty was sudden and stark. The unreal brilliance of the colors hurt his eyes, a scene removed from time. Presently time would start up again with a jerk and the mundane world move on. But the moment and the stillness were a treasure.

Knowing sheep, Padrec found the Prydn variety a queer breed, the wool growing in shaggy twisted strands intermixed with rough hair that had to be separated out after shearing. Ewes and rams alike bore horns, and their meat had little more fat than wild game. The fatter breeds on the downs of southern Britain were stupid, vapid animals, but these had a feral wariness and a will of their own. The dog Rof had to control them constantly, which he did through a precise communication with the herder. Sounds and hand signals would stop Rof short and send him wheeling off on a tangent to execute the new order, shouldering or nipping the strays back into the group, always alert for weasel or wolf or the occasional hawk.

"Rof looks like a wolf," Padrec said to Bredei one afternoon while keeping him company on herd watch.

"Father be wolf." Bredei raised his eyes. "Mother be hound. Like Mother and Lugh. Earth and sky."

"He might have more wolf in him and turn on the sheep. I've seen that."

"Nae." Bredei was positive. "More dog. Heart be dog."

"Not by the look. How dost know?"

"Told me."

"Who did?"

"Rof. Who dost speak of, Padrec?"

"Dogs can't speak. You joke on me."

Bredei only smiled in patience. "Many things speak. Must have ears. Rof! Rof! Rof! Come!"

As the great dog loped up the hillside, yards at a stride, Bredei poured his porridge bowl to the brim with water and set it down for the dog. "Aye, good dog, Rof. Thee's a-thirst? Here."

Rof ducked his great iron-gray snout to the bowl and began to lap gratefully. A dog would always lap water, Bredei explained, while a wolf thrust his whole snout into the water and sucked it up.

"A knows what a be. And thee, Padrec?" Bredei studied the priest leaning on his crutches. "Be more tallfolk? Or human like fhain?"

Rof had a wolf's grayish-black pelt and many of the lines. His normal gait about his rounds had the unique wolf's trot, but when he broke into a run his longer legs thrust him forward in great airborne bounds of fifteen feet or more without touching turf. He looked a nightmare: taller than a wolf at the shoulder, head and jaws much larger and stronger. He caught a fox stalking near the flock. Padrec saw the reddish neck go instantly limp in those jaws as they bit down. Then a vicious shake and toss, and poor Tod-Lowery turned twice, head over tail, and lay without a twitch where he landed. Neniane made mittens from the fur and a carrying pouch from the stomach lining, and her husbands haggled over the luxurious red tail as an ornament.

Padrec knew their speech more surely now. If these were the reincarnated spirits of the dead as legend told, they were reborn wily bargainers with a sly sense of humor. Artcois indicated the tail, his expression and tone pained with noble sacrifice. "Be small and mangy. Not worthy of my brother's fine head. Will spare thee that and take it."

"No," said Bredei in the same selfless mode. "Will hide it from thy sight and promise thee better when Tod-Lowery comes again."

"Ah, no. Would pain me to see thee go with only the hind end of so poor Lowery to proclaim thee."

Bredei began to cloud over. "Dost say thy love's greater than mine? Will shoot for it."

"Oh, well." Artcois sighed like a martyr and reached for his short bow. "But in kindness, brother and second husband to most fair among women, thee would lose."

"Dost say so? Thee's more mouth than bow. Shoot."

"Thee will lose, Bredei."

"Shoot."

"Mother and Lugh will it. Do thee fetch a lamb."

It was in the late afternoon, when their tasks granted them time, that the lamb was tethered on the hillside and the husbands paused by Padrec's resting place to set their rules. When Hawk stooped at the lamb, they would shoot together but with different arrowheads of bronze and flint. Since neither would miss (unthinkable), the tail would go to the mortal strike.

All very well, as Padrec watched, but then they botched the lot by sitting in the open twenty paces to either side of the tethered bait. Hawks could be single-minded but not stupid, and no Faerie under a wolf hide was going to fool them.

The lamb lurched about, helpless and inviting. A number of starlings whirred close in curiosity and flew on. Padrec wondered how long the men would wait before realizing . . .

Before . . .

He blinked and looked again, had to look twice to see them. The grayish hides were two rocks, part of the moor. Even Padrec might believe they'd been so forever.

When the hawk appeared, it was far and high, a black line floating on blue void—slow, lazy, barely moving as it fell off into the wind and let the current pull it into a long, spiraling turn. The hawk spiraled steeper and faster, amber eyes reading every clue to food and danger: the lamb between two humps like any other hump in the earth, the human watching but too far to be a threat. Hawk came out of the descent, wings barely moving, and glided directly over the lamb. Then dark wings folded into dark body. Hawk dropped down the sky like a missile, beautiful and merciless.

The two stones moved.

Hawk seemed to stumble over something solid in the sky rushing up around him. The dive became a pell-mell tumble, and Hawk smashed into the ground a few paces from the startled lamb. A midge of feather floated down after him. Two shafts protruded from his black breast like a pair of absurd forelegs.

"Bredei."

Padrec jumped at the throaty whisper close to his ear. Dorelei squatted there, might have grown out of the earth there, so still she was. "Bredei."

The arrows were very close in the breast. Artcois and Bredei appealed to Gern-y-fhain for the prize. She awarded it to Bredei with no argument from his brother.

Padrec couldn't see it. "How could you tell? The arrows struck home as one."

"But must decide." Dorelei swept her gray eyes over him with a nuance of humor and appreciation at the sight of Padrec. "Watch. Learn. Will need thee as well."

Dorelei was right; Bredei wanted it most, but in the fhain way he had no notion of "mine." He wore Tod-Lowery's tail a few days, then left it for Artcois. Within a week both forgot it.

To Padrec they were all alike as pebbles at first, but as he worked into the ancient rhythm of their lives and speech, fhain emerged as individuals to his eye if not his stringent morality. Holy Church would turn in horror from their marriage customs, if the term was even applicable. They were inbred as royal Egyptian housecats. To say Dorelei and Cru were cousins said nothing; none of them were farther apart in blood than that. In the involuted manner of their coupling, age after age, they were closer than siblings.

They said it brought them closer together in love. The natural playfulness of the others was restrained in Dorelei and Cru. They were more cautious and reserved, spoke less at gatherings but with authority when they must. Padrec was not unacquainted with the fine art of the pagan world. Dorelei reminded him of certain sculptures—not the meaty, sensual figures of Greece and Rome but the delicate work from Alexandria or Minos. Her tiny form was beautifully proportioned, as if God first carved perfection in miniature before turning to larger humans, and Dorelei was distressingly careless in displaying it. She nudged somnolent urges he'd taken pride in conquering long past. In these warm days as summer declined, Dorelei sometimes went bare from the waist up with only a clout of linen about her loins or a skirt of wool fringes that covered very little. Padrec spent much time in earnest prayer for himself as well as Dorelei.

Cru's proportion was as perfect if one excepted the breadth of his shoulders, a peculiarity of fhain men. Truly children of Eden, they had every grace except a knowledge of God. And these were the "little people" of whom Calpurnius' peasants told such dark stories.

Where Dorelei was beautiful in a clean, carven way, Neniane was sweeter and softer. That peculiar set to their eyes, slanting as if to follow the high cheekbones, was more pronounced in Neniane. With the rounded softness of her face it gave her a feline look like a puzzled kitten. Her gracefulness rested in her small brown hands. Her fingers at any task flashed precisely as Minoan dancers, a world of tactile experience in their economy of movement. No task was too precise for Neniane's hands, no object to small to work well, cutting, carving a bone hook or sewing with a bronze needle. Padrec saw why there were so many stories about Faerie cobblers and workers of tiny metals. Small hands and superb eyesight were Faerie characteristics. The clumsiest of them, Drust, could bore and thread the smallest beads for a necklace for Guenloie or groove a willow shaft straight as a rule to receive an arrowhead.

Neniane's husbands were childlike men. Sometimes Neniane was more scolding sister than wife, although she made no distinction between them in her generous affections. Artcois and Bredei could not remain serious for very long. They were quite friendly toward Padrec, also his watchdogs. His legs were almost healed; he thanked them and wished to be free to go. Go? Ah, no, Padrec. Gern-y-fhain said stay, that was the end of it. He would remain.

"But . . . but see here! I am a free Roman citizen and a priest of Holy Church. I have many places to go."

"Stay."

"Not that I'm not grateful, mind you. Not that I wouldn't return to preach to you, but—"

But Gern-y-fhain had spoken. His spirit was released to fhain, and Padrec must stay. In the middle of his protestations, Artcois and

Bredei squatted, one on either side of his legs, each with a large stone in his hand. As tactfully as possible, they explained their position. His legs were broken once to release his spirit. If Padrec remained obdurate, they could be modified again, much as it grieved Artcois and Bredei. Padrec sputtered, swallowed, and looked from one to the other. They'd damned well do it.

In all else they were largesse itself. When the time approached to move north, Cru decided Padrec was too large for a fhain pony.

"Must walk, crutches and all," Bredei sorrowed.

"Or borrow horse," Artcois offered. He appealed to Cru. "Cruaddan first husband, be those horses far who cry out as the pierced heart for a's freedom?"

"Not so far," Cru estimated with an understanding smile, "that fhain does not hear them."

Bredei clapped Padrec on the back as if morning light had routed the last murk from the problem. "Will free one for Padrec!"

"Be only kindness," Artcois agreed. "And thy brother must aid in this."

"I usually—that is, a priest does not ride a horse but a mule," Padrec attempted.

They frowned at him. Mule? What be mule?

"Like a horse, but—"

They couldn't grasp it. Horse be horse.

"You don't know everything," Padrec burst out, exasperated at them and his crutchbound helplessness. "It's half horse and half ass."

Consternation. A new problem. Which half was ass?

"The *mare*, damn it. God forgive my careless tongue."

No real help there. Draft animals and hybrids were unknown to fhain. They'd never seen a mule—nor, come to think of it, a stallion with a taste for loving anything but his own kind. Either Padrec made a joke on his friends whose every effort now bent to his aid, or else he came from a land where animals had customs inscrutable as his own.

He got a horse night-borrowed from a distant village. No one seriously thought anyone would come to make trouble. Padrec learned after a time that anything borrowed by Faerie was never sought by the original owners. It simply disappeared into Faerie-land.

"And much happier with fhain," Artcois reasoned. "See how dost toss a's fine head."

"But you *stole* it." And Padrec launched into a cautionary lecture on the sin of theft: "Thou shalt not steal!"

"And shall nae shout, Padrec. Will fright thy horse. Do nae steal," Bredei concluded on a note of injury. Padrec abandoned it. They had no direct word for theft, as they had only the vaguest

51

notion of property. All came from Mother and Lugh, who would deny nothing to first children.

There was little discord in their lives and that quickly settled. Most of it came from Guenloie. Padrec's direct experience with women as sexual beings was limited, but he knew the sort men regarded as light or easy. Guenloie told him of her Taixali mother and seemed eager to hear of the women of the south and to identify with them. Padrec was sensitive enough to be touched by her open naïveté but insufficiently versed in the gender to know her first-blown, half-child sexuality as ingenuous as the rest of her. Guenloie reminded him of one of his father's overbred roses, too flush and ripe. Fhain women were not promiscuous; no woman invited the husband of another, but Padrec was a gift from Raven and unclaimed. Guenloie found ample excuse to putter about close by. That she did so in full view of her husbands was a measure not of cruelty but innocence. Once she leaned across Padrec to fetch a cup and let her bare breast brush his cheek. He recoiled in confusion, indignant.

"Woman, stop that. Cover yourself. Do you not know what I am?"

Guenloie flashed her radiant smile. "Holy man."

In a corner of the rath, Drust drew his bronze knife and began to hone it on a piece of sandstone. Beside him, Malgon's eyes narrowed with long experience on Guenloie, whose smile now had a teasing quality.

"Dost nae like women?"

"I am a priest. How can I say it? Be promised not to take women. Go away."

The notion of celibacy was as alien to Guenloie as was flying to a dog. She was openly astonished. "Dost not lie with women?"

"No."

"Then how dost get child-wealth?" Guenloie's laughter tinkled in the rath as she leaned forward to stroke his cheek. Suddenly she was jerked roughly away and Padrec felt Drust's knife at his throat. "Drust, no!"—his heart stopped for an instant, then Drust in his turn was thrust aside and Malgon loomed over the knot of them, restraining his brother husband's arm.

"Fool, Drust, *fool*! A knows nothing. Go thee down in crannog. Guenloie!" Malgon jerked his head toward the taut Drust. Not submissively, but in complete understanding and acceptance, Guenloie took Drust's hand and drew him with caresses through the crannog opening in a corner of the rath. Malgon turned on Padrec.

"Come, walk."

"I don't feel like walking."

"Walk."

Malgon pulled Padrec to his feet and steadied him as he set the crutches. He'd made them himself and was proud of their craftsmanship. When Padrec eased himself out of the rath, Malgon led him a little way from it. His gray eyes were almost black with the anger behind them.

"A's love for Guenloie be too full. Like a sickness. Guenloie's be worse. Must be loved by all. Fools." Malgon squatted, scratching with angry knife strokes in the dirt. It was his habitual preoccupation; he sketched constantly with anything at hand. In a few strokes, idly or perhaps to visualize the intensity of his feelings, he drew the head of a wolf with mouth lolled open, laughing or snarling. "Will never be happy, Padrec. Never have enough. Guenloie be a good wife, but fool. Leave be."

Exasperating to Padrec that they could not understand even that much of him or his intentions. "I can take no woman. Leave me alone."

This impressed Malgon no more than Guenloie. "A's in crannog with Drust and will love him now. Leave be." And Malgon left Padrec hunched on his crutches, angry and frustrated as cloud shadows chased each other through the sunlight and Guenloie's tremulous cry of delight lifted from the crannog below.

They understood nothing, these people, nothing of value. While there was no papal rule, celibacy was the approved way of a priest. Some married; many bishops did, but the case for celibacy was incontrovertible and encouraged by Rome.

Not that he was entirely virginal. On two occasions in Ireland, female slaves of Miliuc found him attractive. They excited him. He might have pursued lechery further at peril of his soul if the energy of his youth had not been diverted by God. One wrestled with and defeated such urges; they were not the worst of his personal devils, not even with Dorelei walking bare in his sight. No, the need to be *right*, to be vindicated before all men, to be spiritually triumphant, this was his acknowledged weakness. Meganius sensed it in him, as deadly as lust. The priest of Padrec forever forced his head to bow while the frail, intractable sinner piped his feeble pride.

Oh, Meganius, where have you sent me?

What did these Faerie want of him? He couldn't leave. They claimed his spirit as theirs. Sometimes it seemed Dorelei was waiting something from him, but what? He was almost strong enough now to collect his thoughts and contemplate how to bring them the Word. Certainly no more fallow field existed for it than these incestuous children of Cain, and yet where to begin? What handhold, what common starting point that Dorelei or the rest would understand?

His legs were not yet healed. The continued pain fueled the

53

flush of self-righteousness. Perhaps in her ignorant way, Dorelei had a piece of truth. God had sent him to teach her pathetic people, to save them from the spiritual oblivion toward which they drifted. Their ministered needs would hone his powers, as Drust's knife against the stone, toward the day he faced the Irish chiefs. Even Miliuc would see how the holy strength of Patricius dwarfed his own and confounded his shamans. All Ireland would flock to him. His letters, models of modesty, would impress Germanus by their lack of striving to that effect. The word would go from Auxerre to Rome itself: *In the west, in Ireland, there is a new province for Christ carved by Bishop Patricius whose footsteps led first through Pictland and those fabulous folk known as Faerie . . .*

He was tipsy with the notion of fame; yet as he bowed his head to pray with renewed inspiration, Padrec quelled the pride and tried to think only that God and Christ burned through him in their potency. When he had given thanks, he turned his fierce anger on the distant Venicone village like a sleeping sow in the valley beyond. *You thought you could blunt the sword of God? You?*

But Meganius may have been right—that once. He wasn't quite ready. He would start here with the first small brick in his edifice to God. Savages they were, but not animals, as most people thought. Even giving Him the wrong name, they had a burning need for God. The dead child, the grain, were only a message to their "parents." Send food for ourselves and our flocks, or this death will take all of us.

Dorelei would come to understand. There was an unexpected sweetness in the prospect. He imagined the bright dawn of comprehension in that exquisite, intelligent face. He saw her standing humbly before him, head bowed (befitting, although she never did) and modestly dressed (for a change) to receive at last the truth from Father Patricius. He dressed her in the robes and role of the Magdalene and was young enough not to wince at the indulgence. He saw Dorelei kneel to him, open to the Power that worked through him, and thought the deep flush of excitement and pleasure was pure holy purpose when it was predictably adulterated with simple love for the woman. Being more practical and much more observant, Dorelei knew it earlier and more surely, but then women usually do.

Yet while he strained to change their lives, those lives began to color his own. He sensed a pattern to their existence beyond mere survival, even a music if he could catch the theme and put it to God's harmony. When Padrec's sight began to enlarge beyond his own purposes to contemplate theirs, it seemed to him that he knew them not at all.

Sometimes with sunset red beyond the rath entrance, they would fall silent as if by a single will, frozen on muscled haunches like Bredei and Artcois waiting for Hawk, their gaze on Gern-y-fhain.

"Did speak to Mother in dream last night," Dorelei announced.

Cru waited a proper space to show his respect. "What dream, Gern-y-fhain?"

"As before. As always. Dream of Rainbow."

If Padrec was perplexed, he was not alone. In the circle of stones, Dorelei pondered the other side of the same quandary without the aid of Padrec's dramatic egotism. She weighed the wisdom of a decision snatched out of the air in a desperate moment. Did she read the sign aright? Was it Lugh perched on the stone at dawn, or just a scavenging bird attracted by carrion?

"Cannae turn back now, cannae send Padrec away. Fhain would nae trust me as gern. O Mother, send one of us child-wealth. Fhain would take that as a good sign Send *something*. Cannae understand this Padrec."

And what she did understand was impossible. He was not of Mother and Lugh but of a certain father-god of whom Dorelei knew nothing. There seemed no place for a mother or any woman at all. The abnormality, the heresy made her ears burn. Lugh might depart forever and Mother freeze over for good and all. No place even for a woman in his own life. He said men like himself should not marry. Most strange when he seemed male and vital in every way, comely and a rugged mountain dweller like herself. Dorelei had never seen hair so crisp or angry-red or skin that freckled about the forehead and the backs of his hands. Freckles were new to her, Padrec's word when she asked him. She'd thought Mother was undecided what color to make him at first. He intrigued her. The idea was not beyond possibility, especially in a fhain without children. Padrec might make a good second husband if he could change some of his silly notions about the world in general and women in particular. Yes—a good strong body the man had, built to endure, perhaps even for the delight of loving.

She forced her thoughts back to prayer and need. They must move soon to a new crannog for the winter. In a Venicone hut she'd once admired an ornament of two glass cups connected by a thin tube. Sand ran from one cup to the other through the tube to mark what tallfolk called an hour. Dorelei's own instincts prompted her to move, but she measured by a different glass.

"Mother, if Padrec is to help us, show how. Must ride north with winter coming. Be wise? Be young and new and . . . frightened, Mother. Lead fhain as thee did Mabh. Send me quickly thy wisdom. And some to Padrec, who could much use it."

* * *

The Venicone women gathering herbs on the hillside passed close enough to Dorelei for her to speak to them without raising her voice. Because she willed it so, they didn't see her at all. Through the magic taught by Gawse, she was so still as to be merely a nondescript patch on the heath.

Nothing but her eyes moved when the sound piped over the moor. The song she waited for, no other like it. Dorelei saw the flash of yellow-green plumage as the finch drummed up into the sky. So her own glass turned. When Finch sang, fhain must think of winter. No sign was so reliable, but the Venicone women were deaf as they were blind; they'd be surprised once more when winter came early. They never learned.

Above Dorelei on the hill, Cru observed, "Five tens of days to snow, Padrec. Nae more."

Padrec squinted dubiously. "Will be early then."

"Dost hear Finch? Will start."

"The new crannog? Where?"

"Will be there."

"Where?"

"When do find it. Padrec, dost tire me with asking." Cru waved a bronze arm out over the valley and the world. "See? All answers. Need no asking."

"Those women down there, they walked right by Dorelei. Are they blind?"

"Yes," said Cru. "Like thee. But thy sight be opening to Mother."

Move they must and much to do. Sheepskin saddles were mended, new baskets woven from broad-bladed stalks, available food gathered. Blackberries bursting ripe now in the lowland thickets were marked by day and collected in sunset forays when tallfolk were safely inside. Guenloie and Neniane replenished their stores of herbs for tea and medicines. The men butchered those sheep too old or weak to make the journey and dried the meat. Most important of all, their bronze scraps— broken knives and tools—were packed for travel along with the clay molds for new ones, while Padrec dug with Drust and Malgon into the chalk ridges for usable flints. Few orders needed to be given; each of them had prepared like this twice a year since they were old enough to run behind the ponies. It was their earliest memory.

Fhain ate well the last night before moving on, mutton basted in its own juice and a gravy thickened with the last of their hoarded barley flour, and only when they were down to nibbling and picking did Padrec signal to Dorelei that he wished to speak. He chose his time carefully, since ritual speaking was a precise custom. He must sit cross-legged, hands loose across his knees but with his back erect. Not the most comfortable position for a man used to standing and moving when he preached. Padrec waited until it was clear Dorelei had no ritual speaking to take precedent.

"Would speak, Gern-y-fhain."

Dorelei looked up in hopeful surprise, then nodded. They all turned expectantly to Padrec, as if they'd been waiting for this. "Gern-y-fhain is wise," he began. "Truly have I come from my God, even a shepherd like thee to lead fhain to Him."

"To Tir-Nan-Og," Dorelei murmured. "Do thee speak of it."

"But who will come unclean to his father or mother?" Padrec impaled them all on his pitiless stare. He felt the power of God rising in him like a tide. "*Who* among thee is without sin? Before thou canst come to thy Father, thee must be washed, yea, even in the blood of the lamb, for each of you lives in sin!"

He had their whole attention and alarm at his sudden vehemence. At the reference to lamb's blood, Bredei glanced bemusedly at the remains of the mutton.

"The Grace of God is not cheaply bought, sinners. I tell you it is a narrow door, a needle's eye—"

Drust touched his knee in concern. "Dost ail, Padrec?"

"No, do not ail!" Padrec jerked away from the compassionate hand, banging one of his ankles hard against a stone. He gasped with the sudden pain that shattered his holy momentum. "Which of you . . ."

Clutching the throbbing ankle, he thought of the night the Venicones crippled him. They hadn't understood any more than fhain. He'd thought to build an edifice to God, with fine words about laying the first brick; yet, like an idiot carpenter, he was beginning with the arch of the roof. He rubbed his ankle, seething, while fhain waited politely.

They must be led to Grace, not flogged to it. All right, Meganius. Not the blood of the lamb; for now the gentleness. He looked up at Dorelei, wondering where to begin. When he spoke he used the words and pictures that had meaning for them. For the first time in his priestly calling, without realizing it, Padrec spoke *to* his congregation, not at it. The result was less of a distortion than he would have thought. Dates and years had no meaning to them. Their stories from the past began in a certain way; they would relate to no other.

"Was in the first days in a village like Venicone but far away. A girl named Mary was working in her father's rath when the Raven-spirit of God appeared to her and said: 'Woman, you bear the spirit of

57

God in the flesh. Blessed is the fruit of thy womb. The Son of God shall thee bear and he shall be called Jesu.' "

Fhain nodded thoughtfully. Padrec spoke of strong magic, and any such discussion was a serious thing. For a virgin to carry the child-wealth of Lugh or any god by whatever name was magic of the most potent sort.

"Now, when her time was nigh come to bear the child, a speaking went out from the king of the Roman-men, that each man go to the village of his birth to be taxed. So Joseph took Mary on a mule—see, Bredei? Did *tell* thee were mules—and went toward his village. They stopped at a place called Bethlehem at a large rath where there were so many others traveling alike that there was no room for Joseph and Mary, so they byred in the crannog with the sheep and cattle. Cold winter it was, atwixt Samhain and Brigid-feast."

"Crannog be best," Cru mumbled, picking at a rib bone. "Warmer."

"Always," Malgon agreed. In his view Joseph was a shrewd and fortunate traveler.

"Now, there were shepherds like fhain watching over their flocks in the night."

As a shepherd, Padrec loved the Gospel of Luke. Sometimes, when he shivered on an Irish hill, he thought of those herders on that night of nights and knew exactly what they felt. He spoke of these things to fhain now, and they recognized them. He'd been whereof he spoke and knew the common things familiar to them. The dry, unsalted barley bread dipped in herb tea and munched under the whisper of night wind; the muffled bleating of a sheep here and there, the chill beauty of night and stars; the sense of being alone and naked to Lugh peering through the bright-lit holes in the sky that looked close enough to reach and touch. And one light, Padrec told them, brighter than all the others on this blessed night.

"When the Angel of God appeared to them and said, 'Do thee go to this crannog at Bethlehem where a virgin has borne the Son of God.' So a did follow the light to the place where a found Him in the cradle much like Neniane's. Even the animals knelt in worship, and there were three high gerns from far fhains come with gifts for the holy bairn."

Cru cocked his head to one side. "What did look like? Raven-spirit?"

"Did look a child. The Man-Son of God."

"But if a child," Dorelei asked, "then what did look like? Tallfolk? Red hair like thee?"

What indeed? Padrec was already learning to sketch his pictures to the frame of their imagination. If he waxed canonical in describing Christ or gave the formalized answers, they would have no meaning

58

here. To fhain the halo would only look as if Jesu's head were glued to a flat dish. They needed a picture they knew.

Drust: of all the fhain men the youngest and most sensitive. When his intensity relaxed, when Guenloie had favored him with love, there was a fresh-washed radiance and innocence to his expression. Padrec tapped his shoulder.

"Did look like Drust."

"Who be most fair among men." Guenloie stroked his thigh in approval of her second husband.

Fhain sat rapt as Padrec recounted the wonders of that holy night. How the angel-ravens sang on high; how no dark spirit had any dominion on that night ever after. Fhain hung on every word. His first sermon was a thumping success, although perhaps not as he intended it.

He was still outside their hearts and minds and could not know the things that drew them. Signs, miracles, magic. That a virgin should give birth astounded them. They identified with Joseph and Mary because traveling was part of their lives. And anyone knew a warm underground crannog was the only place for winter children to be born and that it was natural for animals to be present. Their obeisance to the magic baby seemed a lovely filigree to the tale. As for the angels, in fhain imagination they were literally standing on nothing in the sky, singing their hearts out with great wings arustle under the wondrous music. Truly, Padrec spoke well of magic. He gave them new colors to adorn their world. In their generous way they *must* reward him.

Of course, fhain generosity might be taken for assault. When Padrec went outside to relieve himself, the men followed and pounced on him from all sides, pinning him to the ground.

"What is this? Let me up."

"Must thank thee, Padrec."

"Wait! Stop—"

"Must give thee gifts."

"Let me *up*, you little—what are you doing?"

"Do bring thee gifts. Will go as one of us."

Gentle but determined, they wrestled his robe over his head, leaving Padrec in his breechclout, thin linen shirt, and the remains of his dignity.

"Come in the rath. Have gifts for thee."

They left him there and returned to the rath, bearing away his priest's robe. Embarrassed and furious, Padrec finally steeled himself to go in before the women; after all, they went as shamelessly bare.

"Give me my clothes, Cruaddan."

"Cannot, Padrec."

His robe was no more. Neniane and Guenloie had already divided the worn homespun between them.

"Damn you, I am a priest!"

"Do nae shout, Padrec," Dorelei cautioned in an unruffled tone that meant every word. "Be in my rath. Take thy gifts."

"So white," Guenloie appreciated him openly. "Padrec be beautiful."

He was miserable. "Woman, be kind. Do not look upon my shame."

"Thy Briton-clothes be ragged," Dorelei judged. "Not strong enough for rath or riding."

"But you don't understand," Padrec sputtered. "A priest must look a priest. You took my Chi-Rho the first day."

"Was of Blackbar."

"And now you take my robes. They are not just clothes, as I am not just a man."

Cru felt at Padrec's genitals in corroboration. "Be man."

"Stop that! I am a priest of God. I can't go as other men. Can't you understand that?"

"Will now or will be cold," said the inexorable Cru, holding up a sheepskin vest. "Borrowed from Venicone but too big for me. Cruaddan thanks thee."

"And this." Bredei came forward and laid the hide trousers at Padrec's feet with a flourish. "Too big. Must learn to borrow from smaller men. Do thank thee, Padrec."

"Well. Well, I just don't know ..." To salvage his dignity, Padrec stepped into the trousers. A little tight but comfortable. The sheepskin vest was thick and soft.

Malgon held up his own contribution. "Old leggings."

"Borrowed, I suppose."

"From Tod-Lowery. Malgon thanks thee."

Padrec supposed he must wear something now that his robe was destroyed, but he drew the line at the knife they offered him. "I can wear no knife. I can draw no man's blood."

Could not even cut his meat at meals?

Useless. They understood that no more than the rest of what he said. Padrec tried to summon a holy wrath, but it wouldn't quite boil. Profanation or not, the new clothes were more practical than his, which had become ragged and stiff with dirt. Seeing Guenloie with her prized half of the tattered robe and Neniane folding hers with nimble and loving fingers, he saw the trade he'd given them: helpless people who couldn't weave well and had no looms of their own. They'd find good use for the material until it fell apart. Neniane cached her half in the empty reed cradle.

She smiles so little. She never just touches that cradle, it's a caress. The phantom pain from the amputated limb. It makes me feel . . .

"Fhain thanks thee, Padrec," said Dorelei with regal calm.

Oh—botheration. I don't know how I feel. And that was disturbing to a young man with an overriding sense of destiny.

"Did speak of great magic," Dorelei said thoughtfully. "Will this father-god know of Prydn?"

"And of thy fhain. Should He heed the sparrow and forget thee?"

Dorelei beckoned him from her gern-stone. With tactful urging from Cru, Padrec squatted before her in the uncomfortable position so natural to them.

"Hold out thy hands, Padrec."

Dorelei pushed back the linen sleeves of his shirt and clamped the heavy gold bracelets about his wrists. Padrec goggled: each was about five inches long, finely bossed with a design like twisted coils of rope. Ancient work and most like containing some copper and tin, but the gold weight was considerable. In Briton such bracelets could buy a modest house and plot.

"Do thank thee, Gern-y-fhain. Borrowed from Venicone?"

"Nae."

From her cool emphasis, he was conscious of a social error. They joked about many things but never the jewelry.

"Was always Prydn," Dorelei corrected with certainty. "Like Raven-spirit to Ma-ry. Gift from Rainbow."

Outside the rath alone, staring perplexedly at the great stones circling the crest of Cnoch-nan-ainneal, Padrec shook his head and despaired. They appreciated his sermon, one could see that; then why did he feel so confused and unsure? For God's chosen it was an uncomfortable sensation.

Am I the teacher or the taught?

They were ready to move when morning was a mere smudge in the east. Dorelei took from the firepit two unburned ends of wood, which she packed away for travel. They left behind some of the clay pots and bowls too bulky to carry, and like as not the new crannog would have a supply left by the vacating fhain. Over the summer Malgon had decorated most of the clayware with fhain symbols, adding their own fish sign to the older bestiary painted or etched into the pots and walls. His work was remarkably energetic, even humorous. Malgon's fish looked glum and purposeful, like all fish. Reindeer was caught looking back over his shoulder, wary: ah-ah . . . here comes hunter trouble.

"What kind of fish, Malgon?"

"Salmon."

"Why salmon, who spends most of his time in the far sea?"

"Be born here. Salmon will die to go where a must, like Salmon fhain."

The rath was collapsed and packed away, and Cru led Padrec to the new horse saddled for him. The animal was coal black in the early light, a fine gelding with steady nerves, not too skittish at the wild smell of fhain ponies. An army horse from one of the Wall forts, Padrec guessed.

"Taken from Roman-men by Venicones," Cru informed him, adding that all knew what a dishonest lot Venicones were. "A takes so much must have a word for it. A steal anything not tied down."

"Indeed, a brutish and unprincipled race," Padrec agreed with the beginnings of tact. "Help me up, Cru."

When he asked for his crutches to be passed up, Cru only broke them across his knee. "Padrec must be strong as fhain. Like Salmon—move or die."

"Well, I guess I don't need them that much."

"Yah, Padrec."

Silhouetted against the morning, Dorelei looked back to where their rath had stood. "The blessing of Mother and Lugh on this pasture. Better grass for next fhain."

When the sun rose, Padrec knew they were traveling northeast. As they progressed under the brilliant September sunshine, they passed through brief rain showers that barely smudged the azure sky before they ceased. As the Venicone foothills steepened into mountains, the weather chilled and darkened.

Padrec tired rapidly. When Faerie moved, they moved fast, the ponies sure-footed as goats, with a unique gait between a walk and a trot. His larger mount winded long before the others, and it was obvious why fhain sheep were so tough and wiry, living all their lives on hilltops and crags. The reason for lack of cattle among Prydn was equally clear. Compared to these rugged sheep, kine were fragile creatures that needed much pampering and lusher grass.

Guenloie and her husbands brought up the flock in the rear, Rof bounding furiously back and forth in a continual pendulum, nipping at strays, ears pricked up, nose to the ground for any suspicious scent like Tod-Lowery or his vixen.

Villages were distant and rarely sighted. Riding with Cru, Padrec saw the small stockade in the valley to the west of their ridge. "What people are those?"

"Taixali. Cruel folk. Like bear. Sometimes peaceful, sometimes not."

Another look told Padrec more than he wanted to know about Taixali Picts. Far as they were, he could see the human bodies hanging from a rack at the gate. But then something else caught his attention. A horse and rider trotted out the stockade gate, paused for a moment as the rider searched the high ground in their direction, then galloped toward the wooded slope.

"Who's that coming, I wonder?"

"Woman," Cru said.

Lost now in a patch of fir, the rider was too far for definition. "How can you tell?"

"Tallfolk do nae run to meet Prydn unless a need magic," Cru stated with cold amusement. "Oh, *then* will promise much and even keep a's promise on a good day. When Lugh Sun rises in the west. See where a comes, Padrec: woman and bairn."

The rider broke out of the stand of fir trees, much closer now, a woman with a child slung on her back. Dorelei halted fhain as the woman pulled up the horse at a wary distance, dismounted, and took the child from her back. A red-haired woman with peculiarly protruding eyes and a nervous manner. The kind with humors in her body never far from hysteria, Padrec knew. She would not come close to Dorelei but held up the child, her eyes bulging at Gern-y-fhain.

"Faerie queen, I saw you coming along the ridge."

"Did nae come in night-secret," Dorelei allowed stiffly. "Why dost stop us?"

"Help my child, Faerie queen. And I will pay in good Roman silver." The woman held the coins in one open palm.

Dorelei studied her coldly as the rest of fhain walked their horses to flank her. "How does wealth ail?"

Her questioning was distant, even superior. The woman was on Prydn ground. Here Dorelei was mistress, and the woman must know it. The Taixali mother fumbled at the child's swaddling, no cleaner than her own greasy garment.

"My bairn cannot pass his water. Two days now. Those of my husband's house say an evil spirit followed me when I entered the house in marriage. Take it away and the silver is yours."

"What hast done to drive away spirit?"

"A bronze penny in the uisge a chronachadh," the woman answered. She was not much older than Dorelei but already shapeless with child-bearing. "No good did it bring. Take my silver, cure my bairn."

Dorelei motioned to her sister. "Second daughter, will thee drive out this trifling spirit?"

Neniane slid from her pony and approached the woman who instinctively shrank back. "Put no evil on us."

Neniane bit off the words. "Will nae harm it. Have born wealth of my own like thee. Unwrap the bairn. Lay't on the ground."

Padrec was to see this more than once. As Roman physicians specialized in certain ailments, so did Faerie women. Guenloie dealt in love charms and potions to restore virility, a subject that much interested her. Neniane's magic, as her love, was all for children. But always in the women seeking aid was the same need and fear mixed in their eyes. Protective as a lioness over a cub, the woman did as she was bidden. Her protruding eyes singled out Padrec, questioned the sight of him. "You are not Faerie."

"Roman. A Christian priest."

The woman's stiff red braids bobbed in understanding. "The Jesu-Christ. We have heard of him."

"When I am welcome in your village, I will tell you more." By habit Padrec lifted his hand to sign a blessing over the squirming, miserable child. The woman's warning hand shot out.

"Do not curse my bairn!"

"I only give him the blessing of my God, who loves children above all else."

"And well a might," Neniane muttered over the baby. "For do lose so many."

From a pouch at her waist, she took a smaller bag of rabbit skin and laid it beside her as she bent to the child. It was cranky and uncomfortable in its soiled swaddling, which the slovenly mother had not thought to change. The baby's little rump was cruelly chafed. Neniane bit her lip at the negligence: those with good fortune did not always deserve it. The boy's genitals were fiery red, some of it from chafing but mostly with the irritant of a full bladder. Little magic needed here, unless something was blocking the passage. More likely the muscles were confused, sometimes unable to hold or at others unable to let go as needed. Truly, one had to work at children.

Irritated from within and without, the small penis stuck straight up in a comic erection. Although the packet contained nothing more than a powder to make the child sleep, the woman expected magic. Neniane passed the medicine three times over the swollen penis, whispering, then three times the other way. She handed the rabbitskin bag to the woman. With her other hand, quick and deft, she pressed three fingers against the small bladder.

The bairn passed with a vengeance, a fountain effect that spurted straight up for two feet or more before Neniane held the child up by its little shoulders and let him urinate normally, which he did for a remarkable length of time. Padrec began to suspect he was connected to a conduit. When the child was finally wrung out, the mother wrapped him again in the carrying sling.

"Spirit be gone," Neniane assured her. "Let a drink the magic in hot water tonight." She wrinkled her nose at the filthy swaddling. "An't would nae anger thy tallfolk gods, thee might wash a's bottom once a full moon."

The woman was more assertive with her child out of danger. "There's four others at home," she huffed. "I cannot do everything. Here."

Padrec saw the motion. There was no need for the insult except fear and habit. Drawing back from Neniane, she deliberately dropped the silver denarii on the ground. One of them rolled in the puddle of urine. As she turned to mount her horse, a comprehension passed between Neniane and her older sister. Dorelei stiffened in the saddle, her face a mask of contempt.

"Woman."

Even Padrec felt the restraint in the sound, like a hand laid on the Taixali woman. Dorelei's scorn was brittle as frost. Neniane passed her the coins. She held them up. "Did not steal these from Roman-men? Then Gern-y-fhain will send them home."

Slender fingers closed over the coins. Dorelei's other hand passed over it, not touching. Both hands danced a moment, then Dorelei opened them, empty. "Gone like evil spirit. Go thee in peace while Lugh still shines for thee."

Her voice was subtle menace. The Taixali woman needed no urging. She hastened the horse away down the slope. Cru hissed the word with an ocean of disgust.

"Tallfolk."

Dorelei's supple left hand closed and opened again. She passed the coins to Neniane, who flung them away, all her fury in the swing.

"Mother puts wealth in the wrong raths."

"But in yours soon again, sister," Dorelei soothed. "Come."

She moved ahead. Fhain followed.

They traveled for two days, with one night camped in a rocky overhang. Early on the second day a thick, chill fog blanketed the ridges, and much care had to be taken to keep the flocks together. In the animal memories of their half-wild sheep, these high rocks were their earliest home; they saw no reason not to go off on their own.

The ponies had been climbing steadily since leaving the old crannog, following trails worn into the high ridges for thousands of years. No one could tell Padrec where they were going, but all seemed to know. Dorelei led them on with no hesitation. Each fhain knew without need of a map where the available crannogs would be in any season.

"How dost know won't be taken when we get there?" Padrec wondered.

"Will not." Dorelei kept her eyes on the trail, dim in the fog.

"Just waiting empty?"

"Fhain passed in the night."

"What fhain?"

"From crannog."

"I heard nothing." A small lie, but it troubled Padrec like so much about these people. Dorelei gave him the tolerant smile of a mother teaching a backward child. "Did nae come like thunder but wind-whisper."

"The wind . . . oh." Not the Christian but the Brigante of Padrec heard the sounds in the night: faint hoofbeats, fainter voices all spread on the haunted wind. He'd said the most potent prayers he knew and pulled the sleeping robe over his head.

Toward midday the fog thickened. Padrec and Cru fell behind to help herd strays. When they rode ahead again, the three fhain women were pacing their ponies slowly, in single file, along the fog-shrouded ridge. The silence was eerie. Dorelei paused by a granite outcrop, alert and cautious, then moved ahead. When she halted, the others reined in and waited in the still whiteness. Padrec felt the silence seep into him, smothering his question to a whisper.

"Cru, what is it?"

Dorelei's husband pointed to the stone and the fresh figure etched into its face. "Reindeer fhain. Most old, from Mabh's own blood."

Padrec twisted about, straining to see through the mist. "Where are they?"

"Here."

Cru was motionless in the saddle. Dorelei slid off the pony to stand by its head. Fhain froze behind her. Padrec sensed a single tension that gripped all of them and found himself holding his breath. He strove later to recall the moment, second by second, what he saw, what seemed reality. Dorelei alone by her pony, wisps of fog swirling about her. She *was* alone, Padrec was sure of that.

She raised both hands in a queer sign.

She was not alone.

The other woman was simply there beside Dorelei in the fog. Padrec shivered; the skin crawled on his spine. Four, five, half a dozen others ringed them, solid flesh out of the fog. Small men and women like Dorelei's fhain except for the markings on their dark cheeks. He felt they'd been there all the time, stone, stump, hummock, and mist itself transmuted to wary eyes and nocked bows. Their gern was much older than Dorelei, the gloss of her hair clouded with gray and rounded with a gold circlet. She leaned on a stick, obviously injured. Like Dorelei she wore nothing over her upper body but a hide vest. Between her flattened breasts a heavy silver chain dangled a huge blood-red stone in an enameled setting. Padrec supposed it a garnet at first. Not a ruby, not that big.

But it was a ruby.

Padrec swallowed. All his life he'd heard of Faerie wealth, a fabled hoard beyond the imagination of bards or the greed of kings. All true. Fable became truth in a world larger than he suspected and nowhere as tidy.

The stone glinted faintly as the woman moved past Dorelei. Her bare thigh was wrapped in a leaf and poultice dressing for the wound that crippled her, and there were older scars, pale seams through the darker hue of her skin. A hard body and harder face, wintry with the truth of her life and its final defeat. She spoke with still dignity and authority.

"Taixali have a bad year. Have barrowed three of Reindeer fhain, including first son. Salmon must be strong and quick. Mother's eye be on thee."

Salmon fhain bowed their heads in acknowledgment and respect. The gern whispered something to Dorelei, touched the girl's hair, and smiled faintly.

"What's it mean?" Padrec murmured.

Cru's mouth set in a line of stoic acceptance. "Bad year for tallfolk be worse for Prydn. Dead children, poor harvest, nae matter. Will blame Prydn for it. Must go softly among them."

Listening to Cru, Padrec's eyes had not left Dorelei, but even as the words ended, Dorelei stood alone. The other queen and her people had come out of the mist and simply melted back into it without a detectable movement or sound. Cru didn't seem to find it unusual at all.

"Cru . . . where did they go?"

Cru came out of his own thoughts. "Away."

Gawse wintered twice in this place within Dorelei's memory. A good crannog near a small stone circle, usually selected for wintering, with an entrance well out of the wind, a terrace for the ponies, space within the large crannog itself to byre the flock, and none of it apparent to the unseeing eye of tallfolk. The whole looked no more than a rugged outcrop along the high ridge. The stone circle stood on the highest promontory, and beyond it the even slopes of the high meadows where the sheep would have to live on grass already nibbled to the root or forage among the scrubby trees farther down. Not the best prospects, but only part of what weighed on Dorelei's spirit.

Meetings between fhains should be joyous occasions. Theirs with Reindeer was strange. What would Padrec think of them? She knew already he had a kind of pitying contempt for their life, not knowing the music of it. The Reindeer gern and her people met them in caution and sorrow; they had no joy to share. How could they? The gern, Bruidda, saw three of her fhain killed by Taixali, including her own son. They hanged him, said he poisoned their well. Taixali needed no help there. Gawse always said they were dirty as well as cruel. Guenloie would boast less of her tallfolk blood now.

Reindeer fhain was hungry, Bruidda said, and she herself was badly wounded by Taixali. Dorelei shivered. Would she have to shed her own blood like that for her people? Surely if Mother and Lugh heard any of their children, it would be a great gern such as Bruidda. Yet, as the queen melted away into the fog, Dorelei felt a premonition like ice around her heart.

We will all fade away like that. Mother and Lugh are forgetting us. We must find stronger magic.

She mulled these questions sitting on the highest outjutting of rock above the crannog, letting the fresh wind that drove the fog away at evening play its soft fingers through her hair. Cru cantered his pony toward her from the higher ridge, past the stone circle, waving to Dorelei. He jumped from the saddle and climbed up to sit behind his wife. Dorelei was grateful for his arms around her.

"Did see pasture, Cru?"

"Thin."

"Oh—Cru." Dorelei wanted to cry but dammed the impulse to spare Cru the worry. He was tired enough. "No better here than before."

"No worse." Cru shifted about behind her so she was between his splayed legs, her back against his chest. He slid his hands under her vest to cup her breasts. Dorelei shivered with the pleasure and reassurance of his touch, leaning her cheek against his.

"Must love thee tonight," Cru whispered.

"Good." She knew they'd both be far too tired. "Do need it."

He chuckled softly, stroking her nipples. "Will love thee like stag at Samhain."

"Oh . . . large words, small deeds."

"Dost say so?"

"Will be too tired."

"Thee wait. Just wait."

"Cru?"

"Aye, wife."

"Padrec's Father-God that put Jesu into maiden. Dost believe it?"

If true, it was potent magic; yet, by Cru's thinking, there seemed no place for Mother in this paternal scheme of things. Padrec's god was no more comprehensible than Padrec himself. "Nae, Dorelei."

"But if a be true; if this Father-God has such magic—would I be fool to bring it into fhain?" When Cru hesitated, Dorelei twisted around in his arms and let him see her quandary. "Did see Reindeer fhain? Did see the miserable graze? Be child-wealth in crannog? Where be the magic fhain needs?"

"Dorelei, Dorelei . . ."

"Hear! Dost think will nae call Father-God's magic in need?"

"Father with no mother? How can such be?"

Dorelei's shoulders twitched in bleak ignorance. "Who can say? But have much on my mind now, Cru. Much on my heart."

Dorelei's thin face was tight with insoluble quandary. Cru knew the truth of it. The new pasture was nothing to sing about. Winter would be lean. They must try to trade among tallfolk strangers who'd killed their kind that very year. They needed the strongest possible magic. Yet he feared the full extent of Dorelei's thinking. It was dangerous for a new fhain to turn its back on tried ways before taking root. Mother and Lugh might indeed forget them. Cru framed his wife's solemn face in his hands.

"Dost think to turn from Parents?"

"If . . . a turn from us, Cru, would first husband leave?"

"What?"

"Nae, nae, did ask. Would thee leave?"

"Oh, Dorelei." Cru took a deep breath and sighed it out. "Sometimes thee be Gern-y-fhain—"

"Just sometimes?"

"And other times be plain woman and thick." He shut her mouth with a long, tender kiss. "Cru will leave a's wife when pasture moves with sheep."

She needed to hear that. Of all strengths, Cru would not fail her. She remembered hungry winter nights in Gawse's crannog and questioned the providence of Mother and Lugh, especially when tallfolk thrived and fhain weakened. No. Before she watched her people die on a hillside, before they faded into mist like Reindeer fhain with scarce heart for a greeting, Dorelei would bargain with gods and demons alike to survive.

Signs had meaning or they did not. In Mother's world no bird

69

lofted, no mole or worm burrowed without purpose in the wheel of life. Padrec was given to them for a reason, of this much she was sure, must be sure. She would hear more of this Father-God.

For the first night in a new home, Dorelei herself built the fire from the ends of the old one. The crannog was large, cunningly built of dry stone wedged together in the manner Prydn learned from the old broch builders in the north; large but dark, the only light from the fire flickering over Dorelei's preoccupied expression, Neniane and Guenloie cutting dried meat on a washed flat stone, Artcois and Padrec carefully preparing the rath skins for spring use. From now until spring broke they would live underground cheek by woolly jowl with their sheep, but the rath skins needed waterproofing every year, curded sheep's milk rubbed in by hand. Padrec gagged at the soured mess on his hands.

"Stinks, doesn't it?"

Artcois' mouth twisted in a wry grin. "Thee knows spring rain, Padrec. Can smell sweet or be dry."

They went on rubbing.

Neniane and Guenloie prepared a light meal out of dried meat and mutton broth with a few late greens collected about the hill. When the meal was done and the heat from the fire a steady glow in the crannog stones, Dorelei assumed the formal position on her gern-stone.

"Will speak of Mabh. And then Padrec will speak of Father-God."

Dorelei departed from tradition and knew it. The Mabh story was told at Brigid in the dead of winter, when Lugh Sun was far away and all men needed hope, but they needed hope now. Mother did not kindle this fire, or Gawse. She was Gern-y-fhain here and a little reckless in her determination. Salmon would not limp away into fog like Reindeer, looking for a new place that might not be there.

"Was in the first days when the ice was on the land."

Listening to the story, Padrec was confused. He knew the Hebrew writings and had a clear idea of the unfolding of human endeavor from the Creation. Nowhere in Canon was there reference to a sheet of ice covering the flat dish of the earth. Yet this story of Mabh and of ice was central to Faerie belief as the Flood to his. Time, in his sense, meant nothing to them, nor large numbers. Their unit of measurement was in tens as the fingers of a hand and still bewildering to an outsider. "Tens of seasons" could mean two, two dozen, two hundred, even two thousand years, so foreshortened and stylized was their unwritten but queerly consistent concept of history. There was the ice. Its melting had shaped their world anew.

Like all young clerics with some pretense to intellect, Padrec had estimated the world's age from the lives of the prophets in the Old Testament. There was much argument back and forth, but the nearest he could make it was four or five thousand years from Creation to the present. Academic: what need to know how old when the vital question was how long remaining? In this year of God's Grace and dwindling patience, 429, the Second Coming of Christ was an imminent reality. Let some doubt it, the world could end almost before Padrec completed his Irish mission. Virtue, not history, was a matter of urgent priority. Still, as Dorelei spun out the tale, Padrec sensed she spoke of a time impossibly older than his Creation. It troubled him; she didn't speak as of a hallowed legend but of facts accomplished yesterday.

In the first days, in the time of the ice (Dorelei told them), the winters were longer and summers short and wet. Fhains were more hunters than shepherds, sheep and horses still wild enough to want to go their own way. Times were very hard, and all through the quarrel between Lugh Sun and Mother Earth.

The fhain of Mabh lived far south of the ice flow. Mabh was most beautiful of all Prydn women. Her skin was of a hue like copper and smoke, and her hair like washed coal in the firelight, so black it was, and it is said that she wore the skins of animals that melted away with the ice, so who can speak of her clothes?

Times were lean and food scarce, and Prydn said even then: we would hate to be forgotten like tallfolk since even as remembered children life is not that good. Even then the tallfolk hunters harried Mabh's people—until in a certain spring when the melting ice roared down the swollen brooks and rivers, Mabh took a handful of moonstones, scattered them in the circle, and spoke her mind to Mother.

"Where is Tir-Nan-Og?" she demanded. "Where is the mole on our back we cannot see, the place Lugh Sun promised us? We need it now."

So one can see that fhain problems were much the same then as now—if Guenloie and her husbands would pay attention, there being a time for love and another to heed one's gern, but not both at once.

Mother was not feeling too generous herself, half covered with ice. Her eye shone coldly on Mabh. "First husband has left me," she mourned, her voice thin and dry as the crackle of ice breaking up in the streams. "What does Mabh want of me, who have nothing left to give?"

Mabh said, "Now that the snows are melting, we would find Tir-Nan-Og."

Mother laughed at her child, the sound of chill wind through

71

the circle of stones. "That was your father's promise, and thee knows men are inconstant. Has he not left me?"

Mother went on sulking over her misfortune; she wanted to know she was loved before giving anything, a fact that infuriates men but is not all that unreasonable when you know the heart of woman. Mabh knew not what to do except to prove her faith. She laid the first kill of the spring hunt on the altar stone in her circle, a fine red deer. Mother only turned away, clouded over her mooneye, and would not be pleased.

Then Mabh brought to the altar the prize kill of the next hunt, a giant bull of the wild cattle, yet Mother remained obstinate. When Mabh sent her the meat of their next kill, a huge beast who was said to eat with its long curling snout, Mother yet refused it. As a gern Mabh was used to some respect herself and would take only so much refusal. She grew angry and stormed about the circle, never mind the moonstones, and raged at Mother:

"Hear me! Three times have laid gifts on your stone, and this last has cost two of my good hunters to show our love to you. If we cannot waste time crying for ourselves, neither should you. Dost think our life is easy? There are ten tallfolk to every one of us, and all hate us as we do them. Now, dost help first children or dost not?"

"Not," said Mother, who could be short herself, and she closed her mooneye against her daughter. Angry and hopeless Mabh brooded in the circle so that she was not fox-wary as usual. While she wrestled with her own thoughts, great harm stole upon her: an evil spirit of the tallfolk, summoned by devious magic in the shape of a young man to kill the Prydn gern. But being conjured as a male, the spirit had other male purposes aforehand, and he leaped upon Gern-y-fhain Mabh. She threw him off and drew her flint knife, swallowing her natural fear as the evil spirit grew bigger and bigger to kill her.

"Lugh and Mother protect me!" she cried—and hurled herself upon the looming evil. It was a battle from which all humans and animals cowered in fright, covering their ears against the sound of it. Lugh's sky darkened from the dust of their whirling feet. The thunder was the roar of the evil spirit, shaking the earth so that the high rocks tumbled down. The lightning that split the sky was the clash of their knives and Mabh's challenge.

When Lugh Sun rose again, the evil tallfolk spirit lay dead, and in the last strength of her fury, bleeding from a dozen wounds, Mabh hurled the body onto the altar, cut out the heart, and held it high to Mother and Lugh.

"Will this satisfy thee? I have slain the spirit of the tallfolk. I have put down their strongest magic and offer its heart to thee. Have I

72

not proved my love, and will not Prydn be hunted for it? We must go from here. Rouse thyselves from bickering and tell us where."

Mother was truly touched by the desperate gift and the courage of her daughter. "Dost love me so much?"

"That we be shown Tir-Nan-Og," Mabh beseeched.

"Then follow the reindeer north beyond the great salt marsh," said Mother.

Mabh began to fear Mother made a cruel joke or was gone soft-witted with age, for no fhain hunted or grazed beyond the salt marsh. They'd seen the white chalk cliffs on the other side and, just beyond, the edge of the great ice blanket.

"Follow the reindeer," Mother said. "I will break my silence with your father. It is time to forget our differences and think of our children. But lest you grow careless like your father, I give you this law. Each year at spring fire, you will take this tallfolk spirit in whatever form you find it and put it on the stone for me that I know I am not forgotten of Prydn."

In the days of the cold spring, Mabh's fhain collected their ponies and half-wild sheep, child-wealth, and herd dogs and started north in the wake of the reindeer, wondering what they would find. Already they saw that Mother and Lugh ended their quarrel and were together again, for the ice had receded much farther than any hunter remembered.

Now, Mabh's first husband was named Cruaddan even as Dorelei's, only fitting since the name means "first child," and even as wise. When the Prydn wanted to hunt Reindeer for meat, Cruaddan forbade it. Reindeer was not stupid like cattle; to hunt him would be to scatter his herd from the trail they followed. So fhain hunted elsewhere but left Reindeer to point them north. This was a shrewd decision, since tallfolk hunters tracked Reindeer as well. All their conjured demons ran with them, hot on the track of Mabh to punish her for their slain brother-spirit. Not enough they were moving from their hunting grounds, Prydn had to fight and run, fight and run all the way to the great salt marsh.

In those days were parts of Mother half land that wanted to be all sea, and since women are noted for the changing of mind, Mother pushed some into the water and raised some up, but about the salt marsh she could never make up her mind. This caused Prydn a great deal of trouble, sometimes wading and more often floundering and losing sheep until they made rafts and poled their way across the stupid marsh that *would* not be either land or sea. So undecided a place was it (as Dorelei had the tale from Gawse) that fish were growing feet as well as fins to be ready for whatever came. But

Reindeer swam on toward the chalk cliffs that loomed up and up on the far side.

From the first, Prydn knew they'd come to a land of promise and magic. In the chalk cliffs, to be had with a few strokes of an antler pick, were flints of the finest kind, barely flawed or not at all, to yield a wealth of tools and arrowheads. Oh, and up above—sudden as sunlight through cloud—were meadow downs green as when Mother first imagined the color, all aswirl with new flowers and bees busily making the most of it. There were fresh streams bursting their banks from the ice Lugh Sun melted in his renewed love for Mother, and game running so thick they tripped over one another.

But when Mabh's people looked back, they saw their pursuers, too, were rafting across the marsh. Their spirits flew over the rafts darkening the sky with their evil like festering in a wound. Mabh knew they'd come to a place of promise but trouble as well. Nothing was changed. The tallfolk would push them out of the good lands. She ran out on the cliff edge, holding up her flint knife to Mother and Lugh.

"Now decide," she called on them. "Is this Tir-Nan-Og as we were promised?"

"It is a good place," Lugh grumbled, "better than most. The ice is melting. Must you have everything at once? Speak to your mother about it. I'm busy."

Night was falling and the tallfolk rafts were coming closer. Mabh dug furiously for moonstones. She scattered them in respect, and Mother opened her mooneye.

"What does Mabh want now? Your father and I are loving again. You are becoming a nuisance. Give us a little rest from your needs."

"The tallfolk are on us. Look thee where they have almost crossed the marsh. Do something!"

"That marsh has always troubled me," Mother admitted. "Land wants it, sea wants it. I just can't decide."

"If you do not and quickly, you will have no children to honor you," Mabh reminded her, too beset for good manners. "I will decide. Let it be now and always sea."

Now, Mother was not above haggling herself and in a very good position for it now. "Will you honor me and turn to no tallfolk ways or gods so long as Prydn endure?"

"We will," Mabh promised. "We do."

"Will you honor the reindeer who led thee here, wear their mark in remembrance, raise up the stones to measure your seasons by your father's path? Will you give me each year a spirit of the tallfolk on my stone?"

"We will do it," said Mabh—anxiously, for the tallfolk were about to land, their angry spirits howling for her blood. "We will keep apart. Hurry, Mother. Give us the sea. Part us from the old forever!"

In her passion Mabh raised her knife and brought it down as if to cut the earth with the very force of her will. When her knife came down, a great roar filled the world. The seas to the north and south of the marsh reared like stallions in heat and rolled in high waves toward each other until they met with the sound of thunder, swallowing tallfolk hunters, women, children, animals, spirits, all. When Lugh Sun turned his eye on his children again, the land was an island. None could ever agree on what happened, but they saw Mabh's knife slash across earth and sky, and Mother's will was no stronger than Mabh's in her need. One cannot say, but it is known that gerns have great magic, so from the first the island was known as Pretannia, which only later and ignorant men call Britain.

Mabh lived many years as gern and kept the promise to her Parents. She marked her cheeks as Reindeer, laid out the stone circles, and once a year took a child from the tallfolk cradles for sacrifice. Growing older her heart softened, and she often kept the children she borrowed, especially if there were few bairn in the crannog, as in the manner of Guenloie's mother. Now and then in a lean year Mabh ignored the promise altogether and left Prydn wealth among tallfolk so that they might not know hunger. Do not judge; this is not easy for a woman to do. Truly children are to be prized above all other wealth and worth any sacrifice of the heart.

In the long years of Mabh's rule, Prydn became strong, even arrogant. When newcomers came with bronze to break their flint, Prydn borrowed the magic and made even better tools and weapons with it, as they do to this day. And one day Mother opened her eye on the old gern.

"Mabh," she said, "we are both old women and need not lie to each other. You are like these others who have forgotten me. You are my first children and I love you best, but you need a lesson."

Mother meant her words. Times had changed and Lugh with them, being worshiped himself as a god now by the tallfolk, who had the foolish notion he managed it all by himself. Like a man he enjoyed being made much of and allowed tallfolk a new magic to break bronze and flint. And although Prydn tried, they could never pierce the hard magic of Blackbar. A bitter lesson, but the Parents gave this promise to Mabh: Tir-Nan-Og still waited if Prydn kept to the old way. The land of the young was to be theirs alone in a place beyond tallfolk, beyond world's edge. Mother and Lugh had their faults but never broke a promise once given.

When Mabh died at last, her body was placed in the barrow with a hole at each end so her spirit could escape to watch over her people. A long barrow it was, not the round sort of the newcomers, and much better hidden. Tallfolk tried to find it but never did, being too blind in most cases to find their own feet. Mabh sleeps undisturbed, and her gern-spirit rides before Dorelei's pony.

The crannog was warm and dark, the light from the firepit a dull red glow that lent flickering life to the animal figures pocked into the walls. Dorelei finished her tale and leaned to stroke Cru's cheek. There was a general rustle of movement about the fire.

Padrec knew they were tired. They needed rest after a two-day ride with only a rough camp to break it. He truly wished to preach to them about the errors of their marriage ways, yet as he listened to the story of Mabh, plainer and nearer truths crowded in on him. They were wintering in sparse pasture among hostile strangers. Their meeting with Reindeer fhain was anything but hopeful. Mabh's story was one of magic and celestial intercession for faithful children, of a queen leading her folk to a promised land, of courage and triumph. Dorelei was wise to choose it. She made a sign to gather their attention.

"Now let Padrec speak of the magic of a's Father-God."

Later for marriage, when we're all rested. Not much holy thunder left in me tonight. "Gern-y-fhain, I would speak of the magic and of children like fhain who received it."

Dorelei's eyes widened slightly in understanding. "Good, Padrec."

The ritual attitude for tale-speaking was not yet comfortable to Padrec, very tiring on the back, which must be held erect with the legs crossed. His ankles were still tender, but he tried to ignore the discomfort.

"Was in the first days when small children like fhain were held slave in the land of Egypt. Was one of these children called Moses, a shepherd with flocks like to fhain's, living and grazing like thee on the high ground. . . ."

On the mountain slopes it was that Moses beheld God. Padrec told them of the bush that burned and spoke out of its flame: *I am that I am.* He told of the task laid on Moses even as Mabh to deliver his people out of Egypt, of the rod turned into a snake, and the plagues brought on Egypt by God's magic when Pharaoh went back on his word. Warming to his tale, Padrec used Prydn terms more and more, gratified at how little they distorted essential meaning. He spoke in their words of the Exodus and pursuit, of Moses stretching his hand over the Red Sea, which parted to let the Hebrew fhain cross in safety but closed to drown their enemies. Fhain believed him: had not Mabh done as much with her flint knife? Padrec told them of the wandering in the desert, of God's anger with Moses, which they likened to Mother putting Mabh in her place. He recounted the Commandments graven on the tablets and how the children became a great people in keeping this covenant. Aye, great, but always ringed with enemies, even as Prydn.

"Now, Jesu, the Man-Son of God, was of the House of David. Tens of seasons before He came into the world, David was a king who himself was born a shepherd, even as Dorelei. In his obedience to the fhain-way of his people, he made many songs to God, and they are the first words that I would teach you to say with me.

"The Lord is my shepherd. I shall not want. He maketh me to lie down in green pastures. He restoreth my soul . . ."

When Padrec finished speaking, he looked about at fhain. "Truly the magic of God reaches everywhere. His one hand stirs the heart in Salmon's egg while the other sets the stars to move." Padrec rubbed his ankle and bowed his head to Dorelei. "Have said, Gern-y-fhain."

It was Drust who broke the respectful silence—serious, too-caring Drust. Years later, when Padrec thought of him, the love and pain were still bright. Sweet Drust was the tragedy in the seed of triumph.

"Be thy Father-God able to do these things?"

"And more, Drust, when thee will hear of them."

Drust poked the fire with a stick, probing a difficult thought. "Be well a were shepherds. We know the earth and the feel of things. Sometimes on herd watch do look at stars and try to see beyond them."

"Beyond?" Guenloie nestled against him. "What thinks second husband?" she murmured in a voice all drowsy invitation. Drust carried her hand to his lips.

"Do love thee much."

"Need stars for that?"

"Nae, but hear. Do stars speak and point as when Jesu was born? What do stars say to fhain?" The question compelled Drust, complex as it was. "Cannae know. Have thought many nights on this."

"Padrec spoke of chosen people, the Hebrew," Cru reflected. "Father-God looks only to them?"

"Once, perhaps," Padrec told him. "But when Mary gave birth to Jesu, He opened His arms to all men. And suffered for them, as will tell thee soon. All men are brothers who believe in Jesu Christ."

Malgon grunted skeptically. "Brother to tallfolk?"

Padrec laughed at the sour joke. "Even Taixali and Venicone, miserable as they are."

"Cannae believe that," Malgon denied, unconvinced.

"But turn about, Malgon, and see it from another side." Padrec invited him to consider his own wife as example. Guenloie had some Taixali blood but fhain heart and spirit. Now, were she cradle-left in a Taixali hut, would she not still be Guenloie? The difference was the way of life and thought. Thus when different men believed alike, they were brothers and sisters in that unifying faith. Privately, Padrec felt his argument a bit glib, but it led to an inspiration so simple he wondered how it eluded him until now. He took Drust's thinking-stick with its charred point and drew a crude fish on the surface of a flat stone.

"Salmon, who lives in the water whose waves are marked on thy cheeks." Padrec drew a second fish under the first. "And here is the first sign of Jesu, the sign in which his fhain gathered together."

They stared at the two identical figures.

"Except by signs, who knows the way of the stars or of God? Who can say but that I was sent to fhain or fhain to me that I should bring this magic in thy need? Does Cruaddan still ask who are the chosen?"

"Hear."

As always, when Dorelei made the slightest sound or move, the others deferred to her. She sat rigid on her stone. "Does fhain doubt even now that Mother and Lugh have heard thy gern?"

The triumph of the preacher is in the faith he creates. The tragedy may lie in what he destroys to make it. Padrec was no more critical in this than Dorelei, but as he was a natural priest, she was innately a leader, young as she was and grasping at straws. But he proved her right: fish on fish was a clear victory on the stone. No one could doubt it now.

"Padrec be gift from Raven," Dorelei ruled.

She watched her people settle down in their furs and blankets. More fatigued than any of them, Padrec was half asleep when he closed his eyes. Neniane breathed deeply on her side, one leg tucked between Bredei's. Malgon snored softly; Drust was dead to the world, Guenloie's head pillowed on his arm.

Dorelei whispered, "Cru?"

The finest among Prydn men was deep in sleep. So much for the Samhain stag this night, she thought. Just as well. Dorelei lay down beside him, yawning. She didn't believe she could be so tired, but even exhaustion was luxury this night. She could sleep without worry for once. If not yet proven right in all, at least she was not wholly wrong.

Her dreams were not of Cru or Padrec but once again of Rainbow. Waking before morning, Dorelei tried to piece out the meaning and the remembered fragment of the song before it faded back into the realm of sleep.

Be not where but only when . . .

III
She
Who Is
Called Mabh

The music of a soul is made of many songs, and not all of them can be sad. Even Padrec, burning with God like a siege of holy indigestion, climbed out of the crannog the next morning to meet a world that reveled in its own beauty without bothering to define the source. The early sun, not yet bright enough to leach color from the day, heightened it to a drunken degree. Padrec grinned with a child's delight. This dish of the world, with himself at the center, was the paint-board of God. From these hills and high meadows with their rich yellows and blues, subtle lavenders and infinite varieties of green, were the store of colors from which God illuminated the rest of the world. The hues of the morning stabbed their beauty into Padrec's eyes. The stone circle rose a little higher than their crag and looked new-made in the sparkling air. Below the line of scrubby fir trees to the east, a stream winked in the sunlight.

No tallfolk in sight. Where's the village?

Padrec smiled at the thought. He'd used the Prydn word for his own kind, not all that complimentary, since the word meant "stranger" and "suspicious" as well. But the Taixali village was nowhere in sight. This could be the first morning after Mabh parted the land from the continent, earth and sun reconciled and no one but Prydn to enjoy it.

Cru came around the other side of the crag, leading his pony and swigging from a water bag. He offered it to Padrec; the fresh spring water was sweetened with the dark juice of crushed blackberries.

"I was looking for the Taixali village."

Cru pointed to a hill halfway between them and the western horizon. "There."

"That far?"

"That near." Cru's chiseled face closed about his thoughts as he glanced toward the higher crest and the meadows beyond, then into the west again. Padrec divined the thought.

"Better graze down below."

"If Taixali allow."

Dorelei called to them from the terrace as she led out her pony. She came on a few paces and then, as if impatient for the pleasure, bounded up the last few steps to spin around in her husband's embrace. Her mood was fresh as Padrec's, and she included him in it.

"See where Padrec walks without stick. Be well soon."

Dorelei took a long look about their portion of the world. Without fatigue the pure energy of youth and health glowed from her. All prospects looked better now. To Padrec she seemed even younger, if that were possible. She slapped Cru's rump and mounted her pony.

"Will ride, husband?"

For answer, Cru vaulted his own pony, gleaming with good spirits, and kicked it into a dead run down the western slope, Dorelei close behind. Padrec gasped at their wild plunge, but they took the last narrow ledge, cantered out onto a leveling of the slope, charging at each other and circling in play while their silvery laughter floated back to the priest. Rof bounded out from the terrace and leaped down after them, eager to be part of the game, lifting off the ground in great jumps, forelegs braced against the steep descent. One last extension of the long body and a *rowf!* of joy, and Rof went hurtling at Dorelei, who wheeled about to welcome him to morning.

Padrec roared aloud at the comic sight. "Oh, no!" In his enthusiasm Rof bounded up . . . up . . . and landed neatly spraddled over the startled pony's shoulders; right in Dorelei's lap, while she tried to control the skittish mount and help the dog at the same time. Rof snorted, helpless as a beached whale. As Padrec watched, chuckling and shaking his head, horses and dog dashed toward the trees farther down the slope. Padrec felt a swell of affection in his chest.

"Lord God, You must bless these people. They are only truants from Eden. Show me how to help them."

With a chorus of bleatings, the sheep surged out into the day, Drust and Malgon urging them on with bare hands, bending to push or boot at a refractory rump here and there.

"Yah, Padrec!"

The woolly cloud of the flock swirled out from the terrace and along the hillside, Guenloie's husbands hurrying them with pebbles flung with marvelous accuracy, and at last came Guenloie, mounted and leading the other ponies. She called something to Drust, who passed her his water bag. Padrec watched the exquisite feminine grace of the girl as she brushed back the hair still sleep-tangled about her cheeks, the arm lifted, the delicate head tilted back to drink. The white smile flashed from berry-stained lips.

Truants from Eden.

"Padrec?"

He turned to see Neniane behind him, her solemn little cat's face lightened with a tentative smile. She held out the bowl of blackberries and milk still warm from the udder. Without considering it, Padrec reached to touch her cheek. "Hello, kitten."

"Dost call me small fox?"

"Small cat."

Neniane had never seen a cat, wild or domestic. They were rare outside Roman villas. "Cat has kittens like fox?"

Constantly, he assured her. In truth, Cat did little else. Neniane seemed pleased at the likeness.

Well after the last of the flocks disappeared over the last dip before the meadow, Cru and Dorelei broke out of the trees, pushing their ponies toward the crag where Padrec, Artcois, and Bredei sat enjoying the early cool of the day. They scrabbled up the last incline and slithered from the saddles together, flushed and purposeful.

"Scrapes in forest," Cru announced as if it had great meaning.

"Early," Bredei commented.

"Early but there. On ground and trees."

Artcois nodded decisively. "Should hunt then."

Cru looked much happier than the day before. If pasturing was not the best here, the game was abundant and even the stags were starting on the rut early. Clearly Mother and Lugh had not forgotten their children. Cru explained it to Padrec while preparing his weapons and edging his arrows with sandstone. Rutting season, early or not, was the one time deer might be considered careless. Not surprising, Cru allowed, when even men are inclined to be a mite reckless with love on their mind. Of course, deer were never easy to hunt, but with luck there'd be feasting that night. And whoever brought it down, his wife had a fine hide to work or share or give away. He and Dorelei

rode that morning for sheer good spirits, but not blind to the distinc-
tive hoof-scrapes in the needle carpeting under the trees or the marks
on the tree bark where Stag was beginning to scent the hock glands
of does and feel his own need. One of them would fall today.

"Good feasting!" Cru slapped Padrec's thigh. "Good hides!"

"If do not miss."

"Miss?" Cru's brow puckered at the absurd notion. "First bow of
the world was made by Prydn, sent in a dream from Lugh, who rides
each arrow." He snorted. "Miss!"

In some it might be boasting, but Padrec had seen them shoot.
Their bows were shorter than those of the western tribesmen but were
reinforced with strips of antler, requiring as much pull and delivering
the missile with equal power. The problem was their arrows, far from the
best for heavy game. Although compensated by their accuracy, the
bronze head buried in a stag's shoulder needed to be edged almost
with each use. Iron was more efficient, but Padrec knew enough not to
point it out. Fhain had its magic, tallfolk theirs. Iron was not mentioned
directly among Prydn any more than devout Christians joked about
Satan.

"Will pray for thee." Padrec clapped him on the back. "Good
fortune on the hunt."

The courtesy spurred Cru's already jubilant spirits. "Will be
good, close as thee are to Father-God. Pray child-wealth, Padrec."
Cru spread his arms to the sun's benificence. "Tens of children in the
rath, sons and daughters to Dorelei. Artcois! Bredei! Be time!"

A shining day, a day for new beginnings and hopes. Padrec
tested his legs with a walk to the ring of stones and back with no
great fatigue or pain. The sun poised at zenith, then slid down the
long afternoon to evening. The hunters returned with a buck on a
pole, a yearling with a gleaming little four-point rack just stripped
against a tree in his first rutting fury. Being that young, Stag was more
passionate than wary, and he fell to Cru, who grinned slyly passing
Padrec.

"Did say *miss*, Padrec?"

They put up the rath poles and hung the stag for dressing out.
Fhain made the operation into an efficient industry. Nothing was
wasted. The carcass was skinned and the hide stretched to dry. The
fine, healthy stomach, emptied and washed, would serve a variety of
purposes. The small hooves would be boiled for glue, the antlers
worked into an assortment of delicate tools, the head itself cooked in
a covered pit of embers until the bay-and-parsley-seasoned brains
could be spooned out as a delightful pudding sided with jowl meat.
Padrec wondered if they could do anything with the navel. Very
likely.

The head would be tomorrow's delicacy; tonight they'd feast on the loin and haunch larded with sheepfat and dripping its own goodness. The liver, rubbed with wild garlic and cooked in thin strips, would be served to Cru and Dorelei first, then passed around. There would be the story of the hunt, enacted as much as told by the hunters, and uisge to drink.

The uisge was a windfall. Any fermented drink took time, apparatus, and a degree of permanency fhain would reject on principle. Barley beer or uisge had to be traded for, which was what happened this day, more or less, and the getting was the tale to be told at the feast. They all looked forward to it.

People who drank seldom drank poorly when it came to virulent stuff like uisge. Padrec was gratified when Dorelei ordered it well diluted with spring water. He wanted to speak to fhain tonight and could hardly prevail on a prostrate congregation.

The feast was a gala! Youth alone gave their spirits resilience; appetite took care of the rest. When the first edge was off their hunger, when they visibly settled back and picked at rather than attacked their food, Dorelei's voice rose slightly above the contented buzz, with a note of mischief.

"Fhain hunters be best."

"Yah!"

"And wisest. Beside Salmon fhain, the shrewdest Taixali begs to be taught. Were two arrows loosed by fhain, Cru?"

"And two bucks fallen," he affirmed.

Dorelei turned to her people with a knowing smile. "Could ask: where be other buck? Hear from Cruaddan first husband how a did fall."

They were all mellow with food and uisge—watered but still more lethal than any of them, including Padrec, suspected. He found himself sweating, saw the sheen of it on Cru as he rose from his place by Dorelei. As he told the tale, Artcois and Bredei rose to join him, acting out the parts they played in the adventure with a sly good humor that hurled laughter to the stones of the crannog and back again to echo about the fire.

"Here be fhain on the trail of fresh scrapes." The three mimics crouched, wary, moving an arm, a leg, with exaggerated caution. "Whisper quiet. Leaf falls on wind louder than fhain."

"Comes a stag," Cru presented the scene. "There. And here be Cru." He pantomimed the draw, sight, and loosing, graceful as a dancer. "Hah! Down goes Stag, a's spirit flown. But!" Cru held up a warning hand. Bredei and Artcois froze. Fhain waited in expectant silence.

There were two occasions, Cru allowed, when no man, even one with the meager wit of tallfolk, should come between Stag and his object: when he was about to make love, and when he was bolting scared. Not often did one find Stag between these two fires at once, but it happened that very day.

"Were Taixali hunting in wood," Cru said, and one would think out of kindred male spirit and plain common sense that they would at least wait until Stag was done and the doe quick with next year's wealth. "But Taixali? No-o-o!"

"Not them," mourned Artcois.

The three Taixali were just green boys. Not to imply Cru was ancient, even if he did incline to his nineteenth spring fire, but fhain men grew wise early or did not grow at all, and that was no less than truth.

Since tallfolk were quiet as thunderclaps, fhain knew they were in the wood. Stag knew it last, but then he'd had a hard day fighting and losing once already, from the marks scored in his hide. Fhain followed craftily, saw the trees lashed by his sharp horns.

Artcois spread his arms. "Eight points!"

"Nae, nine," Bredei differed.

"Be sure, brother? Thee would not put more in the tale than tale will hold?"

"Did nae see all nine coming at me?"

"Ah, well—nine, then."

A magnificent buck in his late prime, lashing the trees, trumpeting his need, scenting the doe, finding the younger male in his path with the same inspiration and blood in his eye.

"And a did fight," Cru sighed in understatement. "Did come together like Mabh's sea over salt marsh."

"Clack-clack!" Bredei lowered his head and danced at Artcois. "Clack-clack—r-r-*rack*!"

But older was stronger this time and the victor in a mood for love too long denied. As Cru narrated, Bredei bent forward slightly with his head down as Artcois placed both hands on his shoulders. The sexual pantomime was graceful and abstract. Padrec saw the three women lean forward, eyes shining with excitement beyond the hunt, slender bodies moving in subtle empathy. Watching Dorelei, he was surprised at his own promptings, no holier than Stag's. He forced his eyes away and took a large swallow of uisge. That at least was not forbidden him, thanks be to God and a humane clergy.

Cru crouched near the frozen love act. "Fhain waits. But Taixali cannae wait. Or shoot very well. Poor Stag."

"Ah-h-h!" Artcois clutched his rump in huge dismay. The tallfolk boys were so anxious to bring down Stag, they loosed at him in full rut, a standing target, and still couldn't make a clean hit. The arrow aimed presumably for the shoulder hit Stag far south of it, barely creasing the hide in his laboring rump. Stag took it no better than Cruaddan would, being wounded in so undignified a quarter, forgot his doe and shot off in the first direction that came to mind, and that was straight downwind at fhain.

"And to a's end," Dorelei supposed.

Whose end it would be was still an open question. Stag charged right at Cru, saw him, dropped his head to hit Cru with all nine cruel points of his rack. Cru had time for one shot.

"Or move very fast," Bredei amended.

Suddenly Cru's taut body uncoiled in a swift motion of draw and loose. Bredei clapped his hands sharply.

"Boh! One arrow."

One shot in over the lowered, plunging antlers, driving deep between the shoulder blades to pierce Stag to his heart. "And *then* did move!" Cru roared with the rest of fhain in appreciation, because Stag could run quite a distance before Mother sent him the news of his death. Dead as he was, Stag plunged on and might be running still if he hadn't collided with a tree.

"Ow-w-w." Artcois sank to the crannog floor with a vanquished gargle, finished. Cru forestalled applause with a warning hand.

"Hunt done. Trouble just begun."

Out of their own stand, and that with great caution, came the three Taixali boys to claim the kill. Bredei puffed himself up on tiptoe to enact the tallfolk role. " 'Stag be ours,' a says. 'Did make first strike.' "

Ah—but was it so, wondered courteous Cru, nocking another arrow smooth as flowing water. And where was this unerring missile that snuffed the life of Stag? There? Truly a child could take such a wound and need no more than a poultice and patch. Cru's arrow, on the other hand . . .

The Taixali boys were adamant. They'd been drinking from a large skin of uisge during the hunt and would not relinquish the kill. Away, all of them, back to Faerie land before they had more trouble than they could digest.

"Was a better way to decide," Artcois held out open hands to grinning fhain. Neniane nipped his fingers in pure affection. Her husband described a lavish arc with his hand and presented Bredei. "And seen by brother husband whose wit outspeeds Hare when a must."

"Oh . . . was small wit." Bredei shuffled modestly. "But must make large pictures for the near-blind." His solution, to the relishing giggles of fhain, was reason itself. Cru would allow the Taixali to shoot him in the rump as he did Stag. In turn, Cru would put his missile between the boy's shoulder blades. The least impaired could claim Stag. Oh, to borrow or bargain, none like Bredei.

Well, the Taixali blustered and clouded the fine day with talk of the terrible vengeance visited upon troublesome Faerie by their valiant kind. Boys threatening like boys and stoking their courage from the skin of uisge. They boasted of the Faerie skins still hanging on their walls.

"And did know the truth of that," said Cru. "Gern's son from Reindeer fhain."

"Rest his soul," Padrec whispered.

Cru clasped Dorelei's hand. They did not look so young to Padrec then. Perhaps as animals were born with knowledge humans must learn, Prydn were born with the wisdom of survival.

"Be husband to gern. That comes first."

The Taixali blustered on while Cru calmly retrieved his arrow from the carcass and gave himself time to think. The boys really didn't want trouble; they only painted fierce masks on their first-bearded faces. Fhain already had the yearling to take home. Today's meekness might be tomorrow's profit when they traded in the village. Cru yielded the kill with reluctance and concern for the boys' well-being, for he was, he told them, husband to a gern feared through all Prydn for her malevolence.

"Who?" Padrec sputtered. "D-Dorelei?"

No other, the very mother of dragons who would ride such a stag to death up the rainbow and down the storm clouds for sheer spite, or blight a whole crop for a mere headache. But she had her human side and delighted in a bargain. Would the stalwart Taixali give their uisge in return for the buck? As a harbinger of good trading to come?

Quite relieved, they would. Cru received the uisge with profuse thanks, bowed his head over the boy's imperious hand, and, with Artcois and Bredei clowning for distraction, borrowed the purse loosely tied to his belt.

"Ave!" Padrec roared, pounding on a stone. "Ave, prince of borrowers!"

Cru beamed at his people and tossed the purse to Dorelei, his story done. Dorelei was laughing too hard to catch it. The purse plopped into the fire. There was a chattering scurry to snatch it out. The retrieved purse was opened, the coins spilled out: all Roman silver and bronze, which showed the magnitude of tallfolk thievery.

Padrec wiped his eyes, teary with laughter and smoke, mellow as the rest, and a good deal beyond, having drunk much more. "All praise to Cruaddan, Tod-Lowery among hunters, and for diplomacy a very Greek."

Cru needed a definition for both terms but allowed on reflection that the praise was fitting. He filled his cup and nestled Dorelei into his arms. She pushed the hair back from her face with the back of one hand, a feminine gesture poignant to Padrec. He looked away.

I *must love these folk as a people, but no one of them, no woman.*

"Now, Padrec," she smiled at him from Cru's arms, "will thee speak of Father-God?"

Indeed, dappled in firelight and shadow, the cozy group of them made Padrec feel even mellower. He felt a surge of all-embracing love for his new brothers, wanted to open his arms to them all, beckon them through his expanding wisdom to God. Padrec felt exalted. He was Christ on the Mount surrounded by adoring upturned faces, the nimbus of Grace about his head. The drink flared like tinder in his imagination, opening all history before him and his destined place in it: Venerable, Blessed, Canonized, immortalized in mosaic and mural, with his flock (in smaller configuration) about his feet. Not for him the tame congregations of the south or the conversion of fashionable dowagers. He, Patricius, ventured to the wild edge of the world where even the legions did not tread and lighted it with the truth of God.

At the moment Padrec was more drunk than inspired, and he drank no better than any other Briton—furious energy with a sense of music for all too brief a comet's fall before the violence leaped forth to batter at a dark existence, going maudlin and then unconscious. But now Padrec rode the high arc of his comet. Glistening with sweat and sanctity, he faced his congregation, weaving a little.

"Brothers and sisters, I love you all and I bring you God's blessing. But I have said that blessing is not cheaply won, nor by moral sloth. Fhain lives by a certain way, so must the children of God. As the crannog is built one stone on another, so is the Christian family. The man and wife are one flesh."

"Aye, Padrec." And Dorelei put her flesh closer to Cru's as he stroked her.

"As a father gives order to his children, so God to His, and angry when they disobey. Who would go against the rule of his parent?"

None of fhain at the moment. They felt the uisge as potently as Padrec but were urged to a more natural expression of it. His cosmos was founded on the denial of flesh, theirs on its acceptance. As they cuddled dreamily together, listening more to Padrec's music than his sense, their youth and health asserted itself. Neniane lay back between her ardent husbands, Guenloie stroked Drust's loins and whispered to him. They moved back farther into the deeper shadows away from the fire.

Padrec wiped his sweating face, trying to focus his eyes on them in the gloom, then forgot it, wandering in his rhapsody. "The way of God is of cleanliness. His apostle Paul has said the virgin is the most blessed, and was not Mary chosen to bear Jesu because she was so? Oh, my friends, how can I tell you of that squandered innocence, that priceless treasure lost, when the first man and woman looked at each other and knew they were naked; *knew* they were shackled from then on with that knowledge which is carnal."

Dorelei listened closely, vaguely disturbed as Padrec swelled to his theme.

"It is better to be clean and deny the sin, but if one cannot, it is better to marry than to burn. It is better to deny the fleeting illusion of flesh, but if one cannot, then cleave to *one* flesh. For the rule of my faith is, there shall be one husband with one wife."

He heard the breathy assent from the shadows. It sounded like Neniane. Padrec was gratified that they were so rapt; in fact, throughout his exhortation, he'd heard the agreeable sound of their joy as the Word pierced the crust of their errors.

"Aye," Neniane whispered from the darkness. "Nae, do nae stop. . . ."

Padrec paused to breathe deeply in the smoky gloom. He couldn't really see any of them now, but into his outstretched hand Cru pressed a fresh cup of uisge. Well enough; his mouth was dry and his tongue thickening inconveniently. Just a drop to wet it, then.

"And you, my brothers, though you know not the letter of sin, yet do ye sin. You live in sin!"

A smothered sound from one of the men, a coy response from Guenloie. Lying in Cru's arms, Dorelei wondered against his cheek, "What be sin?"

"Do nae know." Her husband's fingers smoothed lightly over her bare belly. "But dost have sweet sound. Sin . . . si-i-n. Like small bells in wind."

No, Dorelei heard more than the pleasing sound of the word, and something in her bridled at the alien sense of it. If unlettered, her intelligence was equal to Padrec's and constantly honed on the need to survive. What he said disturbed her.

"Let you therefore take one wife and one husband."

For Padrec, the crannog had grown somehow darker and closer. The world softened to shadows attentive to his mission. He spoke with crystal reason and the deep music of his faith, and they responded from their symbolic darkness beyond his pulpit by the fire; a murmur, a smothered cry. Oh, yes, they heard. They understood. They thirsted for the truth he poured out to them. In a moment they would come closer again, eager to see as well as hear him—

And then the rising ululation from Guenloie that could not be mistaken for any part of religious fervor: "Drust, oh, Drust, aye, *aye*—"

Padrec broke off. "What . . . what's that? Are you listening to me, Guenloie? Drust?"

He staggered, rubbing his eyes, then seized a faggot from the fire and thrust it aloft, stumbling into the further recess of the crannog, pouring light over the writhing, coital lump of them.

"Jesus!"

They paid little attention to him, Neniane thoroughly involved with Artcois, generous Guenloie unable to exclude either husband from this night's outpouring of her love. Padrec barely quelled an urge to kick them.

"Guenloie! Drust! All of you: what have I—oh, abomination!"

"Stop, Padrec!"

He whirled, reeling, at the whiplash sound of her voice as if she had authorized this desecration to humiliate him. Dorelei hovered like a warning at the edge of his light. "Damn you, woman."

"Be nae more fool than Mother made thee, Padrec."

"Fool?" he seethed. "Fool is it? What have I been talking about? And what to? Aminals . . . animals!" Padrec hurled the stick into the firepit and lunged for the ladder, Cru's delighted laughter floating after like a sting; up, out into the fresh-aired dark to glare blearily at the moon.

"Mooneye . . ."

The uisge and crannog warmth had crept up and struck him down from behind. He was drunk enough not to think what he did at all ridiculous but the reasoned acts of a rational mind. Padrec staggered off across the ridge saddle toward the ring of stones, falling now and then, to reach the circle and clutch precariously at one of the huge liths to steady himself, snarling his challenge to the moon.

"Mother is it? Fat, greasy sow-idea of a god!" Padrec swayed and stumbled about the center of the ring, screaming his contempt at the stones, as if to shatter them with his tongue alone. "Aye, and Lugh Sun. Come up'n I'll spit on you. Is this all you can do for your own? Teach them to rut like animals anywhere, any time they've a mind? Well, I am Patricius. *Father* Patricius. Here I am! Here I stand! Now come and strike me down if you can. Past and gone, the both of you. Frauds!" He hurled his arms aloft. "*I am the sword of God, you hear me?*"

"All the world hears thee, Padrec fool."

He turned at her voice, trying to steady the circle of treacherous

93

stones that reeled sickeningly in front of him. With an effort, Padrec focused his sight on Dorelei. She stood only a few feet away, hands on slender hips, outlined by moonlight from behind. Her face was shadowed, but the attitude of her head and body told Padrec in the small reason left him that she was here for a purpose. Good. Time to pay *her* out, too.

"Indeed," he said with sneering dignity. "Indeed, so they do, so they should. 'Now Padrec will speak of Father-God!' Speak *what*, savage? Speak of God while they rut like animals?"

He was drunk, but her words cut through the fire in his head like shards of diamond. "Teach belief, Padrec? Wise or foolish, words be only words. Did hear the words on the Moses-stones, and so many be what thee shall *not*. Did think on that? All not, all no." Dorelei whipped her arm toward the crannog. "Loving be teaching. *Loving* be faith. Fool!"

"Faith in what?"

"In . . . tomorrow. Thee stands here, near to falling down and dare curse Mother and Lugh? Be nae Lugh and Father-God the same?"

"No, Dorelei. No, ignorant lump, they are not the same. Your sun is only trivial fire that God conceived, that He could snuff out with a flicker of His will."

"Yet thee rage at Lugh as if a could answer."

Blinking at her, Padrec felt distinctly that he was losing his advantage in argument; in fact he had difficulty following it. "Figure of speech. Mere . . . figure'f speech."

"Padrec fool, thee knows nothing worth breath to tell."

"Oh, no?"

"Nae. And do not start away, but hear me!" With an arm stronger than he would have guessed, Dorelei spun him about to face her. In his unreliable sight, she went on spinning with the stones.

"This dirt thee spits in a clean crannog—"

"What!"

"Aye, of marriage: better none at all, but will *allow't* from pity if a must. Better to marry than to burn. No word of loving, none of joy. Thee's ill, Padrec. Must be child-wealth as must be lambs and crops, but thee says to marry is only bare best of a poor bargain. One wife if thee must, but, oh, much better to put love aside for the naught it is and spend thy time howling to Father-God. A will grow tired of thee as Mother tired of Mabh. Give fhain something a can use."

Dorelei tore away from him. Padrec tried to keep her in his failing sight, feeling the tension in her small form, something more than anger.

"Thee troubles me, Padrec. I tell thee, could be wrong in bringing thee to fhain. Could be very wrong."

"Then le'me go."

"Nae."

"Why not?"

Dorelei hesitated. "Parents would not ... lie to a gern," she answered with halting obstinacy. "Where, Padrec? Where the sense in thy teaching?"

He was tired, befuddled, and wanted passionately to lie down in his tracks and sleep. Speaking was a thick-tongued effort. His mouth kept going dry. "D'you not know this world will soon pass away?"

"Oh? When? Afore morning, afore lambs drop or be child-wealth? Must fhain just sit and wait? Mother will not pass, Padrec. Did live with the ice and will live for tens of seasons yet."

"The ungodly are so sure of that."

"Be thee man, Padrec?"

"Oh, not that again."

"Nae, be thee man?" Dorelei came to him and put her hands up on his shoulders. The moonlight washed the expression out of her face; she was all light and dark, whiteness framed in the shadow of her hair, shadow where the light broke on the high bridge of her nose. "Well thee speaks of children, being one."

"Now, tha's enough, young woman!"

"Child." She searched the truth of him out of her own shadows. "Have heard of men who will do anything to run from women. Be thee so? Then will leave thee to tallfolk."

"Fine!" he howled. "Fine. Leave, then. You think I want to spend my life with a damned pack of ..."

He was vaguely conscious of leaning against a stone for support, his own voice coming from a long distance, common sense from even farther. *My God, what's happening to me? Am I really this drunk, this indulgent? Careful ... careful. Enough sin for one night.*

With drunken, exaggerated scruple, Padrec levered himself erect, breathing deeply to clear his head. "P'raps I've had a little too much. Forgive me."

Dorelei's tension loosened in her throaty, sighing laugh. "Oh, thee's wicked, Padrec. Of all men or women, thee's first in the world to drink too deep." Her laughter turned merry and soft as she moved closer, pressing her small body against him. "A drink, a love, these be sometimes joy. And how dost spend thy joy but barking at Mother like foolish Rof."

Tumbling toward sleep, flooded with pity for lost Eden, for all men and mostly himself, Padrec slid down the stone, weeping for all of it.

Dorelei's hair brushed his cheek like the cool of the night itself. He felt her hand stroking his body and yearned toward that balm with the last clear impulse left him. With great effort he lifted a hand to fumble over her cheek.

"Wish you could understand me."

She moved so that his face was against her bare breasts, the dark nipples chilled erect by the night air, rocking him gently, murmuring to him. He tried to catch what Dorelei whispered; it was terribly important, the meaning and answer to all questions in the universe. With a sob he buried his face in the breast of God, Mary, Mother, Magdalene that was all beginning and end.

Dorelei held him.

Next morning, for all his pounding head and queasy stomach, Padrec added an eleventh to his Ten Commandments.

Finch did not sing in vain. Although Padrec began to lose track of days and then weeks, it was less than two months from the song to snow. Not a heavy fall, turning to icy rain on the cutting wind. Wrapped in Cru's huge cloak, Padrec paced his horse along the edge of the flocks with Rof, keeping them together. He welcomed the solitude of herd watch, day or night. There was a serious problem to wrestle with.

To want Dorelei was one thing. To see her walk bare in the sun, unconscious of her lithe beauty, was one thing and a simple thing. A priest was only a man and had to deal with the promptings of his own flesh like any other man. He could manage that easily as a moment's appreciation of sensuous Guenloie. To love Dorelei, to yearn after her, to want to join with her, make her part of him, was quite another thing. To turn aside with lead in his heart when the woman of her reached to Cru, to bury his head in blankets at night not to hear the sound of their loving, to go again and again through the exhausting evolution from longing to exaltation to pain, hate, weariness, and the hope that it would all die, only to see her smile and wave at him and be lost again—all this was another thing and a torture against which Padrec was defenseless.

He was emotionally younger than his years. Like a sick child, he could not imagine a time when he'd not been ill: was sick, would always be sick. Love took him by the scruff of the neck as Rof a marauding fox, shook, and tossed him high. He rose, moved through the shortening autumn days and lay down at night in dull misery, and all the prayers and meditations in Canon couldn't help. In matters like this they never did, but Padrec tried and spent long hours with Drust.

Guenloie's second husband was a joy with the glimmerings of a poet in his soul. "My David," Padrec called him when they stood herd watch together. Above all Padrec's teaching, Drust loved the Psalms, the songs to God of a small people ringed with enemies; the pleas and thanks for help were realities with which Drust could identify. Their music modified to his own world and tongue, they emerged less stately but more direct. The lustier of them Drust loved to hurl ablaze down the wind toward the Taixali village, as if by their sheer force he could batter down their walls like Joshua.

"How long dost forget me, Oh Lord! Nae, how long? How long wilt hide Thy face from fhain?"

"Uh . . . those are not the words, Drust."

"Be right words. See: How long must hide sorrow in my heart? How long will hide Thy face, how long shall tallfolk be . . ."

"Exalted."

"Aye, be exalted over me? But why sing of sorrow, Padrec? Be none in me."

"Well, what the Psalm is saying—"

"Nae, hear. Have no sorrow. Flocks healthy and wolves few, Guenloie a good wife. What sorrow?"

"Am I not trying to tell thee, an will be patient?"

"Dost sorrow in thy heart, Padrec?" Drust twisted around to Padrec. They sat very close together, sharing the large cloak. "Do nae smile anymore."

"Nae, do not sorrow," Padrec evaded. "My heart rejoices."

Like a leaden weight.

"Could wish better pasture," Drust allowed, "but that's nae much. Will trade with Taixali."

If I stay, I go on feeding my heart to the crows. Was any man ever so miserable?

A good many of them at one time or another, Meganius might have told him. Those with some experience in love learned to abridge the drama of suffering, but Padrec was a neophyte and would not delete a pang or a sigh. The colors and the music of creation he muffled under the pall of his anguish.

They won't let me go, and yet I must. If I don't, I simply go on dying with no death in sight. If I go, I've failed, but I'm a weak and sorry priest, no matter.

His impregnable cosmos was crumbling like a sand castle in the rain.

Someone should go to the Taixali with a request to trade for grain and vetch. Dorelei had already asked him to do it. It would get him away for a day at least.

Dorelei's thoughts were as full of him, but her worries were more practical. As they suspected, the graze was not enough even for their hardy sheep. They must trade for additional feed. The best time for trading was high or late summer, when crops were good and the tallfolk mood more generous. With summer festivals, children being born or running about, and young people's thoughts turning to coupling, Prydn magic was welcome and sometimes handsomely rewarded. The stockade gates would be opened, the Blackbar was hidden away, all doors stood wide in a good year. They could use the looms. If there was a scarcity of wool, they might trade some of theirs to tallfolk, and always there was mending work for small Prydn hands—clothing for the women, bronze working for Malgon, who could make and decorate a shield or sword fit for a chief who might fight with a blade of Blackbar but still preferred the artistry of bronze for display. Sometimes at Bel-tein or Samhain, tallfolk and Prydn celebrated at one fire, jumped together over the flames, and drove their flocks between the two sacred fires for good fortune. In good years it could be so.

But now it was late in a bad year for Taixali. They would want no part of Prydn, who had nothing to trade in any case but wool not ready for shearing. Fhain needed much: feed for the flocks, woven wool, oil, vegetables—everything, while they had not even sunshine or goodwill to help them through tallfolk gates.

"Must be a way."

Dorelei told herself that with the sureness of her kind, who did not live long without wile. She rode or walked alone over the high ridges, worrying at her problem like a hound at a bone. She thought sometimes of Padrec, and out of the blend of thoughts came her first answer.

Padrec spoke well. If he was impossible in some ways, there was still music to his tongue. He would go ahead of them to tell the village they came in peace to trade.

The second and knottier question: trade what?

"Padrec, would speak with thee."

She chose her time when all fhain were out of the crannog but the two of them, Padrec summoned from feeding and currying the horses. Dorelei sat formally on the gern-stone, Padrec across the fire.

"Do always look sad now, Padrec."

"It is nothing. What would Gern-y-fhain say?"

She'd already announced him as their messenger; she needed other counsel now. "Thee knows the trade south of Wall. And this season so little to trade with."

"True." Padrec kept his head slightly lowered, eyes on his feet.

"Taixali will ask what thee has to trade. What be most wanted by tallfolk?"

Padrec thought on it, pulling his lower lip under front teeth. Gold and jewels were current anywhere but out of the question now.

Fhain wealth was rarely mentioned, and then only as Rainbow-gift.
Wool, yes, but theirs was not ready. Nothing else worth mentioning.
Were they in reach of Corstopitum, they could get good value out of a
pound of pepper or a few jars of liquamen, but Prydn knew nothing of
commercial spices.

"No wool. No furs beyond what fhain wears."

"Then what, Padrec? Do need to know."

"Can think of nothing else but Blackbar." Informed courtesy made
him use the taboo word for iron to neutralize its power in the
crannog; still Dorelei made a perfunctory warding sign before she
spoke. Padrec shifted on the stone with a trace of irritation. For
anyone else the iron would be money, food, supplies, anything needed.
Here it was unmentionable. And yet she sat there with her gray eyes
solemn with concern and responsibility and worried at him for answers.

"Ponies then?"

"Nae."

"My horse could fetch a fair trade."

"Will need it to move in spring."

"I may not be here in spring."

Her head moved slightly. "Will be here."

Padrec threw up his hands. "Well, there's the rath poles and
skins, but I wouldn't count on it."

"Oh, Padrec."

"Or the stones in the circle, but they'd probably want 'em
delivered."

"Do speak like a fool. Do nae try me, Padrec."

"Why not?" He looked up at her for the first time, hoping Dorelei
couldn't read the thing that ate at him. "You ask common sense and
forbid me to speak it."

"Forbid thee nothing. This word, that, but *say*."

"Rainbow-gift."

Dorelei didn't move. Her eyes opened and closed again without
expression. Padrec pointed to her gold torc. "I speak with your
permission. Gold. Silver. Jewels."

"Nae."

The primitive obstinacy was too much for his civilized mind. "Why
not, Dorelei? Do you know the value of what you wear, that torc, the
stone that Reindeer gern wore?"

He heard the sense of blasphemy in her answer. "Nae."

"Oh, God preserve me, what can I say?"

"Cannot trade that. Will nae think it."

"Someone must think it, Dorelei. I put it to you as gern. What
else?"

"Nae."

Padrec sighed. "Then let Gern-y-fhain, who has the lives of her people in hand, tell what a will trade."

Now it was Dorelei's turn to avoid his eyes. "Gawse would not."

"I venture she never needed it that much."

"Mabh would not."

He knew enough not to contradict her there. Mabh was her own Moses, not to be gainsaid, but she might be an example. "Was not Mabh a bringer of great change? Did not Jesu chide the Hebrew priests mired in worn-out ways? Who can say what Mabh would or would not? I have only ridden with Dorelei, who is wise and strong enough to let Christ into her rath. Will such a gern balk at a handful of cold metal to help fhain?"

"Be more than that, Padrec."

"What then?"

"Magic. From the first days. Real gifts here in hand from Mother and Lugh Sun."

"Then let me ask this: as I am called Father Patricius, will not all of Prydn someday call thee Dorelei Mabh in reverence? Mabh had the courage to change. Does Dorelei?"

A persuasive argument, it pressed on her sense of responsibility and pride. If Padrec could swell to the prospect of honor in the Church, Dorelei might be swayed in her own terms. He was glad she couldn't see him just then, with her head bowed. This feeling toward a woman was new to him and not easily hidden. His love welled up in a surge of pity and understanding that wanted to hold Dorelei, tell her it would all come right. He spoke carefully, then, the truth of both of them.

"Dorelei—my friend—listen. Take back from me what I've learned from you. We must all bend a little from our beliefs sometimes. Bend a little, or . . ."

Her dark head came up, searching him for an answer. "Or what, Padrec?"

"Or go down. Go mad. I don't know." He poked at the small fire. "Have said, Gern-y-fhain."

Padrec lowered his head again, fiddling with his stick at the fire. There was a long silence between them; then he heard the slight rustle of movement. When he looked up, he saw that Dorelei had removed her gold torc, turning it thoughtfully in her hands.

It was a measure of their need that no one seriously opposed the decision beyond some grumbling from Malgon the pessimist, who clearly saw it as a desperation measure, and a few questions in private from Dorelei's husband. Whatever any of them felt, the need was a reality. With Padrec's estimation of Roman gold weights for a standard, a simple clay mold was shaped and baked, the gold broken or shaved from their treasure and melted down into trading sticks of considerable weight. Dorelei was surprised to find how little it depleted their treasure. Not even considering the precious stones, Padrec reckoned it at over a thousand gold aureii and still only a fraction of their hoard or that of other gerns like Reindeer. The wealth, the damned cold reality of it, *there* for years or ages and untouchable, as real a covenant as the Ark. Paradox or madness, Prydn were some of the richest folk in Briton, the most needy, and the least likely to survive.

The Taixali were suspicious of a Briton who came in the name of Faerie, but the gold spoke for itself, solid foot-long sticks of it, notched over the length for easy breaking; fine gold that made the eyes of the village elder, Naiton, shine brightly as the wealth. Well enough: let the Faerie come next day.

Trading was something of an occasion to fhain, the novelty always edged with the uncertainty of their reception. For this day, the flocks were watered and fed and left in the byre. The women bathed and anointed themselves with herbs, chose their best kilt or fringed skirt, the men their least tattered vests and trousers. They shaved carefully, sharing the one ancient copper razor, to show their distinction from Picts. To a man, Picts shaved their whole bodies and beard except for fierce, flaring moustaches, which they dyed or curled or stiffened as their hair. Their women dressed their hair in various plaited styles. In contrast, Faerie men shaved their faces clean, proud as the women of their delicate-boned beauty. The razor was always offered to Padrec but had to be so tediously sharpened after each use that he gave it up and let his hair and beard grow out, much to Dorelei's fascination. His hair was red; how could his beard have red and brown and even a few white hairs, all undecided like the salt marsh?

As for herself and her women, Padrec had never seen them dress their hair beyond a gold circlet from fhain treasure. They washed and combed it out and let it hang loose to the waist. The style was preference, not lack of imagination. A Prydn woman did not put up her hair before or after marriage. It was simply not done.

Scrubbed and shined, the horses curried and gauded in treasure from their ancient chest, fhain set out early in the morning for the village to the west. They would not have to spend much time explaining their needs; Padrec had seen to that. It was a good day to trade or visit, the air crisp and just a trace of overcast as the sun rose higher. The gates stood open, one young man on guard, trying to look more casual than he felt at their approach. Dorelei pointedly avoided

101

the dark skins stretched on the stockade wall. She trotted her pony ahead of the others to rein up before the gate.

"Have come to trade," she requested gravely. "Do ask to enter."

"Oh?" The garishly tattooed young warrior swept low in a mock bow. "And what will you trade with, Faerie girl?"

Dorelei kept her face a blank mask. "Be nae girl but a gern. Do come in the peace of Earth and Sun, thy gods and mine."

"And the blessing of God and Jesu Christ." Padrec walked his horse to Dorelei's side. "You know me. I came yesterday to speak with Naiton. We have his welcome."

The young man stroked the iron charm hung about his neck. "Well, then, come in peace."

Padrec wondered why Dorelei hung back, then he saw the iron bar laid across the gate opening and the sudden revulsion and fear in her eyes. The young lout was testing her courage with something she could not cross.

You mean little bastard ... and five extra prayers tonight for the indulgence of my ungenerous thoughts.

The Taixali waved again, mocking Dorelei. "Come in."

She wouldn't cross the bar and the Taixali knew it; she was to be humiliated at the start. Already some of the villagers had gathered inside the gate to enjoy the sight. Padrec dismounted and approached the Taixali, hands open and spread in friendship.

"You play a silly joke with your iron. Gern-y-fhain, who has more magics than the tree has leaves, will not deign to play with you. As you would not dare the hills at night where the spirits of the air and dark are her servants." Padrec picked up the iron bar and tossed it to one side. "And my God has magics. Think you a God who felled the firstborn in every house in Egypt, who cured lepers and raised the dead will fear the toy-trick in a piece of iron? You waste your time and that of Naiton, boy."

Padrec waved Dorelei past him into the stockade.

It was a day of learning for Padrec. He saw with bemused humor how exotic each people were to the other. The scant costumes of fhain women were as fascinating to Pictish dames as their motleyed and checked gowns were to Prydn. All trading was done in the longhouse of Naiton the village elder, a thick-bodied man who lolled in his mothy ceremonial chair, belly hanging over his belt, picking his teeth while fhain bargained. Dorelei and Cru had organized the trading for efficiency, not wanting to tarry longer than needed. Cru, Malgon, Artcois, and Bredei would inspect and trade for the vetch they needed. Oil fell to Drust and Guenloie, bolts of woven wool were the province of Dorelei and Neniane. They wanted good quality and

102

measure for their gold. Behind his studied insolence, Naiton was eager for trade. He didn't see gold very often.

"There is that which is beside the wool," he announced casually. At a sign, one of his fat wives unrolled a bolt of linen and spread it for inspection. Padrec heard Neniane's little *oh* of admiration and pleasure.

"Dost like it, small cat?"

"Oh, aye. So soft. Could make much from it." Her wise hands danced over and through the linen, twisting it this way and that, catching it into shapes, already measuring and cutting. "Swaddling for child-wealth."

"Who will come soon to Neniane."

Dorelei fingered the linen. "Thee knows fine cloth, Padrec. Be worth our gold?"

The linen was coarse but as good as one would find north of Eburacum. "Fair quality."

Neniane clutched at the prize of it. "Sister, please? But a little?"

Dorelei saw the wanting in her sister's appeal. Neniane desired it for swaddling, as if the mere possession would bring a child to wrap in it. Lovely stuff, but a luxury and far too flimsy for riding. She never saw it outside the lowland villages. Dorelei already felt a blasphemer for spending Rainbow-gift, and yet her hand smoothed over the soft material in a natural caress. So white. It would be as snow against her skin and necklace of blue stones, and Padrec would know a new word for beauty in women, regardless of his peculiar attitude toward it. If it were not too costly . . .

"Perhaps." She put the bolt firmly aside. "Will think on't."

Padrec asked his leave of Dorelei and enjoyed a stroll about the village. Compared to fhain, even Taixali were civilized in some ways. He stopped to watch a potter busy at his wheel, a blacksmith with sparks exploding from hammer and anvil. Taixali houses were sturdier than their thatched roofs belied, the timbers well cut and joined with iron tools. He looked in on Cru, Malgon, and Bredei weighing out vetch, then paused to drink at the well, noticing the middle-aged couple staring at him. Like all isolated folk, their curiosity was direct and a shade loutish, but he greeted them civilly.

"Give you good day."

Still they stared. The specific objects of their concentration were the heavy gold bracelets on his wrists.

"That which you wear," the man pointed. "Is it gold then?"

"Yes."

The man turned to his woman. "Did I not say so? I've seen gold weight in Corstopitum, but none like that. Very little dross, I will be bound."

"A little to harden it," Padrec confirmed.

"Where is it that such gold comes from?" the woman asked.

"From Gern-y-fhain. Faerie queen."

"Ah, the young one. And from where to her?"

Padrec spread his hands. "Who can say? They have had it always. Gift from Rainbow, it is said."

Their expressions opened wider with wonder. "Ah . . . magic, then. There have been such tales as that."

Padrec replaced the dipper and wiped his lips. "You have been often to Corstopitum, then?"

The Taixali man straightened and became palpably official. "It is myself that does the trading with Venicone and Romans."

The wife gave her husband a proprietary smile from which several teeth were conspicuously absent. "Eight fine horses that he loads and that carry back the goods from Wall."

The first rays of a dawning idea struck Padrec. "When do you journey again?"

"Soon, soon." The Taixali rubbed his hands and cast a look at the sky. "While the weather holds."

"Would you carry a letter for me?"

Well, now, for a consideration, for a half notch of gold, mild robbery and Padrec knew it, the man would oblige. Aye, and toss in to the bargain the wherewithal to write. In his house he proudly laid before Padrec a supply of quills, passable ink, and tattered sheets of dark vellum, thin with washing and much use. The trader couldn't write at all. He toted his accounts in a picture code of his own; nevertheless, he felt quite literate owning such materials.

"And there is tea to the fire," the wife blandished as Padrec dipped his quill.

Patricius to Caius Meganius, bishop of Eburacum, that you may know of me and my mission. Ave and the blessing of Christ to your grace.

He wrote of the Venicones and how they crippled and cast him out to die, and of his rescue by Prydn. Padrec paused in reflection and added the word "Faerie" in parentheses. Very likely Meganius never heard of Prydn. Indeed, no one south of the Wall, including himself, had a clear notion of them beyond dark fables to frighten children into obedience. Padrec almost laughed aloud. Frightening? A woman deeply lovely as Dorelei, a man bright as Bredei, vulnerable as Drust?

We are two days north of the Venicones, among the Taixali. God knows where after this, since they are nomads who must follow the herds. My fasting vows have lapsed since it is very hard to know from one day to the next what there will be to eat at all, and I must take no more than my share. Your indulgence in absentia would be appreciated in this. . . .

And for that I love a woman and the love is a thorn. But until I can confess, I will wrestle that alone, Meganius.

Still they have made me one of them and hear my preaching. And so your grace will be pleased to learn I have my first congregation.

Congregation? He rarely felt like a priest these days, more often the prisoner of benevolent jailors or an idiot uncle more loved than heeded. They were yet small vessels for the wine of faith. They could hold so much, and the rest spilled over to waste.

They love the miracles, which are much like their own, and the Psalms for their music, so at least there is a beginning. Farewell for the time. Patricius asks your prayers and sends his to his holy bishop.

He considered adding "and mentor" but could not yet bring himself to it. He rolled the vellum, wrote the name and destination on the outer side, and handed it to the trader with his bit of gold, not concerned about the privacy of the contents. If it got to Corstopitum at all, no one north of the Wall could read it anyway.

Shadows lengthened eastward. Dorelei gave the sun a glance and passed the word to collect by the ponies near the gate. She met Padrec coming out of the trader's house and passed him the bolts of cloth.

"So you couldn't resist the linen," he noted with a twinkle. Dorelei felt secretly guilty over the extravagance. "And why not? Sister much wanted it."

"And you? A fair gown for summer. Perhaps with—yes, the necklace of sapphires."

"Sa—?"

"Your blue stones. They always become you."

"Ah. Perhaps. Do nae think on such things."

Cru and Malgon appeared, carrying baskets of feed between them, Artcois and Bredei laden with more behind. They deposited the goods by the pack animals and hurried back for the second load, all

105

aware of the time and the need to depart. Padrec felt the tension in Dorelei as they worked quickly to load the ponies.

"Need not haste so," he eased. "None staring at us now."

"Be thy first trading, Padrec." Dorelei went on hitching and tying with quick, sharp twists of her fingers. "A do watch always."

"I think it's gone well."

"Will say that when fhain is well gone." Dorelei mentally ticked off her people, wishing them finished and visible. She breathed easier when Cru and Malgon secured their last load to the pack saddles and freer yet when Artcois and Bredei and Neniane were waiting by her side. Only two missing. "Guenloie and Drust? They went for the oil."

Padrec pointed across the village common. "In that storehouse."

"With what tallfolk?" Dorelei demanded.

Cru read her unease and added his own. "That Taixali who laid Blackbar athwart the gate. Did nae like it, but was Naiton's wish."

Hearing it, Malgon started to move. One look between Padrec and Cru and they were abreast of Guenloie's husband as he strode toward the storehouse, Cru subtly brushing Malgon's hand from the hilt of his knife. Padrec was in the lead when the cry rose from inside the storehouse—Guenloie's voice, high and shrill, edged with fear. The door burst open and Drust literally fell out of the house with the Taixali youth after him, knife in hand. Even as the Taixali lunged, Drust rolled cat-quick out of the way and up, knife on guard, circling. Padrec broke into a run, seeing the whole miserable sense of it: the Taixali blood-striped as Drust, Guenloie terrified in the doorway. And now other villagers left off their business, running, eager to see what happened, what would happen.

"Cru, take Drust," Padrec snapped. "I'll take the boy."

"Will do that myself," Malgon hissed.

"No, you won't." Padrec pushed him aside. He and Cru didn't pause at the edge of the fight. Agile Cru slipped behind Drust and pinned his arms as Padrec lunged in front of the Taixali knife that froze its forward thrust a bare inch from his own gut. "Put it up!"

The young man was cut across the chest; not badly, but pride demanded retribution beyond the wound in Drust's arm. "Get out of my way."

Padrec didn't move. "I do only as your own elder would. Put it up, boy."

The youth deliberately placed the edge of the knife against Padrec's throat just under his left ear. "I am no boy to you or any Roman."

His heart pounded so hard, Padrec found it difficult to keep his voice steady. He concentrated all the will into that. "You tried us like a boy at the gate and no better now, testing other's courage where you are not sure of your own. Put up your knife before your women laugh at you."

There was a larger crowd around them now, the women sibilant, pointing at Guenloie in the doorway.

"She's to blame."

"She did it."

"Did what?" one reasonable voice piped, quite lost in the tide of accusation.

"The whore, she's to blame. They're all alike."

The circle began to shrink tighter around them—then quite suddenly the crowd washed to either side like wake from the prow of a swift keel as Naiton plowed through, beefy and choleric. "Now, what is this? What is this?"

In the face of Naiton's unquestionable authority, the youth faltered and whined. "He cut me, Elder. See how he did cut me."

"And you him, and over what?" Naiton jabbed a scornful finger at Guenloie. "That? What happened?"

Cowed, sickened at the blood streaming down Drust's arm, Guenloie could only stammer and choke into silence. Naiton read it as confirmation of his quick suspicion.

"Didn't he pay you enough, whore?"

"Was nae that!" Drust raged from the prison of Cru's arms. "Did try to take Guenloie's circlet and—and touch her. Nae, see Guenloie's face where a did strike her."

True enough. The girl's cheek was bruised from a blow with some force behind it, but that meant little to Naiton, who kicked or cuffed stupid women a dozen times a day. "Only that? Here, give me that knife until you grow, halfling."

The young Taixali handed it over meekly. Naiton turned on Dorelei, towering over the tiny woman. "Out, Faerie."

She didn't move. "Will have our oil."

"What, what?"

"Oil, there in the house. Did pay gold weight for it."

Naiton tossed the order to the crowd. "Someone go fetch their oil. The trading's done. You have your goods. When you have more need and more gold, you can come back. But now take the other whore and get out."

Less of a bully than too used to his word being law, Naiton was surprised when the tiny woman didn't budge. He'd thought earlier her eyes were a queer kind of gray, but not true. They were black now, huge, no whites to them at all, and unswerving from his. The intensity

107

might have unsettled a more sensitive man. She seemed to be sifting through the essence of him to find his center.

"We are both leaders, Naiton, and should not bleat at each other like small bairn."

"You little . . ." Half angry, half amused at the mite of her: barely more than a child and presuming to be his equal. He was holding the confiscated knife; lifting it inadvertently, he saw Dorelei flinch slightly and make a furtive sign. Naiton grinned.

"Afraid of it, aren't you? You know our magic is stronger than yours. See?" His hand darted out and laid the flat of the black blade against her bare arm. Dorelei jerked visibly, recoiling.

"Out, woman. And take the rest with you. Out!" Naiton pushed through the crowd and strode away.

"Whores," someone muttered.

"Get the Faerie out of here."

"They will curse the bairn. Nae, keep the bairn from them."

The Taixali women were in an ugly mood. Cru caught Padrec's eye and jerked his head toward Guenloie. Padrec reached the girl as the first stones flew. A sharp pebble caught Guenloie just under the eye. Padrec covered her with his back, but he recognized the thrower—the slatternly woman who'd brought her baby for Faerie magic. *Lord keep me from the temptation to hate them.*

Now that real danger was passed, the women needed to vent their spleen and frustration on a safe target. They began to throw bigger stones. Padrec gasped as one struck his shoulder, bruising it to the bone. Out of the corner of his eye, he saw Neniane dart in, scoop up the amphora of oil and scurry away to her pony.

"Cru, get Dorelei out of here! Guenloie, come. Come, now . . ."

Covering the shaking girl with his body, Padrec moved as quickly as he could toward the horses. Guenloie's mouth quivered, but it was set. She would not let these people see her pain or shame. Then they were by the ponies, and Drust moved to cover Guenloie on the other side. She mewed sickly at the blood seeping from his arm with no sign of slowing.

"Blackbar knife, husband," she said in a crushed little voice. "Will not heal."

"Nae, nae. Will."

Dorelei stared down coldly at her cousin, holding her arm where the knife had touched it. "Did tell thee, Guenloie," she said in a voice full of terminal judgment. "Did warn thee."

Padrec just stared at her: Dorelei was blaming her cousin as much as the Taixali, but there was no time to consider right or wrong. Some of the younger boys were drifting closer, like purposeful jackals. "Go ahead," he said. "We'll follow. There, Guenloie, will be well. Come now, come."

The Taixali boys edged even closer, excited, eager for their share in the rout.

"Ha!"

One of them ran forward at Dorelei, brandishing a bright-painted arrow with a broad iron head. "Here, Faerie. Good. Take it. Take—"

Dorelei's gaze turned on him almost languidly. The boy froze. His arm, brandishing the arrow, faltered to his side.

"Thee would not," Dorelei murmured in a lulling tone like a caress. "Thee will not." She turned her pony and rode through the gate with Cru after her, the rest of fhain following. Seeing to Drust and Dorelei, Padrec was the last to flip the reins over his horse's ears. He didn't see the boy steal behind him until the inane giggle insulted his ears.

"Ha, Faerie. Look: iron. Magic. Iron."

Padrec turned with a surge of irritation. "Yes?"

Again the silly, pattering laugh from the boy, with the others snickering behind him. "Iron. Take it, Faerie. Take it."

"If you insist." Padrec grasped the arrow, pointedly kissed the iron head, broke the shaft in neat halves, and returned the feathered end with poisonous courtesy. "No, you see, it won't always work. She's stronger than you, and I'm Catholic." He mounted and held up the arrow. "The blessing of my God on you." *And may He spare you the sorrow of age and pardon my wish.*

The stockade gate thudded shut behind him as he cantered after the forlorn trio of Drust, Malgon, and Guenloie, whose distracted concern was torn between the wound of one husband and the disgust of the other.

"Did *naught*, Malgon," she protested tearfully. "Only bargained for oil."

"True," Drust sputtered. "A tried to touch her like Guenloie was one of a's own pig-women." He broke off, fumbling at the wound across his arm. "Do lack word for such men."

"Could offer one but will not." Padrec gave his attention to Guenloie. Her shame and confusion broke forth in a fresh flood of tears.

"*Why* dost Dorelei speak so? Did naught."

None of them knew why, but later for that. Drust still bled.

"Will nae stop," Guenloie quavered over the wound. "Was made of Blackbar. Was cursed."

Then Malgon pointed suddenly. "Padrec! Throw't away."

In the confusion, Padrec had forgotten to discard the iron arrowhead. He galloped out a few paces from them and hurled it as far

109

as he could, hearing it clink against a rock. Guenloie gathered a few broad leaves from plants on the heath and deftly folded them into a makeshift bandage over a handful of moss, while Drust glared at the stockade palings. Padrec's heart went out to him—only fifteen, wounded and humiliated, needing very much to be a man in front of his brother-husband and the wife who worked over his arm with all the love in her hands, fighting back tears of rage so close to the surface.

"Padrec, Gern-y-fhain be *wrong*."

"Hold still," Guenloie sniffled. "Must bind thy brave arm."

Drust twisted about, beseeching the other men to know the sharper pain he felt. He found no words of his own, only the seared music of a beleaguered king. "My soul . . . be among wolves. Do lie down with them whose teeth be arrows. But my heart is fixed, O God. My heart is fixed."

The Fifty-seventh Psalm as Drust remembered it, not perfect, but shaped to his need. He held Guenloie while they both shook, and Malgon embraced them both in silence. Drust might love his wife with the more desperate need, but Malgon understood both of them, which was the greater burden. Padrec felt a deep shame for his own kind. Tallfolk? Wherefore tall?

About a mile from the village, in a small draw between two low hills, fhain waited for them—hovered rather, poised behind Dorelei, who sat her pony in coiled fury, still holding her arm.

"Guenloie, have told thee more than once to turn aside from tallfolk men."

Guenloie bowed her head. "Did naught, Dorelei."

"Thee speaks to thy gern. Naught? Do know thy naught. So proud of thy Taixali blood thee flaunts it for all, even among them, with thy weak little smiles all come-hither."

"Do swear on Mother, did *not*."

"Dorelei, they weren't alone. Drust was there. He'll tell you the truth of it."

Cru warned seriously. "Padrec, stay out. Take no part of this."

"Nae, need not stay out," Drust flared in defiance. "Were but measuring out the oil, and a was paid for. Taixali tried to take wife's gold circlet."

And to touch her in other places with more intimate purpose, as Drust spat out the facts. Padrec knew enough of them to believe it. The Taixali man flustered her. She was never able to manage men easily. Drust tried to be tactful, cautioned the youth politely and then in outright warning. When the man just laughed and thrust his hand through Guenloie's fringed skirt, she pushed him away. Before Drust could intervene, the man struck her hard, knocking her down.

"Dost change naught." Neniane still trembled from the fear she felt in the village. "Did never think but of men, men, any man, like bitch in heat."

"Lie!" Guenloie screamed. "Lie! Lie! Lie!"

"Neniane lies!" Drust choked.

Dorelei held up her hand. "Gern will speak. Look what thy ways have brought to fhain." She showed her arm. Something turned over in Padrec's stomach. Impossible but there: Naiton had barely touched the flat of the blade to her arm, but the reddening, blistered outline of it was like a severe burn. He wouldn't have believed it.

"See the evil of that blood thee prates of," Dorelei said with sick contempt. "And take a's own word for thee. Whore. Go from fhain, Guenloie. Husbands too, if a will yet have thee."

"Dorelei, please." Guenloie slid from her pony to kneel before her cousin. "Send me away when have done what thee speaks, but not so. Did fight the Taixali."

"Was so." Drust spoke respectfully but would not drop his eyes before Dorelei's challenge. Suddenly she lashed out with her foot and kicked Guenloie hard.

"Go, pig."

Guenloie cried out more in desperation than pain. Padrec dismounted and grasped her to him. "Dorelei, for God's love, think what you do. This is not even good sense."

"Did say stay out," Cru warned him again.

"I will not." Padrec pressed the weeping Guenloie to him, glaring up at him. "Not in this."

"Not in this." Drust moved to shield his wife on the other side.

"Will say as much." Malgon got down from his pony to join them. "Let Cruaddan stay out."

Cru started to dismount, but Drust, never coolheaded, snaked his knife from the sheath and leveled it at him. "Cru and all else: do wish to try against Drust as Taixali did? Artcois? Bredei?"

Artcois looked down at his hands. "Thy wife brings ruin to fhain."

"Never to thee, fhain brother."

"Brings Blackbar evil. See where a marked Gern-y-fhain."

"And look at her under Padrec's arm," Dorelei seethed. "Will nestle to any man."

It was too much for Padrec. "Oh, *stop* it, Dorelei. Were thee hurt as she is? Stop it!"

None of them, not even Cru, expected it from Dorelei. In a flash her leg was over the pony's head. She dropped to the ground and flew at Guenloie, flailing at the girl as Padrec tried to fend her off.

"Out, whore. Tallfolk pig. Out!"

"I said—get away!" Padrec shoved Dorelei harder than he intended. The small girl lost her balance and fell, not hurt, but livid at the profanation. No man might interfere with punishment of a woman, not even a husband. Cru moved toward Padrec, but Drust's knife was still out, and now Malgon's as well.

"No, Cru." Dorelei rose, fighting to control a rage she couldn't name herself. "Thee dares so, Padrec? Have said. Guenloie goes with a's husbands. And thee an thy heart be with them, and there done."

Cru nodded. "Done."

"Done," said Neniane. "Husbands?"

Bredei spoke at last, not equal to dissension, hating it all. "Nae, be wrong. Do believe Guenloie."

Cru's anger was audible. "Do we have gern-law, or only the squall of bairn? Thee's heard Gern-y-fhain. Done!"

"Oh, yes," Padrec said. "The word of Dorelei, who is rich in years and wisdom. She raises her hand and cuts a family from fhain as Mabh cut Britain from Gaul, without counting the cost. Has the gern-daughter of a gern so many she can waste three with no loss and winter coming? Believe in my Christ or not, Dorelei, He yet had more mercy dying on the cross than you in your childish ignorance."

When she turned on him, he felt the cold will that froze the Taixali boy with his silly arrow. She might cheerfully cut his heart out now, but her voice was steady.

"Then four will go, Padrec-tallfolk. And thy weeping Jesu who will bring no more good to fhain than Blackbar. Aye, go! Do give thee this night in crannog, but go at morning. Have said."

Her fury translated to energy. Dorelei vaulted her pony, yanked its head around, and galloped away to the east without looking back. Then Cru, Neniane, and her husbands followed at a slower pace. Malgon watched them go.

"Thee speaks well, Padrec. Thee has the truth of it."

"For all the good it did. Here, take thy wife. Where will thee go?"

Malgon shrugged. "Where indeed? Come, wife."

"Padrec be cast out, too," Drust reminded them. "And where will a go who's more man than tallfolk and almost Prydn a's self? Come with us, Padrec. Who will give us the David-songs now?"

Truly, no one. This failure hurt the most. The Venicone only broke his legs.

He didn't know why he chose the ring of stones for his prayers, but that it was the nearest thing to a chapel in three days' ride, and God was everywhere when it came to that. Under the moon that lit the swift-running clouds, Padrec knelt and earnestly tried to pray. He truly needed a confessor himself. The love once wholly dedicated to God was now divided and blurred, seething with human hurt. More than all this, he'd failed, first with the Venicones and now here where the need for God cried out.

No. Better not to pray when his heart wasn't in it but raging at Dorelei. He rose and wandered about the moonlit circle, his sleeping blanket wrapped about him against the wind.

I only tried to help Guenloie. Why did you turn on me? Even your own folk can make nothing of it. I never thought you this cruel.

Guenloie was—well, as innocent as a woman could be with that kind of beauty and so careless in covering it. That was a fault and her only fault, innocent in all else. Why did Dorelei act so irresponsibly? Was that her heathen idea of leadership?

And what is yours of a priest? Wherein celibate when your soul and your eyes have yearned every day after her? Dreamed of her, imagined coupling with her? What part of the sin but the mere act have you omitted? Lord, was I wrong? Was my calling a vanity, a delusion? A moment's answer to loneliness?

It could be; he wasn't sure of anything anymore. His cosmos had turned on its head to show him facets and depths never guessed under Germanus or even Amathor. The world, real and spirit, was larger than his idea of it, and he smaller, weaker, and more contemptible than Padrec ever imagined in his worst moments of self-flagellation. And ignorant as Dorelei. How would he explain the mark on her arm, the inflamed, obscene outline of the knife against her smooth skin, as if the metal were red hot when it couldn't be?

How many times had he sheathed Dorelei in the blessing of God? And what good did it do her when she needed it? There was virulent sorcery in the iron: admit that and admit as well a whole dark, demon-driven cosmos beyond the edge of God's holding where His Grace did not apply, with only fools and failures like himself to make it work. He could preach of the loaves and fishes, Lazarus and the Resurrection, but he didn't know any magic, didn't even know human beings as Meganius did. Padrec was a stupid child trying to build a fire and burning nothing but his fingers.

Where will Meganius send me now? Not even Germanus will give me Ireland if I fail here. I only wanted to tell them of You, Lord. Was that vanity?

What else, liar? Did I not seek my own praise in that service?

"But look at Drust, Lord, how he already loves the Psalms. All of them love the miracles. I tell them in their own way, as stories of magic. Jesu did no less. Lord, I learn slowly but I do learn. If I know not the vessel, I know the wine You would pour into it. To be consecrated Your priest is not enough. Make me one in truth, or put me aside for

113

good and all, as You will divide goat and sheep. Do it now, I pray. Do not bow me down with Meganius' years before I have his wisdom. Let me know men now. Not in safe Eburacum or Auxerre or Rome, my Lord, but here, now, in the forefront of the battle. The iron of me is white on Your anvil. Strike now, shape me now. Give me a sign."

Padrec gazed morosely about the shadowed circle and blew out his cheeks in exasperation. "Miracles . . ."

Miracles and magic: that was religion to Faerie, that and the quaintly unstable marriage of sun and earth. Of them all, Drust might in time go beyond that to true faith; the rest understood nothing but the intercession of magic for good or ill, the folderol practiced with much display by Irish shamans. Tricks, but they believed.

"Tricks . . ."

Failure was the lash he couldn't suffer again; yet to stay he must find a powerful reason now. Hunched against a stone, muffled in the blanket, Padrec tried to order his mind to purpose, glaring up at the moon like a rival: Dorelei's mother of magic.

"Don't look at me. You're the magician."

A piece of an idea snagged on the hem of his thoughts. His frame of mind turned from despair; he began to think slowly, polishing each element before fitting it to the next, doing what would have been obvious at the start to one of the Irish shamans. He tried to think not about Dorelei but like her.

If I were Dorelei, what would I most need now? What would I want? If I were she . . .

To have one side of her at war with the other was new and painful to Dorelei. She knew her needs, but for the first time in her life she could not name her feelings. They were not as simple as before. She'd showed her anger like a child without knowing clearly what drove it, and vented it on Cru in loving that night, biting his neck, tearing his strong back with her nails. He wouldn't know that it was passion of a different color, that she battered herself against a force that threatened her.

"Thee has a hunger tonight," he whispered against her cheek.

"Do need you much." Dorelei writhed against him. "Come to me."

"Again?"

Her arms went around him, tight.

Long after Cru breathed deep in slumber, Dorelei stared up into darkness, reliving the horrible day in the village, the miserable silence around the fire, the wound in her fhain as visible as that on her arm. Her thoughts sifted finer through the sleepless hours, showing her the problem but no way to the heart of it. He was the rock that broke her. Lugh had sent her no help at all. Padrec was a stone around her neck and one with a cutting edge. He defied her when she spoke as gern. He put his arm around sheep-witted Guenloie, who might have killed them all with her weak ways. In the village he thought first to shield Guenloie rather than herself from the hurled stones. For all the magic of Lugh, Mother, and even Padrec's Father-God, all saw how Blackbar frightened her, saw what it did to her arm, and knew her magic was weak. She was shamed and beaten, and future life with Taixali would be all the harder for them.

The men must trade alone from now on, if they went at all. Three of them, all that were left. Padrec couldn't know how much more at stake there was than puling Guenloie, and yet he defied her—this man not sensible enough to reach for a woman. He incited Drust and Malgon to defy her. She'd shown enough of her humiliation this day, when she'd always shielded all but wise Cru from the hard truth of their weakness. They knew now, and when she looked at sullen Padrec across the firepit at supper, Dorelei realized she must rule fhain or he would.

She was glad he was going.

Not true; she ought to be glad. *That* hid itself in passion and made her love Cru until they were both exhausted. *That* robbed her sleep now, the feeling she struggled to catch and drag into the light. A gern must be able to read her own heart before she could read others. What was it that loosed the fury at Guenloie?

Not so much a finding but admitting. Whatever his mad notions of women, Padrec was a man for a woman to treasure and learn from. If her whole life proceeded from belief, so did his, and this made him strong in his peculiar way, strong and stubborn as herself. Aye, and what did he spend this strength on? Guenloie! Always the favored, spoiled child in Gawse's fhain. How her changeling mother cooed over Guenloie and made much of her. And oh, how Guenloie clung to the petting and to her Padrec-protector, wetting his shirt with her innocent tears, all atremble in his arms. . . .

No more, woman. Is that the heart of it? Help me, Mother. I must be wise when I'm a fool, strong where all know me weak, a gern where I am not fit to tend fhain flocks. Help me. Is it all because of him? That I am jealous?

Send him away. And keep the Blackbar evil from us.

Dorelei burrowed closer to Cru's male warmth under the covers. As she moved, her fingers brushed the swollen evil on her arm, and she shivered with the oldest fear of her life and her kind.

Padrec came home late to crannog, and Dorelei heard him rise early, while Neniane was kindling the morning fire. She was not surprised he was gone and his horse with him. Whatever her feelings, that much was done and finished. If a gern could be wrong, she could right it, but she could not give up. Wisdom was never the worse for a sleep. Yesterday's troubles, sifted through a rested mind, were clearer now, the right and wrong of it. Dorelei took small sips from her cup of chamomile and prepared to break the smothered silence.

Guenloie and her husbands were glum and silent in their places around the firepit. They'd already begun to bundle their own things together. Dorelei set down her cup and assumed the formal position on her stone.

"Guenloie?" Her cousin looked directly at her for the first time that morning. The bruises on her face were bluish-black now. The girl had suffered much. "Have spoken with Mother. A would nae have thee parted from fhain."

Guenloie bowed her head in acceptance. "Be innocent, Gern-y-fhain." Dorelei saw the gratitude in her eyes and the vindication in Drust's.

"Mother did say so. Be past and done, then. Fhain will be whole again."

It was the right decision. Dorelei felt the tension about the fire loosen and dissolve in tremulous laughter and snatches of idle talk. She caught Cru's tiny nod of approval. He'd upheld her law but approved the cooler common sense that shaded it to mercy.

"Do speak to all," Guenloie said into the clay cup between her small palms. "Have had foolish thoughts, said foolish things. Nae more. Would open my flesh and spill the Taixali blood from it. Would nae go again to a's stinking village."

"Yah," Malgon agreed. "Wife will stay apart from them."

Now that they were knit again, Dorelei pressed the advantage with further good sense. "Fhain women will not go among them, but men alone and only if a must. And if a's women come to fhain for magic, will set a dear price on it."

Cru touched Dorelei's arm where the inflammation was darkening like an old burn. She shook him away in tacit disapproval: it should not be mentioned, but Bredei did and spoke.

"Was foul of Naiton. A has nae magic but that."

"But that enough," Neniane murmured. "Be Lugh Sun still angry with Mother that a does keep fhain under such a curse?"

"Gods can be wrong," Artcois ventured. "Even jealous."

"Nae, not Padrec's Father-God," Drust protested. "What god stronger? Did part the sea and slay firstborn in every rath of Egypt-land."

"Was thee in Egypt to see?" Cru challenged. "Nae, only that Padrec did say, and a's well gone."

"Gone," Dorelei sealed it. Drust prudently let it drop but couldn't resist a parting shot. "Padrec be a good heart. Will miss him."

They all would. Padrec's absence was more palpable than his presence. Dorelei realized they'd all grown used to the gentle, fussy, incomprehensible *self* of Padrec as part of their lives, but she couldn't bend in this. She couldn't clearly see where his teaching would lead them, nor would Padrec see how she must be sure in that. He would move on, go home. She could not.

When they drove the flocks out to the high pasture, the sky looked ominous, clear blue in the west but an edge of mackerel clouds sliding toward them from the east with a dirty gray smudge behind them. Glad to be exonerated, Guenloie and her husbands jumped to the tasks that Dorelei set out for them. The men went to pasture the sheep, Guenloie descended the west slope to the woods for hyssop to make poultice for Drust's arm and to gather late mushrooms for the supper pot. Dorelei sent Neniane after her, more for mending than needed help.

"Go with thy cousin, sister. A's had a hard lesson."

Artcois and Bredei passed Cru on their way to hunt, grinning.

"Dorelei be wise," Artcois said.

"Aye, did think much on it last night."

The brothers smiled slyly, brimming with fun. "True," said Bredei. "Did hear thee both thinking last night."

"Aye, brother; and see where a did use Cru's back to ponder."

They circled Cru, gravely inspecting every small mark until he shoved them away and slipped into his vest. Bredei assisted him as if he were aged and infirm. Artcois shook his head.

"Be content as husband to second daughter. Do not have the strength for a gern."

"Die in a year," his brother agreed. "Less."

The time for joking was over; Cru tired of them. "Thee were not marked with Blackbar. Go hunt and be done."

That was the thing they could not fight, no matter how high their courage. Dorelei could forgive Guenloie and send Padrec away, but the mark on her arm was burned deep in all of them. Stronger than his bronze knife and his arrows, Blackbar had defeated them since the time Lugh gave it to tallfolk. He could not give in to his fear, being a man, but Dorelei must show more strength than all of them. If his love restored that strength, Dorelei could claw Cru's flesh to the white bone.

The second thought was natural to him. *Where is she?*

As his mind framed the question, he tried to remember. He knew when Dorelei wanted to be alone, but there might be Taixali about, all the more confident since filthy Naiton laid the Blackbar on Dorelei. Cru took the slope in strides and hops on the steeper grade, loping toward the trees.

The darkening sky matched her mood. Dorelei stood by a stunted oak overshadowed by taller firs and brooded out over the glen to the west. Somewhere below her, Neniane and Guenloie moved silently about their gathering. Dorelei shivered and pulled the cloak about her, feeling guilty when she saw Cru coming through the trees. She loved him without question, almost without beginning, since she couldn't remember a time when they weren't together. Yet last night was the first time in all their seasons when she lay in Cru's arms and thought of someone else.

Good that he is gone. If he stayed, the fight would come sooner or later, whether he came to my bed or not.

How could she love what she didn't understand? Some things took more living than thinking about, and Padrec had changed for the better since they found him in the ring of stones. But it was good she sent him away. Difference was one thing, defiance another, and if she felt a loss—well, Gawse must have sacrificed much for like reasons.

She hoped her husband brought no new problems; she couldn't cope with them now. "Aye, Cru?"

"Did think not to leave thee alone."

When she felt his arms around her, Dorelei shut her eyes tight against the loneliness even Cru could not drive away, and was a traitor.

They were not long together by the tree when Guenloie hailed them from a thicket, broke into sight, and sprinted up the wooded slope, Neniane hurrying behind.

"Aye, aye. Thy baskets will spill out. What is't?"

Neniane pointed back down the slope to the moving figure blurred by thicket but climbing toward them. "Padrec comes *back.*"

Then the horse broke out into the open and Padrec called to her. "Gern-y-fhain, would speak with thee."

"Were sent away!" She hurled it back with more force than needed. "May not come back. Will not."

Still he came on, holding a brightly colored stick in his hand. When Cru saw what it was, he nocked an arrow to his bow and drew on the priest. "Stop, tallfolk man."

Padrec halted the horse. "Do not call me that, Cru. It's not a name I'd wear."

"Say that and yet bring Blackbar to curse us again?" Cru's bow was steady on Padrec's chest. "Will kill thee, Padrec."

Padrec held up the arrowhead on its fragment of painted shaft, retrieved from near the rock he'd flung it against the day before. "I'm glad you didn't send Guenloie away."

"Yah, Padrec." Guenloie ventured a tentative smile, wary of the evil in his hand.

"Thee cannae come back." Dorelei took a few paces toward him, placing herself between the evil and her folk. "Will nae mock us so. What dost want?"

"My place, Gern-y-fhain. My people."

"Be nae thy folk."

"You are. If not you, then none."

"Nae, go. Or Cru will shoot."

Padrec dismounted and stood by the horse's head. "But hear me. You believe in the magic of Mother and Lugh. The magic of my God is shown only to strengthen the faith of the believer. I have told fhain of this magic, which is greater than the parting of the seas or riving of rock. Now I must show it. It is all I can give you."

"What magic?"

"When I have shown it to Gern-y-fhain, let her send me away if she will. I wished only to bring fhain to the true God, the Father of Lugh himself." Padrec's voice softened with the admission. "That's all I am, Dorelei, all any priest is. A messenger. My message delivered, I'm not important, but Gern-y-fhain is."

In a different tone, Dorelei said, "Thee knows that now?"

Padrec nodded. "God offers his magic to Salmon gern if she will take it."

Dorelei cursed him silently, disturbed by the challenge of him she felt from the first day.

"If she has the strength to dare as Mabh dared. To change, to hazard what she has for what can be."

"None be braver than my sister," Neniane piped loyally. "Like to our mother."

"And do know it, Neniane. So it is to thy gern I bring this magic." Padrec held up the broken arrow. "The power over Blackbar. Now and forever."

Dorelei made the ward-sign, keeping her face stiff to hide the fear. With a staying gesture to Cru, she stalked forward to within a pace of Padrec, averting her eyes from the Blackbar.

"Will nae leave here if thee harms Dorelei," Cru promised.

"Would harm my friend?"

"What dost speak?" Dorelei demanded in a low, tense voice that only Padrec could hear. "Thee troubles me, Padrec. Have always troubled me."

119

"And you me, fool that I am. But have seen what evil magic did to you and will always do until you know the stronger magic of Jesu Christ."

"Why did nae show't before among Taixali? Why did thee let *this* happen"—she held up her marked arm—"when could fend it off?"

"There were many things I did not know, Dorelei. I thought of my needs, not yours."

"Speak of it."

"It will take courage, Dorelei."

She turned her arm toward him with the obscene mark like a gob of filth. "Dost think would suffer this again?" Not the sick fear that coursed through her when the curse touched her skin, not the nauseous feeling when the mark of it began to swell on her flesh, but the rest of it: her lessening in the eyes of fhain. She was their center, like a queen bee in a hive. She had to dare. "Will see this Jesu magic."

"Then look at Blackbar."

"Nae . . ."

"Look, Dorelei," Padrec coaxed. "Was any danger averted by refusing to see it? Look."

Dorelei did. Behind her, Neniane squeezed her cousin's hand and held on tight. Purposefully, Padrec held the arrowhead pointed away from her, his voice low and sure, and in it Dorelei heard what she'd always loved, the music, often blurred with anger or vehemence, but music when he allowed it.

"Water has always been stronger than Blackbar. See where just the night's dew has rusted it. Water tempers it when a's first taken from the fire for shaping. Water blessed with the magic of God will make it thy friend and servant. If you believe."

"Thee . . . troubles me."

"If you believe. Gern-y-fhain knows the part of belief in weaving magic."

Send him away. Let Cru kill him. Mother and Lugh, what does he drive me to, what does he ask? Am I Mabh that I can cut past from present? Blackbar will kill me. Can I not feel it alive there in his hand, waiting to poison me with a touch?

Dorelei felt the hollowness in her stomach again, but she dare not show the merest sign of it now. She flinched in the village for all to see, that was damage enough. She was grateful there was enough will in her to ward off the piddling boy with his painted arrow. She glanced back to reassure her folk with a smile more forced than felt.

"Did once think to make thee second husband, Padrec. Be past. Now do wonder only if Cru should kill thee."

"That is why my heart was divided with you, Dorelei. I wanted very much to be your husband, and I cannot. As thee said, be past."

120

I knew it, felt it. I lied, Padrec, and thee as well. Nothing is past. I feel you now.

"Dorelei, God knows I'm the weakest, most stupid of His messengers. But let me give you this. One moment's courage or a lifetime of fear and running. When it is no longer an evil, can be a friend, Dorelei. Believe that Jesu can save thee. Call on Him as Mabh called on Mother. Trust me. Blackbar will be as much friend to fhain as I am."

Great shaggy lump with his soft-singing Briton-man's voice, cajoling her. She wouldn't tell him what the sound of it did to her. And yet—if she could master this magic for all of them. Almost too big, too impossible to think. But if she could, as Mabh parted land from sea, as Jesu . . .

"Did say that Jesu died for all men?"

"Aye."

"Saved them for all time?"

"If they believed."

"So Prydn?" She was bargaining like a gern now. "For all time free of Blackbar?"

"And masters of it. Even Mabh was not so."

But I could die as Jesu did.

"For all time, Dorelei. And tallfolk will deal with thee as queen, as gern, eye to eye."

Mother, I am afraid. None has ever dared so. Can he see my fear? He sees so much.

"If thee has Mabh's courage for one moment."

"Padrec . . . do not." A feeble shaking of her head. She wanted to retreat. "Do not."

"Dorelei, you taught me so much. I don't know if I love you more as God's joke of a priest or just a man, but the love is there. I will stop being a child afraid to name it even as you must call this Blackbar by its true name."

Dorelei searched his eyes for truth, found it there. "Could be my life, Padrec."

"Trust me."

Dorelei held up her marked arm. "Thee doubts a could kill?"

"Thee doubts my magic be as strong? Then my life with yours, Gern-y-fhain."

That much was foregone, whether he knew it or not. "Have said. Guenloie! Call thy husbands, tell them to drive the flocks home to byre. Cruaddan, bring Artcois and Bredei from the hunt. Gern-y-fhain will make magic."

The sky was even darker. Dorelei glanced up at the clouds. Lugh sent his own angry warning for trying to change his way of things.

121

But his clouds shadowed Taixali as well. So be it. *Darken, then. Did not Mabh dare thee? So must I. Cursed or killed, I will be gern. I will not be shamed again.*

They gathered by the brook that edged the foot of their hill, wrapped in their warmest against the rising wind. Cru's great cloak was shared between Guenloie and Neniane, trailing behind them on the ground. They stood in little clumps, Neniane's husbands to one side, Guenloie's to the other, Cru alone as if on guard over Padrec waiting at the water's edge. All waited for Dorelei to descend from the ring of stones where she prayed before the awesome thing she would do.

Rof loped nervously back and forth along the stream, sniffing the change in the air.

"Will be snow," Artcois guessed.

His brother sniffed like Rof at the charged air. "Nae, rain."

"One or other. Could nae guess," Malgon confessed. "Strange sky."

Very strange. They didn't want to think on it too much, frightened at what Dorelei would do. Not the strongest gerns, not Bruidda, not even Mabh ever prevailed against Blackbar. In their young lives, they'd seen the marks it left by its mere touch, and a wound from its edge, like Drust's, took twice as long to heal. Blackbar would not break like bronze and stayed sharper through the spell Lugh wove in its creation. An alien thing with so much power must not be mentioned or viewed directly, never brought into fhain. No one ever did until now. The mark on Dorelei's arm was a defeat any gern would answer, but there were limits to what she might dare. Dorelei went beyond courage to recklessness.

Cru's eyes bored into Padrec. Dorelei's husband alone knew recklessness was no part of her decision. Whatever magic the priest might call up, his wife's desperation needed no name. They were both much older for this hard year. He'd seen the girl-fun dim in Dorelei, flashing only now and then under the cloak of her responsibility. She would not make a foolhardy show of power or risk their well-being. She was terrified when she went to prepare and pray to Mother, trying to hide it even from him.

As the rain began, thin and sleety, Cru saw Dorelei walking her pony down the slope. She paced it slowly over the heath and halted a little way from fhain.

"Padrec! Tell thy god that Gern-y-fhain comes!"

Dorelei dismounted and let the pony's reins dangle, her shoulders straight as she moved to Cru. She spoke in a low murmur. "If this magic turns on me, thee was the finest man a woman could find."

"Nae, stay." Cru caught her in urgent arms, feeling her determination in the resistance. She would not be stayed. "Must do this?"

"To be free of Blackbar. Be worth the hazard." Her expression altered subtly. "In this magic, Padrec puts a's life beside mine." Her glance slid to the priest. "See a keeps that promise."

"If thee dies, think a will live? A will be barrowed at thy feet. Thee was mine when did first follow Gawse's ponies. Dorelei, will thee for *once* bow to husband? Be time to stop this."

"Time to do't."

"Be mad, wife. Cannae fight Blackbar."

"Cru . . . stop. Oh, why not Neniane born first? Fhain thinks me to have all answers when would give anything just to bear wealth with thee." Dorelei stroked the loved plane of his cheek. "Did run all our lives from this, Cru. Be time to stop. If Mother takes me, Neniane will be gern with thy wisdom to help." Dorelei drew his mouth to hers in a lingering kiss. "Padrec waits. And dost rain on us."

Still Cru held her. "Do trust Padrec that much?"

"Nae so much as do trust Cru to do my bidding. Let me go, husband."

Reluctantly Cru freed Dorelei to do what she must. She walked away to face her people, standing between them and Padrec. Deliberately she removed the torc, undid her cloak, and laid them on the ground. She held out her bare arm. "Salmon fhain, Blackbar marked your gern. Now see how thy gern answers it. Nae wasting spell upon Naiton, nae *gort a bhaile* to a's fields or flocks, but battle with Blackbar itself." Dorelei whipped her bronze knife from its sheath and held it out to Lugh Sun hidden behind clouds and pelting her with needles of freezing rain out of spite.

"Do draw this knife in battle as Mabh did. Padrec, tell Blackbar that Gern-y-fhain comes against him."

To her confusion, Padrec only shook his head, coming to her with the iron arrow on its broken shaft. When he was at her side he hurled it to the ground.

"*In nomine Patri et Fili et Spiritus Sanctus.* I bless this water and this holy circle." Padrec swept his arm in a wide loop over the arrowhead. "I abjure and cast out any spirit sent by Taixali or by Satan in aid. Be gone. Come, let fhain aid in this. Do not fear, this ground is blessed. Cru, Drust, all of you. Make a circle, help thy gern."

With rising fear, they did as Padrec bade them. The freezing rain pelted them harder now, driven by a wind sprung up from nowhere.

"Look," Guenloie shivered as she and Neniane emerged from the folds of the cloak. "Mark how trees do bend to it."

"The circle is blessed, Guenloie," Padrec said again. "Wherever we gather in Jesu's name, there He is also. We begin the magic by giving the evil its rightful name. Call it up, Salmon fhain! Let it hide no more in the shadows of your own fear. In Jesu's name. Iron! Let Gern-y-fhain say it."

Dorelei swallowed hard and framed her lips to the fearful sound. "Ir-on."

"Let all have the courage of thy gern. Call the iron!"

"Ir-on . . . iron! IRON!"

About to speak again, Padrec saw the wide-eyed horror in Neniane, head turned to her sister and transfixed. Dorelei was rigid, staring into the distance, the wind whipping her hair in wet, black ropes from her shoulders.

"Dorelei?"

No, Padrec does not hear them, he can never hear them. They come. I feel their footsteps falling like those of giants over the heath. The rain all but shows them to me, rolling from their crooked backs. Iron spirit, Taixali evil, all together. I have woken them like hornets to sting me. Ia! Mother! Help me. . . .

The heavy footsteps thudded closer, their vibration shaking Dorelei to her soul. The very trees bent and brushed aside under the fury of their approach. Her fhain shifted nervously. Guenloie trembled. In a moment one, then another would run away. She must hold them.

"Be not afraid, my people," she said, wanting to run herself. "Padrec's magic enfolds us."

"None can prevail against that which Jesu has blessed," Padrec said. "Come, Dorelei. Let the rest of fhain remain safe in the circle."

Padrec led her to the water and stepped into it. The brook bottom slanted deeply from the bank, immersing him to the waist in four strides. "Come."

Shuddering as much from cold as fear, Dorelei waded into the water to reach his outstretched hand.

"Thee's the bravest woman I've ever seen. Any man would love thee."

"D-do nae hear them c-coming as I do?" She quavered through chattering teeth. "Do nae feel them about us, the ones without names?"

"Nae, they cannot harm you. Dorelei, daughter of Gawse, of the people of Mabh, do you accept Christ as your savior? Do you trust His magic to vanquish the iron?"

She tried to keep from shivering uncontrollably in the freezing water. "A-aye, Padrec."

"Christ said thee shall be reborn in Him. Newborn, will need a new name."

Dorelei's eyes were glazed with cold and fear; she felt the spirits pressing against the wall of magic, leaning over it, looking for one small weak point to batter through. "Quickly, Padrec. What name?"

His red hair and beard were wet-plastered against his head, but Padrec's eyes were kind and sure. "Be only one to fit thy courage, Dorelei. Come."

One arm about her waist, Padrec raised his voice to the people on the bank. "Salmon fhain, thee has a gern to sing of. The magic of Christ is only strength added to her own. Let all see."

Holding her small shoulders supported by his hand, Padrec bent Dorelei under the water, immersing her for an instant, then lifted her gasping from the waves. "In the name of God and His only begotten Son, I christen thee Dorelei Mabh. Amen."

He gave Dorelei no time to think about it but led her out of the water to her waiting people, catching up the discarded cloak and wrapping her in it. "Now let Gern-y-fhain take up the iron."

Shivering, miserable, she thought: I *believe in him. Let iron do what it will. Cannot turn back now.*

Dorelei bent to the iron and lifted it.

Nothing—no pain, no magic coursing its evil into her flesh as when Naiton laid it on her. She opened her hand. Only cold metal smeared with wet rust.

"See . . . see," she said giddily, thrusting it out to her folk. "Nae, see! Be dead!"

"Iron is beaten," Padrec said in a low, strong voice. "Iron can only be the servant of fhain now. Thy gern has accepted Christ, and her fhain is in His hand. Yah! Dorelei Mabh!"

"Yah!"

"Padrec, take me to the water," Drust beseeched. "Let me accept Christ as well."

"That can come later, my David." Padrec gripped his shoulder. "As Jesu crossed into death and returned from it for all men who believe, so Dorelei Mabh gives this gift to fhain. Pass the iron among you. Feel the truth of it."

Dorelei held the iron out to Cru, knowing what he fought and conquered in taking it.

"See! Feel!" Padrec shouted against the wind. "Has not fhain beaten it?"

The iron passed more quickly to Neniane, who peered at it in her unmarked hand. "Be just . . . cold. Here, Artcois, feel."

From Artcois to Bredei and through the ranks of fhain. Guenloie spat on it before passing it to Malgon. His artist's curiosity turned it this way and that to see how it was made before passing it to Drust, who held it high overhead, exultant.

125

"Yah! Lugh Sun! See! Do love thee but will nae be ruled."

"Nae more!"

"Iron!" Drust sang out. "Iron!"

"Iron be servant now."

Padrec stood aside as they began to circle the iron where Drust hurled it into the mud. Iron ... iron ... the defiant chant grew in power against the rain lashing about them harmlessly now, turning to snow even as they whirled and leaped in the jubilant dance of their victory.

The dark came early this time of year; the blanketing whiteness of the fresh snow gave an eerie quality to dusk. The world lost its eye for color. There was nothing but white and black and shades between. The stockade gates had been barred this hour as the houses within. The Taixali village was so silent that Leogh, the blacksmith to Naiton, standing on the parapet, was glad to see smoke rising from roofholes as a sign of life.

Rain changed to snow some hours before, and then the wind suddenly dropped to nothing. The falling snow only floated down from a leaden sky as if Lugh had opened all the feather pillows that ever were and wafted the innards to earth. Leaning over the palings, Leogh couldn't see a bowshot beyond them. Gray-white heath blurred into dark sky in profound silence.

Nothing moved on the heath. Nothing. He was sure of that. He tried to remember that later.

Leogh stamped his feet, blinking a snowflake from the corner of one eye. When he looked to the east again, the gasp of surprise exploded from his throat.

The riders were there, an unmoving line of them. One, two, three, four—eight of them behind a ninth, sitting their shaggy ponies in absolute stillness. Leogh fingered the bone charm at his throat and thanked his gods the gate was barred. The figure in front of the line snaked a bare arm from beneath the muffling cloak and pointed at *him*. The motion of that arm was like a missile hurled, like Fate itself choosing out Leogh for death. He felt it as if the arm had struck him.

"NAITON!"

Leogh had good hunter's eyes; he would have seen something of their coming, some movement before they halted, but they were just *there* where nothing was but white a moment before.

Again the woman called. "NAITON!"

For all his summoned courage, Leogh began to shake. The elder should never have insulted the Faerie queen with the iron; Leogh said as much that night at the fire. You don't trust Faerie; you don't

126

back down from them, but you don't bait them, either. Iron-magic was strong, but if their next crops were blighted or newborn bairn deformed, one needn't look far for the cause. The Faerie girl had the unsettling look of a *weird* about her. Did she not stop that fool boy in his tracks when he tried to badger her with his arrow? With a mere look, like an invisible arm holding him back. Leogh remembered that as she pointed at him again. He narrowed his eyes; there was something in her hand.

"NAITON!"

Somewhere in the village, a door opened and then another. Leogh gripped his charm so hard he felt it cutting into his fingers. Three times the Faerie woman called; three times could be the beginning of magic. Nine could be fatal, if so she meant. Leogh hurried down the log steps, pounding across the enclosure toward the longhouse. She called for Naiton, not himself, and Leogh was very glad of that.

Sitting her pony in the white dusk, Dorelei felt her own power sheathed in the magic of the Jesu-water. Its icy memory yet tingled over her skin beneath her clothes. For a moment at the brook she'd quailed at touching the iron; then her courage took hold and she grasped it, broke its power for all time. Changed now, changed forever, reborn, renamed, for doing that which the first Mabh never dreamed. From her own courage was seeded the courage and hope of Salmon fhain. Each of them challenged the iron and proved stronger. Let Wolf warn of the end; where was there fhain like hers, even Gawse's? Nae, they were a wolf pack now. Let tallfolk step aside when they grazed in good lowland pasture. There would be increase and child-wealth, the tightness would go from Cru's infrequent smile, and Padrec, whose magic did it all—who would think it?—would wear the marks of fhain and a Prydn name beside his own. As he renamed her, so she would return it. Padrec Raven, for truly only a gift from the gods could so defy them.

Her sharp eyes picked out the male bulk lumbering to the palings and looming out over them.

"Naiton?"

"I am Naiton," he roared back. "Who calls me? Is it the little bitch dog I marked with iron but a day gone?"

"Be Dorelei Mabh, Naiton. Let thee remember my name. The mark of thy weak magic fades on me even as thy power in the land. See what I hold in my hand."

At Dorelei's sign, Cru and Padrec moved their mounts forward to flank her on either side; then the three of them drew nearer to the stockade. Dorelei held up the iron arrowhead.

"See, Naiton tallfolk?" she challenged. "Iron be tamed. From this time will be fhain's as well."

127

"That is a trick that it is. Not iron at all but a stone."

Naiton was bluffing. Dorelei heard the hesitation in his deep voice. "Come down and see. Here." She tossed the broken arrow to the ground. "Will leave't for thee when Taixali find the courage to come out."

"It is no trick, Naiton," Padrec called. "The magic of Jesu, the Son of God, houses these people like a fortress. Iron has long since bowed to Christ and bent in the shape of His holy sign. Now it is friend to Prydn, no longer yours alone. Let that teach you caution if not kindness, Naiton."

Dorelei barely turned her head. "Cru."

Cru's bow came up. Naiton had no time to duck, but the shaft was not aimed to kill; it merely drove into the palings within his reach.

"Gern-y-fhain has said." Padrec's voice rang like a clear doom in the winter stillness. "And as sign she sends the last bronze arrow you will ever see from her. If you trouble her further, the next will be of iron. And closer."

Dorelei laughed easily. "Will go now, Naiton. And send thee no harm, as thee will not to us. But this magic will go out to enfold all Prydn. Think no more to put iron as a bar in my path. Or if thee must, put a price on the iron, for fhain will buy it."

Dorelei turned her pony and moved away across the snow through the line of her people. Her heart sang with the victory. Other fhains would hear of this. The magic would go forth to all of them. Behind her she heard Naiton say something, then the music of Padrec's strong voice: "Oh, Naiton, Naiton—why be enemy where you can be friend? Don't you know a queen when you see one?"

Dorelei rode on. If a queen, he made her one. Mother and Lugh, but she loved the man. She *would* love him.

IV
Rod into Snake

In the forum of Prince Marchudd's palace, Meganius mused back and forth beneath the raised statue of Mercury to one side of the dais. The forum was empty save for himself, leaving his whole attention to the grubby scrap of vellum covered with minute Latin. He'd read it several times, but Father Patricius' references were as unfamiliar as his extremes were troubling. The letter must remain confidential.

He was searching a shelf for a map when Prince Marchudd exploded into the chamber, rushed as always, hurrying to him.

"I thank the courtesy that makes your grace ever punctual. The rest of my council will be tardy as usual, and I need your excellent common sense."

Meganius went on rummaging through the rolls on the shelf. "Ever at my lord's service. Is it the new Coritani raids?"

"Yes, yes. The war will come. It is coming."

"You will march against them?"

"Wouldn't I love to," Marchudd ground between his teeth, "and won't I just, when I've got something like a legion. For now I can only demand repayment of the cattle. What are you looking for?"

"A map of the north, if there is one."

"Not much there, but—yes." Marchudd drew a roll from a neat stack. "The problem is preparedness. We haven't had anything like a real legion for twenty years, since Constantine took the lot to Gaul and promptly lost most of them."

In British tunic, freed of Roman dress, Marchudd didn't fidget as much but still moved restlessly about the chamber, half his mind on the problems of the next hour, the next day. "The so-called Sixth Legion is a feeble joke now. I've got to rebuild it."

Meganius knew the Coritani as well as Marchudd. "And I doubt the heathen will come to terms."

"I know they won't," Marchudd snapped. "We'll play the old game, and I'm very good at it. They'll delay, I'll insist. They'll haggle, and I'll prepare. And no two of my council have the same idea how to proceed. You know young Ambrosius?"

"The tribune, Aurelianus? I know his family."

"I daresay. Well-connected whelp. Kinsman to the Dobunni prince. My legate pro tem, the only reasonable excuse for a commander I've got." Marchudd bounded up onto the dais and dropped into one of the two chairs, one booted foot crossed over the other knee and jiggling furiously. "A boy! Barely into his gown of manhood, barely twenty. Competent enough, but he's telling *me* how to reorganize the legion. In faith, I could form a cohort from military messiahs alone. They come along every day. A*lae*, no less."

"My lord?"

"Cavalry: that's the sweat from Ambrosius' perfervid genius." Marchudd vented a bark of derisive laughter. "Have you ever seen that dismal lot of errand runners and donkey drivers? The tribune will be in council today, and I tell you under the rose, don't listen to his cant, Meganius. I put my faith in the foot legion."

"Yes, quite." Meganius sat on the edge of the dais, spreading the map before him. "Though I don't imagine the Coritani will fight in neat formations."

"The foot legion can take and hold high ground," Marchudd recited as to a student. "Once taken, they can fortify it in a few hours."

"Once taken."

"And defended while they build, that's the crux. Archers."

The bishop was not a military thinker, but it seemed reasonable. "Ah, yes?"

The prince sounded rather messianic himself. "Massed archers. Dozens, hundreds of them."

"Which my lord has?"

"Wishes he had. That's *my* idea. The damned Coritani aren't going to wait while we haul catapults and onagers into place against them. Archers." Marchudd hunched forward morosely. "The problem is time. Any man can throw a pilum well in a month of practice and be proficient with a shortsword in three. In six you can take a lout who can't keep his seat in a latrine and make a fair horseman out of him. But do you know how long, Meganius, how *long* it takes to train a good archer, the sort to match those tribesmen? Two years, Meganius. Well."

The prince of the Parisii and Brigantes hurled himself against the chair back so hard it creaked in protest. Like all energetic men, he even relaxed at full charge. "Just wait. They laugh at me, call me coward until I'm ready, and then . . ." In Marchudd's parody of relaxation, suddenly there was genuine stillness. His mouth curled in a cold smile. "And then, when they've awakened from the royal drubbing I've given them, those heathen bastards will find they've lost a holy war and been converted."

Meganius looked up with the feeling he'd missed something. "Holy?"

"Oh, yes. You will bless my banners, which will then go forward in Christ's name. I'll annex as much of their northern lands as my soldiers can hold, and your grace will have a larger diocese. Should I expend so much for an odd lot of cattle? Certainly Rome will call it fair trade, they always do. What *are* you looking for on that map?"

"Succatus Patricius."

"Who?"

"You met him in my garden last summer."

"That stuffy little priest? What of him?"

"I've received another letter. He can't write very often, but he's made converts among the—uh, Prydn."

"Never heard of Picts by that name."

"Faerie, Highness."

"Oh, God!" Marchudd hooted. "Not Faerie! Those lice aren't even human. Do they count as converts?"

Meganius mused over the map. "An interesting question. And Father Patricius is a far more interesting man than one would think."

"And how long will they stay converted?"

"He's taught them the use of iron."

"Oh, come." Marchudd waved it away. "They run from iron, always have. All my peasants carry a bit of it for protection, like stinking herbs in a plague year."

"Nevertheless, they're using it. Marvelous craftsmen, he writes."

Marchudd yawned, tired of the subject. "Extraordinary."

"Perhaps my lord will illuminate this map for me. Here are the Venicones and here the Votadini. What lies north of them?"

Marchudd scanned the sparsely featured map. "Taixali, Damnonii. Somewhere . . . here."

The bishop's finger moved up the map. "And this line?"

"The old Wall of Antoninus. Bank and ditch, a few forts. Abandoned in Antoninus' own time. Nothing there now."

"And north of that?"

The prince shrugged. "Moss, rocks, and reindeer. Why?"

The blank space north of the faded line was colored in pale blue. To Meganius it seemed inadequate for what it contained, a man doing miracles and teetering on the edge of heresy. "Well, that is where he's gone."

"Indeed." Clearly uninterested, Marchudd drummed his fingers on the chair arm. Suddenly he launched out of it, off the dais, charging toward the chamber entrance to bark at the guards in the hall.

"Where are those tardy people who call themselves a council? It's late. It's getting late." Marchudd vanished down the hall, trailing concern and invective.

Meganius rolled the map and returned it to the case. *Moss, rocks, and reindeer, that's where he's gone.* Farther than that, much farther.

Is it apostasy or simple truth to say that earth is mother and sky father—nature itself a religion to these folk? They have, after a fashion, an Exodus old as our own. Not that they cannot but will not enter a state of Grace with so much of their belief forced to remain outside, abandoned. While Rome wrangles with Alexandria, and Antioch wars with Athens over definitions of God and Grace, this is a fact that our Holy Mother Church will stumble over again and again, the Council of Nicea notwithstanding, until we see our position anent those we hope to bring to Christ.

It is the doctrine of the Fathers of our Church that these elder and false gods were given to mankind to raise him step by step toward that faith and redemption proved on Golgotha. All true, and yet to fulminate among the idolaters—as you know certain of our brethren can certainly fulminate—to say: Now that you know the correct way, cease the error and practice the truth, is in logic to set a student to the harp for years and then to send him to his first performance with a horn.

Your grace, I do not presume to refute revealed truth but only question methods and strictures laid down by the holy who have never been anywhere but among the converted. These Prydn have no sense of time, of months and years as we have, but have moved with the sun and seasons, breathing in tune with the very humors of the earth they call their mother.

Therein is the problem. He who was promised has come, and the earthly lease of man is circumscribed. By raising man's soul from the dust, we must inevitably part him from the dust, part him from the nature he has known. Illusion or error, this nature, this earth and sky have always been the center of his belief. I could not impart the first word of faith to them until I accepted and proceeded from this fact. . . .

This from a young man who, only a year before, would have yelped "heresy!" at the mere hint of such thoughts. No, Meganius would not discuss the letter with anyone, lay or clerical. He hadn't expected the northern tribes to accept faith in panting multitudes, but the boy had gone far beyond that.

Preserve me, he married her. A *creature of debatable humanity, one half-naked husband already, and he married her.*

God would not lose Patricius, but the Church might.

Only Cru. It hurt her.

All fhain rejoiced in her marriage but him. It wasn't like Cru. Although it was foregone since the time of the Jesu-magic that she would marry Padrec, Dorelei waited until they'd moved the herds north to fresh pasture. Like wealth spilled over from a laden chest, the magic brought other fortune. This year the grass was good everywhere, and the news of Dorelei's new power preceded them as she moved boldly through the lowland pastures. When tallfolk relied on iron to turn them away, Salmon offered to buy it and made impulsive gifts to their astonished but grateful children.

They passed through the bewildered Damnonii without incident, but leaving their fame behind, not so much for Dorelei or Padrec but her sister's love of children. Neniane drew a broken and infected milk tooth from a toddler and cleaned the gum, stilling the pain with willowbark. Not without some coaxing, of course. Children know what's going to hurt. Neniane spoke to her like a merchant about to dicker.

"Do know thee hard bargainer. Let me draw thy tooth, useless as't is, and this night thy head will dream bright on the pillow. When Lugh rises, will be gift under it."

Like her mother, the child had a true Pictish love of bargains. The tooth was swiftly and almost painlessly drawn.

"Now, run and play. Will not forget the magic."

"What is the gift that you will give her?" the mother plied.

"In thy pocket," Neniane said, patting it. When the woman reached to see, there was a bright-burnished little bead of gold. Neniane knew its worth. The woman did, too, from the quick light in her eye.

"Be a blessing from Jesu, but a has moods," Neniane cautioned. "Unless thee places it beneath bairn's pillow, will bring nae good to anyone. And teeth will be harder to draw."

The Damnoni woman took the hint and bestowed the gold where promised. The story passed among her neighbors, canny mothers themselves, and ever after their children shed milk teeth faster and more profitably than others.

Trees were fewer and stunted this far north. On Midsummer Eve, when fhain kept vigil all night in the ring of stones, Mother's mooneye turned the bare, rounded hills and moor to silver. Standing in the axis of the east and west stones at dawn, Padrec said the Jesu prayers, Dorelei scattered the white stones and invoked their Parents. Lugh Sun rose when and where he should, his first ray streaming over the center of the eastern stone.

Dorelei married Padrec on the next night, since there would be no more blessed time until Lughnassadh. A flawed happiness because of Cru, but Dorelei was learning that Gawse hadn't taught her everything, nor were her own instincts infailible in the matter of men. Oh, but the marriage gown, the new linen kirtle! *That* was a triumph. Neniane cut the cloth with her new iron scissors, and her hands were inspired. She fretted and frowned and patted, took a tuck, put in a pin, and thoroughly enjoyed herself, even patient with Guenloie, whose needlework was more enthusiastic than skillful. There were the usual jokes as they fluttered about Dorelei like birds at nesting. No matter how well a fit, was wonder tallfolk women could move at all, so bound up.

Dorelei endured their chatter, satisfied. They were happier, better fed, free of want and fear for once. For the first time they could all see a future better than the past. They played and sang and relaxed. They both carried child-wealth. A gift from Father-God, Padrec said, and who would bother to question happiness? For Neniane pregnancy was a remembered joy, but Guenloie blossomed as a novelty, more beautiful than ever, even a shade plump until the autumn rade.

The marriage garment was a cross between British kirtle and Roman tunica, as Neniane conceived it from Padrec's vague description. Women's garments had never concerned him much.

"Well, they more or less go in at the waist like this, and tie at the shoulder like this, then drape. Fall, you know."

"Fall where?" Neniane asked.

"To the foot."

The result was too tight in some places and too loose in others. Tallfolk women hid more of their bodies, especially the breasts, which seemed pointless in the matter of feeding newborn, and they certainly didn't move as much as fhain women. In such garments, who could? Dorelei wondered when she wriggled and writhed into it. But never had there been a garment so ravishing, and no gern ever had fhain sisters so dear or attentive. They helped her bathe with much fuss, and when Dorelei was tugged and tied into the marriage garment, Guenloie brought the bridal coronet. If they were blessed in new magic, they carefully included the old. Among the summer flowers woven together were bunches of vervain and mistletoe, that Dorelei would be mother to many children.

All the men were out of the rath. This night was as significant for Padrec as for Dorelei, and he himself blessed the knife Malgon would use. Alone with Neniane and Guenloie, Dorelei bade them fetch and place about her throat the necklace of blue stones. Caught in the depths of the stones, sunlight looked young and small, a little light trying to grow. Moonlight turned cold and deep, full-grown, turning old, so that the stones had changing moods like Mother.

This night her sister and cousin would scatter the moonstones in the circle. Her own flower-decked pony was ready. She would ride to her wedding, where Padrec waited alone, where Cru once waited ... no, she couldn't think of Cru this one night.

"Be fair?" she worried as Neniane worried at the hem. "Dost fall like Roman clothes?"

"Will have't on so long to matter?" Guenloie giggled. "Be fair."

"Be that and more," Neniane asserted.

"Most fair," said the flat male voice behind them.

They were surprised to see Cru rising out of the crannog below the rath. He should have been with the men preparing Padrec, but he came to Dorelei with an object wrapped in a length of the new linen.

"Gift for Gern-y-fhain. Would be alone."

He seemed to speak from a great distance; Dorelei could not read him just then, but a first husband had some privileges. "Sister, cousin, go offer the moonstones to Mother. Tell her I come."

For a passing moment, she thought Cru might be drunk on barley beer. She didn't smell it on him. When they were alone, Cru unwrapped his gift.

"Will show Dorelei a be truly most fair. See."

137

She gasped in surprise: a bronze hand mirror with fine loops and curls etched into the back like a flower gone daft with the idea of itself. Briton-men made such mirrors in their fancy, the face burnished bright enough to see her own unblurred face—hair combed into a black river over her shoulders and breasts, the white linen and cool blue of the necklace turning her brown skin into new bronze. All this she saw in the mirror-gift as Cru held it for her. But she couldn't read the thing in his eyes, and that troubled her.

"Sister and cousin be girls. Dorelei be woman."

He'd never said such a thing before, never needed to. She wanted to kiss him, but he turned to evade her. So serious and sad. Dorelei tried to lighten his mood. "Did borrow?"

"Nae, did not!" Cru hurled it at her with such pent fury that Dorelei could only stare at him. "Great Padrec's Father-God forbids borrowing. Did work for't. Shod horse for Damnoni. Leave be." Cru hunched forlornly on his stone seat by the fire.

"Husband?"

"Nae, what husband, what wife? Look in thy mirror-gift. Dost see Cru's wife or tallfolk woman?" He turned mean with the thing that ate at him. "Nae, cannot even walk in thy silly wrapping. Would . . . would have killed Padrec if a's magic harmed thee. Would kill a now—"

"Cru!"

"—if thee said, if thee turned from this." Cru hid his face in his hands. Dorelei heard the ugly, unfamiliar sound of her husband's weeping. In her woman's way, she loved him the more for it. Even wise Cru had this much child to endear him. Gently, Dorelei opened his fingers and kissed them. "Cru, I must do this. Padrec saved fhain; would be nothing without him."

"And first husband so little?"

"Thee asks that, who will always have first place at my fire?"

"But only one place in thy bed." He twisted away from her. "Nae, thee turns from me to him. Do love him."

"Like thee."

"More than me."

"As much, Cru. As I love thee."

"As thee loves me." Cru winced as if she'd struck him. "Do lose my wife."

"Never."

"Leave be, woman. Go, then."

"Husband—"

"Go."

For all she loved Cru, Dorelei felt a twinge of resentment. He clouded over her happiness. If a dear child, there was also a child's cruelty. She would not have charged him with it. "Learn from thy fhain brothers. Who so close to Bredei as Artcois? As Malgon to Drust? And what gern with one husband alone?"

"Mine."

And that only because we were young and new and starting a fhain. I've spoiled him as Guenloie's mother spoiled her.

But for that, the hard year, hard work and dangers, the worry and lack of Prydn men, there would have been another husband. Lugh sent his Raven. It was meant to be. "Give me blessing, Cru?"

Cru managed that much, although he couldn't look at her. "Mother bring Gern-y-fhain wealth."

She bent to kiss him, then moved to the rath opening. "Mirror-gift has great beauty, Cru."

"When thee fills it."

If it is a world of magic, it is also one of pain one cannot go round. Pain when I changed from girl to woman, pain in Cru's bones when he went from boy to man, and our first loving was not without it. The magic brought my blood and stretched his bones, changed us and left its mark like char on wood. Nothing stays, then, nothing goes back. Why should that be a sadness? Yet it is. With all Mother's world to ride, Padrec's Adam and Eve cried for their Garden—but moved on as they cried, and was the old worth more than the new? Moving on is the way of things. Twice each year since I could run behind Gawse's pony, I have left one pasture for another. Fair remembered or fair to come, life went on. They were children in the Garden, Cru. We were children; now we're grown. You and Padrec can both be stubborn children when a woman least expects or needs it. Neither of you knows all my songs, but I need both of you to sing. There is more to being a queen than I knew. Except that nothing stays.

The fresh wounds on his cheeks were agony. The pain made him grit his teeth to concentrate on prayer.

"I have no confessor, no man to turn to, so I pray aloud even where she has shown me how to feel without words. My God, if you will charge me for flesh alone, then I am guilty, but my heart is no heretic."

Around Padrec the ringed stones waited for his words like a council of clerics. Far away across the moor, no part of spiritual drama, Wolf and Tod-Lowery padded on the hunt.

"But they have seen, Lord, and they believe like children who reach for a parent's hand without question; whose faith is like their thumbs in their mouths asleep, a need. For eight brave ones like these and so many more to come, will you lament one vow from one frail man who's no longer sure he was born to be a priest?"

His face hurt too much; he had to pause. Malgon was deft but couldn't spare him this. In turn he tried to be stoic under the blade. If they could conquer a lifelong fear, he could endure a moment of it to bind himself closer to them. He was one of them now, a fhain brother.

"However the world shapes me, I will always be Your priest. Only that the world is so much more than I thought. I've brought them by their own path out of a fear older than Abraham to trust in You. There are new children coming. I've told them it's Your reward for their faith, and so it is. If I have anything to confess now, it is happiness."

He heard the pony snuffle beyond the stones and turned to see the white-gowned figure slip down from the saddle and move toward him through the moonlight. The light was magic itself, shimmering in the stones about her throat, turning her flower wreath to a crown.

"Do come for thee, husband."

He wet his lips and found himself shaking, not in fear but awakening. "I was praying."

"And I." Dorelei reached up to touch his cheek. The woad-stained scars stood out black against his skin. Malgon had been careful, but a few drops of blood had dried in Padrec's beard. Her mark was on him now. "Be pain, Padrec?"

"It will pass."

As mine, and Cru weeping by the fire. Truly this was a night for discovering. She noticed the strip of hide looped in Padrec's hand. This went with the words they would say to Father-God. At a certain point he would bind their hands together.

"As God binds our flesh into one."

"Mother will make us so."

"Then will be the more married, Dorelei."

As always, she had to stretch to put her arms around his neck. "Thee's so far."

"Not so far." Padrec lifted Dorelei and held her close. "See?"

She loved to bury her face in the bristly forest of his beard. It smelled of him and crannog and the heather that sweetened the air of her life. "Untie me."

He murmured into her hair; they were both trembling now.

"Untie me, Padrec," she asked with an embarrassment that had nothing to do with him.

"Why, what's the matter?"

"Oh ... sister's hands be so wise at knots. Did make this kirtle and put me into it."

"Be the most beautiful gown in the world."

"Aye, but do nae know how to get out."

He would marry her by both ways, but hers first. Laughing, Padrec set her down and began to fumble at the shoulder knots, touched at the inconsistency of Dorelei in such a garment. He was used to her mostly bare. The fall and flimsy cloth of it didn't go with her, only showed how small and wild she was. His fingers hurried, impatient with the knots, but they came loose at last.

Lugh is stern but generous as well. If he gave iron to tallfolk, he sent Padrec Raven to me. Mother, see where the mark faded from my arm in but a day. I marry a king, and shall we not bear gerns and sons between us? Mother, thee should not fear nor Lugh thunder; it will be well with Jesu in my rath. Even Cru will see if you help him. Who would think men would have such trouble with love? Yet I am so happy. I am a feast laid for children, a new pasture; like Tir-Nan-Og and the children discovering me, my grass so high the foot falls whispering and world smells green, as Dronnarron, the Good Time That Was, and I wear Rainbow for a crown.

And I thought to confess this? Oh, sweet Lord, I would be liar, hypocrite, to put my face to a musty lattice and beg absolution for my sins. No. Bless me, Father, for I have sung, for I have seen, and no mystery of Yours that I do not see joined to another and revealed. What I struggled to understand with words, I know now without the need for them. Where my thoughts groped for You, my joy flies home sure as Cru's arrow, and just to wake and watch her sleeping by me, just to be alive and close to her is a prayer, and I am more Your priest than yesterday.

Generous themselves, they took naturally to the generosity inherent in Padrec's faith and brought to it an ebullient joy more often attested than felt by many professed Christians. They could forego borrowing, even call it stealing, if that was the word. They could give to tallfolk as extravagantly as to each other, if Padrec bade. The knotty problem was his alien concept of sin and confession. If it was a matter of telling him what they'd done, that was simple enough. They brought all their activities to Padrec, trusting him to separate kernel from chaff. The best he could do was give them the habit of it. The crux of the problem, their marriage customs, remained untouched. Since Padrec was now part of that problem, he could no more than satisfy his intellectual curiosity about it.

"Was from before the time of the ice," Dorelei said.

In this unimaginable antiquity, child-wealth just came as gifts from

Mother to her daughters. Men were not considered part of this woman-mystery. Blood relationship was therefore reckoned from the woman. In any case, women kept the rath and lived longer, while male hunters died every day. Surely, second husband saw the sense.

"But how when men knew children were theirs too?"

When the news broke, Mother and Lugh had long since set Prydn apart as chosen people so long as they followed the old way. What matter the father, since the wealth descended through its mother and belonged to her? Even Taixali and Venicone kept this custom in part. Hebrew-fhain descended through fathers, but then their Father-God had no wife to contend with as Lugh did, and Jesu never had children, which was unfortunate, but there it was.

Still, Dorelei reflected, if they were to heed Jesu and not seem ungrateful for His help, some allowance should be made for His puzzling insistence on one wife to one husband. There might be a way.

"Will confess one husband and be ab ... ab-what, Padrec?"

"Absolved, but—"

"Stay thee: next day will confess the other."

Of course, good manners and rank were involved. A second husband must be confessed first. Padrec would not mind being confessed before Cruaddan. It seemed reasonable.

Dorelei rolled over in the grass to glower down at Padrec when he laughed. "And what dost second husband find to smile at in a gern's wisdom?"

"Nothing ... nothing." Padrec punctuated the words with kisses to her nose and chin. "Will speak to Jesu in the circle."

Dorelei was seriously concerned and proud of her solution. "A be most strange in this. Will understand the right of it?"

"If do put it clear as thee speaks," Padrec temporized. *Well, at least it's a start.*

And Dorelei lay back pondering up at the slow-moving fleece clouds. *Where is Cru? We used to lie together like this in summer. Now he goes alone, speaks little, and that so carefully, I feel the hurt in him. One weeping was enough. He will not show it again.*

"Huff!" Bredei panted, mimicking the sound of the bellows he pumped. "Huff! Bring iron! Huff!"

"Faster, Bredei," Padrec called. "Must be hotter."

"Aye, *huff!* and huff-huff again. Artcois, come help. My arms drop off."

The bellows were only two large hide cups attached to handles that forced air through a long leather snout to heat the coal vitals of

142

the fire. With one brother on each handle, huffing away, Padrec watched the iron turn from red to white, then lifted the ingot and laid it on Malgon's new anvil. Malgon took the tongs and held the iron as Padrec showed him, hammer poised for magic.

"Jesu bless thy arm and hammer. Now strike, Mal! Knives for Prydn, tools for rath. Arrows for Lugh to ride. Strike!"

Hammer swung, iron clanged its song of obedience in a fountain of fire against the falling night, fire-song rising to the sky, falling to the tallfolk valleys, Jesu-song, sacred fire.

"Ai, hear!" Bredei exulted. "Tang! Tang!"

"Hear the music of a's fire," Artcois thrilled.

Tang! Tang! Tang!

The new fire rose from the ancient hill and spread farther than they knew, hilltop to village, to other fhains, one gern to another along the high ridges of the north. They pondered the thing about their rath fires: a gern who turns old ways upside down, who tames Blackbar into slave, the young one called Dorelei Mabh.

They were older and more cautious; not all the news of this young one pleased them. It seemed sacrilege to take such a sacred name. They would know her heart. They would see this magic. They followed Salmon pocked in stone along the ridges, looking for Mabh and the Raven.

They were all awed by this new iron-servant, but Malgon was fascinated as an artist finding a fresh color for his pallet. He could not sing his heart in words or song like Drust, but his passion spoke through his hands, heard the iron, and translated its message to shape. Fine straight blades for swords, keener knives to work with, lethal arrowheads, tiny blades to dice meat and clean fish, pots and pothooks to make their cooking better and easier, to build fire faster through iron's love of flint. Pictures in stone could be more sharply and subtly rendered with an iron awl, a clearer statement of Malgon's sense of order, action, and humor. He didn't laugh as much as the others, but he knew the spirit of laughter and froze it in stone, and so spoke to a much larger fhain than his own.

Malgon lacked the narrow fox-face of his kind. His head was rounder, features blunter than the other men, the difference between a tapered hand in repose and a working fist. Not handsome in Drust's way; even Guenloie said that. Malgon lived and thought and worked and loved with a controlled fire, heated by his own bellows. Neither joy nor sorrow tipped his scale too far. Malgon questioned where he could, accepted where he must, his inner reality always affirmed in stone or with a stroke in the earth itself. Like all artists, he knew the difference between loneliness and solitude. Musing over the new sword, the child of his own hands, he wished Cruaddan knew it.

All three of their women were pregnant at last. Did he bicker with Drust, or Artcois with Bredei over whose loving started it? Bairn would reach for one father as quickly as the other. Three children for one lost. Cru might well rejoice with the rest of them, but no. He rode and hunted alone, stayed away at night, and barely spoke around the fire, though all could see that Dorelei did not favor Padrec over him, only shared herself as she must. Padrec was all courtesy and consideration, never once trying to be first. Wise in all other things, Cru was blind in this, seething like a covered pot. Someone should loosen his lid a little.

Malgon gave one more wipe to the sword with his oiled fleece. It was to be a gift for Cru, the blade etched with Salmon and Stag, Malgon's best work so far, since each working put more of iron's secret in his hands. He could *feel* the balance, tossing it into the air to circle and settle to his hand like a trusting child. Fine. Apt to many more uses than bronze, the working of iron called for more complex skills. The sharpened skill asked keener questions of iron. *What more, what other shapes are hidden in you?*

Padrec emerged from the false hummock that marked their rath, bare to the waist, to stretch and greet the day. Malgon brandished the new blade. "See!" He tossed it high in two full circles that caught the morning sunlight. Padrec whooped and loped down from the rath toward the forge to thrust his head and hands in the tempering trough, spluttering as he wiped himself off.

"Yah! A looks a fine blade, Mal."

"Feel."

Padrec turned the blade in his grip, threw, and caught it. "Thee's prisoned iron-spirit in this."

Malgon watched in surprised appreciation as Padrec's arm flowed through a fluid series of moves with the weapon, rather expert for one sworn not to draw blood. "Was Roman-soldier, Padrec?"

"No, we all learned a bit of sword as boys. I was rather good."

The blade became a wheel of light as it spun, flew, and buried itself deep in Malgon's chopping block four strides away.

"That's how a legionary knows he got a good blade, Malgon Ironmaster."

Ironmaster. Who would have thought such a thing would be? The praise warmed Malgon like strong uisge, but Guenloie took the wind out of his bellows quickly enough. "What master? Cannae make, only shape. Malgon Ironborrower."

His wife meant it as a joke, but women did have a way of bringing a man down. Padrec consoled him: this was the artist's lot. For every caress, a curled lip. Like many other things in a flawed life, Malgon could live with it.

For Cru there might come a time when his level head would find its natural balance, but men need a space to realize new things. He was halfway to accepting Dorelei's right to another husband, but it was her new wealth so quickly come that knocked him flat again and made him blurt out what no Prydn man should ask.

"Child-wealth be mine?"

"Be mine, Cru."

He felt hollow in his stomach. For the first time ever, Dorelei placed herself beyond him. There should be a joy between them at this time; he'd imagined it, how they'd feel, and now . . . ashes in his mouth. His hands ached to touch her, and yet she never seemed so distant. Her moods changed like spring weather now, and everything Cru said came out wrong.

"Should be glad of wealth, Cru."

As if he'd not tried to be. "Yah, Gern-y-fhain."

"Such a 'yah.' Dost turn sour on thy lips."

"Did only say—"

"Oh, thee's stupid! Go hunt." Then, to his confusion, Dorelei turned her back and burst into tears. All the things he wanted to say or do seemed inadequate now. Was it possible she didn't know how much he needed her?

"Need nae hunt," he answered lamely.

"Then go walk, ride, go anywhere, but away."

Her back forbade him like a wall. He knew she felt sick with the wealth, he knew women could be unreasonable anytime. Usually it took only a gentle touching, a holding to let her know all was well. Cru knew this and wondered sometimes if Dorelei had a like knowledge of him. She needed to be held now but would not suffer it. He needed to reach for her and his pride was in the way, and the thought of Padrec. So he left her with the distance still between them and went for his pony to ride through most of the summer day, until he topped a high bare fell where the wind cried like wolf-song. There, between earth and sky, Cru squatted still as the rocks and brooded. Fhain called him wise. He didn't like what wisdom prompted him to now, but he couldn't stop it.

He delayed his return to rath until late afternoon, not liking the way he felt. In his acid view the very green of the hills turned to poison. When he led the tired pony up the path toward byre, he saw his whole fhain gathered on the ridge by Malgon's forge, the men with their new swords, and Padrec practicing with Artcois. Padrec kept the movement slow and precise to show the cuts and parries. What they lacked in size, fhain men made up in speed. More than once Padrec stopped short to laugh in surprise as Artcois dropped low on sinewy haunches and shot up far faster than larger men could hope to.

Cru hovered at the edge of the group, twisting the pony's reins in his fingers. Neniane was wearing Dorelei's blue stones for the whim of it, hands pressed to her swelling belly. Stupid Guenloie had begged Dorelei's bridal gown, her own wealth bulging against the tight waist. Cru wished he could share the happiness they felt; anything to relieve this weight that tightened his jaw until it hurt.

Drust spied him first and waved. "Cru! Come join. Dost make Roman-soldiers of fhain."

Aye, does he not. Cru dropped the reins and moved forward as Artcois lowered the sword to rest. Cru took it from him.

"Now Padrec will teach first husband."

"Right, then." Padrec mopped his forehead with a bare forearm. "Stand so, Cru. Feet so. Sword up in this manner."

Cru circled the larger man, trying several swings. Padrec blocked easily, circling to counter him.

"They'll mostly be bigger than you and go overhand for your head. Like so. And so. Block it square. Get under the blade like a shield. *Under* it, Cru. Good. Again."

Watching her husbands, not all of Dorelei's malaise was due to the child. She chilled with premonition, a wave of it. It could be the wealth that made her instincts unreliable—or sharpened them, she couldn't say—but the chill grew to fear. When Malgon brought her a drink of water and berry juice, Dorelei waved it away; the smell nauseated her now. She drew Malgon close.

"Mal, stop them."

"Do but play, Gern-y-fhain. Blades be not even edged yet."

"Nae, dost hear? Come between them. Padrec, husband—"

The thing happened even as she spoke. As the blades clanged together, Cru slid forward, left hand streaking out with the knife. Dorelei stopped breathing. She heard Padrec's grunt of surprise and pain. He faltered back a step, the thin red line broadening on the under part of his sword arm, then spattering on the grass.

"Cru—"

"Do think fhain scars make thee Prydn?" Cru said in a flat voice. "Then a's one more for thee."

They all hung frozen on the edge of the infamy as the color drained from Padrec's face. Then Drust shot forward, clawing for his own knife. "Judas!"

"Nae, stop!"

146

No need for Dorelei's command. Malgon neatly hooked Drust's arm, spun him around and away, confronting Cru with his own contempt.

"Did know thee angry but nae a fool."

The blood ran faster from Padrec's wound. Guenloie fluttered about him to stanch it. The thing done, it was to Cru as if his eyes had been opened suddenly after long blindness. He saw the mean folly of it and flinched away from their stunned accusation.

"Padrec . . . be sorry."

"Guenloie, tear the gown for linen. Sister, fetch thy scissors and hyssop." Dorelei pointed at Cru, speaking in the same tone she used on the Taixali boy. "Judas. Judas who was false among Jesu's own fhain. Go from me, Cruaddan."

He hung his head in naked misery. "Dorelei—"

"Go from me."

"Cannot."

"Then will speed thee."

Dorelei's own hand was a blur; for an instant in that vicious traverse, Padrec saw the beauty and grace of her go feral as Wolf. One stroke and the shallow red line across Cru's chest. He suffered it without flinching.

"Go from me, Judas."

His bare nod of acceptance was part of the shuddering that took them both. It was not that much; Padrec yearned to say something, to make peace. Cru already had repented of the moment. But Padrec knew enough not to intervene in such a matter. Only time would heal it now. For all his early maturity, Cru was still a boy, and even grown men could stumble on something they weren't ready for. More shocked than angry, his own anger flared and died in understanding. Then Neniane was back with the shears and poultice, cutting at the linen gown. They would rather use that than the almost sacred linen put aside for child-swaddling.

Cru brought from the rath a small bundle, bow, and quiver. He mounted and rode away without a glance at any of them. Dorelei glared after his retreating figure across the back of her own pony as Cru rode south through the last of the light. She felt empty and ill, barely noticing Neniane and Malgon as they slipped up beside her.

"Peace; a's but a man," Neniane soothed. "Will cool and come home the wiser."

"Judas. Will nae step aside for tallfolk, will nae suffer a traitor for husband."

"Be nae Judas but the best of men," said loyal Malgon. "Let a go apart just the while. A day and—"

147

"Oh, let be!" Dorelei hissed. "Go play with foolish iron thy gern did tame for thee. Go."

With a glance at Neniane, Malgon bade her away and went to help Padrec if he could, troubled in his own thoughts. *Aye, bids a go and yet looks after the gone before the stayed.* They were much changed by Padrec's magic. Jesu gave them new gifts, true enough, and new sorrows to wrap them. If he'd not been so fond of his new iron-toy, Malgon might have seen it coming.

Lugh Sun was gone, mooneye rising, but Dorelei raced the pony on, ignoring the labored shriek of its breath. She hated Cru; she would kill him and could not, but if the pony dropped under her, if its heart burst, then let it. Should run the heart out of it and herself. She pushed the spent animal up a brief slope and along a ridge as the sickness grew in her stomach.

Used to her seat and rein, the pony felt the weakened will and sensibly slackened his pace. Too sick now to care, Dorelei let the pony break gait, slow to a walk, falter to a lathered halt. Dorelei eased down to lie on her stomach in the cool moss. After a time she rolled over, letting the freshness seep into her back. The exhausted pony stood nearby, head hanging, too winded even to graze.

I don't care if he never comes back. I don't care. It is not his wealth in me, but Padrec's.

Was it? She didn't know that surely. Cru had not reached for her that much since Midsummer. She remembered the last time, not very tender. There was anger disguised in his loving, as in hers after the Taixali village. It could be Cru or Padrec, she didn't know.

Let him go. I am Christian now. I will follow Jesu with Padrec. He is stronger than Cru. Those that will not follow, let them go back to bronze. Let them try to betray me like Judas-Cru. Oh, Mother, I hurt so inside. Why did he make me send him away?

The flat dish of earth showed no fires anywhere in any direction, no sound but the soughing wind. She wasn't hungry; the thought of food brought a fresh wave of sickness, but she could use a fire to rest and think by before going back. The wind on the hill was alive with things to tell her, once she heeded them.

Sheep passed this way often, the scent old and fresh alike, so the ridge would be full of dried dung. Dorelei collected a small heap of moss not yet dampened by the night dew, then a stock of chips to burn. When her fire was laid, she took from her saddle pouch the tinderbox Malgon made her, thinking how soon wonders became common. She struck the iron against the flint until one of the red sparks caught in the tein-eigin, then shoved the box into her fire pile.

Tein-eigin was sacred moss used for kindling the holiest fires; she felt a bit reckless using it so, but it wouldn't hurt to have one more magic working for her.

The smoke blotted out the sheep smell with its own, but one acrid trace lingered. This trail was marked by Wolf often as part of his hunting range. A path so often used by sheep would be easy food for a family working together. Summer was fat for Wolf as fhain; they were always well fed now, though they might chase a sheep for the fun of it, playful as Rof or Bredei. Tallfolk never thought of Wolf as a person who laughed or liked to play. She heard them, riding before the sun went down, raising their voices before the night's hunt. Dorelei knew the different songs. Sometimes they talked or passed warnings from one group to another, but tonight there was no urgency in the mournful song. Tonight Wolf sang for the love of it.

Dorelei wished she could.

The wind shifted; the urine marking scent was strong and new. Squatting by her fire, Dorelei felt no surprise when her pony neighed and skittered in nervous warning.

"Peace, come here by me." She snuggled her cheek to his forelock. The pony's head jerked up again, wary. Holding the reins, she shifted so Wolf could scent them and come if he felt like it.

Just so, one night, did Jesu climb a high fell where he found Sa-tan, an evil lord of the night who offered Jesu all the kingdoms of the world if Jesu would bow to him. Dorelei found it easy to understand. If gods could bicker, they could bargain. And in just such a place as this, the Father-God spoke out of the bush to Moses.

Speak to me, then. I will listen. What does Father-God say to me?

Beyond her fire, a part of the dark took shape and moved. Light and shadow resolved to gray pelt, two close-set reflections of the fire to amber eyes, muzzle lolling open in a cold smile that seemed to relish the secret joke of the world.

A bitch wolf; like human women, female wolves needed change and play and even a time to tire of her pups and draw off alone. Like Dorelei she could weary of a husband but never left him until death.

That's wise. Mother sends Wolf, not the cuckoo, to remind me of this. Give Cru a time apart, and we will mend it.

The two females eyed each other. "Do come to offer me the world to bow down to thee?"

Wolf seemed amused: why do you trouble night with questions?

"Be the bush that burns and speaks law?"

Will give you law, woman. Taste the air, feel the night beyond your fire. Still. Whole. Would you change that?

149

"Where whole?" Dorelei challenged. "Hunger and cold and dead children always."

And yet it was yours since before Mabh. I hunted on your flank when the first gern cried to Mother, and now we both die out of the land. What matter your new magic and mate; to call him Raven means he can fly? Go the way you know.

"Sa-tan, thee offer old gifts for new."

Do I? Will tallfolk hail you when they believe you spirits of the dead? Will they open gates and welcome you because fhain now carries iron? I will give you law to trust: go back.

Wolf lifted her muzzle; there was a new scent on the night air beside Dorelei and the pony. She rose from her haunches and turned her last pity on Dorelei.

Listen for my song. I will sing for you.

Across the fire, Wolf's form became less definite, faded, disappeared. Now Dorelei heard the newcomers and caught the fhain smell. Her people had followed her. Perhaps ...

"Cru?"

There was no answer out of the dark. Dorelei shifted away from the firelight; after a moment she saw the small shapes squatting motionless in the dark. Out of it, silent as Wolf, came Reindeer gern in her old kilt and vest as Dorelei remembered her, the huge pendant ruby catching her fire and throwing it back. The older woman stood waiting. Dorelei would have risen in respect, but something new stayed her. *I tamed the iron, not Bruidda. I will not put my hands to her belly. That is past. It is for her to do.*

The hard-faced woman gazed at Dorelei with a flicker of displeasure. "Does Salmon forget Bruidda, who blessed thee once?"

"Nae, sister."

"Girl does nae rise for woman, then?"

Dorelei spoke loud enough for the others to hear. "Did call me child. Be woman now with wealth in me. Now gern speaks to gern. Sit by my fire, sister."

Bruidda sank to her haunches, ropy arms dangling over her knees. "Thee grows proud. Do take Mabh's name where a's own blood would not."

"Was reborn in Jesu magic and named anew by Raven. Sister would nae understand."

Bruidda didn't miss the condescension. "Fhains tell that thee ride with Blackbar now."

"Aye."

"By what magic?"

"Reindeer remembers Naiton of Taixali?"

"A did kill my son."

"Did shame him with a's own iron."

Bruidda allowed a slight, satisfied smile. "Did hear. Say then, how was a done?"

"By my magic from Mother. By Padrec Raven. Dost think do take Mabh's name in vain?"

Great or not, blessed or not, the girl was young enough to be arrogant. Bruidda saw that as weakness. She was more concerned than other gerns in this matter. The stags rutted early the past autumn, and the fawns were born before Lugh returned to warm the spring. Many of them died on the summer trail north; many did not live that long. That in itself was a breach in the way of things, as if Reindeer had forgotten everything Mother taught. Among the weak and crippled, Bruidda had found a fawn whose fine hair was not dappled but black all over, so black that it was surely sent by Lugh as Raven in another form, since no fawn was ever dropped with such coloring. The little thing was born with its forelegs only, the others mere stumps. Clearly it was a sign to Reindeer fhain. Since it was dying, Bruidda gave it quick mercy, cut into the sack of entrails, and read the portent. She did not speak in her own fhain of this but only among her wise sister gerns when she met them traveling. Eventually they agreed on the meaning.

That there were forelegs only pointed to a future cut off from the past. There would be born to Reindeer fhain a gern of Mabh's blood, and to her a husband, both from fhain sisters, as was proper. Though the signs did not point to happiness, they would both be great in the midst of sadness. But this girl was Salmon and her Raven of the tallfolk. The signs hinted of the sea in the great one's name: "bright one from the sea," or Morgana, and her husband somehow of the Bear. Bruidda had heard of false gods and false leaders before this, and she was not used to familiarity from girls less than half her age, no matter their sudden and wondrous fame.

"Lugh sent sign of a great gern to come. Do see thee a child who speaks like one, thy belly not yet marked with bearing of live wealth. Does Raven teach you boasting as well? Speak, girl. How was a done?"

Was it Cru or the cold comfort of Wolf that made her do it? Dorelei whipped the iron knife from its sheath and held it up, pointing at Bruidda. "Do nae call me girl."

She saw the averted gaze, felt the flinching in Bruidda under the blunt insult. She felt it in those waiting in darkness and knew she was master here. Dorelei stroked the iron blade across her forearm. "Will try thy magic against mine, sister?"

Bruidda was older and wise enough not to make such attempt where failure was certain. "Dorelei Mabh," she said in a different tone, "do not shame me before Mother and fhain."

Dorelei rose. "Now thee may sit while Mabh stands. Let Reindeer come close. Hear the speaking of Padrec Raven. Only by Jesu shall thee be delivered. Only by Dorelei Mabh shall thee win over iron. My arm will stretch out like the rod of Moses. Iron will go down before Prydn, will kiss thy foot and cook thy food as a does mine. Such gifts will Mabh share."

Cold exultation, kindled from the ashes of fury; Dorelei felt herself growing taller. The night could not chill nor the world frighten her any more than it did Moses, who confronted Egypt-fhain even as she faced Naiton.

"Hear! Will Reindeer tame this iron or run from it?"

As Meganius knew Patricius, Bruidda had some sense of Dorelei— the youth and arrogance and the thrust of ambition. For a long moment she gazed in understanding and a pity quite lost on the younger woman. All was not clear. If this was not Morgana, then perhaps the child in her belly . . .

Bruidda rose, came round the fire. As she put her hands to Dorelei's stomach in respect, her people slipped forward into the light—suspicious, tentative, but coming with hands outstretched to touch the quickened belly of Dorelei Mabh.

Whether Wolf was Satan or speaking bush, Dorelei had already viewed one of the offered kingdoms, and it was that which tempted Padrec.

Other fhains followed Bruidda. Around the summer rath of Salmon, more tents sprang up until the green hill bristled with them. Not entire fhains, who had their own flocks to tend, but if honored Bruidda could travel to see this wonder, other gerns could not hang back. They mulled the portent of the black fawn; whether or not this young gern was the bright one from the sea, if she conquered what Mabh herself could not, then even great ones would come to see.

Other voices talked that summer, watching the ponies move across the high ridges, and wondering. "There is that Faerie queen who is called Dorelei Mabh, and the iron has no power over her. And she gathers others to her. This is not good."

There were those who hated Faerie without thinking on it, because their fathers had. Everyone knew they were evil spirits, that was a fact of life. Such men and women wagged their knowing heads and rolled their eyes and declared that Faerie and iron together were against the natural order of things. And when the doomsayers had made their dark predictions, the cooler heads made theirs, the canny men who looked to profit in any situation and were willing to wait for it. This Mabh and her Raven were young, one heard. Young leaders make young mistakes, overstep themselves. One had only to wait. The time would come.

For the rest who feared more than they thought—that is to say, most of them—the increasing number of Faerie rades along the hilltops was ominous. It was unnatural for so many of them to come together and boded no good at all. . . .

No, he was not humble for all his prayers, far from it. Padrec watched them come, saw the deference to Dorelei, and received it himself. None considered him tallfolk now with the marks on him. There were changelings like himself among the fhains on the hill. Not the size but the heart made them Prydn.

The hill was bright with Lugh's sun, the raths throwing sharp shadows against it. He had preached to them and now they all shared a meal of tea, fish, and a variety of wildfowl and vegetables even simmered in iron pots over Malgon's forge fire. The day of the loaves and fishes must have been something like this, Padrec thought. New people were arriving all the time, paying their respects to Dorelei before accepting food. One of them was a young man with Salmon markings. He put his palms to Dorelei's belly and waited for her to sit before he spoke.

Padrec asked of Malgon: "Would be from Gawse, then?"

"Aye." Malgon noted the ritual movement of the man's hands—stretched out to earth and raised to sky, then down to cover his face. "Has been death in Salmon fhain."

Dear God, not Cru. Padrec and Malgon edged closer to hear.

"Gern-y-fhain," the young man told her, "thy mother be dead."

Padrec would have gone instantly to Dorelei, but Malgon checked him. "Nae. Wait."

Dorelei accepted the news in formal composure, covering her face with the same gesture before speaking. "Say how thy gern did die."

"By tallfolk hand. Venicone."

Gawse's fhain was occupying the hill near the ring of stones where Dorelei first found Padrec. On a false charge of thievery, Gawse and her people were pelted out of the same village where his own legs were broken. One stone too heavy and sharp hit Gawse in the head. She fell and never woke.

Dorelei's face was a mask. "And a was barrowed?"

"Barrowed and wrapped in Rainbow gift, Gern-y-fhain."

Dorelei said no more. The silence stretched out until Padrec felt

153

uncomfortable. This was his first experience with their death customs, but by every Roman and manly instinct, his arm should be about his wife for comfort and Gawse's grave known to them so they could mark and reverence it; if not a requiem, at least prayers to St. Brigid for the honorable mother of a convert. But Malgon schooled him in a few words.

"Barrow be never known, Padrec, never marked. Never asked."

Only that a small opening be left for Gawse's spirit to rise from the cairn. In tens of seasons, even Salmon would forget the place and tallfolk never know, else they'd desecrate the tomb for Gawse's treasure.

And so they disappear into Faerie-land. Drab to find reality behind the rainbow. It leached some of the color from the world. As Padrec looked to his wife, the melody of a childhood rhyme came back with a memory of his slave nurse, and herself singing him to sleep.

Be not where but only when . . .

He couldn't remember more than that. Then the sound sliced across his musing, chilling him in the midday sunlight. He'd heard it some nights in Ireland; at such times his master would not send even a slave to the hills.

"Tonight it is that you will byre the flock and stay at home. The banshee cries in the hills."

The sound, the cry rose from Dorelei, head flung back like Wolf, then from Neniane and Guenloie. Higher and higher through the scale it rose, to dip and rise again in a weird dissonance from all the women on the hill, until the unearthly sound set Padrec's teeth on edge. It licked about the edges of reason and all that was warm and safe, like wind tearing at a thatched roof. *You are foolish*, that voice whispered to Padrec's civilization. *I am the center and you the outsider. Not evil, never evil, but the sound of mourning women. Is sorrow not real? If eternity is beyond understanding, how shall men understand this? You may promise them reunion, but first this loss and the keening of women.*

Banshee . . . he'd said the word so often, heard the meaning blurred by the fearful Irish, who mouthed it without note to its original meaning. *Bean sidhe.* Faerie wife. Small wonder the fear. The keening plucked at the mind with talons of sound, disordered, tore it asunder. *Stop, I beg you.* . . .

They did cease in their own time, fading away to silence like a hole in sound itself. Only the wind whined, the lush grass stirred. The dozens squatting there might have been carved by Malgon. Padrec tried not to notice passing time, but his Roman sense of it would not stand down. The shadows had slid eastward by perhaps an hour's measure when Dorelei rose and beckoned to him.

"Padrec Raven."

When they were alone, Dorelei's stiff dignity evaporated. She shuddered into his arms. "Hold me, husband."

"Thy pain be mine," he murmured into her hair.

"Salmon will move to Cnoch-nan-ainneal," Dorelei trembled. "Among the Venicone."

"Aye, wife."

"My heart be ... sick. First Cru—"

"A will return."

"And now Gawse. And look thee how I must be proper gern in all things before such as Bruidda." Dorelei sniffled and wiped her eyes. "Raven, give counsel. At my word, many of these will follow us south. Thee must help in this."

"Fhains all together? To what purpose?"

"To defeat Venicone, grind them into the dirt. To make iron arrow-heads dipped in hemlock to kill a's elder."

He saw her mood. It was no part of wisdom. "No, Dorelei."

"And in garlic that a dies in pain, dost hear? Would nae give an easy death."

"No."

"Say not? Nae, thee must help!"

"Not to kill."

"Did a not kill?"

"Dost think being Christian is that easy, that you can follow Jesu in the sun and other gods in the dark? That the Psalms and stories are the pretty-sounding whole of it?"

"Will have vengeance," she vowed, "and these will follow me to't."

"Aye, a will follow Dorelei Mabh." Padrec sighed at the brick wall of her. "But know what you bring to them. Know what you bring them to. It is through God that you are strong. Vengeance He reserves to Himself."

"I will kill the murderer."

"Or be killed and undo the blessed work thee's started. Dorelei, hear me. Know what we have started. Be Prydn out there, and never do so many gather together except at Bel-tein or Samhain. Yet they've come, fhain on fhain, all respectful before thee as a symbol like the Chi-Rho. The Hebrew needed Moses to make them one. So a need the living Mabh. Dost think Jesu did not question or doubt or despair? On the night a was sold, a wanted to turn away, avert what was to come."

She was implacable. "Did stone Gawse as a would drive Wolf from a's fires. Must forget that?"

"No, but will forgive."

"Never."

"For thy own sake, wife. For thy soul's sake. I teach the word of my Church. In my Church I can't even call you the wife you are. I stay because I would rather fail Church in that than leave thee. But thy husband will not help thee to death."

Mere words; she hurt and he suffered with her. Padrec squeezed her small body to him as if he could press out the anguish, absorb it into his own strength. *And when did I grow strong but in her?*

"Some believe the black fawn foretold you as the angel promised Christ." And to them, as to the Galileans, everything Mabh did would be symbolic. If she went in peace among the Venicones, her example would sway others, perhaps even the muddy-souled Picts.

"South, then. Let us face these silly Picts and show how weak and useless their magic against a queen who lives in Christ; that she is stronger by not needing to strike back at frail men."

In his arms, Dorelei shook with the released pain she might show him or Cru, but no other. And all of it was there for him to read when she raised her face to him.

"Will need thee tonight to love me."

"Yes. Would now, but there be duty."

"Must hold someone."

And her Cru is gone, Padrec finished for her. If he managed jealousy better than Cru, he could still feel it. "Will be strong together. Will not leave thee."

Not even for God, may He forgive that.

"Fhains wait for us, to see the Jesu-magic." Dorelei opened the fhain chest and took out a heavy gold chain with emerald pendant and hung it about Padrec's neck. "And wear thy gold bracelets. Will trust thee more, seeing my trust."

The grief had washed her eyes, leaving them huge and vulnerable in the rath shadows. "Thee ask much, Padrec. Christ Jesu asks much. But come."

The dozens had not moved since Dorelei called her husband away; it would not be fitting. When she came out of the rath with Padrec Raven, they turned their gaze to her as she moved formally to Malgon's forge. Padrec took the tall pole with its wooden Chi-Rho symbol from Drust and held it high.

"In this sign shall thee conquer. In this sign—here and now, this very day, shall Jesu rout the evil out of Blackbar and make it servant to thee. In this sign are all things possible; without it, nothing."

156

"Let a hear of Jesu!" Drust beseeched. "Speak of the Passion and the death conquered."

"So will I. For Jesu is nae god to tallfolk alone, no wreathed idol for the halls of Roman-men alone. A was sent by God, but born in crannog among shepherds, and a's life was like to thine. When a spoke of God's joy in finding the soul once lost, did tell of a strayed lamb. What Prydn has not rejoiced when lambs were lost and found again in glen or fell? Then know Jesu was born to thee and of thee to bring thee home to God. Let the gerns of Reindeer and Marten, Wolf and Hawk hear and judge the truth of this tale-speaking.

"Was in the first days when Jesu walked the earth. One of his fhain doubted, would not believe, and did sell Jesu to the Roman-men for silver."

"How much silver?" Bruidda wondered out of habit.

"Thirty pieces."

"Was good trade." Wolf gern was scarce older than Dorelei, but coarser-featured and scarred from fighting. "Have been sold for less myself."

"Was it so good?" Padrec challenged her. "Judas the betrayer lies in hell."

"And where be this hell?" Wolf gern asked.

"Where God is not. Cut off from God's light and love, where can it be but hell, as Prydn cut from the love of a's fhain."

Cru betrayed me, and I sent him to hell, Dorelei thought bitterly. *But I would have him back. Does God regret Judas so? Not all of us show our scars like Wolf gern for the world to see. Nothing stays, the world costs, and I know what hell is.*

Padrec told them of Gethsemane and Jesu's arrest and trial, and of Golgotha. Between two thieves he suffered, and to the thief who believed, a man low as any Venicone, he promised Tir-Nan-Og.

"Jesu died, and three scant days later arose in the flesh to walk among a's fhain. Now, here was the manner of it. A did not ask worship but faith. For that faith, does offer to Prydn and tallfolk alike a life eternal. Salmon and reindeer, wolf and marten, the beasts with whom we have understanding, spin out their little time in little life, but thee are blessed. In this sign, in this belief, there can be no death."

"Will cheer my son to know," Bruidda muttered. "A's skin darkens on Taixali wall. Do hear thy Jesu bids us love. Must love tallfolk as well?"

Padrec opened the question to all of them. "Reindeer asks if Prydn must love tallfolk. A wise question."

"None wiser," Bruidda snapped. Padrec burst into laughter with the rest of them.

"Nae, but a would not be funny if a were not true! Open thy heart and see what be inside, even as thee read the entrails of the black fawn. Would pour fresh goat's milk into soured jar? Neither will thee receive Jesu with a heart soured by hate. There's the answer."

It was an image they could understand. Padrec held up the Chi-Rho again. "Salmon gern has learned in her dignity that this is no easy sign to follow, but what fhain has ever known an easy life? This magic is not that thee fear, but that thee *believe*, even as Dismas, the thief who died with Jesu."

Padrec passed the Chi-Rho to Drust and took the iron bar from the forge. "Be gerns here who have made strong magic for a's people. Who will be the first to laugh at Blackbar? Who will be strong as a dying thief?"

"Here!"

Dorelei did it, and Padrec understood why where a year ago he wouldn't. He'd cut her from one comfort, Cru from another, the Venicones from her mother. She darted at Bruidda, took her hand, and pulled the startled woman to Padrec. "The blood of Mabh be first."

"Yah!"

Bruidda was stunned, shrinking as far as possible from the iron but unable to pull away from Dorelei without a loss of presence. "Girl—"

"Sister," Dorelei prompted in a tone of honey and steel.

"Did bless thee once in thy fear and newness, even with my own grief. Thee answers with insult."

"If Reindeer runs from iron, who of these will dare? Take the iron."

"In the name of Christ Jesu," Padrec urged.

The three of them huddled close in that whispered conference, each with his or her grasp of ultimate truth. Bruidda had been forced by an arrogant girl into a position from which there was no retreat but forward. And she must hide the fear from her people, dared by a child yet to bear wealth or see it butchered. She must do this thing but would not forgive it. She glared at Dorelei and raised her right hand.

"Let be, then. Reindeer dares Blackbar by its true name—iron!"

Among the squatting Prydn about the hill, her sister gerns and many others rose in respect. Bruidda took the moment to her advantage. "Even Salmon stands for Reindeer. Hear! Have called on the name and spirit of iron! Feel how a do ring us about. With this hand, and in the name of Jesu, I dare the iron." Her fingers closed about the bar, lifted it from Padrec's hand, raised it overhead.

"Glory to God, Alleluia!" Drust shouted.

"See!" Dorelei sang. "See where Reindeer tames the—"

158

"Ai! *It burns me—it burns!*"

Stunned, they all saw Bruidda drop the bar as if it were blistering hot, clutching at her hand. "The evil marks me!"

Padrec's heart skipped a beat as Bruidda held up the palm with its red mark like a burn. He should have grasped the moment himself, but there was a quicker demon in Dorelei. She swooped down on the petrified Bruidda, snatched at the stricken hand, and plunged it into the tempering trough.

"As did burn me," she proclaimed to all of them, "before the blessed healing water. But a moment and see." Then, in an urgent whisper to Bruidda: "The magic needs belief. Was like burned and like healed. Believe, sister. Jesu be stronger than iron. Believe."

"Does burn like fire."

"Believe. Let go thy fear."

"Thee's shamed me."

"Believe. Be nae pain, nae chronachadh come to thee. Even now the pain lessens, fades, runs away. Believe."

"Burns . . ."

"Would be lost in hell? One moment of belief. Mark how all spirits, good and ill, hover about—aye, thee believe that. Tred on the evil as I did upon the pride of Naiton. *Believe.*"

A rush of sun-sparkling water as Dorelei pulled the hand from the trough and held it high. The red mark of the evil was fading even as the drops rolled from the palm and wrist.

"Now," Dorelei exulted. "Who will be reborn in Jesu?"

Padrec wondered: *She did it, not me. Without my help or blessing, God worked through her.* The moment of uncertainty drowned in enthusiasm. *He loves me no more than Dorelei. Truly there's more to existence than I knew.* "Glory to God, Alleluia!" Padrec shouted. "Come forth, all of you."

"Yah! for the Shepherd and a's fhain!" cried Drust.

"Yah!"

"Jesu!"

A few hung back afraid, but others surged forward, needing no encouragement. The brown hands stretched out to touch Dorelei, Padrec, Bruidda, and the magical Chi-Rho, strong enough to put down iron. In the babble and excitement, Bruidda looked into Dorelei's face and saw the new hardness beneath the triumph.

"What be this we do, sister? What dost bring us to?"

But Dorelei had accepted God's leaven of triumph for her grief. "Jesu treds upon a's enemies! Who will ride south with the flocks of Jesu and Salmon?"

Dorelei stalked through the singing, cheering Prydn, Padrec at her side. Where they walked, the people made way, the sun itself made way for them, and their shadows stretched long and longer across the light on the hill, tall as the Chi-Rho itself. They heard no sound but praise and saw only where their own proud images marked the earth.

Fhains moving together: it was unheard of, but new magic swept old reasons before it. In the warm early autumn, even before Finch's song was heard, the flocks swirled south like an avalanche to Cnoch-nan-ainneal, where Dorelei first found Padrec. They settled not only on the hill but spilled down into the lowland pastures of the apprehensive Venicones, their raths not sodded over but bright-painted as Rainbow. In the flush of the enthusiastic numbers that followed, Padrec did not separate his success from God's. In honest moments, he felt more Alexander than Apostle.

Entering on the easier part of her pregnancy, between the early sickness and the late awkwardness, Dorelei bloomed, basking in the deference paid her by the Prydn who joined the rade south. They placed their hands on her belly in respect, and when the courtesies were done, she asked the question that never left her.

"A man of Salmon fhain, Cruaddan. Who has seen him?"

None at all. Cru had vanished.

For Vaco, the Venicone elder who once cast Padrec forth to die on the hill, this was the worst time to have such compounded troubles shadow his house. A Faerie rade was ill wind any time, a migration of this size plain ominous. They drove their long-horned sheep down into his pastures with mere show of asking permission. What could he do against such numbers, and every cursed one of them mounted and armed and the unkillable Christ-man with them? That one was tougher than Vaco thought; not only throve among Faerie, he led them now, he and his Faerie queen clanking with the treasure they wore. To Vaco's clear logic, the man was incomprehensible: preaching chastity, yet married now. Should have died but didn't. His hair was red—well, perhaps he was favored of Lugh Sun despite his muddled views.

To curdle the milk thoroughly, were not the Romans themselves in his village, thick as flies and friendly as lions pausing among lambs, talking alliance, a new war and bargaining for Venicone recruits?

Vaco had to be a generous and courteous host. He preferred Romans at a distance. Close up they were stiffish, too sure of themselves and brusque—no nonsense, get on with it, that was their way. And their tribune! Vaco had sons older than this presumptuous brat who wore his hair so short and his face so clean-shaven he looked like a picked chicken. His name—almost as long as the boy himself—was Ambrosius Aurelianus. Tribune, mind you, an important son of an important Somebody, very high in the Parisi court. Vaco had older sons, but none of them nearly so self-assured in negotiation, nor so quick to brush aside the traditional courtesies of business transaction with his damned Roman know-it-all. Well, let him talk. He'd get courtesy but no recruits. He wasn't respectful.

Vaco felt truly beleaguered. A fly-swarm of Roman and Faerie. Had he known of Pharaoh, he would have commiserated. They'd be everywhere, so small, so many of them, a man would need a dozen eyes to keep them from stealing him blind. . . .

Not so. They came to his village in a great singing parade behind the red-haired priest and the queen, caroling on flower-decked ponies, and the sight of them was both awesome and laughable, a strain on the eyes. The brevity of their clothing and the breathtaking *riches* they wore like children's beads! When they trooped through the open stockade gate, they scattered gold coins, flashing in the sunlight, to the pop-eyed women and children, who scampered about to retrieve them all.

"We follow the sign of Jesu," Dorelei called to them. "His law be to love and give. We share our wealth that thee know us thy brothers and sisters."

Waiting with his aides beside Vaco and his blue-painted brethren, Ambrosius marveled at the visible wealth among these people whose very existence, until now, had been mostly fable to him. The red-bearded man beside the pregnant queen swung down from his saddle—an Army mount, if Ambrosius was any judge—and strode energetically to Vaco, a fortune in gold and jewels dangling over his grimy hide vest.

"May the sun be at your back, Elder. Perhaps now Vaco will believe in the strength of my God, who once again comes in peace."

"Well," Vaco countered circumspectly, "at least I will listen as carefully as before. Your gods are strong for you."

"He understood and forgave the doubting Thomas. Then so must I. A*ve*, Tribune!" Padrec thrust out his hand to the young officer. "I am Father Patricius."

Ambrosius grasped the offered arm. "A*ve*, Father. Ambrosius Aurelianus. Nuncio from Prince Marchudd."

"From Eburacum?" Padrec brightened. "Then you would know Bishop Meganius."

"To some extent."

"His grace is well?"

"Wise in the prince's council." Ambrosius remembered the benign presence who listened much and spoke little, and then to great effect. "And worrying over his peacocks."

"Ah . . . yes. Forgive me," Padrec confessed, "I've hardly written

Latin this year and spoken it not at all outside of prayer. What news of—oh. A moment, sir." Quickly Padrec stepped to Dorelei's side, where she'd planted herself before Vaco and his brothers in a cool appraisal.

"Be Dorelei Mabh, Vaco. Do give thy people Rainbow-gift to show our love. Will borrow not a stone from thy land. So let be peace between us."

Vaco peered down at the tiny woman. "It is familiar that you are."

"Have summered on the fell before," Dorelei allowed in a noncommittal tone. "And my blood sometimes."

"Gern-y-fhain is held in that Hand which upholds me," Padrec prompted. "Give us welcome, and I will tell your people once more of my God, this time in words that will not offend the dignity of Venicones. Ambrosius, this is Dorelei Mabh, to whom I am priest and second husband."

> ... I could only be polite and reach down for her little overdecorated paw (Ambrosius wrote to Marchudd), and she and Patricius alike fragrant as their sheep when the wind was wrong. Their wealth is unquestionable, most of it visible as Trimalchio's, rattling about loud enough to give one a headache. The woman Dorelei has enormous prestige among these creatures, Patricius is more demigod than priest, and both act like it. To win them to his side, Patricius has gone to theirs—marriage, ritual scars, the lot—with thumping success. The Faerie are Christian with a vengeance, literal believers in the Word. The Venicones are evasive anent my arguments for an alliance and recruits. Under the rose, I would much rather enlist the Faerie, who seem quicker mettle; not only superb archers but the finest horsemen and women one could find, though they ride ponies stunted as themselves. Better mounted and trained, they would make excellent alae. Knowing my lord's views on cavalry, I won't press the point. They are, of course, utter savages and shameless as animals. "Queen" Dorelei goes about bare as a concubine under her jewelry, the swelling of her pregnant belly displayed as a mark of pride. Animals, but loyal as good dogs under a trusted master ...

"Interesting," Ambrosius noted to Padrec as they ambled toward the stockade from the garish tents on Cnoch-nan-ainneal. "You say the Mass in their dialect."

"I know it's wrong." Indeed, the practice troubled Padrec's sense of orthodoxy more than his marriage. "But they must understand it. The

Transubstantiation is very literal magic to them. That and certain other passages I leave in Latin, when they receive the Body and Blood."

"Like a Druid."

"You might say, yes. They have a deep need for magic. The sense of reality is quite different from ours, and there is no linear sense of time. Like Dronnarron."

Ambrosius, fairly fluent in the northern dialects, didn't recognize the word or the weird inflections the priest gave it. "What's that, Pictish?"

"Older," Padrec told him. "God knows how much older. No Gaelic root at all. It means the Green Time, or the Good Time That Was. This island was theirs alone before Abraham brought Isaac down from the mountain."

The tribune's sense of history was totally Roman: fact at the center but myth about the edges. "Really. The Dobunni bards always said it was the sons of Troy who colonized Britain."

"Bards need not be accurate, merely colorful."

"That's true enough. Windy old sods." Ambrosius slowed his stride, matching it to that of the shorter priest, who stumped along on level ground with feet that remembered hills. "All this gold, the jewels and the rest of it: where does it all come from?"

"Rainbow," Padrec answered casually.

"Pardon?"

"A gift from Rainbow."

They were near the stockade now. Ambrosius halted, smiling ironically. "By way of the imperial mint, Patricius. The eager Venicones missed this in the scramble." He held out the gold aureus clearly stamped with the likeness and inscription of Trajanus.

Padrec said delicately, "They have no word for 'theft,' Tribune."

"I'd say not."

"To ask is to be given."

"You taught them that?"

"No, Ambrosius. They taught me. They are innate Christians. Are you?"

"When I have to be," Ambrosius fended, "but I see your point."

"Good; then you must school me in turn. I've been long from home. When I left, the Council of Princes was on the verge of trusting one of themselves enough to call him king. What's the news?"

"Vitalinus is raised to imperator by the tribes."

"The one they call Vortigern?" Padrec weighed the notion. "More of a bargainer than a war-chief, I hear. And this war of Marchudd's against the Coritani: what does he hope to gain from it?"

"Every *gradus* of land they've stolen from him in the past ten years, and an extension of the Church into pagan lands. Missionaries like yourself, Father. Perhaps a new diocese."

Padrec stopped at the stockade entrance to study the ruddy-cheeked young soldier, knowing more of Ambrosius than he declared, a political necessity during his time with Germanus. The tribune was a Dobunni from Severn, close enough in blood and tribal ties to be, in time, a serious consideration for the throne and sword now held by Vortigern. For twenty years, since the withdrawal of the legions, the title of imperator had been only as strong as the man who wore it, and none wore it that well. Vitalinus would scheme and bargain, Ambrosius might—what? Bring back Rome or its likeness? Hard to read in the young face now, but the discipline was clearly there, and the ambition.

"A holy war? If it *is* a holy war, Ambrosius. That word is not to be sullied. The Coritani have a fierce spirit. God could use such passion."

Ambrosius grunted in disinterest. "Surely it's not among the Venicones."

"Perhaps it is, but you'll have to buy it, Tribune. They love a bargain as my people do."

"Um. You're Brigante, aren't you?"

"No, I—" Padrec grinned at the slip. He gestured back toward the raths on the hill. "I meant *my* people."

"Ah, yes. Well." Ambrosius tactfully changed the subject. "I hope Vaco will come to terms soon."

"Quite so. Vaco. Vaco ..." Padrec ruminated, then cocked a brow at Ambrosius. "Named for his mother's tribe, I suppose. The Vacomagii. They're like the Irish; no man can be a chief among them if he has a single blemish on his body. As you can see, Vaco's woad covers a multitude of imperfections. I suspect his presence—his honor—is all the more tender for it."

"Honor!" Ambrosius balked at the word. "How can the man be called honorable when he won't be definite about anything, yea or nay?"

"But he is," Padrec contradicted lightly. "His honor is like our art, very intricate. Courtesy, hospitality, bargaining all intertwine. Inextricable. No doubt he finds you as much a coil. If you'll permit, Tribune? I should say a little less Roman get-on-with-it and a little more observance of his presence. The bargain must seem his shrewd-ness more than yours. You're on his hearth."

"You seem to have learned them well, Patricius."

"At considerable cost. They broke my legs and put me out on the hill."

Ambrosius was genuinely shocked. "By the Bull of Mithras! You could have died. And you came back here?"

"No, not died." The priest's direct gaze might have been unsettling but for its serenity. "God is not through with me."

"I wish I were through with Vaco," Ambrosius sighed plaintively. "Pict food is unspeakable."

"Ah-ha! That's the soft way of the court for you, boyo. Best food in the world up here. You should live more among shepherds. Nothing preserved, everything fresh."

"Hopefully," Ambrosius amended with a dying fall. He stepped aside and allowed the priest to precede him into Vaco's longhouse and further digestive torment.

The feast was crowded and noisy, although the order of seating was carefully planned in concession to the dignity of all. Vaco and his brothers sat at one end with their chief guests—Padrec, Dorelei, and her people, Ambrosius, and one of his aides. At the lower fire pit were placed the other Prydn gerns and the odd Romans of lower rank. The chief wives oversaw the serving. Trying to be careful of courtesy, Ambrosius couldn't remember which wife belonged to which husband.

"Actually they share them," Padrec volunteered.

"Um. Muzzy from a legal standpoint," Ambrosius allowed. "A father doesn't know what to leave to whom, does he?"

Padrec chuckled over his mutton. "Tribune, a Venicone always knows exactly what he's got and how much he wants to leave behind. If he can't take most of it with him to Tir-Nan-Og, he's not going."

"By the gods, Patricius," the Roman spluttered through his drink. "You're not at all the uncomfortable little prig I'd heard of."

"You catch me in the middle of happiness; that does a lot for earnest men." Padrec nodded politely across the fire to Vaco lolling on his greasy cushions, and leaned to kiss Dorelei, who was squirming with the beginnings of discomfort next to him. "How is't, wife?"

"Oh, the wealth. Must always go outside."

The frequency of her need astonished Padrec, who knew as much of pregnancy as he did of building bridges. "Again?"

"Soon."

"Thee looks out of temper."

She knuckled her eyes against the smoke from the fire pit. "Vaco smells of pig and dirt, and the Romans of Roman." And Dorelei was tired of being courteous to Venicones better poisoned than smiled at, and Padrec's faith was sometimes as much a burden as the wealth in her body.

"The feast be nigh done. Will speak soon."

"Speed then, help me up. Will go now and miss nae word of thee."

Padrec drew her close, proud of the swelling that pressed between them, fiercely wanting it to be his. "Do love thee."

The pleasure washed over Dorelei's face; she needed that just then. "Will hurry then. Neniane, come with me."

When the women had cleared away the platters and replaced them with dishes of fruit and nuts, Padrec waited until Dorelei was comfortable, back and hips well cushioned and her feet tucked under Rof's hairy belly before rising to speak.

"Elder Vaco of the Camlann Venicones—a year ago at Lughnassadh, you doubted my words and sent me forth to try my faith against your reality. You have seen the strength of my God, and I have since heard the music of Mother and Lugh. I was a poor and discourteous guest then, knowing little of my host's honor. A year schooled, let me try again."

"His legs are strong as ever," Vaco's youngest brother observed in a malicious murmur. "The wolves let him be, and the damned Faerie made him one of them. A favorite of the gods he may not be, but neither an enemy."

"Perhaps. There is that about the gods that makes me wonder if they know what they're about," said the middle brother.

"Peace," Vaco moderated. "What can we do? Strong he is, but if he is still a fool, it will show." He raised his voice to the hall. "Silence! Peace and silence for the words of Padrec Raven."

"Venicones, I am Padrec Raven, second husband to Salmon gern. Romans, I greet you as Succatus Patricius of Clannaventa. Gerns of Wolf, Marten, and Reindeer: my hands are to you in respect. Once before in this hall I spoke of my God. Like Raven, I spoke with a harsh voice, and the Venicones, knowing true music, sent me away."

Malgon grunted. "Does say much in little."

Vaco called across the fire: "Padrec! Do you still think it better to sleep alone?"

"I still believe in one wife to one husband. For myself at least. I will not speak for other men. Let me tell instead not of laws or the things forbidden, but of the spirit behind the law. The believing, the faith as Prydn have come to know it. There is a tale that will be a lamp to it.

"Was in the first days, and certain of Hebrew fhain served a great king. Now, this king set a golden idol of God at his door to honor Him, and ruled that all must bow to it or die. But Daniel of the Hebrew knew his God would not be presumed in a statue and did not bow down."

They were listening now because he was not preaching at them but telling a story with a beginning, a problem, and an end. He told of

Daniel and how he was cast at night into a den of lions to try his faith against their reality, as Vaco tried his own. In the early morning, when the proud king hastened to the caged pit, Daniel stood unscathed among the gentled beasts. And the king knew the power of Daniel's God.

"So I come again among the Venicone, not to conquer but to give, to scatter among you the wealth of God's Grace as Prydn have flung gold to your children."

Vaco ruminated, nibbling on an apple core. "There is wisdom in what you say. But the tale marks a plain truth with nothing of gods about it."

"And what is that, Elder?"

Vaco belched and patted his pampered belly. "Lions and wolves are less greedy than other creatures. They are merely neighbors when well fed. Hungry is a different matter. Now, it is that I have dogs that are kept hungry all the time to bait wolves and a bear now and then."

"There is no gentling *them*," his nearest wife snickered.

"Would you put even your queen's hound against one of them?"

Dorelei wriggled bare toes in Rof's matted flank as he worried a meaty shoulder bone in huge jaws. "Rof be gentled in Jesu as myself. But even Wolf prays not to meet him."

"Do even wolves pray, then?" Vaco laughed.

"When a sees Rof," Bredei attested through a mouthful.

"Be not a thing of hungry or fed, but—of—faith!" Drust bounced to his feet. "Vaco, be Drust Dismas, honored by Raven to carry the Chi-Rho. Hear me, as have been reborn in Jesu."

Ambrosius regarded him with a mixture of puzzlement and pity. "Patricius, how old is that boy? He looks a child."

"Ask the time in Eden," Padrec said easily. "He's closer to it than I."

"The magic of Jesu be no trick," Drust maintained. "How many dogs dost speak of, Vaco?"

"Three there are."

"Let a come out."

"Against the queen's hound, and himself half asleep?"

"Against me."

Holy Jesu. Padrec choked on barley beer to mask his dismay. He saw Vaco's eyes narrow with a crueler interest. "And what weapons?"

Drust drew his knife and handed it to Malgon, spreading his empty hands. *Mother of God:* Padrec glanced furtively at Dorelei, who seemed calm as Drust. None of fhain turned a hair at the suicidal recklessness. Guenloie even trilled her delight at the challenge.

167

"Drust be most beautiful among men. Be gentle with's poor hounds, husband."

"As lambs," he promised. "Let Padrec shrive me and hounds will sit at thy husband's foot and lick a's hand."

Incredulous reaction murmured up and down the hall. "Boy-child," Vaco rumbled, "it is a braggart you are."

"Nae, be God in my heart as in Daniel's. Do nae carry the Sign alone, do live in it. Will Vaco try't?"

One of Ambrosius' aides, moving up from the lower hall, bent down to whisper in his tribune's ear. "Sir, is that little savage mad?"

"Worse, a total Christian. I'd rather not see this." Ambrosius leaned to Padrec. "Faith or not, this is folly. Can't you stop it?"

"Not now. I know them."

The thing bothered Ambrosius most in that he foresaw impediment to his mission. Negotiations were hard enough in tranquility. "Stop him, Patricius. Surely you fear for him?"

Padrec looked strangely troubled. "I do. And perhaps to the measure I fear, my faith may be less than his. They've not yet learned to ration faith, Tribune. Remember Daniel."

"Fat lot of good that'll do."

"Who can say?" Padrec watched Drust as the proud boy led Guenloie out of the longhouse. "Rome has not all the words for faith."

Faith? To Ambrosius in his self-occupied youth, faith was something kept in a niche and trotted out for ceremony; common sense was quite another. While the excited Venicones readied the contest, no one talked about anything else, nor would they for some time, and even his own men were wagering, giving long odds on the dogs. Whatever the outcome, it took Vaco's mind off recruits. Ambrosius would have to labor longer in this Venicone vinyard of misery.

From the open gate, he watched the boy Drust lead his tiny wife up the hill to a purpled smear of heather, where they began to remove the little clothing they wore.

"By the Bull of Mithras." Ambrosius turned away in consternation and discovered Padrec at his elbow, beaming at the distant lovers. "Do you see what they're doing up there?"

"Making love, I suppose."

"In the middle of the day? In the bare open like dogs?"

"Or Eden," Padrec suggested. "It puts his spirit at peace, opens it to happiness and God. I will shrive him, but Guenloie first. It shocked me once, too. The acceptance is all."

"Rot." Ambrosius felt his sophistication had been tweaked. "Not shocked at all. Seen cruder customs among the Demetae. But civilized men have some sense of occasion."

"Really?" The priest's direct gaze might have seemed rude to the brittle young soldier without its leavening mildness. "You could watch two gladiators gut each other in the arena and even cheer, I daresay. Yet an act of simple loving makes you uncomfortable."

"One has nothing to do with the other."

"You think not?"

"The arena is manly."

"And this is effeminate? I once thought Germanus the most passionate soul housed in a living body. Drust is all of that and love beside. I don't think the soul's joy divides in separate closets."

Ambrosius bridled somewhat under Padrec's scrutiny. The priest had the same expression to his eyes as his Faerie wife and the rest of them, used to open vistas with nothing between himself and the horizon or possibly some other world. *The man looks right through you.*

"Excuse me, Tribune." Padrec bobbed his head. "Drust will be wanting confession before he meets the dogs." He started away, then halted with a footnote by way of afterthought. "The Venicones make love sometimes in the middle of eating. They're on their best behavior for you; didn't want to offend Roman sensibilities."

And he was gone, leaving Ambrosius to seethe over the talent of savages for wasting time and energy.

"Idiots."

He grumbled over the dismal lot of an envoy and the insanity of Drust Dismas, before the Roman of him asserted itself with the cool judgment that would one day make him emperor of Britain. *Make use of it all. Play the game their way, but be the player. Fine horsemen and archers, quicker-mettled than the Venicones. You need only the right time.*

In a small bower borrowed for the occasion, Padrec sat on a low stool, eyes shielded with one hand while Drust knelt beside him.

"How long since thy last confession?"

Always difficult for Drust to think in measured time. "Two days."

"And what sins since then?"

A recollective silence. Drust honestly thought on it. "None, Padrec. But would have thy blessing anyway."

Probably true; just as true that pride in spiritual purity could be the subtlest sin, but Drust would confess the smallest things. Since none of them could really think in terms of sin, Padrec had devised a simpler question to help them along.

"This moment before God, Drust, and His ear turned to thee, how dost feel in thy heart?"

The sigh of contentment was quite genuine. "Good, Padrec."

"In all things?"

"All. Father-God and Jesu love me, and Guenloie. Did feel the warm wealth between us on the hill. Be happy."

"No fear or sin goes with thee to the cage?"

"What fear?" Drust's clear laugh was honesty in sound. "Have nae seen the magic that holds me in a's hand? Nae, look on me, Padrec." Drust sniffed delightedly at his hands and arms. "Do smell of heather and Guenloie."

"Brother, thee need not do this."

"Would show faith to Venicones."

"God knows thy faith and treasures it."

"But Venicone tallfolk do not. Being slow of wit, a must have clear lessons. Nae fear, Padrec. God and Guenloie be about me." Drust looked radiant, exalted. He bowed his head expectantly. "Say the magic."

"*Te absolvo in nomine Patri et Fili et Spiritus Sanctus*. Thee has taken the Body and Blood of Christ into thine own. Go and pray for me."

"Will." The boy jumped up as if he were going to breakfast rather than bloodshed. Then his smile faltered to a shade less certain. "Do remember one sin. The Roman Ambrose has braw horse. Did have passing thought to borrow't."

Padrec ruffled the boy's silky hair. "Nae, hast not horses enough?"

"Aye . . . but Cru would. Do miss Cru."

"So do I, Drust."

"Yah! Come, Padrec. Watch thy brother show God to dogs and other Venicones."

The baiting pit was a wicker enclosure anchored to stout posts with a kennel inside. The three hounds were huge, misshapen and scarred. They looked to Padrec like animated lumps of malevolence with fangs at one end. Rof quivered at the sight and smell of them, hackles rising, whining in his throat. The pit was already circled two and three deep with eager spectators when Drust came forth—Venicones, Romans, and as many Prydn who could wriggle between larger bodies.

"Roman-men give four pieces of silver to one on the dogs," Artcois chortled to Malgon. "Ai! Could we not scrub them clean an't were not forbid by Jesu!"

Malgon only prayed earnestly that Jesu was in a mood for miracles. He crushed his brother husband in a protective hug. "Jesu be with thee."

"Where else?" Drust shrugged innocently. He kissed Guenloie and knelt to Padrec and Dorelei for their blessing. From across the pit, where Vaco's men prodded the dogs to snapping fury with long poles, the elder called, "Is the holy one ready?"

"Ready!"

Drust put his palms to Dorelei's belly, received Padrec's benediction, and nodded to the grinning Venicone at the cage door. Guenloie held on to him as long as she could, her hand sliding along his arm as her husband moved away.

"Thee was beauty in the heather, Drust."

He stepped through the open gate. It closed behind him. Three Venicone youths hauled on the ropes that opened the kennels. The three brutes shot forward. A sibilant rush of breath burst from the crowd. One hand white-knuckled on the wicker, Padrec saw the moment as lethal contrast: the stillness of Drust and the dogs coming like missiles. *God, what you did for Daniel, do it now.*

Before the *oh* of released tension died away, the plunging hounds skidded to a clumsy halt before the unmoving figure.

They were confused.

They inched closer, snarling. Drust's gaze was fixed on the ground at a spot just in front of the nearest dog. The brute pranced and writhed in a display of fury but came no closer. Gradually the pitch of their challenge dulled to bewilderment. Small-brained murder had propelled them at the figure, but their sense of smell gave them no familiar message. From humans and their own kind they knew the scents of danger and fear; that it was absent now disoriented them. The creature did not run, did not threaten.

They were kept brutes, lacking the complex memory that enabled their distant wolf-kin to survive. Faced with quandary, they hesitated and looked for a second sure sign of danger, the hands. To them, the hand was an entity in itself, dealing food and pain. When the palm was down, its smell denied them, there was potential danger. These were turned up, empty and devoid of the fear smell.

Watching, part of his mind always on his own purposes, Ambrosius turned to the squat young aide beside him. "The odds are too long."

"I gave four to one."

"Pity. Even money."

"No."

"Watch."

Confused by a hundred hooting voices, the rattled hounds settled into a stiff-legged circling about the stone of Drust, the rumble in their throats a questioning sound now. They found no clear signals. If the creature bolted or attacked, they would tear its throat out. They relied mainly on smell, and this one confused them, rich with male and female alike, mingled with the trace of sheep and heath, all neutral to the dogs but compounding the enigma. Hackles high, one of the stiff-walking brutes minced forward, muzzle stretched out to sniff warily at the unmoving hand.

"Even money," Ambrosius said again. The boy was beautiful. Useful.

Confused by anomaly and shouting voices, the dogs gave it up. Their small concentration diffused, they snuffled about the earth of the pit for any sign to follow, finding old food traces and their own urine smell but nothing else. When they had quite forgotten Drust, he made his first sound, a low, reassuring whistle.

"Come, dog."

Their heads snapped about. One sure voice in so many without meaning. "Come, dog."

One of them lumbered back cautiously to sniff at the offered palm. Drust gave him ample time to read it all, then slid his fingers slowly over the muzzle to scratch behind the bitten ear. The dog tensed slightly, but no blow followed, only the soothing voice.

"Glory to God, Alleluia," Drust crooned to him.

Padrec felt his own naked awe. *I am a priest and my convert teaches me.*

Drust backed smoothly toward the gate. When the dogs growled, uncertain, he froze again, palms still extended. He laughed low in his throat as if he and the dogs shared a mournful joke. "Be still. Open the gate."

"I will say when it is over," Vaco called with poor grace. He was more than a little afraid. First the damned priest, now this weird boy. And was he not out the length of his wagers, to say nothing of presence lost? "It is not done yet."

"Nae, what more?" Drust's eyes came up to find Vaco, the only part of him that moved. "Dost nae feel the God of Daniel here? Must sing thy dogs asleep for thee?"

The Romans guffawed, knowing it was clearly over; even the village folk began to titter. Vaco read it all and made a poor attempt at not caring.

"Ah, well, then. It is only that I am bored with the small sport in it. Open the gate."

Drust was barely out the gate when Padrec smothered him in exultant arms, lifting him high like a loved child.

"I heard thee, brother. Glory, indeed! Glory to God, Alleluia!"

The rest was a blur of noise and movement: baffled dogs in the cage, challenging Rof for lack of anything else they could understand, Rof roaring back; skipping, yipping Guenloie, who couldn't kiss her husband often enough as Padrec led him to Dorelei and formal honor, shouldering through a tide of Prydn and Venicone fringed with amused but surprised Romans. Ambrosius nudged his stocky aide.

"Get my horse."

"Are we leaving?"

"No. Winning."

Ambrosius bounded from the mounting block into the saddle, sword aloft. "Prydn and Venicones! Here is the light of God, such men as Drust Dismas."

He kneed the horse through the crowd until he reached the dazzled boy. "Mark me all: if Venicones will not war for Christ, why not the very children of Christ? What says Drust Dismas?"

Drust tried to rouse out of a fog of triumph. "Would I . . . ?"

"What say the valiant men of Prydn? What answer from the child of Christ, brother to Daniel?"

The victory over Venicones was no more triumph to Drust than his own stunning, revealed power in Christ. As Daniel, he was touched by God, forever changed beyond that even Padrec could impart. He shot both hands aloft, crying to Prydn and Jesu in the affirmation he was born for. "Yah!"

"Yah, Prydn!"

As the cry went through the people, Bruidda pushed through the press to grip Dorelei's arm. "Stop this, girl. Be dangerous."

Dorelei shook her off. "And the hounds were not? How much magic must thee see to believe?"

"This be not magic."

"Make way for me, old woman." She worked her way to Drust, who yearned to her for vindication.

"Must go, Gern-y-fhain. With all my brothers and Padrec to lead. Salmon fhain be touched by God."

Touched by God . . . the words and the living proof of them swept through the Prydn men. Touched by God—they chanted it, jiggled and danced it in circles about the baiting pit and the silly, impotent dogs who leaped and snarled at the fervor beyond their jaws. Touched by God, and if the stamping, fevered men were not sure which god touched them, what matter? Bruidda might snap at them for fools, common sense might cool them later, but now they were inflamed. They danced and brandished their bows. The Roman masters of the earth had need of them, and all part of the new day come with iron magic. Fhains rode together and pastured where they pleased. The men of Prydn would earn men's honor under the Chi-Rho. The gerns dare not deny them. From this good fortune would come more sheep and child-wealth—*yah*!

If none of them could be sensible now, Padrec still worried. "Must think on this, Dorelei."

"Aye, must." But he saw the fever in his wife as well.

"Pride speaks now, but must think this out."

Yet even as he spoke caution, Padrec saw the Chi-Rho moving forward over the land of the Coritani, the green hills of Ireland in the distance, scholars with polished Latin writing his name in the annals of the Church. "We must be wise in this."

"Truly, husband." *But through me was the iron tamed and the fhains brought together. I feel a larger life in me than the wealth. There will be tale-speaking in the summer raths and winter crannogs, how the men went forth in tens and tens at the word of Dorelei Mabh.*

Almighty God, through whose only Son I hope to be saved . . .

Is this truly right for my folk? It is all so sudden. I only showed them Your magic, and their faith was enough to create more. If anyone is touched by God, as John in the wilderness, it is Drust. If anyone can inspire them, it is Dorelei. If any were born with souls shaped in the womb to Your will, the Prydn are. They are not fools, they would laugh at a tallfolk war, but that it is Yours as well, and being so, they will not be held back.

Their faith is frightening, so pure. How will that gold endure in a world of dross? They tell me to lead them—I who was never a soldier and sworn not to draw blood. Lord, I don't ask to know all, but fall as it will, let my folk have some good of this to their own. They live so much in an old world that this new one might easily swallow them. Drust, Artcois, Bredei, all the young men ready for this holy war like a bright-ribboned fair. They should have something of their own for it. My soul is an open hand to my Lord. Teach me Your will. Amen.

There was little official correspondence on the Coritani war, which was brief and historically minor. In his later years as archivist to Marchudd Rhys, Meganius noted that most of it ran from Ambrosius to the prince. Fitting; they were similar men, aggressive and brusquely competent, and even their courtesy tended to chill. Young Ambrosius was as self-possessed at twenty as the boy Caesar, his cursive style as angular and lean as the thinking behind it.

Drust Dismas now has as much presence as Dorelei or Patricius. By making much of him, I have set up a male pride against the matriarchy that guides them, but it is the young queen I must finally bargain with.

Of course, there were letters never attached to the court record, the property of Meganius himself, letters scratched out on the field, the voice of his own Sochet, clear as a bell but darkening through spring and summer from bright peal to funeral knell.

> Like Uriah the Hittite we are set in the forefront of every battle. We are the very point of the spear. The Chi-Rho goes ever before us....

And then later:

> It is hard to remember even the holiest purpose when you are hungry and wet. There is no rest but always another hill. God is with us, but we are so tired.

And the last letter, the very stylus strokes clumsy, stunned as the hand that dragged it over the smudged wax tablet.

> I have left no vow unbroken now. My marriage, if error, at least erred to the side of love, but not this. Why should I ask God to help me? He may not even exist. It is hard to write. I am wounded and in chains.

Meganius wrote to Auxerre at the end of it, informing Germanus that the reclaimed lands would support a new biscopric if a pallium could be sent. The clergy at Auxerre were puzzled (but relieved) that the heretic of Eburacum did not press for the inclusion of these new parishes in his own diocese. No matter; Germanus was only too quick to nominate.

> There lives in our grateful memory that S. Patricius, once our sturdy help on our late visit, whose strength and resolution in Christ shapes him admirably to the new See. We would know his mind in this.

Meganius carefully mislaid the letter. The mind of S. Patricius then was the last thing Germanus would want to know. One of the earlier letters, perhaps, from the spring, while the bell was still a peal, the men, horses and faith unworn.

> Never have I been so clearly set to God's work or given brothers whose Grace so far exceeds my own. This is, if any work ever, to be a war in the name of God. It is our destiny. It is mine.

V

Glory to God, Alleluia

J esu, I am Dorelei Mabh, first wife to Padrec Raven, who is known to You. The fhains follow me now, and I am a great queen. Shall I do this new thing never tried before? Shall I lift my hand like Mo-ses and send forth my Prydn against Egypt-fhain?

You have given us so much. Where tallfolk have only tale-speaking of Your magic, we have seen and done it. This is only right. We are Mother's first children and have kept magic from the first days.

As Lugh sent the Raven with Padrec, send me Your sign. I would do Your will in this new thing. And now there is one other matter.

Jesu, do not think me ungrateful after all Your gifts, if I speak to You of forgiveness, which is much of your teaching. Padrec has told of Judas and how he betrayed You. Do not think me ignorant; I am a gern and must know the way of the heart. Cru betrayed us, and we have all forgiven him, even Padrec whom he most wronged. Cru and I are as finger and thumb, made to touch, and I would have him home. If I can forgive my Judas, it is only fair and reasonable for You to forgive Yours. Look you, Cru struck out of pain because he could not understand a love too large to fit just him. Might not Judas have done as

much? Standing there with the knife in his hand, Cru was repen-tant
before Padrec's blood flowed. Poor Judas, then, with the mean silver
in his hand, and did he not feel much like Cru? What man hanged
Judas but himself?

Remember the lost lamb and the rejoicing when it was found.
Would do You no harm to think on it, Jesu, nor grudge that the
thought comes from a woman. You and Father-God are too unbending in
the matter of women. It is the only fault I find with you.

Beyond the moonlit circle of stones, Bruidda waited by her pony,
chosen out of respect by the other gerns to hear Dorelei's decision
and give what counsel the headstrong girl would accept. For all her
magic, Dorelei didn't listen well. Bruidda watched her in the circle and
pondered which was the greater cruelty: to be too old for the able
use of wisdom, or young with too much power, like an overfed child
that sickened on plenty even as it cried for more.

Dorelei's hand moved as if she were sowing seed, scattering the
offered stones. She had waited for the full moon, since it would be
unwise to make any important decision on the wane when Mother was
no better disposed than any other woman just before the flow of her
blood. Evil alone could be worked in the dark of the moon, and this
was to be a work for good.

Ia! Mother, hold Gawse in your bosom and guide her spirit to
Tir-Nan-Og. She is young forever now. Take her my greeting.

See my offering and know you are not forgotten in this new time. If
the men go forth for Jesu, it will not be until our wealth is born and
the new lambs dropped. If the Roman Ambrose cannot see that spring is
a time for increase, then Jesu must do without Prydn. As always, when
Lugh came to you in summer, our men came to us. We quickened and will
bear in spring as our flocks, and our men will be there to help, to see
life come forth and know it comes from you. Ambrose finds this hard to
understand. To him it is woman's business alone, but he is only
tallfolk.

Mother, I would do this new thing, not only for Jesu but for that
I or my daughter is the one promised by the black fawn to raise Prydn
to greatness, despite what Bruidda read in the signs. Such signs
have been unclear before, and Bruidda has old bitterness like cataracts to cloud her sight. Let me be wise and strong before her, as
Gawse was.

And for Cruaddan, first husband, let Lugh ride his arrows. Let
your breast whisper to his foot as he walks and turn it home again. I

would say this to no other woman, not even Neniahe. I wronged Cru before he ever struck at Padrec. There are more sins than those second husband speaks of. I love Padrec, but there is a place in my heart like a barrow.

Dorelei saw the figure by the pony, the gold of the torc flashing cold with moonlight, the ruby pendant and bracelets that shimmered when Bruidda moved.

"Dorelei Mabh, thy sisters would speak through me."

Dorelei might have squatted with the other woman, but her belly made it hard now to sink into the position of rest. She remained standing before her sister gern. Neither of them hurried to speak. Bruidda would meditate first on Mother's mooneye to add wisdom to her words. Eventually Bruidda asked, "Thee will rade for Jesu?"

"If a send no sign against it. Be in my heart."

"And in our men. Thy Drust be like Raven now, like a god."

And so Salmon fhain grew in presence. Dorelei kept silent, making the older woman reach out.

"Sister, let us be plain," Bruidda said. "This new fever be a man-thing. A see the power thee gives Padrec Raven and be like Lugh breaking free of Mother."

"Will go when I say."

"Be patient and hear, Dorelei. Real power be always patient." Bruidda rubbed at the scars on her arms. "Roman-men have much of patience and more of wile."

"A's wisdom be small beside Prydn."

"As bee's sting, yet may thee feel it. And our men fall over themselves to fight a tallfolk war."

"For Jesu. Dost nae see the power we have now?"

Bruidda chose her words carefully. "Do speak of power. Thee hast it now, even that which should be carried by thy sisters. Remember in this power that Mother's world has many tallfolk and few Prydn. What little Prydn did get from them, did shrewdly bargain for."

"Ai, Bruidda, speak thy mind." Despite her courteous intentions, Dorelei was wearied with the weight of the child in her that made riding difficult now and her walk like a silly goose in a pen. She yearned to lie on her side with Padrec's arms and voice to lull her to sleep.

"Tir-Nan-Og be nae here, child, and the Green Time will nae come again."

The woman wasted her time. "Mother told thee this?"

In the darkness she missed the subtle softening of Bruidda's mouth. "Nae, bairn. The cold in my bones a-winter. But hear thy sisters:

thee scatters Rainbow-gift like sand among tallfolk. Cannae always be generous and wise in one day. If thee send our men with Ambrose, get a price in return. A *braw* price, Dorelei. For the days of thy wealth."

That was wisdom. Dorelei thought much on it. Bruidda and her sister gerns, backward in some ways, were still women of experience, pondering consequences while the young men dashed about on their ponies and gabbled of nothing but the adventure, even in bed, which was a place and time for better things. But tallfolk had been known to give short weight in bargaining. Dorelei lay awake with her back curved into the warmth of Padrec and pressed his hand to her stomach. "Husband?"

He nuzzled the nape of her neck. "Mm?"

"This rade: we can give a to Jesu and ask only a's blessing."

"Truly."

"But from Ambrose and the tallfolk prince, we must have a bargain."

"Was in my mind too, and wise. Marchudd will pay. A has money and cattle. What will thee ask?"

The child in Dorelei stirred many new instincts. Things once trivial or totally alien became important. Money and cattle were not the coin of these promptings. Dorelei was a little awed by the reach of her thoughts.

Roman-men have land without reckoning, from Wall to Middle Sea. If Dronnarron will not come again, we could make our own for the days of our children. Then they could stand at a locked gate and say who entered and who did not.

Frightening even to think it, so big. None among Prydn had done it, not even Mabh. But iron-magic was once a locked gate that opened before her like Jericho. They would have a place....

I couldn't say [Ambrosius wrote to Marchudd] whether one bears a Faerie child or simply drops it like a sheep, but we must wait for both if we want the Prydn archers, which means spring at the earliest. That was my estimate in any case, since VI Legio will not be ready to march before then.... S. Patricius has presented his wife's price for their men. Not gold or cattle, but land within Parisi holding and granted in perpetuity by treaty or patent. You must deal with this as you will, but they are quite serious. Land for service.

... as if she were Mother herself, earth itself heaving in its deep recesses to loose this force into the world. Dorelei bit hard on the cloth and pushed when Neniane told her to. Poor Padrec looked

182

white. For all his magic, he wasn't used to this greater wonder. His kind made much of the end of life but waited outside at the beginning.

The pains were so close together they seemed one. Padrec's fingertips were dark red from her grip. She must bear live wealth. Neniane and Guenloie had already brought their daughters to fhain, the good milk spilled from their breasts. She must do this. She must push. Yet it was like pulling on a giant bowstring of earth. Pulling like Cru, drawing the arrow to the head, aiming life at a world not left to tallfolk alone.

"Now, sister. Do have a's head free. Now."

Cru . . .

She loosed the arrow.

Guenloie took the bitten cloth from her mouth and swabbed her face as Neniane deftly handled the aftermath of birth. She cut the birthstring and laid it by the fire to dry. Guenloie had willowbark tea ready to rout any lingering pain and clean water to wash Dorelei's body. The birthstring must be blessed by Padrec. This was the strongest magic for the child in the first perilous year of its life. Padrec was barely listening or coherent. Yes . . . of course, he would bless it, anything. He saw only the exhausted face on the pillow, the lips that barely opened to call him.

"Padrec . . ."

He took the cooling cloth and pressed it to her cheeks. "Be alive and whole, sweet."

"First daughter?"

"A Prydn man."

"Oh . . . did thee sicken?"

"A little. Be strange but a wonder as well. Here." He coaxed more tea to her a sip at a time. "A wonder. Why do women hide such miracles from men, such strength?"

She passed a limp hand over his cheek. "What man be brave as my husband? Thee sees now how quick life comes."

"Quick? Seemed hours. Here, drink more."

Wan herself, she tried to smile. "Thee looks pale."

"Nae, but . . . there was a man, a priest like me. I dedicated myself to him once. He called the organs of life the center of all evil. '*Ecce unde!*' he said. 'That's the evil spot.' And I believed him."

"Dost seem a troubled man."

"Yes. Here, drink more while's hot."

"Nae."

"Come. Drink it." He put his lips to her sweaty cheek. "Let me bully you this once. Come, now."

The tea worked with her exhaustion to dull the pain of being

183

stretched farther apart than she ever thought possible. "In three days, if a takes good suck and thrives, thee will christen my son as Crulegh."

He wouldn't let Dorelei see his disappointment. After Cru, then. Not him. "And what in Christ?"

"Padrec. Crulegh Padrec."

"Must be holy. Mine be just a name."

She lay with her eyes closed, thinking on it. "Mo-ses."

"No, Dorelei. You see—"

"Father-God spoke to Mo-ses as to Paul."

"Paul would be better. Moses be from Hebrew-fhain."

"What difference? Did hear the same voice. Mo-ses." His silly differences were lost on her. She would have no other name. Padrec said it meant "from the rushes," which grew at the edge of water. If Crulegh was not the promised bright daughter from the sea, he would be close. "Have dreamed of water, Padrec. A great, crashing world of water."

Crulegh took to the nipple like Cruaddan to the bow, a messy but efficient engine of digestion. Padrec was concerned for Dorelei, worse than an old woman at it in some ways, the more because no one else seemed to regard the gern as fragile. They all thought it quite proper when she rose within hours of her labor, while Neniane nursed the infant for his first feeding. Padrec's male protectiveness was outraged.

"Go back to bed at once."

"Why?"

"*Damn* it, woman, you need to. Why, a woman at home would—"

"Tallfolk women be soft." Dorelei dismissed them with audible contempt. She must be up, and there an end. Soon they would move to new pasture. With the young men gone to holy war, there would be more work for the rest. She must be strong enough to ride. Child must toughen through spring and summer to survive the autumn rade and the winter again. For all their Rainbow-gift and iron-magic, there were things Prydn could never afford, and frailty among them.

"Be time, Padrec. Take my child and let Jesu hear a's name."

"The wind still draws a knife across Cnoch-nan-ainneal. Can do it here by the hearth."

"No." Dorelei wouldn't consider it. "Will be cold on rade. Bairn must learn it now."

Padrec wrapped himself and the bairn in Cru's big cloak, and Dorelei put on her new one bought from the Venicones. Together they left the crannog and went to Malgon's tempering trough. The few people about the ridge saddle made way for them, as they were on solemn business. About and below them, the bright rath-tents were being struck, the sheep being counted and culled of the sick. Weak or deformed lambs would be butchered for eating now and salting for the rade. Far down in the meadow, the stallions kept jealous watch over their mares. Padrec dipped a bowl into the trough and consecrated the water. He pushed back the heavy folds of the cloak to expose the tiny forehead, still soft and misshapen from its passage into life. Padrec touched a finger to the fine dark fuzz that would grow someday to black silk like Cru's.

Ave, my son, as well you may be. I don't know exactly what day you were born. I am forgetting my kalends. No matter. We Prydn go by our own signs. Look, son: the hazel and alder are in bloom. The kestrel flies north again, and Tod-Lowery cries for his vixen. These are your kalends. They tell you to ride as I must.

Padrec dipped two fingers in the bowl and signed the Chi-Rho on the tiny brow. "In the name of the Father, the Son, and of the Holy Ghost, I christen thee Crulegh Moses. Thy sins this water washes away as Christ took upon himself those of mankind. And no iron shall have power over thee."

Crulegh. Small Cru, it meant. He could be Cru's son; there was nothing of himself that Padrec could see, and he'd certainly searched, worked at it. The baptism was done. For the moment, Padrec ignored the cold wind and the uncertain future.

You are God's for all time. For this one moment be mine. I loved your mother. Let me think you are the bright piece of forever we made between us. I have preached of miracles, but you are the meaning. I've prattled of love and know now it was only a word, only a sound. I have read of God's only begotten Son until the phrase blurred in my soul's sight. Until now. To think of it: if God is love, then He felt this pang of mine so much more keenly, sending His Son, a little thing like you, to begin that short, sad journey in a byre, to trust such a tiny spark in so miserable a place. Did He look down as I do now, wondering and exalted and terrified, and feel unready for it, as I do? Jesu was part of Him, *was* Him, and yet—I can see how He must have missed the boy sometimes. Could he inspire the passion and anguish of the Psalms and not feel this? Yes, God must have loved the world very much.

"Padrec?"

Dorelei had to call him twice. He placed the swaddled child in her arms. "Done. Take thy wealth to crannog."

"And thee?"

"Would be alone." He said it too gruffly, eyes averted. "Please."

She understood. He never asked as Cru did and yet must be asking in silence every day with every sight of the child. There were times when even a gern should simply shut up and be a wife. She walked back toward the crannog, jiggling the baby with a fierce tenderness.

"Ai, sweet. Ai, Crulegh. Thee will marry sister's wealth and be a braw man."

Neniane's daughter had been named Morgana Mary for the prophecy. Bruidda might curl her lip at the presumption, but there was nothing amiss in helping along what was to come. And Guenloie's child had been named for Bruidda, so the woman had really nothing to complain of.

Under a light spring drizzle that brought all the rich smells of the heath to life, the milling Prydn gradually separated into two groups— the women, children, and older men with the wet and ill-tempered sheep, and the young men prancing their ponies about, supposed to form a military line behind Padrec and absolutely no notion of how to go about anything so regular.

Watching them from his stockade walls, Elder Vaco felt enormously relieved to be rid of Romans and Faerie alike. "True it is, brothers, that it is almost worth eating the body and blood of this peculiar Jesu to be quit of his priest."

The parting threatened to evolve into reunion as wives ran back to husbands to hold up their children for one more kiss good-bye. Padrec twisted about in the saddle, searching for Drust and Malgon, who were in place not a moment ago. Then out of the chattering press, Drust emerged with Guenloie in one arm and little Bruidda curled in the other. He kissed the child once more, tucked it in Guenloie's hip sling, caught her in a last crushing embrace, then stood aside for Malgon to make his (absolutely) last farewells.

"Drust, Malgon. Come. We must start."

Fine intentions, but then didn't Dorelei dart forward with Neniane close behind, to tug at Padrec's leg. "Down, husband." And he had to dismount again to kiss her face and rain-straggled hair and not show how hard she made leaving. Her mouth crushed to his.

That was the best of us, Padrec remembered later. He must have said something then but couldn't bring it to mind an hour later. Those gone from Faerie-land said they wandered outside of time itself and never found their way back. *None of us did*. He remembered his heart squeezed tight with feelings that turned meaning to mumble. The Prydn word for love was old as Mabh, beggaring attempts like *amor*.

"In my knowing of thee," Dorelei's lips murmured against his. "Will be empty, will be filled with thee. Jesu and Mother bless thee, Padrec."

Drust set the tall Chi-Rho in its socket. Padrec raised his sword. "God's benison on our holy cause. One fhain in Christ, one rade in God! To Eburacum!"

Corus had never seen northern tribesmen before. The novelty appalled. He did not even ask their business at the gate, just ran to summon the bishop. Meganius had just stepped out onto the portico when one of them came down the walk with a lithe stride. A Pict by the look of him, dark with sunburn and dirt but jangling with a fortune in jewelry, red hair caught in a headband from which dangled the pinion feather of a raven's wing. Meganius stopped dead in astonished recognition.

"Sochet!"

His surprise momentarily forgot its Latin. He hurried forward to embrace the young man in an effusion of Brigante. "Magon Sochet! Good Jesus God, boy, and look at you! I didn't know you, and yourself half dirt and the rest finery. Dyw, lad—if this were Babylon, I'd think you a graven idol."

The grimy, gaudy apparition knelt to kiss his ring. "Ave, your grace."

"I am very glad to see my priest, Father Patricius." The young man who rose before Meganius was a year older and somehow physically different. Stronger, stiller, more concentrated. "So. These are the . . . Prydn?"

"I've brought them to Christ as you bade me."

"By a debatable route, perhaps."

More than strength, a new ease. The laugh betrayed it. "Your grace means my marriage."

"But brought nonetheless. Corus, bring us drink. What news, Sochet? You've seen the prince?"

"And have his promise of land for service. That's his word. And with my folk, a word is a contract."

Privately Meganius hoped it was so with Marchudd. He steered the conversation elsewhere and his priest toward a nearby garden bench, amused when Padrec ignored it at first and squatted out of habit like the small men waiting near the gate. "No, sit here by me, Sochet. Good Lord, and aren't you a sight! I hope you wore canonicals to the palace."

"My last canonicals went to line a cradle." Padrec settled himself on the bench. "Not very practical up there."

187

"And when do you march?"

"Perhaps tomorrow; soon, at any rate. Ambrosius is snapping at his officers to be ready."

"And you are his archers?"

"And his cavalry. All he's got, so it appears. We receive our orders today."

"I see." Meganius did. He might never look on Patricius again. "You'll want confession then."

"Yes, I suppose. Though it won't be much."

"After a year and more? There's arrogance, boy."

"Is it, your grace?" Padrec smiled across the atrium at his brothers. They were following intently the movements of the bishop's peacocks, having never seen one before. How dost fly and why dost cry so mournful with such beauty on's back?

"Would it be confession?" Padrec posed the question out of the serenity that covered him like a cloak. "There's more broken vows in me than a brothel, and I've never felt happier or closer to God."

"To God, Sochet, or merely a man's acceptance of himself?"

"I've considered that too. I've a wife. I may have a son."

"May? Preserve us!"

"One can't be sure, and one doesn't ask. It's a matter of good manners. The only thing I could confess now is joy and pride. How strange it is to err in love and through an error to find the right. To find how much I love *them*. The truants return to Eden. Their sins are like tiny flecks of dust on God's notion of perfect. One flick of His finger and they shine again. Suffice to say," Padrec admitted with a sidelong glance, "I am no longer quite an Augustinian."

The bishop shrugged. "I cannot grieve for that."

"Rome can haggle the boundaries of Grace, but these people . . ." Padrec lifted his head to the waiting men. "You should know them, your grace. They are a definition of faith in themselves, perhaps one forgotten since Peter."

"Oh, Sochet." Meganius tried to mask the sorrow in his sigh.

"No, hear me. I've learned a deal since I brayed damnation at your parishioners. Do you recall the Gospel of Mary?"

The bishop knew it better than Padrec: no longer included in Canon, but a cryptic and troubling testament to many literate clerics like himself.

"There is more spiritual power in women than men will acknowledge, Caius Meganius. And more in men than the Church remembers. My people *live* that power. It's like apotheosis."

Meganius felt constricted by his learning and urbanity. He knew Marchudd and Ambrosius to their hard core and how these Faerie, unworldly as their priest, came to squat at his gate. He was grateful when Corus appeared with their refreshment.

"Did you urge them to this war, Patricius?"

"Not I. They couldn't be stopped once Ambrosius asked."

"Ah, I see."

"And I must lead them. They'd follow no one else." Padrec laughed suddenly, a clear, free sound. "Can you imagine me as Hannibal?"

"Oh, quite. If you can refrain from preaching to the elephants." The bishop tried to sound cheerful. In that the Word would spread to pagans, the war was holy. This he could not deny—nor a small, clammy wish that Ambrosius would not sleep too well henceforth. The holiest aspect of the war was sitting here on his bench. "Some wine?"

Corus served them and hovered in the background. "Did your grace wish something from the kitchen? There are pastries just out of the oven."

"No, but wrap some for Father Patricius and his men. And bring me the box from the table in my closet. I want you to write to me, Sochet. As often as possible."

"Surely, if there's that to write on."

"I have a gift for you."

The bishop's gift was a birchwood writing case with six new wax tablets and a good stylus. Padrec's fingers caressed the treasure. "Do you know how rare such things are north of the Wall?"

"I didn't know when you would come but bought it anyway. As much a request as a gift. Write to me. It is Church privilege. The post riders will bring them straight to me, unopened. Well. I send John into the wilderness and he comes back Joshua. Write to me, Sochet."

And care for him, my dear Lord. Such men must always drink too deep. Drunk with You and now with life, which he has found rich in his path. I imagine he came to the woman as to faith, like a child astonished by joy, and no hair shirt in his pack. I saw the taste for life in him the first day he came. Do not grudge him the woman or the happiness, Lord. What holiness he's found, there will be none in this business. Take care of him.

"If your bishop asked you ... if I excused you by clerical privilege from this?"

"Nonsense." There was something definitely patronizing in the way Padrec patted the old man's hand. "They'd drag me anyway, Drust and the rest. Didn't I say they are a definition of faith?"

Padrec sprang up from the bench like a child bidden be quiet too long and now released, holding his gift high. "Yah! See! Father-Raven sends us gifts from Jesu to go with us. Come bless them, your grace. I am a magician to them and you the father-raven who sent me." He hauled the old bishop to his feet, gentle but not to be denied.

"And if they offer you gold, take it for the poor. They are more than Christians, they are Galileans."

With urgent respect, the young man propelled Meganius down the atrium walk, calling to his brothers.

The drilling centuries wheeled back and forth, splashing through shallow puddles of last night's rain. Along one edge of the bald quadrangle, the wagons lumbered into line, filled with supplies. Stone slingers carried bundles of arrows and pilums to be tallied before inclusion on the vehicles. Over it all, centurions bawled orders and curses to hurry them to completion before sundown, while the mounted tribunes dashed here and there like Rof on a busy day.

Padrec and his Prydn were bunched in a corner of the quadrangle, the men in the rear spilling up onto a sodded bank. Padrec stood before them with a sharp stick and three empty wine jugs. With these he would draw them an image of their part in the war. A crucial part; with the exception of a few messengers and wagoneers, they were the entire cavalry of VI Legio, one hundred eighty men divided into three small squadrons of sixty each. There was no usual complement of stablers or blacksmiths. The alae were to be light, totally self-contained, modeled on the Goth horsemen but more disciplined.

To be sure, VI Legio itself was a reconstruction. The original force was twenty years lost and gone in Gaul. This was whatever Marchudd's father had been able to scrape from the barrel bottom, pat into shape, and pass on to his son. Very few were soldiers in the old sense, none had the old legionary spirit that simply fell in and marched on order for its allotted twenty years before settling down to a government bounty, house, and plot of land. These men had never fought and hated the idea of leaving comfortable homes in safe Eburacum. They were led by officers like Gallius Urbi, who grudged the time to cram themselves into harness and drill infrequently on the quadrangle. Now suddenly it was all too real. Holy, justified, or gilded, they were going to war, and people died in wars; going now when Ambrosius must have known they weren't ready. Padrec grasped that much from the meeting at the palace. With Malgon as his lieutenant, he'd stood in the forum and listened to Ambrosius. The tribune had strong ideas about cavalry that none of the other officers understood, let alone agreed with. A great deal of responsibility fell to the Prydn in this campaign. They were attached to the First Maniple commanded by Gallius Urbi, a first centurion who didn't like the idea at all. Was it the tribune's command?

Ambrosius squared him off. "It is. You are the leading maniple of

190

foot. They are the point. In supply and quartering, they are to have the best and the first."

In practice they got the worst and the last, though that was the least of their problems. Standing before his men, Padrec tried not to shade them with his own dissatisfaction. Some were as young as fifteen, none over twenty, waiting and trusting to him in the gray afternoon.

"Was a braw speaking at the great rath," he began heartily. "Mark the manner of it." He tried to make them laugh as they learned, mimicking the iron stance of Ambrosius, spear-straight and no nonsense. *I will make this body of horsemen into something new.* Step, step. Halt. Sharp pivot. *There will be a number of army horses assigned to you.*

"And must be returned," Padrec cautioned.

"If a do not first get lost," Malgon amended.

A few only for scouting. Patricius, you will impress on your men that scouts will never engage. Step, step. *They will observe and, by Mithras, get back with the information. Now. Weapons.*

"See!" Padrec held up the army arrow with its well-fletched feathers, tooled shaft, and triangular head. "Better than at home. Will be a wonder with Prydn bows. This spear be called pilum." He hefted the balanced spear that ended in a two-foot iron rod and standard triangular head. "Each man will have to his saddle as many as a can carry."

If you were fighting in flat country, I'd remount the lot of you. But your own ponies are better for the hills.

"So thee will most times ride a friend," Padrec assured them. "Now, the words of Prince Marchudd-Rhys." Abruptly his pacing became more agitated, lunging.

Land, you say? Land where? How much does she want? Well, it doesn't matter now, with a hundred other things . . . wish you'd brought it up some other time. Yes, yes, there will be a patent of land. I can't say where just now, really. I must get on to the matter of supply.

"Be a's word," Padrec told them. "As we be Christian, we live by the given Word. For this land-gift, now learn our task. Come closer."

Padrec drew a wavering line in the muddy earth and another three paces away, roughly parallel to it. Between these he placed the three wine jugs in a wide triangle.

The first line was the River Wye, which they must cross. There was a bridge, but they must assume it destroyed. Ambrose must know for certain, the first job of the scouts. Once across Wye they would not make war on each settlement of Coritani but take and hold the three jug-forts between Wye and Churnet. With this strategic wedge deep in his holding, Rhiwallon, prince of the Coritani, would come to terms and his people to Christ.

"Now—here be the hard part, brothers."

The old tribal forts, no more than circular earthworks, were to be modernized and rendered impregnable. Circumvallations were to be dug around them. Committed to this work, the engineers would be vulnerable to attack. The Prydn would defend them, mounted or afoot.

There was only one comment on that, from Bredei. "Who takes this great hill so diggers can dig?"

"We do." Padrec added quickly that they would be followed in by foot troops after the mounted assault to deliver a second blow on top of the first. The Prydn stared at the picture-war on the ground. They were mountain men and knew what mountain ponies could do. They would be the first blow, moving uphill with no protection but speed. Most of them did not think in words but saw the problem in terms of success, no matter how difficult. Their word was given to Padrec and Christ. They didn't know or care that they were an experiment, but they proved its exact worth with no uncertainty. As Ambrosius later acknowledged in a classic of understatement, all new ideas need refinement.

Padrec and Malgon sat their mounts at the top of the last hill before River Wye. They could expect to engage Coritani at any time now. Padrec hadn't expected to find the bridge intact, but there it was. Mere ants in the distance, two scouts from Hawk fhain nosed the approaches to the bridge, crossed it, and dismounted on the other side.

Padrec's stomach felt queasy leading men in an enterprise so foreign to him. Not much consolation that officers like Gallius were no more seasoned beyond the drill ground. He would lose lives from now on and feel each loss like a blow.

Malgon munched currants from a cloth bag, offered some to Padrec, and bent forward over his pony's mane to feed him a treat. Below them on the road leading to the bridge, the long worm of Gallius's maniple inched toward their hill.

"They're coming back, Mal."

Their scouts wheeled the big army horses and cantered across the bridge, stretching out into a gallop when they cleared it, making straight for the hill. Good that the bridge was whole. Gallius was bad-tempered enough and never subtle in his contempt for Faerie, who got the oldest and leakiest tents in any camp they pitched. For rations, what was left over from the other mess units. Padrec wondered why Ambrosius served them this way after such hearty promises.

192

The scouts worked their long-legged mounts up the slope, riding like small monkeys high on the animals' necks, clattering up to Padrec and pointing back at the bridge. Coritani had been there not long ago. Many tracks, both sides of the river.

"How long?"

In their own terms, the scouts knew exactly how long, but it was still hard to think in the Roman way of time. They pointed to the sun and then to the east: about three hours, a large mounted force had come to the river. Some had turned south again, others crossed to this side and veered northwest.

"Braw work, brothers." Padrec brought the black's head around. "Now we go home."

Until the bridge was secured, First Centurion Gallius Urbi's mission was specifically scouting. The annoying priest had brought him good news for a change. A number of points along Wye were fordable, but if they were attacked in the middle of the stream, they were helpless.

"Intact, you say?"

"Yes, but they've been there today in some force. I'd say we were expected."

Gallius glared at him. The centurion was one of those florid, tallish men, once in fine condition, who'd gone to fat concentrated all in his stomach, an incongruous paunch. His bullhide breastplate had to be specially shaped. It helped him to be a little more imposing.

"Anything else?"

One of the scouts mumbled rapidly to Padrec, who translated. "There's probably a goodish force of them this side of Wye now."

"Can't these ignorant mules learn enough Brit to speak for themselves?"

"They are learning. It is much easier than their own language. Orders?"

"They'll be coming. That's all for now. And take your . . . flock with you."

It was the midday halt. Gallius received the report sitting in the shade of a tree while his meal cooled, barely tasted. He had more problems on his mind than the priest and his monkey-squadrons. Into his fortieth year, Gallius suffered from chronic indigestion. The potbelly was a cathedral for suffering that dampened good humor even when he felt disposed to it.

He prospered as a seller of foodstuffs, building the business from a failed stall owned by his father-in-law to a white-plastered edifice of respectable proportions in Eburacum's marketplace, with a mosaic sign of his trade set into the paving before the door. Would that satisfy his miserable wife? Did she appreciate the comfortable life he gave her by being shrewd at trade, an acumen bordering on banditry and, on occasion, crossing over? No, it did not. The woman and he tolerated each other like oxen mired together in a peat bog, merely used to each other's proximity. He didn't like her much or their three screeching children, who were more energetic in filching from the store than working in it. Both he and his wife were relieved at the mobilization. Gallius wasn't at all sure of himself as a commander, but at least it got him away from her for a while, not to mention he'd go back with a tidy profit, but let that pass. Gallius wanted the leading maniple. There was prestige in it beside the money. He wanted to return to Eburacum with honor, something that, if meaningless to his dull wife, was at least a part of him she couldn't get at. *It was at the River Wye, nothing in front of me but the enemy and a bunch of scouts I couldn't trust. Ambrosius was miles behind. The decision was mine, and I made it.*

The decision was his. He made it. Gallius called for a tablet and a messenger.

Wye bridge intact. Will cross and secure/G. Urbi

The message reached Ambrosius at almost the moment the leading maniple halted at the bridge, the worst news of a bad day. Ambrosius sent the messenger flying back: on no circumstances would Gallius cross until the main body came up and the bridge was thoroughly inspected. The tribune forked his own horse from a dead run and galloped back along sweating ranks to hurry his officers.

Not half an hour before, a horde of naked, screaming Coritani horsemen had dashed down on them to hurl spears and arrows, sweeping away unscathed. The casualties were light, mostly inexperienced troops who panicked when there was no need. The shaken men had to be pushed on. Gallius was green as the rest. He could panic and be cut off very easily. Ambrosius tore off his gold-plumed helmet and plowed agitated fingers through his hair.

"He had no orders to cross. The bloody fool was told to scout. The alae are forward. In other words, no one up there who knows what he's doing." He settled his helmet with a fatalistic tug. "Hurry them on. Run them."

A small square stone set at one end of the bridge claimed it as the work of VI Legio only five years since. The clayed wicker of its surface was underlain by sturdy logs. On the downstream side, flying struts reinforced the structure against the current. Upstream, triangular break-waters of three timbers each pushed the flow to either side of the supporting posts, minimizing stress overall. Padrec admired it as he waited with Malgon for Gallius' order to cross.

194

The first centurion walked his horse away from the ranks of foot to rein up at Padrec's knee, shielding his eyes against the sun's glare. There was very little level ground on the other side; the hill slope began almost immediately.

"We'll set up the bridgehead right away," he ordered, not referring to Padrec by name, which he did as seldom as possible. "You and your Faerie get across, scouts first. Establish a perimeter with one base there on the bank." He described a semicircle. "To about there upstream. Center point out there where the hill begins. When you're in place, the foot will cross."

Absorbed in his first tactical problem, Padrec answered casually, "Yah."

"The word is *sir*," said Gallius belligerently. "And didn't anyone teach you to salute?"

"No. Sir. Nor that nor Roman gear nor decent quarters or mess. Perhaps when there's time we can address those questions."

Gallius' florid complexion deepened a shade. "Get across that bridge."

"Delighted, sir." Padrec swooped a broad approximation of a salute and trotted away to his squadrons. "Scouts out. Squadrons by twos."

In the trees overlooking the slope, Rhiwallon, prince of the Coritani, lay behind a fallen log, digging a silver spoon into a bowl of cold porridge and eating with relish as he watched the horsemen flow onto the bridge. So it was true: Marchudd was using Faerie. Good horsemen armed with bows. Not "squared off" like the rest of the filthy legion, they had no more sense of straight lines than his own men. The scouts crossed, then the first squadron straggled after. They began to take up a ragged arc about the bridge.

And the dear bridge could go at any time, with every supporting timber sawn half through just below the waterline. *Dyw*, wouldn't that be a lovely sight, the bridge and every man on it sinking like the sun in the west, like Rome itself.

"But not yet," Rhiwallon prayed. "A few more fish in the net, and then . . ."

Rhiwallon's people had been only nominally subjugated by Rome. Little of the culture rubbed off. Not a barbarian, he still believed in government by force, tribute in cattle. What he took was absorbed by his chieftains, but Marchudd Rhys was not going to reclaim cattle or territory allotted him by Roman decree when the ancient rights were clearly Coritani.

The prince offered his porridge to the small boy beside him, ruffling the child's long red hair in good humor to ease his tension. "Hungry, Cadwal?"

"No, Father."

"Mind, when I say move back, there'll be no argument from you. Out of trouble. There will be time later for you to be brave. Years."

But for now, although he wouldn't say it, it was good to have the boy with him, to show him what he must do someday and a look at this joke of a legion. Rhiwallon glanced back into the trees to the men waiting at their horse's heads. The day was warm. Most of them were naked except for sword and shield. Cadwal tugged at his father's sleeve.

"Look."

The Faerie were in place now, the foot troops squaring off their ranks into columns of five abreast to cross the bridge. That was less interesting to Rhiwallon than the two riders who walked their mounts back and forth in front of the perimeter line. The red-haired man on the big army black: that would be the priest said to lead them. But the other . . .

"Does he not have a notion now? That one's Faerie, Cadwal, one of the little folk. You won't see men or ponies like that this far south, not every day." He studied the small figure. A smile played about Rhiwallon's mouth. "And if I've the kenning my good mother gave me, the wee man's no fool."

Not ordered, but Malgon wanted to see the woods at the crest of the hill. All the Prydn were on this side of the great bridge now. With Padrec's permission, he started up the slope, waving the two scouts from Hawk fhain to join him.

"Will see the woods, an be clear of tallfolk."

"An be not?"

Malgon looked at them. "Hawk rides the wind and knows its taste. What says thy heart?"

"Not."

"Would know." Malgon urged his pony forward. "Come."

He threw one more glance back at the bridge. The first foot ranks were stumping across, square as a tallfolk box, pilums all at the same angle, like grass bent in a hard wind.

He and the scouts moved up the slope, fanning apart. Malgon's mouth felt dry and his stomach fluttery. He needed to relieve himself when he just had. He must keep his concentration on the woods, but some went to quiet his fear. He thought of Guenloie and the sweetness of her in their last loving. It was the first since her daughter was born, and Malgon burst almost as soon as he entered her. But the power returned quickly, and the second time was long and rich. Her skin felt like cleansing water as it brushed and crushed against his. She drew the long, heavy need from him, brought him balm, and he wished he could speak it in words like Drust. . . .

Almost there. No movement in the trees, not even birds. There should be birds. His pony worked effortlessly up the slope. Malgon felt his skin go clammy. *Should be birds.* He should hear or see them this close.

He drew up a few yards from the tree line. Somehow he found it difficult to breathe deeply. The pony snorted its own question, and then Malgon smelled the foreign horse-scent. There were men and horses in the wood, or lately had been. Which was it?

He kneed the pony forward, bent low over its neck. To either side, the scouts followed him. They were at the trees now. The hard knot in Malgon's gut swelled like a pig bladder, stretched tight—and exploded in a searing wave. The command that twisted the reins was a silent voice. The image of Gern-y-fhain flashed clear in his mind, arms up, warning him back. Malgon cringed into the pony's shoulder, part of it. He wheeled the animal about and kicked it into a flat run down the slope, the scouts dashing after.

Behind their covering log, the boy Cadwal turned wide-eyed to his father. "How did they know?"

"Because they are as much animal as the pony. And the rest is boucca-spirit." Rhiwallon watched the retreating figures with sour admiration. Agile as cats, they slid from one side to the other in the saddle, zigzagging to make harder targets, keeping the horse's body between them and the Coritani.

Clinging to his pony's shoulder, pounding down toward Padrec, Malgon heard the sound he couldn't identify at first. Out of range of the hilltop now, he hauled erect in the saddle to see the bridge alive with men from end to end, pouring onto and off of it, then—

"Ai, Jesu!"

The sound grew louder, drew out, ripping and splintering. The ranks on the bridge swayed in a brief, grotesque dance as the whole structure tilted and slid over to the downstream side in a surging stew of timber, spears, shields, and floundering men.

And high above it all, Rhiwallon hummed as he stroked his long moustaches. "Is it not a dear sight, son? Just lovely." His arm swept forward and the Coritani horsemen boiled over the hill, through the last of the trees, and down the slope.

Under his natural flush, Gallius Urbi went pale and froze for an instant, seeing that force coming down at him, then roused, whirling about to his men.

"In ranks! Shields up!"

197

Padrec himself surrendered an instant to terror before instinct propelled him to safety behind the line of archers. Less than two centuries had cleared the bridge. A few men were safe but astonished on the other side, the rest washed downstream, clutching at each other or fragments of wreckage, whatever would keep them afloat in their heavy gear. Malgon whacked his pony on the rump, sending it toward safety, then ran for the archers, who were beginning to shoot raggedly into the charging horsemen. Padrec found a hoarse quaver for a voice.

"That's it. Keep shooting. Keep shooting!"

He stumbled to Malgon. "Together, Mal. Tell them to loose all together on your signal. That's all will stop them."

Malgon ran forward of the archers, sword held high. "Ai! Brothers!"

The flight loosed with the sound of a million maddened bees. Atop the hill, Rhiwallon almost lost his porridge at the sight. The men who rarely missed hawk, fox, or squirrel had much larger targets here. Rhiwallon swallowed hard. The leading edge of his charge lurched, buckled, and simply folded under the next as it ran over them with no time to veer aside. Even as it happened, another flight was drawn and loosed. But his men pushed on. The first of them crashed through Padrec's unprotected men, the naked riders flailing viciously with sword or clubs before they were unhorsed or scampered away. The archers, wherever hit, were simply run underfoot and lay where they fell. *Helpless*, Padrec cursed, running toward his last sight of Malgon. *Where're my people? Oh, God, I'm frightened.*

Someone was screaming at him; dimly he recognized Gallius' voice; then a tattooed rider plunged directly at him. Padrec leaped aside, and the man drove on. He'd not even drawn his sword, not that he could use it. *How many dear men out there, still shooting, and won't they be trampled?*

"Spears, Padrec!" The small, strong hand spun him about to Malgon's grimace. "Spears!"

The whirlwind of horsemen swept back up the slope, managing shields nimbly against the hail of arrows, waiting for stragglers before rushing in again. Malgon and Padrec panted up to Gallius, standing in place before his remaining foot ranks.

"Spears, Gallius. Move your men up in two ranks. A wall of spears in front. They need the cover."

Gallius didn't hesitate. A good idea; he should have thought of it on his own. He ordered the first three ranks forward through the archers but grabbed Padrec by the front of his grimy shirt.

"Why wasn't this bridge inspected, you fool? Anyone can see that—"

"Could *you*?" Padrec twisted himself free. "We weren't told to inspect it. Let me go. I've got to get up there."

He sprinted away after Malgon to rally the archers. Already they were dragging their wounded away from the line. Through a stinging veil of sweat that flowed too fast and hot, Padrec saw the Coritani force pause and shuffle about. The spearmen were out in force now, three staggered lines of them, pilums jammed into the ground. The Coritani hesitated. While the Prydn sent another flight at them, a raucous horn sounded from the wood and the horsemen broke formation, galloping back up the hill, losing another half dozen to the descending arrows.

Barely more than a few minutes, but to Padrec it seemed hours. His body was an open floodgate for sweat, and his head stung. No man should sweat that much. He didn't know just how or when he went down on the trampled ground, but it seemed an excellent idea. Lying on one arm, he wiped at his face. The hand came away red. Who . . . what? *I never felt it.* Then Artcois threw himself down on the grass at his feet, exultant.

"Did see me, Padrec? Was Lugh a's self with my arrows."

"Oh, aye and aye again," Bredei sang, skipping toward them, half walk, half dance. "By Jesu, do know who comes against them now, do a not! Neniane will hear, brother. Such tale-speaking a-nights in the rath. Ai!"

Padrec could only shake violently. "Brothers, am I hurt? My head . . ."

"Oh, a scratch. A passing bee. Drust! Malgon! Here!"

Drust stood like a monument in front of the archers, screaming at the hilltop. The spearmen waited for another attack that never came. Behind them, Drust brandished his nocked bow, bellowing to the high woods. "Philistines! Philistines, see David come against thee!"

"Fhain brothers. Here to Padrec."

They came then, Malgon leading his pony, and squatted in a circle of four about Padrec. On the opposite shore, the trailing century of Gallius' maniple milled about in frustration. It would have been their first battle, and a safe one with few casualties, and all they could do was look on, impotent, while the few men on the other side hogged the glory of it. They'd have to listen to it all blown up four times the size of truth for days to come. Men were creeping up out of the river, wet, angry, and feeling foolish. Many, unable to swim, had been sucked under.

Then the black birds, soot flecks in the sky.

"Look, Padrec," said Drust. "Thy omen-bird. Ravens."

After that day they never remarked on the birds or how quickly they smelled the battle. Not omens, only scavengers. There were always ravens.

They watched the ravens settle anywhere they weren't waved off.

"Must see who's fallen," Padrec said huskily.

"A must be barrowed," Malgon said.

Another horn, a legion buccina. Behind the eagles, the first elements of the main force jogged toward them. The blood began to cake on Padrec's forehead.

It galled Gallius Urbi to take orders from a boy like Ambrosius, reputation or no. However, if the boy tribune, nicknamed the Beardless Mars by the older men, were not a cool-headed commander, the first centurion might have been relieved and disgraced. The bridge should have been inspected before crossing.

"You should not have crossed without orders. You could have lost your whole command there, foot and horse. Lost enough as it is."

Step, step. Halt. Sharp pivot. "And you, Patricius. You have neither the temperament nor the instincts of a soldier. I have no time to teach you, but you could at least think on your feet."

"Yes, Tribune."

"However, you cost Rhiwallon dearly. Both of you. And you didn't retreat."

Step, step. Pause. Gallius and Patricius could both be charged with serious dereliction of duty by regulations, but neither was that experienced in the field. Neither was he, and now he knew Rhiwallon would not fight a textbook war. Score it to experience and carry on.

"Tribune." Padrec stepped forward. "We'll be wanting more spears out front when we're afoot."

"Nursemaids," Gallius snickered.

"Spears, you say?"

"Dismounted, we have no cover. We're naked. Nothing between us and the enemy but good aim."

"I sent my men forward with a line of spears," Gallius offered. "It was the only thing that saved them."

"Spears. Yes." Ambrosius chewed idly at a knuckle, considering it. Of course. In this kind of battle, with archers needed to fight on foot over unditched ground, it was the most logical defense.

"Dismissed, both of you."

Quite right, of course. Alae are valuable only in motion or attack. Dismounted, they are a liability unless defended. I made incredible blunders myself that year, excusable

only in that I was a mere student myself and had to pretend to experience, else my officers would lose faith in me.

For Rhiwallon, pondering where to strike the invaders next, the skirmish was not all boasting. He learned with Ambrosius. Of those men and horses wounded, almost all died or were useless afterward. The Faerie poisoned their arrows whenever possible. Since they made much of being Christian, he would honor them accordingly when the time came.

Pictures in the mind, fragments of a scattered mosaic that never afterward quite rearranged to coherence in Padrec's memory. Pestering Gallius for rations that didn't come or were never enough. The long, plodding marches in the rain, the mounted head of a long serpent moving toward the first of the three crucial forts. The brief pleasure at the smell of watered spring earth before it turned to muck underfoot. To Meganius—

... costly lessons, but we learn. The bank and ditch go up no matter where we are at evening. That is when the Coritani are most likely to attack because the foot troops are vulnerable. We ride a circuit around the camp like herd dogs. When the Coritani come, we shoot from the saddle or dismount and form lines of archers behind a picked detail of spear carriers. If all works in time, the Coritani pay for it.

And so do we. My Latin is plain, my Greek crippled. How can I describe the sound of them, screaming as they come, or the desperate necessity to hurl ourselves like a wall between them and the engineers? What they lack in discipline, the Coritani make up in courage. Sometimes, when it's over, you see a Coritani down on the ground, wounded and perhaps dying. There is always the pall of shock over them, a queasy surprise, like a thoughtless child fallen from a tree. He doesn't know why he hurts. Sometimes, when I look a second time, I find it is one of my own men. The face is always the same.

The diggers work on behind us. When it is over, someone tallies our dead. Sometimes I wonder what matters most, the deaths or the fact that someone records them. Armies and civil governments are much the same. My Prydn have their own customs regarding death ... my squadrons are thinner, tiring. So many missed Mass yesterday that Drust jeered "Philistines!" at them. Most of them had simply fallen asleep when they had the chance....

201

Small miseries grown large for lack of relief. Being stiff and sour with damp from sleeping in the rain or mist. Comfort narrowed to dry clothes and a fire when any deadwood found had to be dried out and burned with more smoke than warmth.

A foggy morning, Ambrosius striding down the line of the returning patrol to hail him.

"Patricius, you forgot to report yesterday. How many dead?"

He wanted a number when Padrec remembered faces. "Nine, Tribune."

"Inform Gallius and try to stay regular with your tallies. There'll be a burial detail for the Christians and cremation for the rest."

"No need, sir. Each is barrowed by his own fhain brothers."

Ambrosius cocked an eyebrow at the unfamiliar word. "Barrowed?"

"Interred."

"So that's why I've never seen dead Faerie. Where?"

A vague gesture to the hills around them. "Under the hill. I don't know. One doesn't ask. They are taken away."

"I see. Well, watch for patrols from the fort from now on. We're that close."

More pictures. Sharing the windfall of a chicken with his brothers. No one else in the legion bothered to pay for such things when they passed a trev. The hapless fowl was merely neck-wrung and lugged off, but Prydn paid in silver scrupulously counted out into the astonished owner's hand. It galled Padrec's sense of right: they weren't getting their proper rations. He was losing weight; the sodden clothes hung loose on him. Bad food, a constant state of fear and feral alertness. *Where does Gallius send our rations? He and his own men eat well enough. That potbellied bastard, Jesu forgive me, hasn't lost a pennyweight since we marched.*

And the incongruous turns of war, like the old army brothel. Until fifty years ago, the imperial roads were busy as the arteries in a man's body, thousands of miles of graded highway dotted with army brothels every twenty miles or so. Gallius' maniple thought it foresight of an admirable breadth. The one Padrec's scouts encountered had been supported by Marchudd's family during the Parisi hegemony. When Rhiwallon reasserted his claim, he saw no reason to close it. That the remaining women were worn as the road did not daunt the maniple. They had only one scruple, which Gallius relayed with relish to Padrec.

"You. Priest. The men have made it clear they want those Faerie of yours kept away from the house. I won't be responsible if you don't."

Padrec lounged against the back of his reclining horse, eating a leek flavored with crumbled salt. The priest rarely rose when Gallius addressed him. Now he didn't even interrupt his lunch.

"No difficulty, Centurion."

"I wouldn't be so casual, holy man," Gallius glared. "They mean it."

Padrec chewed languidly. "We've been there and back. The ladies gave us gifts from their garden. But Prydn's picky in the matter of love. To them the women are unclean."

Gallius brayed at the absurdity. "*They're* unclean!"

"Very unpleasant smell." Padrec took a noisy bite of the leek. "House, musky perfumes, a clout of scents the men don't trust because they can't recognize them. Dirt. Incense. Cheap wine. God knows what else. It would be like drinking from a muddy hoofprint. But don't let it deter you, Centurion."

In point of fact, Gallius intended to make lusty use of the house. He felt his taste clearly slighted by this odd priest and wouldn't leave the field without a victory. "I've heard you have one of those Faerie women yourself."

Padrec's eyes slid up to him. He got up, dusting salt crumbs from his hands. "My scouts are waiting."

"Tell me." Gallius' manner became confidential. "What are they like?"

"Pardon me?"

The grin of knowing intimacy became actually repugnant. "You know."

Padrec regarded him gravely. "Do I know? Ah, how can I put it? It is beyond description, but I will try. Last year, far north of the Wall, a black fawn was born that some say held prophecy for those who could read it. Yet I could not. No, truly." Padrec leaned in to the larger man, utterly serious. "And the Egyptian priests of Amon said that while God was a black cow, look you, Isis was definitely not a bull. Do you believe that?"

"What? Of course not. What are you talking about?"

"That is a wise question," Padrec said. "Thank you. Excuse me, my men are waiting."

After the fear was the dampness, never being dry, the plodding on, struggling up hills, slipping and sliding down the other side. The monotonous creak of the heavy-wheeled onagers and catapults, men groaning and cursing as they strained with the oxen to haul the wheels from one mire after another. Sometimes there was good road, more often the paving stones were gone for other building, and the heavy equipment had to muck along snail-pace. More and more, Ambrosius stayed forward with the alae now, sniffing ahead for Coritani. *Where are they? Will they hit us now, or wait in the fort?*

And then that first godsend victory, more blunder than skill, when the outcome rolled loose like a dropped ball on a playing field where either side could pounce on it, and Ambrosius did.

Pictures . . . the thinning trees before the long, fog-wisped meadow. The *whirr* of a wet-winged bird from one branch to another, shying Padrec's horse. *Be still, you damned fool.*

That morning the scouts picked up fresh tracks near this wood. They were very close to the hill fort beyond Wye now, and Ambrosius chose to ride with this patrol: Malgon, Padrec, and forty-odd Prydn of the first squadron under a young man from Reindeer fhain. Ambrosius rode with a pilum in his fist.

"From the other side of that meadow, we can look across the glen straight into the fort when the fog clears. Almost count noses."

He wanted a look at it before committing his force, what new ditches or ramparts, if any, and an estimate of strength. Ambrosius was daring but not rash. The tribune read Caesar in his tent and played chess against himself when he could find no other opponents.

"The sun's burning off the mist," he remarked to Padrec. "Let's get across the open while it'll hide us."

Padrec relayed the order to Malgon, who moved soundlessly up the line. "My men say the Coritani are very close. Closer than the fort."

"How do they know?"

"They feel them."

Hardly conventional, Ambrosius privately felt Faerie instinct a bizarre way to search out an enemy, but he wouldn't argue. Caesar was a rule-flouter and would readily employ any advantage at hand. He gave the command to move out by twos, taking his place ahead with the squadron leader, Padrec and Malgon at the rear. They left the cover of the wood and moved silently along a thicket of blackberry and briar, the ponies shuffling through the soggy meadow grass. In wet like this, they rode with bows unstrung and spent much time straightening warped arrow shafts over a fire. Padrec and Malgon clopped softly out of the wood behind the rest. Ambrosius by now would be near the other edge, ready to slip into cover on the other side. For no good reason, Padrec glanced toward the white swathes of mist swirling over the meadow south of them, and there were the Coritani horsemen.

In the instant he had to see it all, before the explosion of discovery, it was comic. The Coritani patrol, their groping counterpart, were plodding across the open meadow to enter the wood they'd just left. A little farther apart in thicker mist, they would have passed unseen to compound the ridiculousness. Then someone in that ghostly line saw them and pulled up sharply.

"Look!" And then, redundantly, "There they are."

The astonishment was mutual. Padrec never knew who gave the order, and later it was irrelevant. In the crucial seconds when the two lines gaped at each other, two riders dashed along the Faerie ranks, brandishing pilums, Ambrosius and Drust, his fhain brother, singing out in Prydn:

"Spears, brothers. Spears. We *go!*"

The men from Reindeer fhain were a touchy lot. Almost all were new fathers away from wives for the first time, worn mean by fear, hunger, and fatigue, just waiting to ignite. Padrec saw the pilums lift and dip forward. Then Drust shot out, spear couched, low behind his Chi-Rho shield, Ambrosius just behind him, roaring to the rest.

"After us! After us!"

The patrol spurred forward in an eager, ragged line. Padrec had no spear, only sword and shield, and in the instant they collided with the unprepared Coritani, he saw the enemy had no spears either. He heard the high-pitched scream of a mortally wounded horse, raised his shield as someone cut at him clumsily with a sword.

The Coritani could not snatch back the lost initiative. They went down like stuffed targets, quite often with their Prydn aggressors, ill-braced in their saddles, on top of them. Then someone hamstrung the beautiful black, the long-ago gift from Cru. The animal stumbled and pitched Padrec into the grass. Someone kicked him in the ribs. The air bellowed out of him. The blow rolled him over against the agonized, writhing horse, and he blinked up at the tattooed face, saw the sword raise—and freeze, as the pilum thrust outward from the painted body like another arm suddenly grown in the middle of his chest. The man fell sideways, and Drust yanked the pilum from the body.

"Padrec, be hurt?"

"Just kicked."

Drust swooped and grasped him under the arms, dragging him clear of the roil. "Thee must fight," he worried. "Must use thy sword."

"Cannot. My oath."

"Ai, then thee'll be downed for sure again and me not about to help. Must *fight.* Have I not lost good horse, too? Guenloie, pray for me."

It was over quickly. A number of the Coritani dead, the rest sensibly turned tail, pounding away toward the fort and the fog. While Padrec lay in the wet grass trying to catch his breath, Drust scampered about the meadow, calling in the mist.

"Malgon. Brother, cry out. Where?"

Padrec retrieved his sword. One of Malgon's best. He couldn't use it any more than he had, for parrying his way out of trouble. He would not kill with it. . . . But was that so? If there'd been time with that painted lunatic, visible death coming at him? Just silly luck Drust was there to save him. Next time he could die, and for nothing. If there'd been time, would he have used it?

"No."

The Coritani lay where he fell, the blood startling against the coiled designs in blue woad on his chest.

No, I would not. I will not.

He was trying to sheath the weapon with hands that didn't work too well, when Ambrosius strode toward him, pilum angled jauntily over the shoulder of his bullhide breastplate.

"Patricius, look at this. Marvelous!"

"What, then?"

"This." Ambrosius snapped the pilum off his shoulder, hefting it with intense purpose and satisfaction, boyish as Drust with his new sword. "It'll work. Huns and Goths have used it. There were Sarmatian foederati who used it with the Second Legio at Caerleon. It'll bloody well *work*, I tell you."

"Have we lost many men?"

"Not a man. Not a man. Lances . . ." Ambrosius subsided, still in his dream. "Cavalry with lances. Should be longer. Heavier."

Drust and Malgon returned with handfuls of bloody, pinkish meat. They offered Padrec a generous share. Ambrosius' enthusiasm paled by several shades. "What in hell is that?"

"Coritani horse." Padrec chewed hungrily. "All the meat we get of late," he added meaningfully. "At least it's fresh. Do have some, Tribune."

"No . . . thanks. Don't you people eat mutton?"

"Mutton!" Drust hooted through a mouthful. "What mutton be that?"

"Your regular ration."

"Last sheep to cross my sight did still walk," Malgon informed him.

"And the last hint of pork at Eburacum," Padrec said. "Horse isn't at all bad. A bit tough, better cooked. Orders, Tribune?"

"Let's get on. If it's clear enough. I want to see the fort before that patrol stirs them up."

The three of them grinned sourly after the retreating tribune. "Dost nae care for horse, brothers," Padrec shrugged. "Cut me some more."

"Did speak of mutton," Malgon wondered suspiciously. "What mutton?"

"Who knows? But by Saint Alban, will find out, brothers, and that with speed." *We must have better food. The tribune sees what we're eating. I'm going to complain again and keep complaining until something is done.*

They learned in time to slice the horsemeat thin as shavings and cook it on green sticks over a fire, when a fire could be had, one of the basic lessons of war besides sleeping dry and staying alive. Along with the others, Padrec took to catnapping when he could. Rest was precious as food. Half the habitual prayers of his day, like fast days, were a thing of the past. Sometimes his Mass was perfunctory if not half skipped. He missed sharing things with Dorelei, the sound of her voice, grave or gay, riding beside him or before they fell asleep at night. At other times he felt the simple male need of her body as a tightness in his loins, although that became less and less as the campaign wore on. Hunger, worry, and fear were water on that fire. In the spiritual fervor of taking his first orders, he convinced himself that flesh was the smallest part of a consecrated man like himself, a mere afterthought to keep soaring spirit humble. In the musky heat of loving Dorelei, he knew he was male and mortal, and this coupling not a taint but a seasoning to all else in life. He was the better priest for it, but so much for asceticism. He yawned, dozing with his head against the saddle. *Ai, listen to me. Were she here right now, I'd be too tired to do anything about it.*

He tried to draw the image of her with him toward sleep, pull her small, dear body against the sensuous fatigue in his.

All he could see was the long slope bright with tomorrow's sun, and the men at the top waiting for him.

The first fort fell easily. There were less than two hundred warriors behind the earthwork ramparts. Padrec's squadrons walked up the slope until the first arrows fell just short of them. Behind the horse was an entire cohort with scaling ladders. When the alae mounted and spurred forward, the infantry followed at a run.

The main attack was centered on the well-defended entrance to the hill fort and for several hundred yards to either side. The slope was gentle with no serious obstructions. Padrec's men swept back and forth like fish swimming just offshore, sending flight after flight at the ramparts, keeping Coritani heads down while the assault troops moved in. The attack was beautifully clear in principle but didn't allow for frightened men in the furnace of their first battle, or being slowed by the defensive ditch before the ramparts, dropped ladders, foot and horse getting in each other's way, and enthusiastic Faerie charging right up to the walls to loose again and again and running short of arrows too soon. When the walls were breached by Gallius with his first wave, some of the Faerie didn't hear the horn sound for recall;

the rest simply ignored it. The Coritani tribesmen were lunatic with battle rage, some of them leaping down from the walls to certain death, running into the Parisi ranks, screaming and swinging their swords.

An eddy of confusion: the attack faltering as foot soldiers, ladders, and milling horses snarled together. Padrec reined the bay gelding cruelly. The animal had more endurance than Cru's gift-horse but was not yet used to Padrec's rein or seat. Padrec saw the attack slow, then Malgon rising from his arrow-shot pony, and spurred forward to scoop up his brother. Malgon hopped nimbly up behind, hugging Padrec's middle.

"Jesu, Mal! They never heard the horn." Padrec pushed the horse through the advancing foot, sword raised, shouting to the Prydn, "Back! Back!" until he was hoarse. Little by little, out of the roil of men swarming over the ditch and up the walls, clumps of small riders broke off, trotting or running afoot down the hill to safety, to form again their never-clear notion of squadron order behind Padrec, some of them skipping and dancing with pure excitement until Ambrosius rode up, bawling at them to cease.

"Damn it, Patricius, don't these fools know the signal to withdraw? Do you know how many of them could have been lost just for lack of discipline? By Mithras, I've seen more order in a troop of clowns. Just lucky you didn't lose more. Just lucky."

Ambrosius cursed and fretted and won the day, moving his engineers into the fort to make it impregnable, and added another line to his lessons.

A mob of tribesmen on horses are just that, a mob. Not clowns they need to be but dancers, horse and man part of the same body and will. Otherwise far too many horses will be lost, as we did, beside a few Faerie whose bodies simply vanished afterward—into Faerie-land, I suppose.

As Ambrosius learned, so did Rhiwallon. He no longer joked with his chiefs about Parisi cowardice. They saw the plodding line of the legion and what it could do, and the word "inexorable" came to mind. Skirmish warfare with cavalry could delay but not defeat them, and nothing short of fifteen thousand men, more than Rhiwallon could ever field, would retake the hill fort at Wye. If VI Legio was not yet an inspired fighting force, it could build with awesome speed. The simple bank and ditch at Wye became two in as many days. Rhiwallon's scouts said it looked like a colony of ants gone berserk. The inner ramparts were now palisaded with stout posts interlaced with wicker; the outer *vallum* prickled with tree trunk obstacles, fronted with triangular ditching in which "lilies" were planted—sharp, fire-hardened wooden stakes to take the impetus and the fight out of charging Coritani. Three-tiered archery towers reared at regular intervals.

On the move, the legion was learning even faster as the boy tribune recalled for them the military genius of a fading empire. No tribal loyalties, no favoritism. Minor offenses were punished with fatigue details, more serious ones with flogging, and there were several summary executions for attempted desertion or disobedience in action. The great snake coiled around a hill, nested briefly to make it impregnable, and moved on. Rhiwallon sent Cadwal home for safety. He could afford one lost hill but not two. Two gone, the third would fall in a matter of time. Churnet Head had to stand. He would command the hill himself. Churnet would be much harder to take than Wye, better manned, the approaches steeper and more thoroughly prepared. The outer ditches would be planted with the Roman sort of lilies and a few tricks perhaps the boy tribune hadn't encountered in his Caesar.

Padrec had to admit Ambrosius was right about discipline. It saved time and lives. When they stopped to camp even for one night, the defense ditches were dug, tents up in minutes, smiths at their endless repair, cooks readying a meal even as the camp filled out its familiar rectangular shape around them. Food was on Padrec's mind as he clumped down the line of tents at sunset. The mess situation had gone from bad to intolerable. They were the hardest worked and the worst fed. Not a question of shortage; the foot ate well all the time. After continual complaints, Ambrosius called this accounting. Briccu, the tribune's tent guard, recognized Padrec and saluted respectfully. He was a Christian and often heard Mass with the Prydn.

"They're here and waiting. Father?"

"Yes?"

Briccu was a mountain man like Padrec himself. He spoke the archaic Brigante dialect Padrec had known from birth. "It is that I would be asking confession of you, Father."

"And where have you found the time or opportunity to sin, busy as we are?"

"Och, it's not that much. But I am new-betrothed. . . ."

"Bless you, I have a young wife myself."

"Well, then." Briccu shuffled a little in embarrassment. "You'll know what I mean. When we passed the old army brothel . . . well, wasn't I drunk at the time, and lonely."

Padrec smiled. "Drink's been known to do that. A man can lose his way."

"Can he not?"

Padrec couldn't resist the chuckle. "Jesu, those worn-out old—well, Briccu, I'll be hearing confessions tonight. We should speak of taste as well as transgression. Rest you gentle until then." He patted the man's shoulder and passed into the tent.

The tribune was seated on a plain stool next to a camp table on which had been set a jug of wine and a covered plate. Ambrosius lived as plainly as any of his men in the field. Harness discarded on a rack, he received his officers in a plain Dobunni tunic and trousers of red and green checks. Gallius was still in gear; since the victory at Wye, he'd exchanged the potbellied breastplate the other officers joked about for a good coat of scale armor scavenged from a dead Coritani chief. It made less comment on his paunch. He pretended to sniff the air in distaste when Padrec entered.

"Whew! Don't the Faerie ever wash?"

"We're always last at the water ration and other things. Sir."

"The tribune said you asked I be here. Well, what is it? I have other duties."

"Centurion Urbi," Ambrosius began, "Father Patricius has lodged a formal complaint about alae rations. A number of them, to be precise."

"He went over my head?" Gallius rounded belligerently on Padrec. "You sidled up to the tribune and whined—you little coward, you won't even use your sword in battle."

"I may not."

"How convenient. So that if a man, a real man, has a grievance with you, don't you have the whole Church to hide behind."

"Enough," Ambrosius broke in. "I want to get to the bottom of this and clean it out. Now. Gallius, my records show that dried pork, mutton, and lentils were purchased in ample quantities for your maniple. For thirty-two *contubernia* of eight men each. More than enough to allow for spoilage, waste, error, and the predictable thievery of cooks. There should be more food than men to eat it." Ambrosius unrolled a papyrus and waved it under Gallius' florid nose. "Thirty-two. Where are they?"

Gallius looked convincingly bewildered, offering the small roll tucked under his own arm. "I signed for only twenty-four, Tribune. The quartermaster has my receipts."

"So he does. A shortage in rations for sixty-four men."

"Well, I'm a merchant myself. I've never seen supply records tally since I took service with the Sixth."

"Your own men don't go without," Padrec shot at him. "Or yourself, one notes."

Gallius backhanded the smaller man across the face before Ambrosius could intercede. "You wish to note that, Father Patricius?"

"Stop!" Ambrosius caught Gallius as he moved to strike again, spinning him around. "I could charge you with that, Gallius Urbi. For the moment, I will only remind you not to mistake a moment's valor for a sense of honor, you . . ." The tribune's voice was frigid with contempt, his restraining hand an iron clamp. Gallius subsided, quite satisfied in any case.

"He knows what I think of him."

"And I of you," said Padrec. "Let me tell you, storekeeper, it takes a full man to be a priest."

"Square off, both of you!"

Force of habit snapped both subordinates to attention. Ambrosius turned away from them to take the edge of anger from his thoughts. "Acting Centurion Patricius is stating a fact, Gallius. I've eaten with your men and observed the Faerie at their meals." His hand, resting against the base of his spine, closed in resolution. "Guard!"

Briccu ducked his head inside the tent flap. "Sir?"

"Take Centurion Patricius and a detail of five men to the quartermaster. They will draw extra rations, which will be charged to Gallius Urbi's supply manifests. Go get your rations, Patricius. And heed Gallius in this, at least. Use your sword hereafter. Since your men will follow none but you, it'll muck me up properly if you're dead, won't it? Dismissed."

When they were alone, Ambrosius waved Gallius to a stool by the camp table and poured two wooden cups of wine. Gallius was disappointed that the trib entertained his officers with the same ration swill the men drank. He noticed, as Ambrosius sat down, that the vital young frame seemed to slump a moment, sloughing its youth like a wet cloak falling from the shoulders. Then Ambrosius recovered himself, shook off the weariness, and drank.

"Thanks, Tribune. Thank you. Things get lean in the field."

"Indeed."

"A touch of home. It helps."

"I hope you have an appetite," Ambrosius invited cordially. "I want you to take supper here."

Gallius brightened. "Of course, sir. Better than at home, actually. I find I've a taste for soldiering."

Don't you just. Ambrosius knew Gallius' domestic circumstances. This would be a holiday for such a man, and he was a fair soldier, valiant enough in the balance. He'd gone over the walls at Wye with no hanging back. Surprised at his own valor, Gallius was now a little pompous, even dropping incense to Mars on one of the portable altars. Yes, he'd crow at the priest's timidity, his own lack of it being such a relief. *One good scare, that's what you need.*

211

"Centurion, Patricius is a rather naïve man, hardly bred to war, and leading a mob of enthused children who happen to be the only archers we could raise. I have no special regard for them, but they're better than the Venicones would've been. More wine? It's good for the appetite."

"Thank you, I will."

Ambrosius refilled the cups, spilling a little. Gallius observed that the young man's hand shook slightly.

"Forgive me, I'm that tired. It would be sheer joy to have nothing else but war to contend with."

"Quite understandable to a soldier, sir."

"Every officer in my command has signed the *regulae* of the Sixth Legio, as fully understanding their import. You remember the forty-second article."

Gallius did not at the moment.

"Then let me refresh you," Ambrosius went on easily. "It states that any officer knowingly falsifying a report or manifest shall, in garrison, be flogged through his command and dismissed in disgrace with forfeiture of any monies due or pension to become due. Or, in the field, shall be put before archers and shot with arrows. As my archers are all Faerie, the execution detail would be voluntary and meticulous, not to say inspired. Do I make myself clear?"

Ambrosius watched the other man blink and swallow. *Yes, you understand well enough, merchant. Easy enough to short-route part of a shipment and lose it now to later profit. I'll never find those lost rations, but you will, and no one will ever be able to prove it because there isn't time.*

"Am I accused of theft, Tribune?"

"No. Merely reminding you of regulations." Ambrosius turned a corner of thought and brushed the subject aside. "Now, then: hungry?"

"Famished, sir."

"Good." Ambrosius lifted the linen cover from the plate and offered it to Gallius, whose nose quickly advised the rest of him away from it.

"I prepared it myself," Ambrosius informed him mildly. "And sampled it, so I know what I ask. Eat it, Gallius."

"For God's sake, it's rotten."

"Just pleasantly ripe." The plate was thrust in Gallius' face. "A direct field order, refusal of which is punishable by death. Eat it, you larcenous son-of-a-bitch. And let it be the last raw horse any man in your maniple has to swallow."

The hill dreamed in the early sunlight.

A morning of such beauty and peace that Mother seemed to open one drowsy eye and then, reassured by tranquillity, turn over for another short nap. Drust fed turnip to his pony and breathed deep of the sweet air, gazing across the valley at the fortified hill. "Malgon, Padrec? Would be a braw place for a church."

"An abbey," Padrec said. "A whole community for God."

A little forward of them, the scout from Wolf fhain rested in the saddle, one leg hooked around the pommel while his army black switched lazily at marauding flies with its tail. The scout beckoned Padrec forward: it was time.

"Should be with thee," Malgon fretted.

"Nae fear, be no great Gallius," Padrec assured him. "Will not play at bravery before I must, only look."

Before we're committed to it.

Drust and Malgon watched the progress of the two riders, intent, as if concentration alone could protect them. They were almost to the first ditch, drawing apart as they moved. Then Drust sucked in his breath. "First arrows."

The tiny figures flattened out as they broke into gallop, sliding to the protecting shoulder of the horses, dashing in opposite directions around the far side of the hill.

For most of a mile, stretched back along Churnet Valley, VI Legio waited in ranks. Under a tree a little distance from the first maniple, Padrec crouched over a bare patch of earth, drawing lines with his knife while Ambrosius absorbed it all.

"The first ditch is wider and deeper than at Wye, with sharpened brushwood all through." Padrec went on with his knife point to the next line. "Beyond the ditch, there's *stimuli* planted, not too many, but the hooks can give a horse or man a nasty slash." The blade trailed toward the rampart line. "Past that there's the ditch with the lilies."

"All the way around?"

"All the way." Padrec wiped his sweaty forehead on a grimy sleeve. "He's learned from you, Tribune."

"How far from the lilies to the rampart ditch?"

"About forty-five *gradii*, sir."

Ambrosius looked skeptical. "Are you sure? Those Faerie of yours don't think in straight lines or numbers."

Padrec gave him a tentative smile with the confession. "I measured it."

"Damn it, Patricius! I told you not to go nosing about the hill yourself. And what happens? Don't you go prancing up to measure a distance a bare forty yards from the rampart. What if I lose you? You're the only one who can understand your men, let alone order them."

Padrec contemplated the lines in the dirt. Violence in still-life. "After today, it may be academic."

"Don't talk rot, that won't help."

"There's one more thing, sir. The entrance to the fort. I got pretty close while I was at it."

Ambrosius turned despairing eyes to heaven. "Oh, very good."

"Not to worry. I didn't linger; they'd got my range by then, but they were more interested in throwing insults than wasting arrows. This is the manner of it."

Padrec sketched what looked like the open end of a torc with a spur growing out of one end to curve in front of the opening. Ambrosius knew it immediately.

"The fort was built by Marchudd's grandfather, who apparently read his Caesar. The Venelli used this in Gaul." He borrowed the knife and drew an alley from the opening into the fort. "See anything like this?"

Padrec thought he might have but couldn't be sure, moving fast as he was. The alley was angled at forty-five degrees from the rampart.

"The heavy concentration of archers will be on the right," Ambrosius explained. "The unshielded side for men with swords. Efficient."

"A beautiful place, for all that." Padrec stood up, sheathing his knife. "A braw site for a monastery."

"Hm?"

"A monastery, Tribune. We are to convert them, are we not?"

"Oh. Yes. To be sure."

"A monastery school. In serenity like this, a man could not only read the voice of God, he could hear it. Shall I form the alae, sir?"

Ambrosius remained crouched over the battle diagram. "Yes. I'll send orders through Gallius. By the way, I hope you had a good breakfast."

"Did we not!" About to fork the gelding, Padrec grinned impishly. "My stomach's been rumbling with gratitude all morning."

From the ramparts, Prince Rhiwallon watched the human squares below him elongate to rectangles. Bloody Romans, they even thought in straight lines. Still, he owned a grudging admiration for the discipline that could move so many men with so little argument or confusion. Rhiwallon could see the intent: each wave about to hit his stronghold was now separated from the others and poised behind its commander.

Crammed into Churnet fort and bristling for battle were near a thousand of his best warriors. He estimated Ambrosius' superiority at between four and five to one.

214

"But that's mere numbers, not heart," he cheered his men. "Most of them have fought one day to your hundred. After the first attack, the odds will be lower."

They had to be, but the prince refrained from the comment. The first two assaults would be crucial. Those repelled, he could last out Ambrosius. If the rest of Rhiwallon's warriors waiting downstream heard nothing from him by morning, they would move to engage VI Legio from the rear. The boy-bach Ambrosius would have to split his force even further and eventually break off.

The Coritani's best archers defended the fort entrance, which was choked with sharp-branched tree trunks.

He felt the new tension in his men before any movement. They pressed closer to the rampart, leaning over, stringing their bows. Prince Rhiwallon shaded his eyes against the sun. Ranged before the center of VI Legio, the Faerie riders were dismounting as shield bearers moved forward through their ranks.

"Here they come."

If Ambrosius was younger than Rhiwallon, he learned faster from mistakes. Cavalry against such a radical slope crowned with such defenses would be lunacy. Wye taught him their best use was open, level ground. Archers would move on foot behind shield bearers with files of infantry among them. Once in position, they would fly continual volleys of arrows while the foot went forward to clear wide lanes across the first ditch.

"Because when we go through, Gallius, we'll go fast. Your maniple will be in the lead."

"Yes, Tribune."

Not so much fear that twisted Gallius' already suffering stomach as a kind of evolution. The novelty of soldiering and his own physical valor had worn off on the long road from Wye. His reaction now was much more typical. *Why us?* He wondered if the trib was still punishing him for the Faerie rations. He set that straight, didn't he? Ambrosius wouldn't know or care the cost to Gallius' stomach to eat that bloody ripe horsemeat. None of them knew. He didn't noise it about, but for years he'd not been able to digest much of anything but plain boiled millet and vegetables cooked to mush.

You'd think the Beardless Mars would be satisfied, ease off a little, but no—always the first maniple: first in, first over. *Jesus. Always us. And I asked for it.*

Gallius was becoming a soldier in earnest. Like wise foot soldiers through the ages, he no longer volunteered for anything. He found

Patricius, absurd in his scavenged armor, and passed the orders. The Christly little man just nodded and looked away up the hill to the waiting fort. Even he knew what this day would be for all of them.

Gallius prayed with silent fervor. *My God, I hope those stupid children can get along without me, if—ah, that's no way to think. Well, the woman will squeeze every sestertius, always did. And there's men here I'd miss more than her. Holy Mary Virgin, we're going to catch it today.*

He drank from his waterskin, wiping his lips and beard.

"Don't drink too much, you'll be sick."

Ambrosius was at Gallius' elbow, serene as the priest. "Move them out."

"Yes, sir."

"I'm coming forward with you. That ditch up there's the only place I can see it all."

All the archers were slung with extra bundles of arrows, as many as could be carried. Padrec hefted three himself, trying to look confident for Malgon and Drust.

"Will be an easy day for horse, brothers. God with thee."

He stepped out in long strides, turning to wave his Prydn forward. Drust sprang to his side, swinging along, the bundles bouncing on his back.

"For Jesu!" he sang out. "For Jesu and Dorelei Mabh!"

Coritani arrows were flying before they reached the first ditch. The Prydn crouched close behind the line of shields. Padrec raised his sword, waiting for the order.

"Ready . . . loose!"

The first *wush* as the flight shot home, aimed a foot over the ramparts. Gallius scurried forward under its cover, leaping into the ditch with his sappers behind him. "Four lanes—four good, wide lanes. Clear 'em out!"

Padrec called for each flight as Ambrosius signaled it. "Loose . . . ready . . . loose! Malgon, ready a detail of six men to carry shafts from the rear. We can't let up. Ready . . . *loose!*"

Behind the shield wall, as far forward as he could get, Ambrosius saw the strategy working, the sappers working maniacally in the ditch, hurling tree trunks this way and that, scooping fill-earth to make the paths, and only light opposition from the ramparts. If anyone raised his head, down it went again, or he lost part of it to a Prydn arrow. Then Gallius waved his sword, crawled out of the ditch, legs churning under his heaving paunch, back toward the shields, his men dodging after him.

"Four lanes clear, Tribune."

"Good. Patricius, hold off until my order. Save shafts. Gallius, tell me when your maniple's ready to move up."

Gallius tried to wet his mouth with a dry tongue. "Right, then." He hurried away. Ambrosius hissed his impatience: the damned Faerie were still loosing at the ramparts. "Hold *off*, I said."

Padrec had given the order twice over, but the battle-fevered Prydn didn't hear or didn't care. He bounded up over the forward rim of the ditch, shouting at them, "Hold off!"

They began to break off raggedly as Gallius' assault and ladder teams started forward. Shuffling back and forth, the shield bearers had allowed a temporary gap. Yelling at his men, Padrec's back was exposed to the ramparts, where men were already fitting arrows to their strings.

Artcois saw it and sprang monkey-nimble out of the ditch at Padrec. "Mind, brother. Down." He swiveled about Padrec to herd him back into the ditch, his own back to the ramparts. "Pad—"

All so fast. One arrow whined by Padrec. Then Artcois' white grimace went red as the arrowhead shot out of his mouth like an obscene tongue. The boy fell against Padrec, sliding down his body, still grasping at him. Below the nose, Artcois' face was a red mask. His eyes moved once, finding Padrec, then nothing at all.

Padrec made a sound like a sick dog.

The leading edge of the assault pushed toward the wall. One man tripped, stumbled; another went down, dragging his end of a ladder with him. Gallius caught an iron goad, cursing as the hook gouged his leg. Then they were clear of the goads, running forward again with the second wave after them. Readying the third wave, Ambrosius knew only that his attack faltered. The Coritani were up and shooting, heedless of the arrowstorm peppering them.

"They're slowing down," he said aloud. "What in hell is happening up there?"

With the first of his men, Gallius leaped over the narrow lily trench, dashing forward toward the rampart ditch. He stopped, turning to urge them on and so missed the second, disguised trench—two inches of carefully laid down soil over thin wattle and sharpened stakes. The first line of Gallius's maniple went into them, onto them, and when the second line faltered, the Coritani sprang their trap. Out from the fort entrance thundered half a hundred horsemen, trampling over the floundering first wave, scything with longswords, and sweeping on around the hill.

Gallius heard the buccina with only part of his awareness. He stared down at his own gashed leg and the blood seeping over his shoe. Someone called to him with the queasy sound the wounded make. Only then did he link the braying horn to a meaning. Recall. The second wave was already running or stumbling back. Gallius went to the wounded soldier and lifted him up. His mind worked stiffly as a frozen hand. He hoped they could get back to the ditch alive.

Ambrosius stalked down the ditch past the wounded wreckage of his first three assaults, those that got back. They were stopped dead, lost all initiative. Recall was necessary.

The reserves were up now and just to his rear, waiting without enthusiasm for the order to move forward. A moment's rest, then, while he sorted frantically through possibilities, knowing the one thing harder than starting a difficult attack was starting a failed one up again. He passed Gallius Urbi on his rump in the dirt, cursing feebly as he wrapped linen about a slash in his leg.

"Get them standing to, Gallius. We'll be going again."

Gallius and several others gaped at Ambrosius in what was left of surprise. Again? Go up and get this done to them again?

"You don't want to spend all day in this rutting ditch, do you?"

Gallius went on cursing over his leg like muttered prayers. Ambrosius moved on, stepping over and around men who hunched or huddled alone with their fear among other lonely men. He almost tripped over Patricius, who sat with a dead Faerie in his arms. The priest's hands were bloody. In the dirt by him was the arrowhead pulled free of the fatal wound.

Ambrosius knelt by him and spoke softly. "Put him down. You can't mourn one man like this. It will demoralize the rest."

"He was my brother. I'd be dead but for him. His name was Artcois. You might just remember it. And I will mourn him." But there was something about the priest not so still as mourning, that moved and coiled. "I confessed him this morning and gave him the last rites just now for whatever sins he incurred while walking up this hill for God. It should be God's, this place. And now, if you have no immediate orders, I would be alone. Sir."

Then the arrow detail hopped down into the ditch, tossing their bundles to waiting hands, Bredei crowing with breezy cheer. "Nae, did tell thee would be swift back. Artcois?"

Drust and Malgon only stretched their hands to the sky and down to cover their faces. Then Bredei saw what Padrec held.

Without a word he came to lift his brother husband from Padrec's arms.

"Did say the magic even as a died, Bredei. Thy brother will not stay long enough in purgatory to know the place."

Bredei kissed his brother's forehead and laid him down on the earth. "Remember how Neniane called us children? True, we were." He smoothed Artcois' long hair. "Was all play to us."

A sound like a purr began low in Bredei's throat, soft at first but rising in pitch and power. Malgon took it up, then Drust and a dozen, more and more swelling the eerie wail that went through Ambrosius like a fingernail down slate.

All along the ditch, the Prydn were rising as they joined their voices to the ululation. Ambrosius felt his skin crawl and the tribesman in him shiver. The sane world he knew held no place for such a sound. It was like a dark always hidden behind sunlight, suddenly bursting through to give sanity the lie. He kept from covering his ears only by an effort of will.

The Parisii and Brigantes shuffled about, unnerved by the wail. On the ramparts, heads rose curiously, ears cocked to identify that which had no name but a niche in their fears older than time.

There was a word Padrec had never heard before, a harsh, percussive sound like hardness breaking against hardness. The word cracked from Bredei's lips, then Malgon's, echoing along the ditch as the Prydn men rose. Bredei drew his sword, tossing away the scabbard and belt, hooking the shield over his left arm.

"Prydn will end this for Ambrose, Padrec."

Malgon's sword belt dropped across Bredei's in the dirt. "Can nae win from here." A brief, muttered word to Padrec, and they scrambled out of the ditch, running downhill toward the waiting ponies. More Prydn trotted after them, ignoring Ambrosius.

"What is this?" he demanded of Padrec. "Are they retreating? I gave no order to pull back."

"No." Padrec snaked the blade from his own scabbard, discarding the belt. The priest looked ashen but his mouth was set. Ambrosius looked down the hill after the small, darting figures.

"Are they deserting? What did they say to you?"

Padrec picked up his shield. "In literal translation, they mean to borrow your tallfolk war. Tell Gallius to follow us in. Close."

"What?" Ambrosius didn't relish surprises not authored by himself. "Follow you . . . ?"

"Into the fort. Tell Gallius to be close behind and everything you've got after him."

Insane but true: the Faerie were running back up the line, leading their ponies. "Patricius, are you mad?"

"No, but they're sick of the smell of fear and losing brothers. They're going in."

219

Ambrosius recovered himself, restraining the little priest with a hand on his arm. "Centurion, you will not *do* this."

Padrec only shook him off. "I must; they'll go anyway."

"A mounted charge straight through the ... it's insane!"

"*Of course it is!*" Padrec pushed the younger man back from him. "And you can't stop it now any more than I could the day you called them the children of Christ. Get away."

Malgon rode up, leading Padrec's gelding. The priest jumped his saddle, lifting his sword amid the keening that sounded to Ambrosius like the buzzing of maddened bees. "This hill to God, Ambrosius. And land to the Prydn. Remember it." Then Padrec joined in the keening as the Prydn rode toward the paths filled in by sappers.

Ambrosius couldn't stop them all; it would be chaos and demoralize the rest of his badly shaken men. The Coritani, with no arrows to duck, just stared at them a moment before they responded. Totally mad—undefended horsemen stringing out by twos this side of the ditch.

Ambrosius pounded down the ditch to Gallius, fiercely hauling the big man to his feet. "They're going in, Gallius!"

"What? They're what?"

"Are you blind? *Look* at them. I can't stop them, but I'm not going to waste them. The priest said for you to follow them in. Get ready. First maniple over. Now. That's an order."

Ambrosius leaped out of the ditch, running toward the centurion of the second maniple. "Be ready. We're going in."

Stunned as Gallius, the centurion pointed forward at the moving Prydn. "What in the name—"

"You heard me. We're going in. Third maniple, up to me!"

Ambrosius heard the rumble as the Prydn spurred into a gallop, sweeping toward the fort entrance. His breath burst from his throat in a gasp of sheer disbelief. The lunatics were doing it.

He couldn't stop it, had to use it, make insanity into a weapon, follow it with another and another, his whole force if that's what it took. Once the entrance was breached, Rhiwallon would have to draw men from other parts of the wall, and then ...

Ambrosius whirled in his coiling excitement, expecting to see Gallius' men halfway to the fort entrance.

Oh, no. Jesu, Mithras, and Mars, no ...

The first maniple was just moving out of the ditch, while the Prydn were already disappearing around the spur defense into the fort under a shower of arrows. Gallius would be late by that much when every second meant a man dead in that alley.

Gallius knew it for madness, and he'd been given a mad order on top of it when all of them were glad merely to be alive in the safe ditch. Through the fort entrance—a solid line of large targets in a narrow trough. His men were on their feet, none of them wanting this any more than he did, and somehow the order stuck in Gallius' throat as the seconds bled away. Then the fear turned to anger. Ambrosius would cheerfully execute him if he didn't move. Die now, die later, small choice. Somehow his hand grasped a high rung of the ladder and pulled him up a step. Gallius stared at the hand. It belonged to someone else who stole his own raw voice.

"Shield bearers out. Follow me. Let's *go.*"

Plunging around the turn into the fort alley, Padrec had no time to look back at their support. He rode in the pack of his brothers still keening their death-song. There was no leader, only a single drive to close and kill.

The first arrows began to take them.

Padrec pushed his horse high along the side of the sloped ditch after Bredei, practically able to reach out and touch the archers drawing on them. Still they churned on, mindless of the milling confusion behind them, men and horses slowed by the underbrush choking the entrance. Screaming, flattened over their ponies' necks, the Prydn bounded straight up the ditch walls to cut down the archers or be impaled.

Malgon's pony took two shafts full in the chest and neck, and Padrec caught a brief flash of Mal going down under the stricken animal. Then Bredei screamed high—off his dead mount and swinging his sword two-handed as two Coritani leaped at him. In the swirl of close combat, his heart pumping like a blacksmith's hammer, Padrec caught a glimpse of the spur they'd just passed. *Not there, Gallius isn't there. I told him to follow. He betrayed us.*

Then his own horse stumbled and went down on its foreknees, dumping him into a pile of sharpened branches. He felt the wood cut into his back and legs, not deep but jarring pain that bathed his brain in a sudden red light. Pain roared into rage. The rational fear that wanted to live melted away in lunacy as the tattooed tribesman leaped down at him, spear thrust forward. At the last instant, Padrec knocked it aside with his shield and windmilled his sword at the copper-haired skull.

. . . Screaming, only dimly aware of a warm wetness about his body. The splintered shield had been lost somewhere. There was another man with a sword in front of him, slow and clumsy, far too slow for the feral speed in his own arms. He felt immune to pain, immortal. Whatever touched or even broke his flesh, Padrec knew it only from a distance, bellowing as he followed the swing of his arms and the beautiful scarlet sword, roaring at the pitiful doll figures that went down before him. Screaming at nothing, at air, at the sun, at the sudden but useless iron against his iron. Falling across the ripped belly of a dead horse, to see the shield bearers trotting up the alley, the running men between them, shields overhead, pushing farther into the fort, brawny sappers tearing the obstructions out of the way.

. . . told you to follow us . . . why did you wait, Gallius?

His hands shook on the sword. The arms worked beautifully, inexhaustible, but something was wrong with the rest of him. He was down on one knee. The other throbbed dully, didn't want to bend at all. And now there were more Coritani running pell-mell toward them from the south wall to mend the breach, but too late. Behind Gallius' maniple—too late, far too late—fresh foot soldiers were pouring in too fast to be checked.

Padrec giggled weakly. "Too goddamned late, all of you."

Then sanity, like a polite servant, cleared its throat in the rear of his brain. *Excuse me, sir, but you're bleeding rather badly. It's your leg, sir. Do lie down.*

"Yes, certainly." Padrec obeyed with idiotic reasonableness. The leg wouldn't bend because the muscles above the knee were badly lacerated. Oh, a big one. A large rent in his trousers and a lot of blood. Where did that happen?

Above and around him the shield bearers, slingers, and spear throwers were pushing forward as more and more men trotted through the now undefended alley. And over the south wall, the first assault ladders were poking up, then helmeted heads. Lying down was an excellent idea. *Should have thought of it before.* Sharp in the center of his red consciousness there were red hairs stuck to his sword blade in a mess of something sticky and pale white. When he fell over on his side, his outthrust hand mucked in something wet. Padrec concentrated very hard to recognize the remains of the face. He shaped his mouth to the name, but it didn't work very well.

"Spears, spears! Follow me!"

Someone was roaring orders. *It's Gallius, Bredei,* he told the broken thing beside him. *Listen to the hero. Late? You can damn well believe he was late. He can make his excuses to you, Bredei.*

Bredei's left eye was gone in the wound that spilled his brains over the dirt, but the right eye was open and quite clear in its judgment. *Must die for this, Padrec.*

"Oh, yes," Padrec agreed gravely. "No question of it."

*   *   *

222

The walls were breached, Ambrosius throwing everything he had over them. He took the insanity of a moment and turned it to advantage, made a decision that cost him a full cohort, but once committed, he did not falter. Century after century went through the alley and over the walls, faster as the breach widened, knowing it was just a matter of time. And if the Beardless Mars sickened at the extravagance in blood, or wondered what god gave him such license, he never voiced it then or later. He was one of those private men who must be measured from the outside by those who knew him. Marchudd always spoke with cool respect of his abilities, knowing the ambition that fired them. Young Arthur Pendragon adored him, and it was with Arthur that the old emperor shared what leathery heart he had: *Don't ever expect them to love you, Artorius.*

Running toward the walls with the rest of his reserves, his shield a pincushion for arrows, Ambrosius knew what he'd paid for what he'd won, and the prize was worth it. He hooked the shield farther up his arm, leaped at the ladder, and hauled himself up toward the rampart.

"Come on! Don't stop, don't slow down! Come on!"

At the last minute, Rhiwallon and his leaders left the fort, escaping on swift horses by a prearranged path, dashing down the unbesieged north slope. The retreat was neither despair nor cowardice. He'd led the counterattack himself when Gallius' men poured through the entrance, personally rallied his men when everything was lost, but he would not stake his last throw on that. He gave the order to surrender, to save what was left of his men, then dashed away to where a fight could still be made. His war was two thirds lost. He wouldn't depend on the last stronghold to turn the balance but would hunt these Roman bastards like a wolf, whittle them down until they had nothing left to make a stand with.

And yet it stung, such a defeat. He was not like the chess player who came against him. He left his heart in Churnet Head. From the shade of a stand of trees a mile from the fort, Rhiwallon brooded on the scene of his defeat.

"I would not think such foolhardiness of a Roman," one of his chiefs observed. "It should not have worked."

"But it did," Rhiwallon cut him short. "Nail it in your skulls, paint the truth on your eyes. It did. And it was *them* that did it, those Faerie. Have you not heard all your life of them and what they are. Do you think . . ." He was as surprised as his men to hear the voice in his

223

own throat strain so tight. "Do you think praying at such creatures makes them human? Leave me alone, all of you. Ride on."

Rhiwallon pretended to fuss with his helmet thongs to hide the tears.

It was over. The last troops and wagons filed slowly into Churnet Head. The engineers were already marking out the work to be done, agrimensors squinting along plumb lines, lumber details busy on the riverbank below. In the alley, to one side of the trudging men and creaking wagons, the remnant of Prydn waited for help that didn't come. Their signal, an upended pilum stuck in the ground, went unheeded as the surgeons plied themselves elsewhere.

Padrec dragged Bredei's body with him to the side with the rest. Malgon sat with Drust's head cradled in his lap; around them huddled the remaining Prydn, no more than eleven, all wounded.

"Surgeons here!"

"Why did a not come after?" Malgon kept wondering in a dull way. "Nae, Drust, do not try to move."

"Hurts, Mal."

"Surgeons!"

"Lie still, brother, lie still. Do nae move."

"Did nae come after," Drust croaked. "Must pay dear for that."

My God, that's Urguist. I can see the inside of his throat.

The boy from Reindeer fhain lowered his squadron leader to the ground. "Urguist be dead."

"Surgeons! For Christ's sake, *help* us!"

The surgeons heard, they heard well enough. Padrec hated them silently. *They'll get to us last, they always do, like everything else. Only eleven left . . . no, not even that.* Limping from one body to another, Padrec knew there'd be less than that to walk away from Churnet. If they could walk. Bredei was dead, that sunlit, unshadowed mind, most of it spilling out of his skull. *You wouldn't think him capable of such rage. And what of you, Sochet? You thought you'd be sick at killing; you can't even remember what the buggers looked like.*

Drust whimpered with the jagged wound in his shoulder, squeezed against Malgon's chest. "Say the magic for me, Padrec, while be time."

"Will not need it. Will live long to have more wealth with Guenloie."

Urguist dead, two boys from Reindeer dying. There was a sick color to the dying. A man learned to recognize it.

"Where was God?" Malgon burst out. "Where a's magic?"

"Surgeons!"

Drust reached up to pat his brother's hand. "Jesu knows did

take this hill for Him. Be a's children." Only wound shock in Drust, wearing off into pain, but no bitterness. "Would nae let us die forgotten, would a, Padrec?"

I can't answer you, can't even pray, I've forgotten the words. Let God do it, if He's home.

"Priest!"

Padrec looked up out of his dull hating to see Gallius Urbi standing over him, weaving with fatigue, sword bent, his armor torn and splashed with blood.

"Right then, you little bastards, we did it. You started it, we finished it, and devil if I know how. You're not soldiers, any of you. Rutting fools. Savages."

"Where were you?" Padrec peered up at him with the dull patience of exhaustion. "Why did you wait?"

"I was right behind you fools if anyone was. Jesus—"

"Too far behind," that Lazarus voice denied. "You've killed us. Why did you wait?"

"What did you expect?" Gallius exploded. "It was insane, even Ambrosius saw that. No one could go in like that."

"We did. Why did you wait?"

"Wait, is it?" Gallius still stung with shame for those too real moments of hesitation in the ditch when he found his courage, like most men's, a thing of seasons. "Wait? We went as soon as we got the order, mad as it was. Don't put it on me, priest. It wasn't me."

Malgon considered the upended spear quite within his reach. He laid Drust's head gently on the ground.

"You waited too long," Padrec croaked. "This is what's left of us because you—"

"All right then," Gallius flung back. "Go on, run to the trib and tell him. That blood on your sword's the first you've seen since we started and probably the last."

"Gallius, please." Padrec got to his feet with difficulty, wavering on his bad leg. "Get the surgeons over here. They see us. Do that much at least."

"When it's your turn, priest. After the better men you got cut up in there." Gallius threw one last contemptuous glance at Padrec's people. "After the humans."

Gallius started away.

Malgon moved like a shadow. As the spear poised at his shoulder, Padrec wrenched it from his grip. "No!" For an instant he stood, wobbling on his injured leg, hearing the sound of their pain around him. Betrayed, all of them. The spear sent its own judgment to his hand and arm, and Padrec obeyed.

"*Gallius!*"

225

*   *   *

When Ambrosius and his praefect reached them, they were still
sitting by their own dead. Malgon had frugally salvaged the scale
armor from Gallius, who would no longer need it. They ignored the
stunned tribune, keening with that indescribable teeth-on-edge sound.
Only Padrec stood apart, a ruin in sunlight.

Ambrosius finally found his tongue. "Patricius, what. . . ? Oh,
shut them up. Make them be still, you hear me? Patricius. . . ?"

But the priest's voice rose with the others. His eyes were quite
mad.

> AMBROSIUS AURELIANUS at Churnet Head, to CAIUS
> MEGANIUS, bishop of Eburacum—
> Your grace, I enclose the last letter of Father Patricius,
> written when I relieved him of duty along with the rem-
> nant of his command. I transmit his letter with the seals
> unbroken. Since Patricius killed his superior officer, I
> had no choice but to put him and the others in irons.
>
> Your grace, many things happen on a battlefield that will
> never be just or even clear to reason. This is to inform
> you that, as legatus pro tem of VI Legio, I will not oppose
> Church immunity in this case. For the time, I had to
> condemn him even as he was put aboard the invalid train
> bound for Wye.

Meganius mourned over the laconic enclosure from his priest that
might have been posted from a suburb of hell. He learned indirectly of
the outcome through field dispatches to Marchudd. It was plain that
Rhiwallon's need for immediate vengeance over balanced his judgment.

> AMBROSIUS AURELIANUS at Churnet Head, to MARCHUDD
> RHYS, princeps Parisii et Brigantes—
> My lord, today the wagon train of wounded bound north
> for Wye was ambushed and taken by Coritani raiders.
> Naturally we are in pursuit. I will not allow this insult to
> yourself or VI Legio, but we must assume that all the
> wounded are dead. Since Father Patricius was among
> them, I trust my prince will speed my condolences, et
> cetera, to his grace.

Et cetera. So easily ellided. *There's an agile conscience,* Meganius
noted acerbically. Of course he would have claimed Church immunity for
Patricius, moved all of Britain and Auxerre had there been time.

Most like Ambrosius would never think to number rape among his
virulent sins.

*   *   *

The Coritani moved from wagon to wagon, finishing off the tallfolk wounded. The Prydn were reserved from the ordinary slaughter. Eight of them were put on the wagon, three died before the blue-painted men rode down on them. Near their tree, the two dying boys from Reindeer fhain lay where their captors dumped them. The great dark-browed Rhiwallon had a special interest in Prydn. It seemed superfluous: two dying, Padrec cloudy in his wits, Drust like to die if his shoulder was not tended.

They were going to die: not meaningless to Drust and Malgon, but not the whole of their concern. Before they came to Christ, they were children of earth. All things went back to Mother. But Padrec had left them; not the body but the soul of the man they knew. He lay like a sack against the tree, chained as they were. When they tried to give him water, most of it dribbled down his lips into the overgrown beard. His eyes moved now and then. They wondered if Padrec knew what was happening. Going to happen.

"Dost pain, brother?" Malgon asked gently of Drust.

"A feels hot."

Festering. The poison would reach Drust's heart if the wound weren't treated. Malgon would not speak of that, but happier things. "Lambs will be fat in new pasture now. When Finch sings, where will a rade, thee think?"

"North among Atecotti. Grass be good this year."

"And Guenloie will carry wealth a–sling through winter, but will a nae be walking afore Bel-tein?"

"For sure."

"Braw bairn," Malgon remembered softly. "And wife. Guenloie could be dumb as sheep sometimes. . . ."

"But such a woman." Drust shifted slightly to ease his shoulder. "Most beautiful. A song."

"All of that. A picture."

"Malgon?"

"Aye, little brother?"

"Have thought much on't. Do think bairn be thine."

"Och." Malgon just shrugged. "Who thinks of such things?"

"I do. Now," Drust said in a voice so still, more than one meaning could be heard in it, "dost favor thee."

"More like my brother."

"Speak so? Does Bruidda have my beauty? Nae. And while thy hand has the power to mark the earth with beauty, thy face has none, nor bairn's. Be thine."

Who takes gifts from any god without something in return? Before

227

Jesu brought the iron-magic, was Drust not the one most jealous of Guenloie, most urgent to lie with her, while Malgon took only his reasonable share of her heart, happy enough with his pictures in earth and stone? Then Padrec came and called Drust's heart away from small desire to a greater one.

"Thee did bed Guenloie more than me last year. Be all from one well." Drust winced at the ache throbbing in his shoulder. "Knothead, wealth be thine."

"Fool."

"Nae. I must father a different life. As in the baiting pit."

They watched impassively as the bodies were hauled from the wagons already buzzing with flies. Their Coritani guard, naked except for tattoos and ragged breeches, leaned on his spear and leered at them. "Don't worry, small ones. They'll be coming for you. You are the sweetmeats to follow the feast."

The guard deflated somewhat when his taunting evoked no response in the three of them, but then one had wandering wits, and the others were not really human.

"Thee has more Briton-speech, Malgon. What says the great blue Coritani?"

"Do nae know. Padrec . . . Padrec?"

The shaggy head turned to Malgon, looked for him with difficulty through a welter of images. Brown eyes: Malgon always found that strange in a man with such coloring; then later one saw the warmth it gave Padrec. The eyes were sunken now, the color of trodden dirt.

Malgon gave it up. "Be sick inside. Would nae think one small death would take him so."

"Gallius tallfolk?" Drust snorted feebly. "Smallest of all."

"Did much want to do it myself," Malgon admitted seriously. "This very hand lifting the spear, and Padrec took't from me."

"Like Jesu the sins of the world."

"Poor Padrec."

"God left him: all a said to me, Malgon. God left him. Could such be?"

"Oh, Drust. I don't know. Be not much God in me this day."

Then truly, Drust knew, I hold the magic of Jesu and Father-God among Prydn until it return to Padrec. I do not know why I was the first to feel the magic in me, to know Padrec's faith for truth, but I must give it back to him before I die. Jesu, I will not deny you now at the end, but you must forgive Padrec when he's fevered a-mind. Come into me now and into Padrec as you were with Dorelei when she tamed the iron. As you were with Daniel and me in the baiting pit. I will miss Guenloie and the bairn, but it is not a foolish sacrifice, Jesu, nor do I act from heart more than head. We have become frugal of death in this place of so many. Only give me the power of heart that Padrec will see and believe again. Come back to him.

Cold in the sunlight as on the chill nights in Ireland before the Spirit of God filled him. No, not God. Never. Satan took him to a high hill and showed him the prizes of the earth, among them a fatuous belief that he knew of and lived in Grace. Only a man and a poor one, no priest at all, but no longer blind. Following in Germanus' footsteps, deluded as he, adored by Dorelei and other innocents, puffed with a little success, he flattered himself that he was touched by God.

The ultimate vanity: that Jericho would tumble before God's voice speaking in his own. He was much clearer-sighted now, thank you. Not God's war but a private comedy of conceit with himself the leading player. He even saw it sometimes in himself and Dorelei. Blind faith and success gave them the illusion of infallibility. Blind faith fed that illusion while it cried for more and more. Look you, he was more than man; he was Raven in the flesh, sent by Lugh as Jesu was sent. Subtlest of all sins, doing Satan's will in Christ's name.

The play was ended, the bodies carried off to funeral strains. An entire generation of young Prydn men. From somewhere in the high seats, there spattered gratified applause. *Make an end, actor.*

Killing him would be redundant, but make an end.

Christ Savior—

Never heard of him.

Yeshua. His father did carpentry, and I believe his uncle dealt in tin.

Oh. Him.

What's this? Doubt from the immaculate soul of Succatus Patricius?

Shut up. Where was I? Dragged Bredei over to one side . . . we were all hurt. Ambrosius let me write a letter. No, that was later. I carried Bredei, and he told me, before the brains leaked out of his skull, that Gallius had to die.

I agree.

Would have forgotten, you know how those things are, but Gallius came himself to remind me. So there it was. I did it.

And very efficiently, too. Went through the armor like hot grease, through the Parisi hide of him, whatever courage he found, all that small man's prejudice, the food he stole from your men—then out again, layer after layer of whatever life he called his own. Thee's a good arm, Padrec.

Poor Gallius.

So why are you laughing?

It's funny. Comic. He was so surprised. Did you see the look on his face when he went down? Like he'd lost something, or it was all a ghastly mistake.

Which would be righted, of course, as soon as VI Legio's *notitia* caught up with facts. Yes. Just so.

Isn't it strange how poets and priests try to make meaning, even drama, out of such banal muck? Must've been this dreary at Troy and Carthage.

His last act in life was to foul himself. Not so unusual. Take the female roach: pregnant, the egg sack so big she can barely stagger along with it. When you hit her with the swatter, she writhes back and forth, trying to leave the sack of eggs in life before she goes. Leave something. The same with men. They twist this way and that to leave something of themselves. Gallius left shit for a signature. The dead don't look peaceful, do they?

Just done with it all. It's the living who still look lost.

Who's that coming? Rhiwallon: he looks like Gallius, something lost and he can't for the life of him put his finger on it. Wish he'd speak up. Can't hear him. Look at him there, moustache ends stiffened in lime, bristling like his wounded pride. What's the fool saying?

Complaining, what else? That's what the live ones do.

Tell him to go away. I have nothing to do with him now.

Two dying, these other two wounded. They weren't important. It was the priest Rhiwallon would confront, the one who led them.

"You are the Christian priest, the one called Raven who brought them here?"

The shaggy head turned indifferently to Rhiwallon, then away; the mind within retreated into its own questions. Rhiwallon seated himself on the ground before the silent man.

"See? I do not make you kneel, but sit and speak as one man to another. You might be surprised to learn that a barbarian can speak Latin and even a little Greek."

The Raven did not look surprised or even interested.

"I was born at Churnet Head, in that very fort on the very night my father went to defend the sovereignty of my tribe against the benevolent civilization of Marchudd's Christian grandfather. Civilization had the larger army, and by the time I'd come into the world and was washed, Churnet Head belonged to the Parisii.

"We took it back because it's ours. We barbarians. That is a strange definition, Raven. In my hall there have been contests among bards so unequaled that no man could judge among them, only weep at the wild beauty that spoke through their hands and voices. I have given hospitality to historians and mathematicians and set them to

230

school my children. Goldsmiths and the blowers of glass, far travelers and even Christians like yourself have sat at my board, and I have listened to them all. And nowhere in the sweet song that is life have I heard such discord as comes from your kind. There was a man of the Afric desert much like you, Raven. God to him was like the pitiless sun on rock and sand. No green, no peace, only heat and more heat. I sent him away without insult but without gifts. He poked hot iron into the still coolness of reality and made the world hiss with it. I think you are the same."

Rhiwallon glanced over his shoulder at the wagons. "So they die and go to be born again in a new life or to your sick God, whatever their belief. I don't know or care. But we will leave you for Ambrosius to see. Your madness took my birthplace and honor for the second time. But for you, I could have laughed at the boy tribune. I heard you screaming as you came; no human sanity could have done it or would have. Only these creatures you have dragged out of dark into daylight."

The prince stood up and dusted his hands where they'd pressed hard into the earth with his tension. "Are the beams ready? Then set them up." Rhiwallon searched the three blank faces under the tree. "Which of you will show the way of your god to the others?"

Drust did not have the gift for Briton-speech that his brother husband could boast, but it seemed the tallfolk had nattered on for a long time. "What did a say, Malgon?"

"A would know which of Prydn knows the way of Jesu and Father-God."

That was clear enough. "Oh. Help me up, then." Drust got to his feet unsteadily, leaning on Malgon's arm. "I am Drust Dismas," he managed in labored British. "I am the one touched by God, bearer of the Chi-Rho."

"Marvelous." Rhiwallon beckoned his men. "Put this one up."

Since the hills between Wye and Churnet were constantly patrolled, Ambrosius knew of the captured wounded within an hour and that Rhiwallon himself led the raid. Senseless as it was, the news brought a cold elation to the tribune. Rhiwallon knew he was beaten and was dragging as much down with him as he could. On the instant, Ambrosius comandeered every horse left at Churnet, most of them captured, and every man who could ride, and was off across the hills at a killing pace. By late afternoon, the Iberian scout, riding ahead, signaled a halt and waved Ambrosius to his vantage point at the top of a high hill but shrouded in thick trees.

From the crest, Ambrosius could see half a mile across the intervening valley to the bare top of another hill. They saw the horses first.

231

The grizzled little Iberian was one of the few alae riders left behind when the legion departed twenty years ago. He subjected the hill to a long scrutiny. "Thirty horses, no more."

"How many does it take to attack an invalid train?" Ambrosius scanned the valley. Good tree cover all the way. With any luck they could get close enough before discovery. His force was larger, his riders armed with three pilums each in addition to sword and shield. It would be as at Wye, when the flash of genius lit his mind and Drust's at the same moment—intense boy; of all the funny little faces, Ambrosius remembered Drust's most clearly. The spears seemed to leap into their hands even as they spurred out in front of the squadron.

The scout touched his arm. "What's that they are putting up?"

There was no mistaking the silhouettes against the skyline, or what hung on them. One by one, heavy with their burden, the crosses rose against the sky and settled into their pits.

Ambrosius turned away from the sight. The scout couldn't read his face at all just then. It was not the Beardless Mars. Ambrosius scrubbed a hand over his face and chin, blinking. He stood up, reaching for his mount's bridle.

"Back to the patrol. Pass the word to get ready."

"Yes, Tribune."

"And tell them . . ."

The scout paused. The tribune was having trouble with something.

"There will be no prisoners, tell them. No ransoms. I want—" Ambrosius paused for a deep breath or two that he seemed to need very badly. "I want every Coritani on that stinking hill dead. I'll give a gold aureus to him that brings me Rhiwallon's head. Anyone who brings me a prisoner gets five lashes for dereliction of duty. Go on."

They put him up between two others, but Dismas should not be in the middle, so tiny and broken on the heavy beams.

They said the sky darkened and the wind rent the veil of the Temple, but wrong, there's not a bit of wind. And the sun is bright and opaque as the eye of a god with cataracts. Why do men fear evil in the dark when horror works as well in sunlight? The sun splinters in shafts through the trees, and this obscenity is as banal and unremarkable as the eating of a spider by its mate.

Which of you will show the way of your god to the others?

My brother stepped forward. Not me, not the one who should, but Drust: saying the words slowly for that self-vindicating Coritani to understand. *I am the Chosen.*

Mal is weeping. I've never seen him weep before. The Coritani are surprised, didn't think Faerie could do something so human. Pity my faith died before I will. It wasn't me who stood up, but Drust.

"Padrec?"

Someone calling me. Must be my turn. Only Mal and me left. Please to report, O Lord: the timbers are ready, and I'm posted to decorate one of them. Golgotha, that's the style. What, Sir? No, it doesn't really matter, not a question of faith at all, actually. Sorry to wake You. By all means, get on with oblivion.

"Padrec . . ."

O Pia, O clemens. Oh, words. When did I truly believe? When was it more than my bloated need for grace? The artifice of pearl between the oyster and his pain.

". . . Dizzy, Padrec. Pray for me."

He forced himself to look up at the reality of what he'd learned as symbol. Such heavy beams for such a small life. A butterfly spread on black cloth by a zealous but clumsy collector, the exquisite, fragile beauty trembling a moment before the pinioned life left it. Between the wings, the small body yet live enough to sense eternity.

He felt his lips moving for the first time in hours. Days? "I cannot pray."

"Nae, thee can. Hurry," Drust gasped. "Will nae be long. Head be full of cloud."

"Oh, my sweet brother—"

"Thee can pray. Be nae writ? 'All these things I do, ye shall do an ye only believe'?"

When did I believe as you do now? When? Why can't the nails drive at least consciousness out of you? Your belief shames me, your strength condemns me, and yet I can't believe. I never knew Golgotha until now. "Drust . . ."

"Hard to breathe. Heart be like Mal's hammer." The boy writhed suddenly. "Malgon!"

"Stay for me, brother," Malgon choked. "Do come with thee."

"*Pray for me, Padrec.*"

I will give you all the truth in me now. I loved thee more in thy innocence than any god in a's wisdom, or all the citizens of heaven. Why not? You showed me all the God I shall ever see. You show me life. You show me how to die. May I do it as well. They'll never know the deception.

"First words thee did teach me—"

Don't.

"The Lord is my shepherd—"

The lowered is my septic and shall not mount. He leadeth me

beside stale waters. Drust, you were the reality of my love, not that. Without you it was only echo, a dream of vanity.

... someone shouting. *Parisii! Parisii!*

Padrec peered about dimly to see men scurrying, frightened to horse and weapons, a lethal flurry of movement. In the center of it he recognized Ambrosius, white-faced, galloping nearer behind the lance, and after him the needle-pointed spears coming like a river at flood tide.

"*Roman—*"

Rhiwallon, transcended, making a poem of his death. Drawing his sword, poised to meet Ambrosius' lance. Oh, yes, Rhiwallon would do that. For him life was still poetry, and the ending should rhyme. Look at him bellowing his defiance against that tide, and doesn't he love it? Now *he* is the center of drama and meaning.

In the middle of screaming, far removed from the unreality of such things as men, horses, and retribution, Padrec knelt at the foot of the obscene cross where love was impaled.

Drust's eyes were glazing now, as the carpenter at the end, no doubt, going into darkness that held nothing, only a name that men used as excuse. Now Drust knew it too, must know it. Why forsaken?

"Dost forget ... words, Padrec Raven?"

Fixed, but there was no darkness in the eyes, no shadow of it over the light that shone there. Drust's head lolled forward. "I shall not want, Padrec. He maketh me to lie down ..."

The final convulsion. The death.

I will not look away. I will remember this and tell Meganius. A man who speaks of crucifixion should see it once to know what he's prating of.

Crouched by Padrec, Malgon was brushed close in his soul by that death and began to keen softly. They had not moved when Ambrosius strode up, hoping to save the three men. The boys from Reindeer fhain were more than half dead when Rhiwallon put them up. It would have helped nothing to take Drust down even then. Thoughtful Rhiwallon had even pierced his side with a spear.

Padrec understood little any of them said to him, even Malgon. Not important. Padrec crimsoned his hands from Drust's wounds and smeared his face with the blood. Once more he worked his hands over his dead brother's broken body, pattering the words of the Mass more purposefully than ever before in his life. He bore the hands before him like the Host, to where Rhiwallon lay dying. Padrec smeared the proud mouth and moustaches with the offering. The last thing Rhiwallon saw was a coiled madness that worked over him while the febrile laughter spattered in and out of the words.

"It is the blood of the lamb, tallfolk. And none so deserving as you and I."

The Iberian scout reflected with comfort how little the mad priest's worship differed from his own. There was always blood. Men could understand that.

Meganius hurried his servants along the street, heedless of the chair jouncing about over the cobbles and doing nasty things to his digestion.

The holy war was over, the Coritani capitulated on Rhiwallon's death, the last fort opened to VI Legio with no resistance, and Marchudd's message required him at the forum on a matter of Church authority. Sochet, alive by a miracle. Meganius would burst the lungs of a hundred lazy servants to get there.

"I said hurry. You call that hurrying? Run!"

They just dropped down in front of the palace, run out. Meganius puffed up the steps through the entrance where the guards knew him too well to question, and caught his breath in the hallway leading to the forum.

Prince Marchudd sat in his chair of state on the dais. His leg was draped over the chair arm, but the sandaled foot jiggled nervously. A study in detached contrast, Ambrosius Aurelianus lounged against a pillar, arms crossed. The tribune was crisp and simple in a white tunic under the lightest ceremonial breastplate. Still a picture of young vitality, but much of the starch was gone from the Beardless Mars. He looked used.

Marchudd rose to greet his bishop. "Your grace. Our thanks as usual for your promptness."

"My lord, thank my servants. They certainly won't thank me."

"It's a matter that won't take too much of your time."

"Formality. Your priest." There was a faint tinge of distaste in the shift of Ambrosius' glance to Marchudd. "I am quite willing to dismiss charges, since Patricius is really your responsibility."

"But we must still adhere to judicial form," Marchudd stipulated. "All right, bring them in."

From a small antechamber off the forum, two guards waved in Padrec and Malgon. They were not bound. They'd been given clean garments of linen and homespun, but their alae boots were disintegrating from every mile of the long summer's march. Padrec did not kneel to the diocesan ring.

"Meganius."

"I am very glad to see you alive, Sochet. I prayed for your safety."

"Thank you."

"And this is Malgon, if I remember."

"Aye." The small man stayed close to Padrec, suspicious of houses so big and roofs so high that evil could slip between to do a man harm. To Meganius, a sensitive man, there was a peculiar coldness that surrounded the two like a bog. "And your men, Sochet? How fares your company?"

"You are looking at my company."

Surely he doesn't mean ... there were a hundred eighty of them.

Padrec spared him the question. "We sustained ninety-eight and the half percent casualties. I am one percent of the survivors." He touched Malgon's shoulder. "Mal is the odd half. The rest spread the faith. Glory to God."

"Alleluia," Malgon mumbled.

They look dead. I've seen cadavers with more life in their eyes.

Marchudd unrolled a notitium and gave it swift perusal. "Father Patricius, I have my tribune's full report of your offense. The killing of your superior, Gallius Urbi, in the field—Father, do I have your attention?"

Barely audible. "Yes."

Marchudd snapped. "Yes what?"

"What would you like?"

"Don't be insolent, priest. Both I and Ambrosius are disposed to clemency in this matter. Do not insult your way back into jeopardy. The killing of your superior officer, which the legate pro tem of the Sixth Legio is willing to mitigate. Are you not, Tribune?"

"Um? Yes." Wrapped in his own thoughts, Ambrosius responded absently. His face was thinner than Meganius remembered. "As convening authority in the field, I press no capital charge against Succatus Patricius."

The prince accepted this mildly. "None whatsoever?"

"None, sir. Since this inquiry is under the rose, as my report to you, I declare that Patricius struck in self-defense. Gallius raised his sword first."

"I see." To Meganius, Marchudd seemed far from concerned and barely curious. "Quite. We remand the prisoner to canonical authority. But for the record, Tribune?"

"For the record," Ambrosius appended, "guilty of dereliction of discipline in the field."

"And the specifications?"

"Faulty judgment." Ambrosius moved to Padrec. "Insubordination. Accordingly reprimanded and fined two sesterces. Let the record reflect the penalty."

Not like a man delivered out of the lion's mouth, Padrec just stood there like an ox. "I don't have any money." He stripped off one of the heavy gold bracelets and held it out.

"Oh, put it away." Ambrosius gave it up. "Yours, your grace."

Padrec spoke then. "Since I am acquitted, I ask the prince to keep his promise."

"What?" Marchudd's head came up like a nervous spaniel. "Man, you've been given your life. What promise?"

"Land for the Prydn, which you pledged in return for our service. I must collect it for those who could not appear today with me. For Dorelei, who stipulated the bargain to Ambrosius."

The tribune shrugged politely. "I was merely the conveyor of terms."

"What land, what promise?" Marchudd demanded. "Must your bishop describe for you the blessings and indulgence you've already received? You are free to go, and I advise it."

But Padrec persisted with the wan patience of a ghost. "You promised land in perpetuity to the Prydn. To Queen Dorelei. It was the very basis of our enlistment."

"What memory I have of that wholly unofficial discussion was that I would consider it." Marchudd lunged off the dais to Ambrosius. "Do you recall or have you recorded such an agreement in the terms of their enlistment?"

The tribune was a study in innocence. "Not I."

"I thought not. Father Patricius, have you about you written memorandum of such an agreement, signed by myself?"

"You did not give us a writ."

"Ah. Well—"

"Only your word as a man."

Marchudd stung under the implied reproof. He turned on the smaller man, ready with all the thunder at his formidable command, when the other voice, gentle but weighted with authority, checked him.

"Father Patricius said as much to me, my prince," Meganius declared. "As I recall, the first word out of him after greeting. On the very day they enlisted."

And you, Brutus? "Indeed? Your grace remembers so?"

"Clearly. And as your spiritual father and counselor—"

"Yes, yes."

"Father Patricius' converts, while not Augustinian," the bishop parenthesized meaningfully, "are still a light of God among heathens and deserving of the support of a Christian prince."

"Well. Well, then." Marchudd bounded back onto his dais and hurled himself at the chair, frowning. From a pile of rolls by his foot, he scooped one up and tossed it to Patricius. "Find Churnet Head on the map."

The fort was marked with a tiny circle. Entirely inadequate to what happened there.

"From Churnet Head, we give you in perpetuity the land north to River Dane, south and west to the Cair Legis road."

Studying the map over Padrec's shoulder, Meganius knew the impossibility of it. *He asks a flame and gets ashes. The violation is complete.*

Padrec saw the circle on the map and past it to ditches where men drew and loosed, drew and loosed again. Under a ghost-clamor he lay with Bredei's brain on his fingers. He knew that hill and those around it. Mostly forested, miserably suited for sheep, still full of Coritani trevs. Everything Dorelei or any gern called her own in such a place would be disputed forever, never truly theirs any more than what they had now.

And it was small for people used to changing pastures each season. Even a handful of fhains would find themselves cramped in competition with each other. Move a day's ride to new grass, and they would be outside this pathetic portion, among people who hated them as virulently as the Picts. Padrec controlled an urge to ram the map down Marchudd's smug throat.

"They can't live there."

With plodding patience, Padrec told Marchudd why. The prince was not impressed. "There was no mention of seasonal migration. Or of where you would settle them. The land is there. You have my redeemed pledge. I wash my hands of it."

"You give them nothing. They are not farmers or town folk. They must move. Like the salmon or reindeer, it is their way of life."

"Priest." Marchudd folded his arms like a barrier and leaned back behind it. "I have said and you have received, and other business calls me. Your grace, take this so-called man of God and school him in obedience."

Padrec moved toward him. Prudently, Meganius intercepted, but the priest shot it at Marchudd anyway. "They cannot *live* there."

"Well, if you will not take the lands freely and generously offered, then let the Faerie seek it where they will." Marchudd spread his hands. "In Gaul, for all I care." He laughed suddenly, pointing at Malgon. "Or at the end of the rainbow, for a start. Isn't that where the pot of gold is supposed to be, in Faerie-land? You are remanded to your Church. Guards, escort them out."

"Come, Sochet." Meganius put his hand to Padrec's shoulder, only to have it shaken off.

"Leave me alone."

But the bishop persisted in a soft voice. "Sochet, there is the reality of God and that of secular princes. There is nothing without a price. There will be missions to the Coritani and a biscopric. Whatever else, you did do God's work."

"And other horrors. Leave me alone."

Padrec stalked away with Malgon between the guards.

"Your grace," Marchudd invited carefully, "will you have some wine before you turn to business? We must consider Auxerre in this new biscopric."

"Thank you, no." With no more excuse than flat refusal, Meganius nodded curtly to the prince and followed after Padrec. Alone with Ambrosius, Marchudd took a wine decanter and two cups to the edge of the dais and sat down. "Some wine?"

"I don't believe I will, sir."

"I was being polite," Marchudd said with an edged weariness. "Sit. Here. Drink."

Ambrosius settled himself dutifully and took a cup. "So much for Patricius."

"Uncomfortable little man. Picts would have been far less trouble; pay them and forget it. Well, it's done. Except for the matter of Gallius' widow."

"My lord?"

"She's been talking to some of your men about the manner of her husband's demise."

Ambrosius considered it over his cup. "I was your legate in the field. It's my word against theirs."

"Of course, but I like to be tidy. I want this ended, Ambrosius. Was Gallius Urbi a good soldier?"

"He might have been, in time."

"But valiant."

Ambrosius sipped his wine without relish. "Now and then, like most men."

Marchudd's observation was distinctly curdled. "It never changes. You always have to buy people, and you never get the best for your money. Give the woman a gold laurel of valor."

"What? For merely following orders, and tardily at that?"

"Tribune, subside. Call it a matter of judgment. He was not tardy. You understand? He was an exemplary soldier who led the first foot into Churnet Head at great personal risk. For this, the posthumous gold laurel and a full pension to his grieving widow."

"Hell, why not a eulogy?"

Marchudd didn't even smile. "Why not?"

Ambrosius understood the prince's drift. Being quite self-possessed, he accepted it. Many things didn't matter now. "Why not? I'll write a commendation."

"In glowing detail," Marchudd suggested. "Something she can show the children and visitors."

Ambrosius reserved his private thoughts for the bottom of his cup. "Jesus."

"Precisely," said the quite capable prince of the Parisii, Brigantes, and now a considerable number of the Coritani. "You know what Rome has said to Vortigern? 'Fight your own battles, boyo, we can't help.' There's only one real power that stretches now from the Wall to Jerusalem, Ambrosius. The Church. And I need trouble from them no more than I need it from the plebes. Meganius wants no part of the new diocese. You saw how he forced me just now."

"He's your man, isn't he?"

"Meganius is Meganius' man. We travel the same road enough of the time, but not today. He has an attachment to that painful little priest. So does Germanus."

Marchudd refilled his cup. "And Germanus thinks his favorite disciple is still in the Augustinian fold. I need his cooperation toward a bishop I and the Coritani can live with, and the price of *that* was the gentle treatment of Father Patricius. I think we have managed it all rather well." When he elicited no response from Ambrosius, he put his arm around the young man's shoulder. "Come, you heard Meganius. It is all God's work, isn't it?"

As mentioned, Ambrosius Aurelianus was a private man even in his youth. He wrote his own final word on the matter more than forty years later, in the last months of his reign as emperor of Britain.

The lessons were dear. I began with a large idea and larger ideal. If what I ended with was leaner, it was at least a workable truth. The value of disciplined cavalry has been proved by Artorius Pendragon. This last year at Eburacum, his use of cavalry in attack thoroughly shattered the Saxons under Cerdic. I passed to him a knowledge of the strengths and limitations of alae as I learned them against the Coritani. Although Marchudd was never convinced of its value and caviled at the waste of horses and equipment, my standard for both was clearer for this experiment, and of course the Faerie were expendable from the first.

VI

The Road
of the Gods

Summer was waning and the evening cool, but Meganius lingered in his atrium to see the western sky go from blue to smoky indigo, a hint of orange deepening to blood red as the sun sank to a narrow border of light on the horizon. His tarrying was not entirely aesthetic, although the meditation sometimes took the edge from his concern for Father Patricius.

A week since the shameful hearing, and his priest had disappeared. Worried, still Meganius could not send out the praefect's men in search of an ordained priest as if he were some errant husband. Discreet inquiries among the city's decurions and minor clergy were fruitless. Patricius had not been seen in any place one might expect to find him, not even in the shops, certainly in no chapel. The taverns, of course, were beneath consideration. Meganius threw it over. If the man was gone north again, he might have said good-bye, but what else could one do?

The light in the west was a mere thread. Meganius felt the chill. He rose from his bench and turned toward the portico. The tentative knock at the gate made his heart thud. He hoped.

"Never mind," he called to the servants within the house as he hurried down the walk. "I'll go myself."

In the gloom, he recognized Patricius folded belly down over a smaller form that wove unsteadily toward him. "Malgon? Oh, preserve us, is he hurt? Not dead?"

He helped Malgon lower his burden to the ground, as it couldn't stand on its own. The Faerie tried to straighten up; the effort destroyed what balance remained to him. They both reeked of cheap uisge. Malgon made a slurred attempt at speech.

"Padrec be much . . . much in need."

"You're drunk."

Sodden as Patricius, Malgon collapsed on his rump, gazing blearily up at the bishop, then wilted down beside the other body. One of them belched.

Meganius counted to ten and then, drawing on a patient character, counted his blessings. *At least he's come home.*

"Corus!"

How many days was it now? When Padrec could think of things like that, he seemed to remember handing one of his gold bracelets to the obese tavernkeeper. What before that? Hazy. He left the palace and walked with Malgon. They found a dim little tavern near the south gate that made up in squalor what it lacked in charm. They drank wine at first, then called for uisge, then after—how long?—the fat man asked for a reckoning. *That's when I paid with the bracelet, told him to keep the uisge coming.*

The tavern never seemed to close. It was light outside, then dark and light again, and after that he couldn't see as far as the door and it didn't matter. One of them must have ordered food. A bowl of something appeared in front of Padrec.

Wine-drowned chicken? Oh, I can't, your grace. It's a fast day.

The uisge floated them into a raucous, orgasmic laughing jag until the laughter turned morose, and then they cried until exhaustion took them, and they bellowed for more uisge. Somewhere in one of the light periods, when the tavern bustled around the sodden island of them, they began to keen, but the other customers complained.

Sing if you like, but stop that—whatever it is.

The complainers had a Coritani look to them. Padrec and Malgon quickly agreed on evident truth. Any tallfolk who objected to the voiced soul of Prydn was not in harmony with Mother and should be cleansed from her.

They managed to rise.

Padrec woke in one of the darker periods. He was lying on the floor with the taste of blood and vomit in his mouth. His lip was swollen and split. With great care, he hauled himself onto the bench again. Red-eyed Malgon was hung over the table like a garment carelessly thrown at it. When Padrec shook him muzzily, Malgon opened an eye like a hemorrhage.

"Tallfolk man says must go, Padrec."

"That was this morning," the tavernkeeper told them in a tone drained of patience. "Out, you two."

"I'minute." Padrec thought about the distance to the door, then melted over the table and lost consciousness again.

No, not near enough to oblivion. He could still think and dream, the dreary treadmill still turned, unable to stop. He dreamed of foolish things less painful than others: Marchudd princely in his chair of state.

Everyone knows Tir-Nan-Og and the pot of gold at the end of the rainbow. Weren't we going to sing, Mal? No one said we couldn't sing.

The treadmill turned, cranked by Ambrosius, and Marchudd prompted him in the words everyone knew, *everyone knows.*

Padrec moaned, lifted his head with effort, and turned the other way on the tabletop, the pillow. He dreamed of Dorelei humming softly before sleep, stroking his hair as he lay with his mouth against her small breast.

Be not where but only when
The Prydn hoard be seen again

"Not the right words," Padrec mumbled into the pillow.

It seemed he slept on forever, a Tir-Nan-Og of the mind. The rest of the world and time hung on a rack, waiting while he dreamed. Of course he knew the right words, knew them from the cradle, from the time he left his mother's breast and fell asleep on his old nurse's lap.

Beneath . . .

He never wanted to take his nap in the afternoon but would delay and evade Nurse's coaxing until he was cranky-tired. Then she would haul him up onto her big soft lap and, thumb tucked safely in his mouth, he'd drift away listening to the Brigante hill songs from her own childhood.

Beneath the greening . . . *something, something.* He remembered the rhythm more clearly than the words. *Greening hollow sods,* that's it.

The treadmill churned, too tired to cease.

Dorelei had the words wrong. He hurried back through the maze of exhausted sleep. As he drew near enough to call, he remembered the words in a burst, all at once.

"Dorelei! I've found the words."

His wife's head lolled forward between her arms pinioned on the cross. "Thee's lost the words, Padrec."

He opened his eyes, then squeezed them shut against the brightness of whitewashed, sunlit walls. While his head throbbed softly, his cheek felt damp. Someone had wept on his pillow.

Though he was strong enough to carry Padrec home, Malgon was much sicker. The tallfolk uisge tainted his mind with strange pictures. Padrec could sleep it out of him, but Meganius called the court physician whom Marchudd had placed at his disposal. The slight Parisi doctor came eventually, fashionable in his Byzantine robe, and inspected the sweaty, trembling lump of misery on the couch.

"Your grace, who . . . what *is* this creature?"

"Faerie."

The doctor subjected Malgon to professional scrutiny: an acute inflammation of the stomach, possibly a nonfatal dose of poison.

"A week of uisge, master physician."

"Um. Very like and not the best, I'd say. But that's the least of it."

The physician's examination was thorough and pitying. An accumulation of maladies. Bad food and not enough of that. Exposure. Skin looks unhealthy. Exhaustion mostly. Never seen one of these creatures before, you must realize. They must subsist differently. Well, give him fresh milk with the cream unskimmed. Eggs, boiled only, no condiments or spices. Let him rise when he will. That will be some days yet, by the look of him. Both of them, come to that.

The physician surrendered to his curiosity. "Where have these two been?"

"Doing God's work," Meganius said. "Some wine before you go?"

Malgon crawled shakily from his sickbed, hoping to find a thing lost. This world was not his, nor were Guenloie or the child anywhere in it. He was homeless as Cruaddan.

Truly lost now. I cannot feel Guenloie on my one hand or Drust—
No.

In his sickness, Malgon dreamed not in words like Padrec, but images and sounds. In the meadow beyond the hill of his dreaming, he heard Finch sing and sensed an unmeasured passage of time. He couldn't find Guenloie anywhere. He went off on some foolish errand and told her to wait, but she couldn't any more than Mother would forestall autumn. Somewhere he'd lost her completely, lost the way home altogether. Perhaps he really was old as he felt, slipped through the squared-off sieve of tallfolk time with its sundials and hour-marked candles, lost forever to Guenloie.

Malgon squatted alone over the soft patch of courtyard earth, smoothing it out. There was a thing in him that clamored not so much to be said as expelled from his soul. He felt inadequate to the task with the skills he knew, but he began anyway in the language familiar to him.

He drew the line of men, a stiff procession of them with bows in their hands, the rampart, and a line of defenders. High over it all, Malgon etched a radiant sun with a face and fire for a beard. Lugh. Father-God. The truth as Malgon saw it. But somehow not true.

"No."

He knew the tread that stopped behind him, the voice that found his picture false as he did.

"Be nae the way of't, Mal."

"Have lost it."

"And I."

Padrec squatted beside him. They both contemplated the image and its inadequacy. Malgon's gift was for more enduring images than spears and men. This was how tallfolk would picture it, trying to take time as seen by the mere eye and freeze it like river into ice. Yet under the ice, water flowed and fish swam, motion and reality did not cease. So with men. In his head, the center of the soul, a frozen man could be running in terror, soaring with rapture, racing with the impetus to create, a cataract of energy behind a single gesture or stillness itself.

Although the notion was alien past recognition, this was what seethed in Malgon, stumbling over itself to be born. Not the men but the truth of them.

Tentatively, under the god-sun, he began to sketch the Chi-Rho. The knife hesitated, then obliterated the lie with vigorous scraping. False, all of it. No lines of men, no Father-God. For sure, no Jesu sign. Nothing of gods at all about that place.

"Nae," Malgon said. "This."

With angry strokes, he smoothed his patch of earth again and let the truth spill out. Aye, that was the sun that drew their sweat from them, beating down in hard—straight—lines with a demon energy of its own, like *so*. And there were the twisting snakes of mist that chilled them when they woke, that wet them through as they toiled up and down the hills, rolling along the picture-ground. The head of a Coritani spear darted out of the mist here and there, as it always could. More strokes: not stiff men, not men at all, but the force lines of their forward movement pointing ahead, the strength of Prydn that uncoiled under a keening and launched at Churnet Head. Now, jagged runes for the sharp branches that speared them in the alley.

"Yah, Mal."

Malgon felt Padrec's sharing like a warmth in his hand, guiding it.

247

The knife moved faster. No Chi-Rho over it, no neat symbol but truth as it burned into him: two deep slashes in a cross for a cruel thing that men died on.

The dance of the knife slowed, became deliberate. Truth, yes, but there was part of truth that could not be shown as eye saw it. Malgon scraped the bottom of his soul for the truth that would never be scoured from it.

He drew a mouth, open in pain, distorted to gasp out the bleak question at such betrayal in payment for such faith. The mouth was Drust's and his and Padrec's. All of them. It was beautiful and obscene and it hurt.

The knife paused. Malgon roused himself from a concentration like troubled sleep. Quickly, to one side of the mouth, he etched a sweeping curve: a wing, the spirit of all wings that ever flew.

"Finch."

"Aye, Malgon. Must go home."

"I can't just pray with complacent faith. The words must mean. They don't anymore."

"Then how do I find you here in my chapel?" Meganius asked mildly.

"Asking questions," Padrec said.

The lift of an eyebrow. "Of a silence, you will say. Oh, Sochet."

They stood at the altar of the small oratory that formed one chamber of the bishop's villa. Outside, Malgon waited by the saddled and provisioned horses. Thinking only to say good-bye, Meganius was surprised to find Padrec here, livid, readier for confrontation than prayer. "You are a priest. With the faith or throwing stones at it, you will be that forever. Why do you pester God so?"

The old bishop deposited himself on a stone bench. He tired earlier in the day now, and these last days with Padrec wore him down even more quickly. "You weary me much as my age does. Obsessive priests."

"Obsessive?"

"Yes, that. You woo God like a suitor and then rage at Him out of the same jealousy. Not God you love, but yourself. I, I, I. Pity the world's less perfect than you can endure, but you are a priest. You must work with fallible sight through fallible souls to prepare for the union of God and man. To that you are consecrated. Stop sulking like a rejected lover and do what you have to do."

"What's that?" Padrec glowered.

"I don't know; what honesty prompts you to. You might start with tonsuring to help you at least look your calling. Don't you tire of the exotic?"

"Only when I can believe in what it stands for."

Meganius rubbed at tired eyes. Since Padrec's return, he'd not slept that well for concern and soul-searching of his own. The man was justified in his righteous disgust, as far as it went.

"So you have lost your faith, Father Patricius. The first time, I take it. A moment ago I compared you to a jealous lover. Say then that you are married to God. Do you not imagine in any marriage that lovers grow bored, disillusioned with each other, see how common and clay-footed the loved one can be, unwashed, unshaven, unpleasant in the morning? How perfection can decline? Do you think I have not lost my faith a dozen times over, sought an answer in marriage as you have; that I haven't rutted and reveled my way through every dreary vice the uninventive world has to offer, only to find myself wearier of error and indulgence than I was of faith? You haven't lost your belief, it's merely indisposed."

Padrec tried to shape with his hands what words failed. "You—you are—"

"What, Sochet?"

"So damned *smug*. How do you presume to know what I feel?"

"Because you are not apathetic toward God, but angry at Him."

"Yes." More than angry; Padrec felt the cold suet of his rage begin to heat and stir.

"No one hurls invective at an empty room. Still, let it out."

The younger man's eyes shot to the Chi-Rho. "At that?"

"Why not? Every union has its quarrels. And God, since we are made in His image, is man enough to hear you out."

"Then I would ask . . ."

"Let it out, Sochet."

"Why?"

"Don't whine. Yell. You're that angry, aren't you? Yell!"

"W*hy*?" The force of it pulled Padrec around to the Chi-Rho panel, pointed like a weapon at his betrayer. "Why? If you are there and you hear me, I want an answer. I—they . . ."

His fists beat against his thighs with rising fury. "Never since the Apostles were there children so sure of you, so ready to your hand. They believed. You placid, omniscient butcher, they *believed*! Do you know what that costs? Any tonsured eunuch can bend his knees and babble *aves*, but they did miracles in your name. They turned the other cheek, gave their substance to those who hated them. They were so ready to fight for you. And they were betrayed, that's the word for it. Betrayed by those who pray to you and act in your name.

"You hear me, God? You stir yourself now off your smug rock of ages and . . . and t-tell me . . . what good can come of this, what divine plan? My God ..." Padrec swayed forward, trembling, toward the symbol. "My God, you sicken me. We were better treated by Coritani whores."

Meganius winced at the taut back. "With men and fools, a little patience."

"I'm not a fool," Padrec snarled at him. "Don't tell me that, old man. I was there. You saw how they sold us at the end, sold us all through it."

"I did. But Marchudd and Ambrosius have at least the purity of their motives. They know what they are and what they do and that they dealt with a fool."

"And you knew this would happen?"

"Not the end of it, no," Meganius denied. "Only the ultimate purpose. The Church must grow in Britain and Ireland if it is to grow at all. We may be the thorn in Rome's rump, but we have a genius for faith, no matter how troubled. And nothing and no one could have filled your expectations, Sochet, or those of your wife. Marchudd's motives were at least cut to a world he knows. Yours ..."

Meganius lifted his hands and let them fall with the impossibility. "And now God sickens you, eludes you in His design. Why not use the original words: 'Why hast Thou forsaken me' "?

The force of Padrec's anger seemed to stumble on something. "What?"

"Surely you remember them?"

"No ..." Padrec crumpled to his knees, collapsed in on himself, face buried in his hands. "He didn't say that."

"Sochet, what is it?"

"He never said that. I was there."

"What do you mean?"

"I was there, Meganius. I heard him. Saw him. He believed to the end. He never said that."

Padrec was weeping now. Meganius martyred his old knees to kneel beside the miserable priest, holding him. "Let it come, boy. There's no shame. Let it come."

Padrec swiped at his tear-blurred vision. "Have you ever seen a crucifixion?"

"Once. A long time ago."

"All these years, babbling by rote of Golgotha ... no one should die like that. You know what happens to a man when they hang him up like that? No, listen. Remember. None should speak of Christ's agony without seeing it. The hands are too weak to support the hanging body, so the nails are hammered through the wrists. Very quickly the man grows faint, dizzy. He finds it hard to breathe, then impossible. The

250

heart fails. I used to think the *crurifragium*, the breaking of the legs, was a pointless cruelty. It was a mercy. There used to be a *sedile* for the man to ease his weight. When the legs were finally broken, the man could not support his weight, and so his heart failed the quicker and ended his suffering."

Padrec was calmer now but still insistent. "Rhiwallon wasn't that expert. They just—just nailed Drust's wrists and his feet and left him hanging. Oh, they gave him the irony of the spear in the side. And before he died, he tried to help me." His voice broke again. "Hanging there, he tried to h-help me pray. He went on that stinking cross, Meganius, because he believed where I didn't, couldn't. Even Jesu doubted then, but Drust didn't. What god would allow this? Play him so false, ask his belief, and have it *given*, purer than any psalm, and then . . ."

It was too much. Padrec clung to Meganius while the ugly, wracking sounds tore from the pit of his stomach. "W-what kind of god, Cai?"

"Was nae Father-God, but thee, Padrec."

Malgon hovered in the chapel entrance, still, his voice with no accusation, only truth. "Was thee told us to believe."

Padrec looked up at him, haggard. "Yes." He rose wearily. "Yes, I did, didn't I? Will I ever earn your forgiveness for that?"

"Thee was sold as well, fhain brother." Malgon beckoned. "Come home."

"You can't go now," Meganius implored.

"He's right, Cai. It was me."

"You can't go like this, not apostate. You need time to think, meditate."

"On what?" Padrec asked desolately.

"Don't just shake your head at me, Father Patricius. Will you accept the responsibility, the fact that you are God's priest and always will be?"

"Priest?" There was a mocking weariness in the sound. "I don't even have the faith to pray before sleep. But it was me."

"Oh, God in heaven, is there no end to your vanity even in guilt? Can't you be as human as your own Christ and forgive yourself?"

"When I think of faith, it's not Christ, but Drust hanging there."

If it's his crisis, it's mine as well, Meganius thought. *What do I tell him when only time will make him know it? One of us has to believe in him.*

He could only be a man and hold the open wound of Padrec close to him. "Sochet," he murmured, "I can't presume to speak for Christ, but I know something of the men who give Him their lives. No wonder you admired Augustine; in that much you are still like him, a blunt fist, a battler. You've not left God. You couldn't. He'd have to draw you like an aching tooth, roots and all."

"Come, Padrec," Malgon said, half turned to go in the doorway.

"Aye, Mal. Farewell, your grace."

"Will you not wait at least a little?"

"There's my family. I must find them." Padrec turned absently and genuflected to the Chi-Rho. Meganius smiled.

"You still have at least the habit of God. That will have to do for now. Some men never have any more than that. I suppose you should know: Germanus has nominated you bishop to the Coritani. Something of an honor, I suppose. He was your mentor once."

Padrec said something in Prydn to Malgon; their laughter was not pleasant. "Shall I suggest what Germanus do with his biscopric?"

"Good Lord, no."

"I don't think I could quite find the right words. On the other hand, perhaps I could."

"I'll convey your regrets."

"Thanks. Are the horses ready, Mal? Farewell, Cai."

"God's blessing on you. And will I see His toothache again?"

"I don't know." He gave the bishop a lopsided grin. "Hast nae heard? Holy war be over." Padrec didn't kiss the ring, merely embraced his friend—"But I will miss Cai meqq Owain"—and followed after Malgon.

They had two fine army horses; swords and shields, and a bow and army arrows for Malgon. That Meganius knew where to procure them quickly was a measure of his awareness. That Ambrosius personally supplied them at no cost commented, perhaps, on a peripheral sense of guilt. The bishop sent a formal note of gratitude.

There were no prayers on the road. Malgon did not ask them, Padrec didn't offer. They followed the army road north to the Wall fort at Camboglanna.

"Brigantes call it Camlann," Padrec waved ahead across the undulating moor. Malgon knew it, a British village cut from Britain when the Wall veered south of it. Deserted now, used as a casual resting place by traders and hunters. To the east, tucked among the hills, was Vaco's stockade and Cnoch-nan-ainneal.

Some time after crossing the Wall, the fort well behind them, Malgon drew up, alert. It seemed odd to Padrec: the horses would have sensed any real danger first, but they were oblivious.

"What is it, Malgon?"

Malgon listened for a space. He studied the milky sky and then the hills ahead. "Ravens."

Padrec saw nothing. "Where?"

Malgon's visage contorted with the mystery. Padrec sensed a sudden distance between himself and his fhain brother. Malgon's eyes were clouded with something when they moved on. Padrec read nothing in the sky but coming rain, probably before night. They skirted south of Vaco's stockade, then northeast toward Cnoch-nan-ainneal to spend the night in a known crannog. The few shepherds they glimpsed were tallfolk, and none of their own long-haired sheep. Malgon's tension began to infect Padrec, licking about the edge of his senses. They walked their horses slowly across the level heath toward the hill of the stone circle. Suddenly Malgon threw his leg over and dropped to the ground to pause with the feral stillness of his kind. He handed his reins to Padrec and walked forward, searching the ground.

As Padrec watched him, he was also aware of profound silence. There'd been an east wind before. Nothing now. The world had gone mute, leaving them in the wash of eerie quiet. The grass and flowers about them might have been painted by an uninspired artist unable to convey even the suggestion of life.

"Padrec, save us!"

"Mal. . . ?"

The horror was already bright in Malgon's eyes. He raised his hands to the sky and down to cover his face in the death sign, sinking to his knees, and Padrec went cold to the bone as the sky darkened rapidly, far too rapidly for any natural element, from milk to gray.

Malgon moaned and covered his head, rolling into a small defensive ball on the ground. Padrec felt his skin crawl in the charged, unhealthy hush.

No, not hushed. Shadows that were not of clouds rushed over the ground—faint at first, then louder and nearer, a sound grown too familiar in places like Churnet. Fighting men. The air sang with the whine of arrows. The whine deepened to a roar topped with terrified voices, the scream of a dying horse, all battering against Padrec's ears. Even as the darkness grew, the tumbling shadows were darker still, racing over and around them, the shapes of men—running, stricken, falling, panicked horses. Padrec covered his ears against it, squeezed his eyes shut against the shadows.

It is not real. Or I am stone mad.

For the ravens were there on the ground, more swooping from the sky. Stretching away around Padrec and Malgon, the heath was

253

littered with arrow-shot knights, each with a blazoned shield askew on a dead arm or lying near. Queer armor covered the bodies: not leather or scales but flexible coats of minute metal rings looped and sewn together.

Nothing moved but the feeding birds.

I am not mad. They are there.

Malgon's dark head lifted to the top of a low hill just beyond them. Against the skyline three riders looked down on the slaughter.

Malgon got up carefully. "Stay, Padrec."

The two of them seemed ghostly intruders on the reality of the carnage, the watchers on the hill, and the gorging ravens. Padrec found he'd stopped breathing. Then a slight movement to one side . . .

The young Prydn stood in the middle of the bodies, his gaze fixed on the three men watching from the hill. A handsome youth, his body rose from kilted waist to naked, scarred shoulders in proportion that might have been sculpted by a Greek. Only the face marred it somehow; not a male handsomeness but subtler, a deceptive, womanish prettiness. And something else.

Whatever sorcery gripped this place, Padrec knew the marks of Reindeer fhain. "Mal, it's Reindeer. Yah!"

"Nae, Padrec!" Malgon faced the youth, whose whole being was focused not on them but on the watching riders. In the silence he grated a name.

"*Belrix.*"

"Reindeer!" Padrec jumped from the saddle and strode toward the man. "Be Salmon fhain."

The youth turned on Padrec, his smile malignant as the eerie light over them all. Padrec faltered, feeling as if he'd moved into a clammy room. The youth's beauty was that of a twisted angel nourished on hate. Then suddenly Malgon was between them, blocking Padrec's way.

"Be nae woman there, Padrec."

"Woman?"

"See."

The unnatural cold went deeper into Padrec's senses. No man of Reindeer, no slaughter of men, no scavenger birds disturbed the summer heath. Wind stirred the moor grass with its fresh promise of rain, nothing else. The hilltop beyond was bare. Padrec shook his head to clear it. "No woman but man."

"Was Bruidda, Padrec."

"Thee's daft, I saw him."

"Was Bruidda."

"Nae, did speak."

"Speak?"

Padrec considered a moment. "A kind of name. Belrix."

Malgon seemed more frightened by the portent than the vision itself, the naked fear in his eyes fueling Padrec's own.

I am gone from God now, and hell knows it. These visions are of that place. Different or no, we both saw them.

His hands trembled as he gathered his reins.

Malgon roused himself, vaulted his horse from a dead run, and lashed it toward Cnoch-nan-ainneal.

From the edge of the stone circle, Padrec could see the Venicone stockade in the distance.

"Was here Dorelei and Cru found me when Vaco broke my legs and I believed in no magic but God's."

"Were ravens then, too," Malgon reflected. "And now a come again in dreams."

The first drops of rain spattered them. They led the tired horses toward the rath and byre. Both were obviously deserted. Prydn would have shown themselves to their own kind long before this. They rubbed down the horses with moss and then ventured into the disused rath.

Disturbing: from the signs scratched on the hearth stones, a clear record of habitation could be read for many seasons past. Newest of all was the curved line of Marten fhain, some of whom must have lingered at least part of the summer. Padrec had to interpret for himself, bemused Malgon only nodding absently at this or that observation.

"Rath poles be good, skins whole."

That added to the mystery, as did the iron cooking utensils abandoned. No fhain left good skins, which were considerable work to obtain and used until they wore out. Marten had gone in haste.

Padrec made a small fire and boiled some tea from their provisions. They shared a supper of bread and cheese, listening to the sound of the rain. Malgon stared into the fire, silent. Finally he spoke, not in Prydn but the army-learned jumble of Cumbric and camp Latin. "Padrec, what is it that I am called in your tongue? Have no word for it. He who speaks in pictures?"

"Artist, Malgon."

"Ar-rtiss?"

"Be thy gift."

Malgon tried on the strange sound like a new garment. "Ar-tist. Dorelei has gern's gift of sight. It is to women that such pictures come, not men." Malgon faltered into silence for the space of a few breaths, haunted by thoughts beyond language. "Thee saw the men dead and the ravens. And those who watched from the hill."

255

"So much I saw, like thee."

"But a Reindeer man where I saw Bruidda. A spoke name as thy vision did."

"Belrix," Padrec confirmed. "As one would name Lugh or summer. Lord of fire."

"Nae, Padrec."

"Brother, did hear it."

Malgon only shook his head. "Artos. Name was Artos. Briton-name."

"Artos?" Padrec squinted at him across the fire. Not a British name; more like Britonized Latin, their attempt at *ursus*; that seemed more reasonable. "It might mean 'bear,' Malgon."

Malgon drank his tea, pensive. "Such sights be given to gerns alone. When men see them, sign be sure as tracks in snow."

He put down his bread. Food was far from his mind now. In the rath entrance, the slit of daylight faded, and shadow deepened around them. Padrec accepted his brother's silence and didn't press to share his thoughts. When the words came, they were in Prydn and Brit together for the alien mixture of truths Malgon had thought out.

"Did see Reindeer alike. Thee a man, me Bruidda. Was Bruidda found the black fawn."

Padrec listened without comment, open now to many more beliefs than were schooled into him. If Paul could have a vision to the profit of the gentile Church, or Constantine to that of an empire, why should he disbelieve his own senses or those of Malgon? What was holy, who blessed or elect?

Malgon spoke carefully, choosing his words. "A thing was to come among Reindeer fhain. The Bright One from the Sea. And the Bear. Alike thy man and Bruidda looked to the hill, alike did speak a name. Firelord and Bear.

"A thing has ended," Malgon whispered. "Or will end. May not yet be begun. But did see the ending this day. Lugh dimmed a's eye and turned from the sight of it. World be a circle like the stones. Like life, Padrec. Reindeer came first, Reindeer will end. Tens of seasons will come for Taixali and Venicone, but Prydn will be gone." He smiled thinly at Padrec. "Perhaps Lugh will keep a's promise and show us Tir-Nan-Og."

"When, brother?"

Malgon shrugged. For all his bond to fhain, Padrec Raven yet thought in the illusion of tallfolk time, so he must use their queer word for it, a word that stopped the wheel of life and plucked from it one hurrying moment as more important than another.

"Soon."

Death for Prydn was only a turning of the wheel to youth again, but no longer. Dim but near, Malgon had seen an edge, an ending.

*   *   *

The rain washed the world clean and deemed it worthy of sunlight. The morning shone, the last sprinkles of rain sparkling on the heath. Over it all, as if to say, "Now, there's beauty," Lugh had drawn a rainbow flowing out of cloud down to the undulating hills.

Padrec drew water for the horses and then washed himself in the tempering trough. Malgon came out of the rath, dazzled as himself by the colors of the world. Last night's shadows seemed unreal in such radiance. Malgon lifted his head and sang to the rainbow.

Be not where but only when
The Prydn hoard be seen again.

"Rainbow song, Mal? Sing more."

"Do forget the rest." Malgon came down to the trough to splash himself. "Be most old."

They breakfasted on bread and tea sitting outside the rath in the gift of sunlight. Something niggled at Padrec's memory.

"That's a Brigante song. My nurse sang it to me."

"Prydn," Malgon corrected with a trace of condescension.

"Do remember dreaming it when the uisge made us sick in Eburacum. Be called 'The Road of the Gods.' Have not remembered it for tens of seasons."

Malgon chewed stolidly. "Rainbow song."

"There's strange for thee."

Most strange: his old nurse came out of the hills, where they spoke a more antiquated dialect than in Roman Clannaventa. Their word for rainbow translated literally as "road of the gods."

Malgon sang the couplet again at Padrec's urging, all he or fhain remembered of it. But the words were wrong, the lines didn't go that way. Padrec's hand remembered the rhythm on his knee, the way his nurse crooned it to him, and as they later sang it together. The fragments rearranged themselves in memory as he tapped them out.

Beneath the greening, hollow sods,
The Faerie gold be seen again.
The road is pointed by the gods,
So be not where, but only when.

"Do remember, Mal. Mark how't goes—"

"Thee mark." Malgon stopped him, ear cocked. "Dost hear?"

The distant but unmistakable song of Finch, which told them the days of good weather were numbered.

257

They traveled cautiously, keeping to the high country but below the skyline, hiding from tallfolk while searching in vain for any sign of Prydn. When they came down from the high Cheviots onto the plain before the ruined Antonine Wall, they were in Taixali country. The crannogs were empty. No sign of Salmon at all. When they neared the crannog where Padrec gave iron-magic to Dorelei, they moved even more carefully. These lowland glens were Naiton's, and they'd already glimpsed his hunters nearer the high fells than Taixali usually dared.

"As if do know Prydn be gone," Malgon worried.

Once they risked asking an old Taixali shepherd with no one else about. Padrec offered him a few small coins, but the ancient kept his distance.

"Where are the Prydn, old man? Where gone?"

"North." A gesture of riddance. "North."

What's happened? Where are the women? Where's Dorelei?

Even the hardy pines thinned out as they left the Taixali behind and moved through the barer hills of the Damnonii. The wind grew colder and sharper each day. At night, Wolf's song was more purposeful as the adults spoke, den to den, of prey seen and the hunting lessons their cubs must learn. Sunlight waned to monotonous gray, and a day came when they could gaze full circle about the windswept bowl of earth and see nothing but brownish moss stretching to infinity. No tree or human, not even sheep.

"Atecotti land," Malgon said. "Most old, like Prydn. Friends, but will not see them till a come to speak."

The loneliness was oppressive. They'd found no crannog to stay the night, and they camped out of the wind under a rocky overhang, hobbling the horses to keep them close. Wrapped in cloaks and a blanket apiece, Padrec and Malgon lay close to the small fire. Even fuel was difficult to find, a few chips of dried sheep dung and moss, the flame guttering in the never-still wind that carried many voices. There was a tacit knowledge that since the vision at Camlann, they'd gone past the edge of the known, but known or not, the women had gone or been driven even farther. All that day they'd seen pony tracks across the hills, most of them fresh. If Prydn were that near, they were aware of any newcomer within a day's ride.

"But do nae show themselves," Padrec mused across the small circle of light. "And no fhain signs, nothing to tell—"

Pure learned reflex jerked their bodies aside at the brief, whined warning of the arrow. It drove deep into the dirt beside the fire on Padrec's side.

"Do nae move, Padrec." Malgon's voice was tight. "Did nae mean to kill, but could. Be still. A will come."

Deliberately, Padrec pulled the arrow loose. A bronze head, the straight lines painted on the shaft clear as a written word. "Reindeer."

Malgon wetted his lips, waiting.

"Reindeer? Be Salmon fhain. Brothers."

The second arrow lodged even closer, an inch from his knee.

"D'nae *move*, Padrec."

They waited. There was the dark and the wind—and then Bruidda stood in the fringe of their small firelight, flanked by two grizzled Prydn men with nocked bows.

"Gern-y-fhain," Padrec said. "Where be Salmon?"

Bruidda ignored the question. "Where be our sons, Raven?"

"Thee's nae heard?"

"In part."

"Gone. Dead. All dead," Padrec said heavily. "Romans were false to us."

The woman's mouth twisted in a hard grimace. "Could have told thee as much, fool. And thy proud wife."

"Do seek her, Gern-y-fhain. Where is she?"

"Was a fool always, like thee. A child who found evil and thought it a toy. And brought it with thee into fhain."

Padrec stood up carefully, hands spread to show them empty. The two bows lifted with him, deadly birds poised to fly.

"All dead." Whatever Bruidda felt did not show in her firelit face. "And what saved thee, Raven?"

"God knows. Or the gods. I don't. Tallfolk prince offered us land where Prydn could not live and then laughed at us. We wish only to find our wives. Where are they, Bruidda? And where are Prydn? Have seen none even where a should be."

"Nor will thee," Bruidda told him. "Fhains now do nae dwell anywhere close to tallfolk. Dorelei has done that."

"Gern-y-fhain." Malgon stretched his hands to her in respect. "Blood of Mabh, hear me. There are strange signs. Thy spirit was seen at Camlann, in a field of dead men and ravens."

Bruidda barely looked at him. "Speak."

"Did see spirit-battle, and thee did call to the Bear. Have seen that which we cannae know. Where be Guenloie? What ill be on Prydn that hides my wife from me?"

The fire-flickering image of the woman did not move. His first nervous fear wearing off, Padrec felt his patience thinning. "Bruidda, answer him. We've already seen the terrors of the dark and worse in daylight. Thee cannot fright us more. I was betrayed by tallfolk as thee." He glanced with pity at Malgon groveling before the gnarled woman. Then the pity turned hard. "Put up thy weapons. Have seen more death in a day than thee in all thy life."

259

Malgon was horrified. "Do nae speak so to gern. Bruidda, do honor thee. Did see the dead and the ravens and thee calling to the Bear. Was thee who found the black fawn. Be a thing that has ended? Tell me."

Bruidda's eyes closed and opened again. "Ending has begun." She moved closer into the light, the two fhain men gliding after her. With great reverence, Malgon made the mourning sign and put his hands to her belly. Padrec did the same. They stood in respect before her as she sank to the position of rest, speaking with icy vindication.

"Did rade north from Cnoch-nan-ainneal, all fhains together and Dorelei higher than all, even Reindeer. All in the name of thy Jesu and Father-God."

But would the girl be counseled? No, she led them through the lowland glens in pride and daylight. They were seen by Taixali, even Naiton and his murderers who killed Bruidda's son. Would Dorelei even then have the caution of a dull-witted sheep? Would she think of her people before her pride? Nae, nae, all be changed now, all be in Jesu's hand. Had she worked miracles any less than Padrec? Will give Rainbow-gift to these tallfolk. A will see that our strength be in peace and love, oh, yes. Trust Dorelei: she will go among these Taixali thus. And so she did, with many words from the Father-God's book.

"A's strength might be in peace and love." Bruidda spat into the fire. "But nae Naiton's."

The Taixali elder was not awed but vengeful. He nursed grudges against Dorelei for lost presence. He fell on them in daylight, following a night of dark moon, after making magic of his own. Then Prydn saw how wise Dorelei had grown in Jesu. She raged through the survivors, seeking a vengeance she called God's on Taixali she called Egypt-fhain. The other gerns knew they followed only madness and left her. They threw away what iron they had and cleansed themselves in the circle and begged Mother's forgiveness. None rode with Dorelei but her own fhain women and their wealth.

Bruidda rose off her haunches. "Salmon swims where a must. Should not jump from river to run on dry ground, nor Reindeer breed in water. Malgon first husband, dost still pray to Jesu? Dost still believe?" She waited for the answer. "Speak: dost still believe?"

The answer was slow in coming. "Drust did."

"And where be Drust now?" Bruidda demanded in a flat voice. "Leave this lying fool of a Raven. Find thy wife, an a still lives."

"Where, Gern-y-fhain?"

A bare shrug; that was not Bruidda's concern. "Where dost wind go? Nae fhain will give place to Dorelei. Nae rath a can rest in for long. Be spit on now, cast out, and this Raven as well. Leave him, Malgon."

Bruidda and her men did not move back into the dark, it simply closed around them again. "North . . ."

They were alone again.

When Padrec woke next morning, Malgon was squatting motionless across the cold ashes of the fire. Padrec had the impression he'd been the object of study for some time. When they were ready to ride, Malgon unhooked the quiver of army arrows from his saddle and tossed them away. He drew the iron knife and held it out to Padrec.

"Thee'll have need of it, Mal. Braw work of thy own hand."

"Will have nae more iron. A's magic turns bad." And there was something else that Malgon fought to confess. "In the night, did almost use it on thee."

Padrec's throat went dry. "Jesus."

They looked at each other.

"What stayed my brother's hand?"

Malgon took his time to compose the thought. There was a quiet dignity to it. "Be bonds between us, Padrec. Have fought together, have shared things beyond fhain, beyond what any woman, even Bruidda, could know."

"Bruidda. Visions." Padrec dismissed them with contempt. "Ending? Death? Death's been common as salt to us. I'm sick of religions, yours and mine alike. Keep thy good knife."

But Malgon hurled it into the ashes of the fire. "What are we, Padrec? Where are we? Lost!"

"We're going home. Come here." Padrec engulfed the smaller man in wiry arms. "Going home, Mal. Then we'll think on what to do."

"Could nae do't, Padrec."

"I know."

"Did want to. Was so feared in the night. Feared all summer of death, of being lost and never to see Guenloie again. Feared a would put *me* on the cross when believing be gone anyway. Feared of Bruidda, and how . . . how could rid myself of all that fear and thee, once and always. With one blow." Malgon shuddered in Padrec's arms. "Did almost."

"Look at us: lost beyond finding and not a faith or a god to patch our souls with. But we have women and children somewhere."

"Dead," Malgon whispered, broken.

"Nae. Listen." Padrec shook Malgon hard. "Listen! Are we dead? Mal, I've a gutful of gods and omens. Enough."

Padrec stumped away to his horse, threw his saddle over, and began to cinch with angry, decisive movements. "Gods awake, gods asleep, gods who don't give a deacon's damn. I am *me*, Mal. I am here

261

between earth and sky. A poor joke of a priest, but a man like you and undeniable. We have a family, and I'm going home."

Padrec's grin was a defiance. "Pick up your knife and arrows, man. Iron couldn't kill you all summer. Cannae hurt thee now."

Malgon felt barely encouraged, but the artisan in him hated to leave such fine work. And then didn't Padrec wink at him, heaven and hell forgotten, unimportant.

"Will rade with thy brother, Malgon, or stand weeping in the cold?"

Malgon retrieved his weapons. "Will be insult to Mother."

"Mother's managed since before the ice," Padrec threw over his shoulder, trotting ahead. "A's a big girl now."

That same day, following River Findhorn to the northeast, they came on the solitary stone covered with symbols. Most of them were ancient: Rainbow-sign, the marks of Wolf and Hawk fhains, even old Salmon marks. But far down and quite new were the waved lines of Salmon again, shallow-scratched into the crumbling granite surface.

"You see, Mal? It's them. We'll find them."

Between this stone and the sea, Malgon remembered only one crannog and that rarely used by Salmon in his lifetime. They wrapped their cloaks tighter against the cutting wind that smelled of salt now, and pushed on. When they reached the low, bare rise that Malgon pointed out, they called to announce themselves. Their hopes leaped for a moment when they seemed to receive an answer, but it was only their echo, lonely as themselves, wandering over the hills and gray river and back again.

The crannog was empty, the newest signs months old.

"No, look." Padrec crouched at the gern stone. "Salmon."

"Gawse." The terminal discouragement was audible as Malgon sank down on the stone. "Was a boy when a cut it."

"Well, then, they've gone on."

"*Where*? Be nothing but sea and world-edge. World-end." Malgon covered his face with dirty hands. "Where, Padrec? Did hear Bruidda. None would help them. Will thee byre horses? Be tired to death."

"Here's dried chips. Will make a fire." Padrec reached out to scratch at Malgon's unkempt growth of beard. "And must shave, brother. Will Guenloie kiss such a forest of a face?"

The cheer fell flat on Malgon. While Padrec bustled with pretended energy over the fire, Malgon just sank lower into his gloom.

"Have lost them. Have lost all."

"Ah, belt up," Padrec grumbled over the tinderbox. "I'm going to make us a fire."

"Here to sea be nothing. Should never have taken Blackbar. Mother and Lugh turn from us."

"Such a worrier." When the chips caught from dried grass hoarded in the tinderbox, Padrec settled himself on a stone. "A man can wallow in guilt like uisge, Mal, and grow as sick from it. I could feel guilt: did thee not say as much in Eburacum? Was not Father-God but me. I brought thee to the iron and to Jesu and asked thee to believe. Did nae come as well to fhain?" Padrec touched his scarred cheek. "Crulegh may be my son. My blood flows with fhain's. Was not easy to stand in two ways at once. Truly, with guilt for a knife, a man can cut out a's own heart." Padrec spread his arms. "So, do think a man must reckon his guilt carefully and pay what's due when it's due, but no sooner and no more."

And that was the gospel according to Padrec on this particular bleak day. He felt at his own dirty beard; if nothing else, they'd both feel better for a clean face. Padrec took up their goatskin water bag, chuckling as an incongruous memory tickled his mind. Years ago it was, in Auxerre. He hadn't seen the humor of it then. He laughed aloud.

"I just remembered something. When a man takes his final vows as a priest, he puts on a white robe. The day in Gaul when I was ordained—oh, Malgon, I prayed all the night before, hoping God would find me worthy, piling objections on my hopes, seeing all my unworthiness like a great debt to be paid. Bishop Amathor was worried I'd make myself ill with fasting. When it was time, I was in such a state and haste to get to the church, I ran from my cell and went *plump!* in a mud puddle.

"Well, like the black fawn, I thought it an ill omen of the degree of sanctity I'd achieve as a priest, and no better than I deserved. Malgon, I didn't even have the resolution to get up. Just sat there in that puddle and started to cry."

One hand on the ladder in the brightening firelight, Padrec laughed again. "Then Amathor, God bless him, he was just on his way to the church—he came and offered me his hand up. He saw how miserable and foolish I was, and he just laughed and said, 'Succatus Patricius, God will accept you. Once you get mud on a white robe, what else can happen between here and your vows?'"

The laughter rolled out of Padrec again, a clear, healthy sound. "Look at the two of us, where we've been and what we've seen. Gods, gerns, or demons, what in hell can they do to us that's not already been done? So let's wash our faces and go home."

In the spreading light, Malgon's attention was caught by something else. "Padrec. Here."

In the loose dirt by the stone wall were the impressions of small, bare feet. Not old, not so much as a season. Like Rof on a scent, Malgon traced about the wall. Nothing. Then he delved in the space

263

between the firepit and the wall, the warmest spot in the crannog. The scrape marks were clear as a stag's in rutting season, and the tiny impression of an infant hand. A baby crawled here.

"They were here. We're close, Mal."

Next day, following the riverbank, they found the arrangement of small stones: the water sign of Salmon, and an arrow pointing north to the sea. The discovery helped put heart into Malgon but posed a mystery as well. They'd left the last crannog behind; there were no more between here and the sea. Land ended, world-sea rolled away to its edge, to nothing.

In this place a man could believe himself at the end of the world. The sea wind drove the rain like a whip into their faces. The few birds they sighted were feathered dull gray or black above, fish-white below.

"Cannae be far to sea!" Malgon shouted against the wind. "See? World-edge comes to meet us!"

Ahead of them, the leading edge of the storm obscured everything; the land simply disappeared into it. Padrec wondered where they'd shelter for the night. There was nothing in this place, not even the nomad Atecotti, whose land it was supposed to be. Only the storm and the harsh-voiced seabirds driven before it or huddled on the ground.

Plodding ahead, hunched against the rain, Malgon straightened, suddenly alert. "Guenloie!"

Not waiting for Padrec, he pushed the worn horse ahead into a stumbling trot, then a lurching run, squandering the last of the animal's stamina. She was near, unquestionable as the footprints in the crannog. Beyond this storm was nothing familiar, but if anything lived in it, Guenloie did. Malgon felt her like a heartbeat.

The horse could do no more, breaking gait and slowing to a walk. *Well enough.* Malgon wiped the rain from his cheeks and slipped to the ground. He hugged the animal's drooping, matted neck. *Far enough.*

He was gazing ahead at the dark shape looming up out of the storm when Padrec drew up and jumped to the ground, exasperated. "There's thick, Malgon. Poor beasts dead as it is. Will have to walk them now."

Malgon only pointed ahead. "Broch."

The tower reared up perhaps fifty feet from its foundation on the edge of the cliff that dropped off to the sea beyond, broad at the base but tapering as it neared the top; in this bleak place, perhaps the loneliest reminder of man that Padrec had ever seen.

"Did say was nothing atwixt crannog and sea, Mal?"

"Not that Prydn use."

"Then what's this?"

Malgon just dropped his reins and moved ahead on foot, leaving Padrec unanswered. Against the slate sky, a darker smudge rose on the wind over the tower: smoke. Malgon began to run.

"Yahyahyah! Guenloie!"

Leading the spent horses, Padrec felt the urgency and need in that last headlong dash. *There might be folk at least, even if not ours. Let them be kind. Give him a reason to go on.*

A cloaked head appeared in the tower's single low entrance, peering out into the rain at Malgon. Then the woman forgot the rain and let the cloak go flapping down the wind as Guenloie shrieked and ran to meet her husband. They collided and tumbled in a heap, laughing, trying to kiss and talk all at once, nipping at each other like fierce, joyous puppies, rolling over and over in the wet, weeping.

And Padrec swooped down on the drenched pair to embrace them both. "Sister! Oh, sister. Did tell thee, Mal. We're in the puddle all the way. What else—aye, kiss me, sister—what else can happen but joy? Ai, sister, and hast nae grown even more fair than before ..."

Another small head appeared in the entrance, a face with the intense set of a curious kitten, and behind her the other woman with a graver beauty and a small boy in her arms.

Padrec moved toward them like waking from a dream.

They passed the winter in the broch that was almost as old in Britain as Dorelei's folk. Not even the Atecotti remembered who built the towers that dotted the northern shores from here to Catanesia, but it was long before the first word of Padrec's tongue was heard in the island.

The round broch-tower rose fifty feet from its base, built with a dry-stone technique cunning as Prydn crannogs. The single entrance led into a short passage that gave on the circular interior of the tower. There were no upper tiers; the open inner space reached from ground to the open tower rim, but the thick-based walls had separate chambers built into them. Open to the sky, the tower had been partially covered with Salmon's rath skins to protect the ponies and few remaining sheep. This done, peat could be cut from the heath and brought inside to be dried and burned for a fair degree of comfort.

A place of stone, as they were used to, but with subtle differences. The chambered tower afforded them a degree of privacy not available in a crannog. By common consent and with no argument, Padrec and Dorelei claimed one chamber for their own, Malgon and Guenloie another. Neniane slept in the chamber used for eating and meeting together. The new separation was less surprising than the ease with which they grew accustomed to it. Each of them had more reason for solitude now.

The infants tumbled about the chambers, crawled among the sheep, and made life busy but warm. Mealtimes were sometimes chaotic as the children grew stronger and more rambunctious. Someone always had to leave off eating and tend or scold them. Padrec and Malgon took vast delight in playing with the children and lavishing love on them, up to a point. The men were changed since spring; there was a detachment to them, an incoherent but catalytic male experience the women couldn't share. There were times, like most men, when they didn't want to be bothered with children. They spoke of the vision at Camlann, sharing that with their wives, but never the war. Now concerned them more than then. They could winter here and give the children strength. The broch-tower was an adequate truce, a stillness, not a future. The future must be thought on.

Of the three women, Neniane was the most natural mother, a blessing since she was alone now but for Morgana Mary. Padrec reflected it was better, if such a thing had any good in it, that Neniane's men were lost than Guenloie's. They were no different than any women in this. Some could fill their lives with children and be content, but Guenloie defined herself by the presence of men, her daughter dear but secondary. She was quite willing to let Neniane's surplus love spill over Bruidda. Malgon was home and center to her life now, if even more laconic than before. He loved her, his body said what his tongue could not. They tore at each other like starved foxes in the language Guenloie knew best, but Malgon grew moodier through the winter. The tower was an alien place to him. This last year had wrenched his life into a tangle of twisting channels impossible to follow. He grew less tolerant of Guenloie's prattle or teasing. Malgon didn't know why any more than she, except he'd been in a place of men where women need not be considered at all. If strange, that was sometimes a relief. And there were other thoughts to haunt him that Malgon understood not at all.

"Ah, woman, be *still*."

Wanting to understand, Guenloie would twine herself about his neck before the fire in their chamber. "But dost love me?"

A sigh for the inexpressible. "Truly."

"Then come lie with me."

"Not now."

Guenloie ran her tongue over his neck and ear. "Now."

Malgon only parried her absently. "Later."

It put her off. He'd never been the one to say when, neither he nor Drust, that was always her prerogative. "Did weary thyself with tallfolk women?"

Malgon lifted his eyes to Lugh. Understand? She couldn't even fathom why he laughed. "Oh, aye. Did pass them out three to a rider, like spears."

"Malgon!" She was horrified. "Dost have second wife?"

"Oh, peace! Dost nae have wealth? Then look to her. Must Neniane be a's mother always?"

Remarks on her lack of maternal instinct hurt Guenloie less than an unreachable man. It left her helpless and resentful. "Drust would nae speak so."

"A was a gentle man."

"And thee, sad lump, will nae even speak of thy brother husband."

Silence, his back to her. She had no way through the wall of him. "How did Drust die?"

"In war. Holy war."

"How?" she screeched, capable of anything when he rejected her. "A's daughter would know in seasons to come."

A cruel insult, the most degrading a fhain wife could level at a husband to speak directly of parentage and deny his. But Malgon's smile was even crueler when he turned to her with acid invitation. "Thee's a marvel, Guenloie. Did say thee wished to bed? Come, will lie with thee."

No, she couldn't couple with such frigid distance. "Malgon . . ."

"Nae, come. Did wish't."

Not an invitation but a thrusting away. Guenloie felt lost. "Thee do nae want me."

"Oh, come." The contempt froze the words. "Do have nae better to do. And thee'll not prattle the while."

Guenloie slapped him hard. To her absolute shock, Malgon back-handed her sharply and left her alone to understand why.

Dorelei did not fly to punish Malgon for the breach of custom as once she would have, but it troubled her on a deeper level. They were not really fhain anymore.

"Just people," Padrec murmured as they lay together. "You're growing, all of you. Men and women now. Leave them be. They'll manage."

The peat fire made the small stone chamber warm and sweet. Gazing into it, Dorelei's profile had a firmer set to it than Padrec remembered. The exquisite girl was a woman now, harboring her own silences within her as he did. With no wisdom to give her out of any conviction, self-excommunicated, he could only put his body to hers like a bandage. Yet even their loving was different. Joining with Dorelei, tender or fierce, he could feel the space between them and hear a deeper echo

267

from the woman, as if her own war eroded sea caves in her soul. Not a lessening of love but a greater complexity.

She came to this tower because it was safer, partly because she had to go apart to deal with things she didn't understand. Padrec gave her magic, and through what she deemed a love of her people, she brought them to ruin. She trusted, was a fool, denounced and deserted. She felt betrayed as the rest of Prydn, apart from Jesu and Mother as well.

To Padrec, it was the bleak but logical consequence of his own truth as confessed once to Meganius. *By raising man's soul from the dust, we must inevitably part it from the dust, the nature he has known.*

He brought her his faith and told her to believe. That was his mission. But although he called himself Christian, his own acceptance of faith was innately more self-centered than Dorelei's. The Greeks had done their subtle work. Man stood apart from himself and thought on belief in abstractions with names, making it all the easier to part one dust from another. Dorelei made no such division. Earth, sky, body, faith were all one. She existed in a wholeness from which, intended or not, he had riven her. Dorelei would never distance herself from faith by meditating on its nature; it would be part of life or not exist. Any move she made now would be toward that wholeness again, by whatever name she put to it or road she followed.

Not a subtle woman, still Dorelei knew the difference now between real and false pride, and the figure she must have cut before the older gerns. That hurt less than the thought of those who followed without question. Until the Taixali fell on them through her own blind folly and arrogance.

Until I punished Cru, I never put a knife to human flesh before, but the day of the Taixali, I did it with blood cold as brook water. When the boy ran at Neniane with his spear, I knew I would do it. He turned on me, roaring to frighten me, hoping to kill me. He hoped but I knew. That was the difference. His spear slid across my shoulder and my iron went into him as if it always belonged there. And then trying to pull Guenloie and Neniane and the wealth away from danger, Crulegh screaming with fear, blood on Guenloie's hands ... I needed to be sick and yet had to deny it and stand straight before Bruidda and the rest, turning sickness to rage, crying for vengeance mad as the rest of it. And they turned away. The youngest and lowest of them turned their backs on me.

Sweet Mother, we grow as used to darkness as worms and to death as the smell of sheep. I do not need presence as Bruidda does, not any longer, but somewhere it must be found and life itself must be found again, if only for the wealth.

The weight on her heart overbalanced the squabbles of Malgon and Guenloie. "True. Will let a heal't alone."

Padrec drew her down beside him, wrapping the covers about her new-scarred shoulder. Dorelei squeezed tight against him.

"What be happened to us, Padrec? Do nae believe anymore."

"Why should you?" He stroked her cheek. "All a-sudden we live in the world like everyone else. Not special, not chosen. I imagine every disillusioned Jew who ever cut off his ringlets felt much as we do."

"But can nae live in a tallfolk world."

Padrec raised up on one elbow over the dark head of her, the glossy tumble of hair, the features delicate-carved as any Egyptian's. "So quick to say what thee cannot? You're no different from anyone else."

"Speak so?"

"Just smaller. And more truly religious."

Dorelei squirmed up to huddle her knees against her chest. "Be small to purpose. Have always been first children. Who else be given Rainbow-gift?"

"Who can say? But even Brigantes have a song about it."

She flatly disbelieved that. Brigantes?

"My father's folk."

Dubious but intrigued: "Say."

Why not? He was bored with matters cosmic, feeling drowsy and loved and sufficient. "Thy Rainbow song: thee hast the words wrong. Mark."

Padrec sang it softly to her. The phrase "Faerie gold" Dorelei knew as "Prydn hoard" and sometimes just "Rainbow-gift," but undoubtedly the same song. She was astonished that something so much a part of Prydn should be familiarly used by tallfolk. "A did borrow't from us."

"Why not of both peoples? Did not say we all live in the same world? If you can't see the mole on your lovely back, there's always someone who can. Come here to me."

When Dorelei was lying against him, one slender leg warm between his, Padrec began to caress her back and hips. It was a sensual pleasure to her as well as relaxing.

"Dost want me again?" she murmured.

For answer, he extended the stroking to her shoulders and between her thighs, moving his hand in long, soothing movements. "I want to be simple. Yes, I want you." Padrec smiled to himself, thinking of Meganius. "Let's give the poor gods a rest."

Their loving was simplicity, more deep than passionate, a pleasure and a bonding between bodies that knew each other well enough to trust. Not joyful children now—older and full of shadows that neither expected the other to banish, and thoughts they could not share.

I am not in their world and never will be, Dorelei knew silently, her mouth against Padrec's shoulder. *What will I do now?*

She wanted to be simple, too. She found it a relief sometimes to be alone with nothing to do but feed Crulegh. To him she could pour out the worry in baby-prattle as he nestled against her.

"What shall thy mother do, Crulegh? Ask Mother for a new world like Mabh? Ai, bairn, kiss me and tell. Kiss me, Cru. . . ."

Cru, where are you gone? Tell me what to do.

To speed him toward sleep, Dorelei crooned the Rainbow song to her son, the new words Padrec taught her. Brigante or not; something in them felt right.

Padrec woke when the early winter light was filtering through the skin roof, and smelled porridge cooking. He paused to wash in the open space now rank with the smell of their animals, and then climbed into the common chamber, where Neniane had a bowl waiting for him. She worked over the food with her daughter dangling in the sling on her hip. Malgon and Guenloie were there, and a glance at the two of them, close and content, Bruidda tucked between them, told Padrec their differences were mended.

"Where be Dorelei and Crulegh?"

"Riding," Neniane said.

"Where?"

Neniane only shrugged. "Dost so often now." She settled in her place, lifted Morgana Mary to the front, and spooned porridge to the dark child. Her small cat-face was serene at such times. Neniane completely lacked the restlessness of her sister. She had none of Dorelei's complexity and was, very like, the happier for it.

Padrec missed the boy this morning. He would have enjoyed playing with Crulegh, who'd taken his first wobbly steps this last week before collapsing on his swaddled rump. Prydn young were tougher than tallfolk and walked earlier. Unlike other infants on the threshold of speech, they rarely prattled. They traveled a-sling with mothers who themselves were not garrulous, and many of their lessons were wordless. They cried or burbled like any infant but very quickly learned the stillness of their kind and touched more than they spoke.

Crulegh's first recognizable word was "nenna" for Neniane, then "puhrk" for Padrec, "Durry" for his mother. Malgon he left for later and a nimbler tongue, and Guenloie he couldn't manage at all beyond "gwish," usually mangled through a mouthful of porridge.

Holding him sometimes, Padrec was filled with a peace that went far to compensate for things lost or mislaid. This small, palpable wonder was enough for the time, although Padrec worried, like any father, *What sort of world will I leave you, and what place in it?*

The question niggled at Malgon, too. "Do much wonder on't, Padrec," he confessed in private. Whatever they'd left behind in spring, they'd not found the way back. Perhaps they never would, Malgon feared, caught forever in tallfolk time.

And Dorelei rode apart herself.

She dreamed the night before of the sea again, a round world-dish of sea, no land in sight. All her life she was used to dreams as the voice of Mother speaking to a gern. But gerns must be able to understand the signs, and Dorelei was confused, her confidence gone. The sea-dream came back and back, while Prydn melted away from her, deserted her. Now visions came to men alike, as if sight were taken from Dorelei for being unworthy. The vision at Camlann . . . Bruidda said a thing was ended. Perhaps every ending was a beginning. But where?

She rode the narrow strip of beach below the cliffs, Crulegh straddled in front of her. From the day just past when her son bunched his untried legs under him like a new foal and stood for a wavering moment, Dorelei discarded the sling and held the boy before her on the pony to curve his soft bones to the animal's back from the start. For his first years, he would walk, then run behind the pony. By his fifth year, Crulegh would be legged up to his own pony; by the sixth, his springy limbs would launch him unhelped, but it started here in the cold rain. If nothing else, she could give him this much of the heritage her folly disordered.

I am not a girl anymore, Mother, but a woman with the marks of bearing on my belly, and a fool who can no longer hear your voice. Padrec and I are a braw pair, lost to his god and you alike. We have a word for faith and magic, no more. When the magic was with us, the word was not needed. I will go in the circle this Bel-tein, scatter the moonstones, and pray to you, but I will understand if you choose not to answer. Mabh tried your patience as well. Must I live to her years to hear you again?

When the rain slackened, Crulegh peeped from the folds of his mother's cloak. Dorelei bent her head to kiss the fuzzy crown of his head. The fuzz was lengthening and darkening into the gloss that would be his pride through life. She pointed to the clearing sky.

"See? Will be a good day. Lugh begins to smile."

She joggled Crulegh to make him laugh, proud that he took to the pony with no fear, as he should. The beach grew rocky here, hard even on a Prydn pony. Dorelei slid down with Cru, leading the animal.

Some distance beyond them, small and slender on a shelf of rock thrust out into the surf, an Atecotti woman in a sealskin cloak spread a net wide and tossed it into the white foam with a graceful motion, waiting, then hauling it in slowly. She was small and dark as Dorelei; one couldn't tell the two peoples apart but for fhain marks, which Atecotti never wore. Good folk; one could be neighbors with them without fear of betrayal.

"See, Cru. Rainbow."

The Atecotti woman looked up as she did, enjoying the wash of color across the sky and bending to the sea.

"Thee's heard Rainbow song enough, Crulegh. Come, sing with thy mother."

As she sang the last notes, the other woman straightened up and called to Dorelei in the soft, liquid speech of her people. "Rainbow song?"

"Aye, friend. Thee knows't?"

The woman, a little older than Dorelei, busied herself snatching fish from the net and flopping them into a large wicker basket. "Did hear it now and again. And of Dorelei Mabh of the iron magic."

"Truly. And this my first bairn, Crulegh."

"Did hear Dorelei Mabh was cast out by Prydn."

Dorelei's smile faded. She did not want to talk about that. "And thee?"

The fisherwoman shook her head. "Life be too short for that. Be too much to learn. Like Rainbow. Does Dorelei Mabh truly know the rainbow and where it goes?"

Queer question. Dorelei swept her arm up to the bright daub across the blue. "Down to sea."

"Or from sea down to us." The woman plunged both hands into her catch and held up two large wriggling plaice by their tails. "Help me cast, and thee can share."

A generous thing to do, but a strange thing to say, that Rainbow led depending where one viewed it from. True enough, but Dorelei never thought much on it.

She wrapped Crulegh in her cloak and helped the Atecotti woman with the net. The sunlight, rare for this time of year, turned their brown skin to gold as they worked. It was good to have the woman's company.

That evening's meal was ample but chaotic. Dorelei stowed her share of the catch in Crulegh's blanket, so that her son rode home sheathed in fish. As always, the children roamed free during the meal, eating from dishes here and there, Prydn-fashion as they pleased. The custom reinforced a child's feeling of security within fhain but didn't do much for serenity.

The fish were wrapped in seaweed to cook and sprinkled with Neniane's hoarded sweet basil and rosemary: delicious and plenty of it. The children could disrupt supper for a time, but when Dorelei nodded to their mothers, they were whisked away to bed—another tedious process. Growing faster than tallfolk children, they were already learning, and reveled in, the beautiful concept of *no*. No, they weren't finished, no, they weren't tired, and no! they didn't want to go to bed.

"Think again," Padrec advised Crulegh. "Bed."

"Bed," Malgon ordered his daughter and turned back to his meal.

"Just like men," Neniane muttered to Guenloie as they dragged the children off. "One grand judgment and leave the work to us."

But the supper fire was warm, and when the children were finally subdued, the three women came back to sit with the taciturn men, stir their tea, and meditate over the fire. Dorelei was more thoughtful than usual, but not depressed for once. With the men home, there was that at least to help them feel human, not alone, and she was careful to include Neniane in any cheer they found. The thick stone walls had become a world for them—gloomy, but at least they would not be reminded of their shame by vindictive Prydn.

"Padrec," she asked, "sing Rainbow-song."

"Again?"

"Would think on words."

Padrec sang the verse to her, Malgon joining in toward the end.

Beneath the greening, hollow sods,
The Prydn hoard be seen again.
The hoard be pointed by the gods,
So be not where, but only when.

Neniane spooned the last of the basil and rosemary from her wooden platter and licked the spoon. "Most queer. Not green, but green-ing."

"So did think, sister. Green be green all summer. Green-ing be only in spring."

They considered that. Padrec admitted he'd never thought on it much before. None of them had, but it made excellent sense.

"And hollow?" Dorelei's narrow brow furrowed with the puzzle. "Why hollow?"

"Ai, did think Gern-y-fhain would know that," Guenloie offered.

"As all have seen, cousin, be many things thy gern does nae know," Dorelei replied with gentle irony. "Tell."

"Rath or crannog." Guenloie stroked her husband's bare thigh. "Malgon be the silent thinker nowanights. Be nae so, husband?"

His round head moved up and down in slow affirmation: a sodded-over rath or crannog would be the only hollow sods he could name.

"And the treasure," Padrec finished the thought, "be that hoard every gern keeps."

"Kept," Malgon commented dryly. "Did give't away as Jesu bade, remember?"

That wasn't the best subject for peaceful supper talk, and Dorelei deflected it. "But why green-ing then? Why only in spring? And pointed by the gods. Do think ..." She broke off, small fists rapping excitedly on her knees with the insight, frustrated for lack of words. "Be a road somewhere, a ... a *picture* of roads. Tallfolk word for picture of land and roads, as Ambrose had. Padrec, help me."

"Picture of roads. You mean a map?"

"Map!" she clapped her hands in triumph. "Could be so, a map. A picture of land."

"Land where, wife?"

"Do nae *know*." And she didn't, but all the same ...

"Nae where, but only when?" Guenloie wondered. "Can be picture of when?"

Padrec warmed his tea with more from the pot, intrigued with the odd logic of the doggerel that fell into place more neatly than one would expect, once scrutinized. He tried to order the thoughts; after all, Prydn riches were no mere song. They might—must have—come from a larger hoard. And suppose—

Everyone knows ...

Lifting to his mouth, the cup paused. *Everyone knows.* Marchudd made a cruel joke of it, referring to the nursery tale so old Padrec wouldn't have thought twice about it. The pot of gold at the end of the rainbow. Every Parisi or Brigante child knew the tale from the cradle, and that it was impossible to find, truly in Faerie-land, because the rainbow began and ended nowhere. Was that what the song described? The road of the gods pointing to a fabulous hoard somewhere in place and/or time? The more he considered, the more it made a tantalizing kind of sense. An interesting puzzle, and fhain had so little to keep their spirits up now.

"Among my father's people, there is a story," he began. "A great hoard of treasure at Rainbow's end. Now, just suppose ..."

It began as an intriguing riddle to divert them from matters too hopeless or painful to dwell on. Padrec dreamed too often of Churnet Head and a place like Golgotha but with more familiar faces. He turned to the riddle as an escape, paraphrasing its lines into plain statements for consideration.

In rath or crannog, in spring/ the Prydn hoard may be found again/ this rath or crannog is pointed by the rainbow/at a certain *time* in the spring.

He liked the neatness of his thinking, but even deciphered, the results were meager. Obviously after a spring rain, which often occurred several times a day at that season. Still no clue to where. Quite possibly there was a line lost in the telling through the years. Rath and crannog were suspect because all of them were known and used.

Brigid-feast came with early February. They slaughtered an old ewe who would not live to rade again in any case. Dorelei told the traditional stories of their ancient covenant with Mother and Lugh, and the coming of Mabh to Britain. She spoke slowly with care to the words, addressing much of it to the children. They wouldn't understand yet, but in another year or two, the ritual tales would be part of their memory by pure sound and rhythm alone.

The Rainbow riddle took Dorelei's mind off her failures and the hard truth that many of them were her own fault, but not all. She *would* rade north in triumph through the lowlands. She traveled in a haze of vanity, a folly of confidence that infected her younger women but alienated the other gerns. She showed herself in daylight in Taixali land and gave gifts in Jesu's name to those she met.

When Naiton attacked, Dorelei found how much of a Christian she really was. As she wanted vengeance for Gawse, she ordered it on the Taixali, *demanded* it, with no prudent Padrec now to temper her rage with sense, only the aged, the very young, and women—many of them wounded, some of them dead. They'd simply lost too many, and all the young men gone. The other gerns moved against her then, led by Bruidda. They laughed at her openly, called her no gern but a stupid, willful child. They said things that were not true, and it was clear much of their betrayal was envy. She'd taken presence over them on a tide of enthusiasm and new magic that seemed strong but failed in the testing. They left her with the warning that Salmon could henceforth expect no rights or place in any rath or crannog. Bruidda, descended of Mabh, branded her false. She was not the promised Bright One, nor was any child of Salmon. They threw away their iron and left her outcast, goaded by the jealous gerns whose power and presence she'd blithely put below her own. So be it: she was young and arrogant in her power, but they, with all their talk of wisdom and prophecy and endings, were only too quick to avoid the new. Did she not have to plead with Bruidda to challenge the iron, and then save the woman's dignity by sheer quick wit?

Neniane and Guenloie were blessings. They might have gone with other fhains but remained loyal, thanks for that. But there was the hard reality of three women traveling alone with infants, pack ponies, and sheep. Word of their disgrace preceded them. Every rath warned them off or avoided them. They slept in the open, huddled against their ponies, curled around the children to keep them warm. The wolves took Rof one night while he circled the remnant of their flock. More than one, for sure: Rof was a match for any one wolf.

They didn't feel safe until Mother's mooneye shone over this barren Atecotti land. Atecotti, of course, knew all that happened to her but made no judgments. In their soft, throaty tongue, very close to hers, they guided Dorelei to this ancient broch and even found a few oddments to spare by way of provisions. Few and shy, like Prydn, but they understood reality as Dorelei knew it. Perhaps like her own folk, they would fade from Pictland with no trace but the sinuous animals pocked into stone.

If she was a fool, who played her false? Not Padrec: as faithful and as sold as the rest of them. And he came back to her, not with prayers or Jesu-reasons, but because he needed her. Dorelei knew how much without words. The need was in his hands when he made love to her, not even caring when Crulegh woke to watch, fascinated, which happened often. Padrec's body against hers was like sea sponge in its need to absorb her everywhere, and nothing enough at such times. She felt the fear as well as the need in him, as if she must make up, if only in loving, the other things lost or no longer believed in.

Well, they were all a long way from Dronnarron. She loved him, not by any of the comfortable, sustaining things once clung to, but because he was there and both of them terribly alone. It was lonely to be godless. The joining proved them real, like the stark tower itself against endless sea and moor.

Frightening at first to be gone from any god at all, but in time it removed walls from Dorelei's thinking. Slowly, hesitantly, she began to place one fact on another toward her own tower of existence. She wasn't sure Prydn *could* live away from Mother, but she could think beyond Bruidda's small scope and for once beyond the pale of gods.

With the prophecy of the black fawn and the vision at Camlann, then clearly, as Wolf once told her, Prydn were not to be long in the land. Grant this, then perhaps the older prophecy was as true. Perhaps Rainbow-song *was* a map and Lugh Sun could point them to Tir-Nan-Og as well as treasure.

"Will be no rath allowed Salmon in spring. What fhain gets, must take, this side of Tir-Nan-Og."

She confessed it to Padrec as they rode together trying to ferret a hint of spring from the sea wind knifing over the bare, low hills.

276

Propped before his mother, Crulegh rode swaddled in blanket, red-cheeked in the cold air.

There *was* a nuance of the turning of Mother toward Lugh in the weather, not so much warmth as less gloom in the cast of sky, less edge to the air as it filled the lungs. Coming spring meant more than rade. This time it meant decision. Dorelei had no more leisure to brood over folly or wrongs. What to do, where to go *now*?

Like their tower, any human sign stood out sharply against the windswept world around them. Dorelei hooted with sudden delight, pointing.

"See, Padrec! Atecotti."

Far to the west, the four small figures trekked along the side of a low rise, distant but quite aware of them. Dorelei waved and received their salute in return.

"A never come close," Padrec remarked, "and yet do feel them neighbors."

"Good folk." Dorelei thought of the fish net left outside the tower, worn but needing only a little mending in Malgon's clever hands. She nudged her pony on. "Did come in the first days and bring the bronze for Prydn to work. Have always been friends."

Her own folk were once spread over Mabh's island, but Atecotti came to this northern place, and here they remained. Perhaps the remoteness appealed to them.

"A's barrows be still marked in the land as ours," Dorelei concluded. "There: be Atecotti barrow, one of them."

The small hillock rose ahead of them, worn with age and situated so as to seem a natural part of the rolling barrens. Padrec knew Prydn barrows by now, even harder to separate from the landscape than this, and long where this was circular. He would not have noticed this one by himself.

Dorelei explained the mound to him as they walked the horses in a slow circuit around it. In the days of Prydn and Atecotti greatness, such were the customs of burial. Great slabs of stone were cut from the hills or sea cliffs and dragged into position to form the core structure, which was then covered with smaller stones and earth and left undisturbed until Mother made the barrow part of herself again. The great ones from the first days slept in Mother's breast, which still breathed around them. Nae, look where even now the first green showed—

Dorelei jerked the pony to a short halt, wheeling about to Padrec, radiant with discovery. "Barrow."

"What?"

"Barrow!"

As Padrec looked on, mystified, Dorelei lifted Crulegh and jumped to the ground, dancing away along the edge of the burial mound.

"Barrowbarrowbarrow!"

She capered, bouncing and jiggling Crulegh into a paroxysm of squealing delight as he tried to imitate her.

"Barbarbar!"

"Barrow!" Dorelei whirled and leaped in a savage triumph that totally eluded Padrec.

"So? A barrow. What other thunderbolt hast thee to shatter the world with this day?"

"Dost nae see?" Dorelei wheeled her arm toward the round cairn. "Greening hollow sods. *Barrow*, Padrec. Did think Rainbow could be map, but nae sure until now."

She spun about in the thrill of realization. "Barrow! Where else? Prydn gold be barrowed with the dead. Will yet find this treasure and Tir-Nan-Og. Yah!"

She forked Crulegh over the saddle, jumped up behind, and cantered away toward the broch while Padrec stared at the mound and the absurd possibility of it all. He shouted with glee at the sight of Dorelei, happy for once, prancing the bewildered pony in circles for sheer good spirits while her victory floated back on the sea wind.

"Barrow! Barrow! Barrow!"

If they raded, it must be soon. Food for themselves and the stock would not last forever, and here at the end of winter even the benevolent Atecotti had little to sell or trade other than fish. There must be graze or vetch; that meant movement, and this gloomy tower, warm and well built though it was, would never be home to Prydn.

These were urgent matters, but nothing beside Dorelei's discovery, which was turned this way and that by fhain, like picking the last meat from a bone. Neniane ladled out barley porridge while Dorelei, excited on her gern-stone, held forth with such thoughts as not even Reindeer gern would dare, may her shriveled spirit be forgotten of the ages, never to be young again.

Dorelei's shadow danced on the fire-lit walls of the chamber. Now did they have all the pieces of it, look you: beneath the hollow sods of a barrow, a secret, sacred place, at a certain time in the spring, Rainbow will point to the Prydn hoard.

"And how dost know this be truth and nae only song?" Neniane objected.

Before Dorelei could lay out her reasons, Guenloie spilled the porridge she was spooning to Bruidda, and it splattered over the child's chin, making her howl. Reasons were forgotten in the ensuing clamor that bounced off the walls as Crulegh set up his own wail,

278

joined by Morgana Mary. Clearly a problem for the women. Malgon just poured more tea, and Padrec growled, "Can't those bloody children be quiet one moment in a long day?"

So it was a while, with quieting the wealth, and coaxing them to bed, before the women got back to the fire and Dorelei's point.

"Nae, then," Malgon challenged, "an a day in spring, what day?"

"Think on't," Dorelei teased him with a cool smile. "What great, unchanging day would be the choice of Malgon first husband?"

His lower lip jutted in concentration: nothing.

"Bel-tein," said Neniane, and Dorelei rewarded her with a kiss. "Truly. Bel-tein."

"But only an be Rainbow," Malgon argued.

"But should be Rainbow then," Padrec said. "Be most common then. Will rain at Bel-tein often as't will not. Oftener."

"Should open our eyes and see this Pictland have lived all our lives in," Dorelei judged. "Spring and autumn can give three and four kinds of weather to any day's sky."

Still, Malgon was not convinced. "But why only Bel-tein, Gern-y-fhain?"

"Why not? Can think of better day to mark from?"

She was sure of her reasoning, but each thought was hard-won. She wasn't used to thinking in what Padrec called "logic," or even in words most of the time. He called her thoughts an "assumption," and she paraded it over and over through her mind: on Bel-tein in a certain place, the rainbow would point to a barrow that held the Prydn hoard. But Rainbow fled before the watcher, faded even as one tried to see it all. . . .

The answer came when they were all on the beach with the mended net, casting and hauling in fresh fish. Padrec and Dorelei worked apart, scraping fresh salt off the rocks. Dorelei looked up at her people working on the same rock where the Atecotti cast her net.

"Do remember, Padrec."

"Eh?"

"Atecotti woman. She said . . . about Rainbow."

"Said what?"

"Where a goes."

"And?"

Dorelei bit her lip, picturing the woman on the rock. "A did ask me where Rainbow went." She lifted her arm over the water. "Down to sea, I said. And a made answer: 'Or from sea down to us.' "

Just then a wave higher than the rest broke itself against the rocks and they had to dash up the beach to avoid being drenched.

But Dorelei's insight was clear in her mind, although she had no words for it.

"Must be *one* place thee must stand. Nae, more. What is't do try to say, husband? See."

Not at all sure what she tried to express, Dorelei took up a driftwood stick and smoothed a patch of sand, scratching indecisive figures with the point of the stick: the curve of Rainbow, a figure with breasts for herself, lines connecting them. "Help me, Padrec."

He didn't quite know how at first. She groped for something, not even sure of its shape, only that it was there.

"Do stand here," she poked at the woman-figure. "Rainbow there. An Rainbow point . . ." Dorelei ransacked her small tallfolk vocabulary for the word. "De-pend-ing on where do stand, then—ai, Padrec, what is't do try to say?"

He concentrated on the drawing. Not much for clarity, more like the stylized conceits on stone slabs. "About what?"

"What be atwixt me and Rainbow?"

"Oh. Well. Space. Distance."

He thought he knew a piece of what Dorelei was fumbling at through pure intuition. Geometry. Angles. Stand in a fixed place . . .

"A ring of stones! It's the only place that makes sense. Fixed. Unchanging."

"Yah!" She yipped her excitement and pulled his head down to be kissed. "Do have the wisest of husbands. Circle!"

Where else? The very center of all Prydn life, like Jerusalem for Christians. Padrec smoothed over the sand and began afresh. A mere vertical digit for the watcher. A circle about it for the ring of stones. Then the rainbow and two lines radiating from it, one to the digit, the other from the downward end of the rainbow to earth. Dorelei hung over his shoulder, wide-eyed.

"What be that?"

"An attempt at mathematics, and don't I wish I'd listened more carefully to my tutors. Was never shrewd at it."

Yet Dorelei's people must have been using some of the principle for ages. The stones in the circle were precisely arranged so that at Bel-tein the sun rose over a certain one, at Midsummer another, and so on through Lughnassadh and Brigid-feast in order to know the precise times for moving with the flocks. With his stick he could give Dorelei some sense of her own insight.

"On Bel-tein, Lugh rises over a certain stone. Now, watch." Padrec jammed the stick upright in the ground to show the position of its shadow. "All day on the first of May, a stick placed in the center of the circle will have a certain relationship . . . well, let me put it so:

an thee stand all day in the center, will see Rainbow in certain places."

"De-pend-ing?"

"Yah. Right. Depending on the time of day. Where Lugh Sun is after rain."

The vertical stick would indicate true meridian. In the morning Rainbow would appear in the west; in the afternoon to the east, but dividing it would give them a smaller area to search out the long barrow.

Dorelei's eyes glowed with belief. "Hoard be there, do feel it. The road of the gods. But . . . which circle?"

No, he wouldn't let her dampen her own victory. "Circles come later. Come, were gathering salt."

"Ai, what needs salt when—"

"We do."

"Which *circle*, Padrec?"

"Have nae come to't yet. Peace. Have just been brilliant. Must be God in the next breath? Salt."

Dorelei sighed at the enormity of it. "Must be tens and tens in Pictland."

"Hundreds."

She sifted the loose sand through her fingers. "One grain from the whole of't." She inclined her head toward the others working at the net, and the children. "Still, must have something to believe in for them. Could a be true, husband?"

"Could."

"But where?"

Gloomy truth to match the weather's treachery. The wind shifted, and fhain trudged home with their catch through a pelting rain. A late winter pall hung over the tower, shadows too deep, the smell of the close-mewed sheep for once too rank for Dorelei. Drying her hair with Neniane and Guenloie, Dorelei gazed about the dreary place they'd come to. Suddenly she swore gustily. "Gray, gray, gray, and what be not gray be black or brown. All shadow, all dark. Enough!" She swooped down on Neniane and Guenloie, linking her arms through theirs. "Tonight we comb out our hair to shine in firelight. Tonight we open fhain treasure and wrap ourselves in the brightest left to us."

Guenloie squealed *yah*! for the notion, already seeing herself in a riot of color.

"Thee, Neniane," Dorelei kissed her cheek, "will wash off sadness and wear the color becomes thee most. Green, sister. Green for thee, scarlet for Guenloie, and gold for thy gern." Dorelei felt lifted up just for deciding. "Let the men see us most fair this night."

Malgon and Padrec must be sick of the dark as they, she knew; as any crannogbound fhain in late winter, starved for the feel of warmth on their skin, the smell of fresh green in their noses.

So supper had that much color to it: Dorelei on her gern-stone, heavy with gold, Neniane ladling mutton-bone soup in an emerald pendant set in obsidian, Guenloie noisy in silver bangles clustered about a modest ruby, wrists clanking with copper bracelets inset with jade.

The men were pleased indeed, especially Malgon, who couldn't make enough of Guenloie in her brushed and rain-softened hair and flashing finery, and of course the children had to tug at the jewels and try to swallow them. Dorelei's simple stratagem worked. With the aromatic peat fire and warm soup, her people were at least content this night, and she led them in remembering good things from the early times when they were bairn themselves, barefoot and black-dirty to the knees, trudging after Gawse's ponies on rade.

Now and then Dorelei's glance slid to Padrec and his silent enjoyment of their sharing without needing to be part of it. While they chattered on, he'd not spoken for some time, holding Crulegh in his lap and gazing over his tea from one woman to the other. Then he put down the cup and said:

"Dorelei, it *is* true. It must be."

"Nae, wait." She silenced the others with a gesture and turned to him. "Say, husband."

"Thee did ask this afternoon, in all the mathematics and reasons, if Rainbow-song could be truth."

"Do much believe't."

"More true than not." Padrec leaned past her to finger Neniane's emerald and obsidian pendant. "Bredei said once that many things speak an we've ears to listen, eyes to see. The treasure thee wears: did see it and nae see it before this moment."

Like holding a truth in each hand without the plain wit to join them together. Look at what Neniane wore: emerald set in obsidian. Emerald came from Africa, obsidian nowhere but near volcanoes. He had to describe a volcano for fhain, but the point was made. Were none in Britain, and they were grateful. The ruby Guenloie wore came from nowhere near Britain but from Cathay in the Far East, alike the rare green jade. All were foreign to Britain but not to Rome, whose wealth came from all points of the known world and beyond, and much of it brought to Britain in the days of the long peace. Did not most of the coins they flung to tallfolk have a Roman's face on them?

Padrec grinned slyly at them. "Dost know what I think? A was borrowed."

282

Indeed? This fhain could appreciate.

"For who be more skilled night-borrowers than Prydn?"

"Borrowed!" Neniane hooted, and then the others with her, the children shrieking in chorus to the joke.

"So Gern-y-fhain's belief be more true than not."

Guenloie winked like a conspirator. "Will nae tell an thee'll not."

A braw joke on tallfolk. The good spirits bubbled around the fire, but Dorelei was reflective, turning the clay cup slowly in her palms. "Would think on this. Padrec showed how tallfolk numbers could make Rainbow help us. Now, an hoard be borrowed, was done south of Wall and carried north."

"And must think in tallfolk time now," Padrec said.

If he was right, Rainbow-gift was not ancient at all. Roman citizens like himself and his family were traders and importers for centuries. The wealth of the world poured into Britain to adorn the villas. But about eighty years ago, the Picts and Irish started to raid the coasts for whatever they could carry away, including slaves, as Padrec himself was taken to Ireland. As the strength of the regular legions depleted and then vanished, the raids grew bolder and more frequent.

"My own great uncle buried a's wealth as did others. Many fled to Armorica, many were killed before they could return."

In fact, Meganius told Padrec that only about fourteen years past, shortly after Padrec was taken by the Irish, there was a great collecting and burying of treasure against such raids. So it could all be that recent, didn't fhain see?

For Prydn, all the past was like looking at the world with one eye closed: all flat, no depth. But open the other eye, and some things are farther away, others nearer. Like Rainbow-gift.

They ruminated on the new concept in silence. Dorelei wondered, "Eighty years be how much?"

"Three hundred twenty seasons, Gern-y-fhain."

The number was meaningless. "Tens and tens."

"Tens *of* tens. Hoard might have been barrowed in the time of Gawse's mother."

"Then much was borrowed," Malgon guessed. "Look thee at the treasure each gern held so long."

"A *great* borrowing," Guenloie agreed. They all approved heartily; somewhere in the notion shimmered a pride. "A braw rade such as Artcois, Bredei, and Cruaddan did make for horses," Guenloie continued. "Come like shadow, go like wind. But how fast could wind fly with such a heavy load, or how far? Would take many horses and the silent speed of Tod-Lowery to get it across Wall in secret. Were many men on the Wall."

True, it would ask much even of Prydn stealth. If the hoard came even from a series of borrowings, the loads would be considerable. Padrec estimated their worth in millions in Roman gold, no stretch of imagination when he'd seen a million's worth or near it jangling from more than one gern's neck. Across the Wall with all this, then through the thieving Venicones and dishonorable Taixali after them? Difficult. Perhaps impossible. Dorelei realized that all this truth, dazzling as it was with tallfolk numbers and history, still left them where they were before.

"Where, Padrec? What circle out of hun-dreds?"

"Well, Gern-y-fhain." Guenloie's laughter tinkled in the stone chamber as she gathered the cups and platters for washing. "Thee dost nae make hard work harder."

"Cousin has new thought?"

"How many tens of seasons have raded with Gawse and thee?" Guenloie sighed. "And who was't must always help load fhain treasure? Did always need three ponies for the whole of it, and a did need much rest on rade."

Guenloie looked from one to the other of them to see if her point was followed; it was not. "Well, then: with a great rading into Briton-land and out again, and the ponies all lathered under treasure-weight, look thee, how far would wise Prydn go afore sharing some and barrowing the rest?"

Padrec nodded carefully. "Dost make sense."

"Would carry it through Venicones or Taixali, whose blood I curse in my own veins?"

"Wait." A spark from Guenloie's idea caught fire in Padrec's imagination. "Be only certain places to cross, and those only in the dark."

"On moonless nights or in storm," Dorelei prompted.

"And those crossings . . ." Padrec tried to picture the army maps of the Wall and the crossing places he knew. Camboglanna, Brocolitia, near Cilurnum. The notion made excellent logistic sense. *My God, the perfect place, not a day from the* Wall.

"Cnoch-nan-ainneal!"

"The Hill of the Fires." Dorelei glowed with vindication.

"Thee's right, right, *right!*" Padrec swept Guenloie up into his arms in a thrill of excitement, flustering her.

"Nae, Padrec, *stop.*"

"Why did thee nae tell thee was genius, cousin?"

"Oh . . ." There was no vanity in her self-effacing blush. "Did nae ever ask me." A furtive glance at her fhain sisters. "Tallfolk blood be always last in fhain."

"Cousin, thee's been long clean of that," Dorelei said.

"But was habit, Gern-y-fhain. Gawse did call me slow and stupid, and thee and Neniane. So." Guenloie shrugged ingenuously. "Did think't myself."

Malgon toyed with the new notion, liking it. "Why *not* Cnoch-nan-ainneal?"

"Why not?" Dorelei sealed it. "Hast been ours since first days and closest to Wall. Mabh herself put a rath on the hill."

The simple truth of it awed Padrec. They might have walked over the Prydn hoard many times. No longer a mere puzzle to divert them at supper. So the song-map was heard by Brigantes trading across the Wall and taken home as doggerel for lulling children like himself to sleep, already half forgotten by Prydn with their own foreshortened sense of the past.

Until now.

The Hill of the Fires. It could be.

Dorelei crossed her legs on the stone, back straight, arms resting on her knees in the formal position for gern-speaking.

"Salmon fhain will rade early this season to Cnoch-nan-ainneal. Will trade with Atecotti for what be needed even an be naught but fish and vetch. Will take our flocks. Those that die on rade will be eaten, the fleeces saved. Will be on the hill before other fhains even think to move."

She paused, distilling the cold remainder of her thought.

"For other fhains, a's cast us out. An a try to take rath from us, will be a's misfortune. If Salmon be no longer of a's blood, then they none of ours. Will find this treasure for Salmon alone. Will walk again in Mother's breast, but alone."

Padrec bowed his head toward her. "Yah, Gern-y-fhain."

The others agreed sibilantly. Y*ah*.

"Be a thing to end or begin, be there't will happen. So speaks thy gern."

End or beginning, her people, even for a little while, would have a new faith and purpose. Beyond that hill there was nothing for them but Tir-Nan-Og.

Mother, it is I, Dorelei Mabh. There is no circle here for you to find me in, no moonstones to please your eye. We lose many things in this new world, but we learn as well. The other gerns cast me out, so we are no longer bound by Prydn law to share or be a part. They are not as wise as I once thought. Truly, I think Bruidda is only a tired old woman and a frightened one. The world is more than I knew; I am not on the edge of Bruidda's world, but in the center of my own. Mabh had the sight to see and the courage to change, and though she angered you, she was your first great gern, like Mo-ses. Watch over our rade.

Lugh Sun, let Rainbow point us to the hoard, and as well to Tir-Nan-Og, which you promised in the first days. Be much needed now. Show us the mole on our back that we cannot see, for we can wait no longer. Let ending be beginning. There is no place else for us now. I promise when we come to the first circle on rade, I will leave my last gold torc for you to remember with. Send us Rainbow at Bel-tein.

Jesu, Son of Father-God—I leave farewells to the last. We are very sorry to leave You, but we must return to what we know, to Mother and Lugh. Will be hard for You to understand, but we must go where the magic lives, even beyond world-edge. I will be promised no longer, but will have Tir-Nan-Og for my folk. You, who are a god of the small soul, will understand. Mo-ses only listened to the bush that burned. I must go into it, take the god by the hand, and demand miracles, not for later but now. You will know how low hope can burn in gerns who are only human women.

Even when You spoke in riddles, You were a gentle and generous god, Jesu. You gave us iron-magic. You gave me Padrec, who is my joy, and though he is gone from You, have eye to his care now and then. I do not think he can live without his gods any more than I without mine.

You were a braw god, Jesu, but ... You and Your priests have very strange notions about men and women, like Padrec when he came to us, but marriage cured him. It would have been better if You married. You would have known a little more about women. But You helped me find not only the name of Mabh, but Dorelei as well. You helped me say my own name aloud in the world. I will not forget. Father-God bless you. We go.

VII
Where the Magic Lives

I t was still March and the wind sharp when they led their ponies up Cnoch-nan-ainneal and entered the stone circle. With Crulegh in her arms, Dorelei turned slowly in a full circuit about the center.

"Was here I offered my first stones to Mother as gern, Cru. Here we found Padrec." *And here we could end.* "Here we begin again,"'she announced firmly to her people. "Be much to do."

She assigned their tasks. For this day, she and Neniane would take charge of the children and consecrate the new fire with unburned fragments of the old. Malgon would hunt (and be frugal with good arrows, mind), Guenloie would search out and prepare moonstones to offer Mother.

"And Padrec will make the magic of the tallfolk numbers. The mathe-matic. Let us begin then."

Alone in the circle, Padrec noted the position of the afternoon sun moving into and out of cloud. It could be a beginning; failure wouldn't be for want of trying. They'd traveled nigh the length of Pictland, from Moray Firth to the Wall. The few encounters with tallfolk

289

tribes were ticklish but bloodless, since they kept to the high ridges. The decision to rade early was wise. No other fhains were yet on the move. They used bits of gold and small jewels from the last of their treasure to trade for barley and winter vegetables, and now and then they butchered an old ewe for mutton. They met no fhains on the way, and very few signs were observed. Beyond the generation that died in the holy war, the rest of Prydn seemed to have melted away.

Were there so few to begin with that less than two hundred would make such a difference?

Why not? Last year the fhains massed on this hill numbered less than a thousand, and all said it was the largest gathering in memory. From here to Catanesia, there were probably less than half that in all now. Vanishing.

Lord God, no matter that you and I are not getting on, but these people gave more than I ever did or will. Let's not haggle faith or the purpose of miracles. They need one now.

He picked up the sharpened stake by his foot and began to pace the circle, which was more elliptical than round on an east–west axis. With the Roman gradus as measure, he estimated as closely as possible the exact center of the stones and hammered the stake upright with his sword hilt.

Begun.

Padrec noted the position of the sun and the pale shadow angling from his sundial-stake. Not quite gone two of the clock. No hint of rain, not yet. But a generous distribution of rain and sun with accurate notings of time could give him a spread of rainbow positions, morning and evening. On Bel-tein the sun would rise directly over the most easterly stone; thus it was aligned.

If he was right, and if they were in the right circle out of hundreds, if the sun shone enough to help his perilous mathematics, if it rained often enough at the right time of day, and if his theory was correct to begin with, if another fhain didn't challenge them for the hill or the Venicones drive them out, they just might be within arm's reach of the miracle they needed.

The next morning at dawn, he and Dorelei were waiting by his stake to see where the sun rose. Dorelei had no word for complex numbers but knew exactly how many days to Bel-tein.

"Four tens and five."

"Forty-five days." Padrec grinned at the wry coincidence. "The Ides of March. Caesar died on this day. Did make great roil in Rome."

She looked anxious: had they begun on an ill day, then?

"Just for Romans. Look, see what Lugh tells us."

He drew a circle in the earth with his knife, two lines slicing into it at close angles, one for this day, one for Bel-tein morning. Knowing this much, he could halve and quarter the difference and virtually predict where Rainbow would appear and point in the world-dish round them, even before the day came.

Dorelei flushed with admiration. What other man could, with a few scratched lines, so foretell the movements of Lugh? Truly Padrec was Raven-gift and his magic awesome, but she could still help in some things.

"Barrow will be higher in the west than east. And must look sharp. Will be hard to find."

The weather warmed day by day. They moved out of the crannog, set up, and sodded over the rath, wondering when the Venicones would notice them, and one day Malgon found out.

He was hunting in the wood north of their hill just after daybreak, hoping for a buck deer. Doe was forbidden now, still needed to mother the new fawns, nor was it the best time of year for Stag, and Malgon apologized to his spirit beforehand, but food was needed. The hunt should not be difficult. Fhain knew all the thickets favored by deer and their morning and evening trails to water. He planted himself upwind of the freshest trail and waited as morning grew brighter.

Tallfolk notion of quiet was laughable; he knew Venicone were near long before they showed themselves. They'd been spoiled by a whole autumn and winter of free ranging on the slopes with no Prydn to fear, and here they came clumping through the thickets, secret as a thunderstorm. Malgon debated showing himself and decided it was the better course. They should not be allowed too close to the rath or know how few lived in it. He stepped out of the thicket directly in their path, one arrow nocked, another ready.

It was Elder Vaco himself, one of his brothers, and a much younger man, probably one of Vaco's nephews. To the Venicones, his appearance was startling as it was silent. They halted, unprepared, their bows not even strung yet. The unmoving little man could impale all three of them before they had a chance. Vaco tried to read that face. A year ago it was impassive; now there was something darker and tacitly dangerous.

"So the Faerie are back. We heard it was that you were all dead in the war of the Romans."

"Many are returned to Cnoch-nan-ainneal," Malgon assured him.

The other two men edged apart from Vaco as if to encircle Malgon. His bow lifted slightly. "Do but hunt this day."

"This hill is ours now," Vaco claimed. "We have grazed our flocks on it."

"Will be as't was before. Glens be Venicone, hills Prydn."

"Put down the bow," the young man said in what he hoped was a threatening voice. His hand itched toward the knife at his belt. "Elder Vaco will be merciful."

Malgon shook his head. "Do hunt. Thy noise frights game. Go."

The youth mistook Malgon's stillness for indecision. He took a step forward. His hand touched the knife. The stillness of Malgon flowed into motion. The bowstring thummed loud in the clearing. The youth jerked and howled as the arrow pinned the fleshy part of his right arm, protruding from it. In the next eye-blink, the other arrow was nocked and ready.

Vaco recovered himself. "You little—"

The sentiment choked off as the cold metal edge touched his throat, the voice as cold. "That would be foolish and wasteful, Elder Vaco. You would die for nothing where no harm is intended you."

"Who," Vaco sputtered, off balance, "who is it that is behind me?"

"The Jesu priest," his brother said sourly.

"So you see the truth my brother speaks. The Faerie once again claim their ancient hill. Don't move, Elder. Your youth is lucky. Malgon need not have taken just his arm, but the arrow is tipped with aconite, so the wound should be quickly tended."

Padrec removed the knife from Vaco's throat and stepped out to face them at Malgon's side. No, the cold of them was no mere impression. They were different men than those who feasted in his hall the summer past. It was as if some of the life had been leached from them and replaced with iron. It glinted in their eyes. Padrec drew his sword and leaned on it.

"We are not of your world, nor will we be long in it. Dorelei Mabh, who tamed the iron, now seeks for Tir-Nan-Og. Our flocks will not graze in Vaco's meadows. Our magic will not take from his presence. A little time only will we be among you, then no more. Will Vaco be wise enough to see there is no war between us? We have already seen war. There is no profit in it and no honor."

Vaco hovered between two fires—the need for presence, and the quiet force of this weird Jesu-man. He and his wife broke the age-old magic of iron. They came bearing gifts, one of them quieted three vicious dogs with a look, were rumored dead and gone, and now stood here before him, and he seriously doubted in his superstitious soul if the priest, the demon-bitch, or any of them *could* be killed. The priest was once an easy target for ridicule; now his very stillness was formidable. He dangled the sword casually, motioning Vaco to one side in private speech.

"Vaco, let us end this. Take the boy, mend his arm, leave us the hill. We ask no more. Do that, and this night you will hear the bean sidhe cry out our bargain to the gods. Will it be so?"

"You will stay out of our glens?" Vaco demanded in a loud voice for the others. "You will work no magic against the Venicone, man, woman, flock, or field?"

"None."

"Then I grant you the hill." Vaco sealed the bargain with an expansive gesture. "So long as Faerie keep their place, agreed?"

"Agreed. The Venicone are old and mighty in the land. Get the boy home before his arm festers."

And that was, happily, the last they ever saw of Vaco. His presence acknowledged and the Faerie respectful, he allowed them what he would not have labored to take in any case. He and his brother helped the shaken youth away down the hill through the trees.

And Malgon was very pleased Padrec happened by at such an opportune time.

"Luck. Was on the ridge and saw them set out for the wood." Padrec sheathed his sword. "Will be no buck this morning, brother."

Malgon agreed reluctantly, not with such noisy tallfolk in the wood. Stag would be far away now and running yet. Malgon might as well wait the evening or try for smaller game. They squatted in the thicket, grinning at each other as the sun rose higher through the trees.

"Must keen tonight, Mal. Did tell them bean sidhe would sing on the Hill of the Fires."

"Be none dead."

"Be nae poison to thy arrows, either. Will nae tell an thee won't."

Malgon sifted the idea. Very tallfolk it was to make profit of a belief, but shrewd in this case. "Will sing Venicones to sleep."

"Tonight and often." Padrec sniffed at the air. "Will be showers. Must watch from circle."

That night the wind whispering about Vaco's stockade was haunted with the dark song of the bean sidhe. No man, for his life, would go near Cnoch-nan-ainneal when the shadows lengthened eastward, and few during the day. Fhain breathed easier.

Sighted from the center of the stones, the sun slid each day closer to the Bel-tein stone. Rain showers were brief and frequent but not always followed by a rainbow, so another variable factor had to be worked into an already fragile hypothesis. The length of time between cessation of the rain to the clearing sky and sunlight. To compensate, Padrec estimated the time at optimum: a rain shower with no fading of sunlight, which happened quite often. He marked the morning and evening position of rainbows, no matter how faint or brief. For each observation, he set up a sapling rod notched at the top which, from his center, he sighted on that point where the rainbow would touch earth.

Forty days to Bel-tein, thirty-five. Thirty. The center of Dorelei's worship place now looked rather complicated. Padrec's rods became a cage in which he gradually mewed himself up. Each sighting called for an investigation. One of them, whoever could be spared, would saddle Padrec's horse, the fastest they had, and ride out sometimes for miles to the sighted point. One rider alone could more easily elude Venicone detection. The truce was unbroken, but they would ruffle no feathers meanwhile.

Report was always the same. "Nae barrow," Guenloie said, slipping down from the saddle.

"Did look sharp?"

"Until my eyes pained, Gern-y-fhain. None."

Prydn barrows were not that numerous or easily detected. From the first days, the bones of the dead were stored in temporary houses, split, dismembered, and stacked neatly until the death of a person of note, usually a gern. When the gern died, the barrow would be put up and communal ceremony done for all the waiting dead, who would then be interred with the great one.

So it was in the first days, Dorelei told Padrec. Many of the oldest barrows were forgotten, all kept secret. Was never good to let tallfolk keep count of their deaths with Prydn so few in the land.

Twenty-five days to Bel-tein. Twenty. Fifteen.

"And . . . midpoint." Padrec drove a notched rod between the two stones and swung back to Dorelei with long strides, flourishing his writing shingle peppered with calculations.

"Fifteen days past, fifteen yet to come. Mind the rod, don't jar it. See."

She dutifully admired the incomprehensible bird tracks, curves, crosses, and odd scribblings. "Most braw. What dost say?"

Padrec was rather pleased with himself. "More than it did. Have marked where Rainbow went down for fifteen days. Nine times: six of the evening, three of the morning. Beginning to get some sense of distribution. Proportion."

Dorelei was impressed. Mathe-matic was sorcery to be reckoned with, but . . . proportion?

"Well, percentage."

No light there, either.

"Be simple." Padrec swept his arm over the southern horizon. "Because of where Lugh Sun is now, Rainbow shines south of our hill. Southeast in the evening, southwest in morn. Be nae so close thee can put the point of a pin to it but can make areas to search. So."

He carved two short arcs in the dirt with his knife, two more under them, joined by straight lines into two warped rectangles. "Twixt now and Bel-tein, Rainbow will nae wander that much." Padrec bent over his latest planted rod, squinted through the notch to the southwest. Not an hour before by his sundial stake, there was a shower so brief the sun didn't even bother to cloud over. The colors bent to earth only for a few minutes, but Padrec was there, like Cruaddan on the track of deer, to mark it . . . yes. So.

He straightened up and pulled Dorelei close, planting light kisses on her mouth and narrow cheeks. "Will Gern-y-fhain ride with me?"

"Where?"

He pointed again to the southwest, delineating two points. "Atwixt there and there."

Dorelei's gaze narrowed like an archer's, fixing one point, then the other, and the ground between, a rumple of sparsely wooded low hills, rarely used for graze or anything else.

"Come."

The approximate area of search was about a mile square, the winter grass turning lush with mild spring rain. Violets peeped from the humus at the foot of young trees, and oak saplings were coming into leaf. Padrec and Dorelei rode as much for the beauty of the afternoon as for any quest, but her awareness of the place was as much instinct as sight. Coming out of the trees onto a little knoll, she pointed to the stone slab lying flat, slowly disappearing under moss.

She'd seen it often, year by year watched the faint etchings wear and be covered. Ancient animals, ancient memories of them. The bog elk: a few were left in Ireland, Padrec said, but long vanished from Britain.

"Be most old," Dorelei murmured over the stone. "Should nae be forgot."

She scraped at the encroaching moss near the foot of the slab, casually at first, then with more purpose as it became clear that the moss obscured more than she'd thought. Under her knife, old fhain signs appeared—Hawk, Marten, even Salmon, pocked into the granite with a bronze awl by some dim ancestor. The knife scraped over the surface, the only sound in the silent world around them, even the wind's whisper fallen to nothing.

"Padrec, look."

So worn it was barely readable, already ages old before Mother grew over it. "Reindeer fhain. Long before Bruidda, that's sure."

"What be older than hundreds, husband?"

"Thousands."

Meaningless to Dorelei, but other things were near as yesterday. "Be tale-speaking that Mabh put first rath on the Hill of the Fires and raised the stones."

She gazed thoughtfully at the sign. The young grace of her, the antiquity of her unhistoried people in this land . . . Padrec felt a sudden, vast pity like a requiem. Egypt, for all its unimaginable ages, was real as Jupiter in enduring stone: temples, tombs, pyramids whose unreadable inscriptions could yet say, *Here we were. Here we lived, a people.*

And here his wife like a last flower in a garden sinking under bog. Where were the fhains of even a few years ago? Where the thousands that flourished after Mabh and greeted the bronze-bringers? Mere hundreds now, scattered over Pictland, trekking from one crannog to the next, even their long-haired sheep an antique curiosity seen nowhere else. Stones in a lonely, shunned circle, shadows slipping over a hilltop. Faint marks in stone obliterated by the very Nature they worshipped, fewer and fewer to read them or care. People who never wrote a word or needed to, and there the difference. But for the writing, even Christ might be forgotten, who was to say?

He saw Dorelei clear with her narrow head bowed over the stone. A tiny woman in half-cured sheepskin and skirt of ragged wool fringes, usually hung with thistle or burrs, that even a tattooed Pict would call outlandish. Yet she had been to him in reality what he once asked of God. Through her he was born again as surely as if she'd forced him from her own womb with Crulegh. She gave him eyes to see the world he lived in, and even now in her doe-graceful youth, he saw her dead and gone as those who scratched the fading marks on this stone.

"Dorelei."

She couldn't understand why he hugged her so close and hard.

"Because I love you."

Because you have made me whole, I see the whole and that there will be an end, and I dread it. That must be what makes the light so lovely, knowing it will go. We see the parting and know we'll never be ready when it comes, yet we go on and even dare beauty. If not worthy of Grace, at least that keeps us human. Let me write my own gospel, my Book of Dorelei, that men remember you and this moment you filled. Hell, they'll forget both of us anyway, so stay the moment in my arms and let sunlight be our psalm.

"Husband?" She touched his eyelids. "Dost weep."

"Nothing. Sometimes I . . . nothing. Foolish."

"To touch be never foolish."

"Come, let's ride on. Be late."

Dorelei rode ahead in a gradual circuit between the marked points, much more able than Padrec to note any human incursion on the ancient hills. The sun was only a finger's width on the horizon when they gave it up for the day and turned back toward the rath, riding close together. Dorelei was anything but discouraged.

"Be many days to Bel-tein. Thy magic will yet point us. Ai, smell." She breathed deep with pleasure at the damp air. "Do love spring. A time to quicken." She kicked playfully at Padrec's leg. "Must bear more wealth, husband. Be nae good to have but one child and that a man. A gern must bear a gern."

Neither of them spoke of the future such a gern would be born to, but her grin was mischievous. "Do nae spend *all* the day on mathe-matic."

Just then a few of their sheep appeared over a rise, Guenloie riding on their flank, leading them to water at the brook south of Cnoch-nan-ainneal. The setting sun bathed the hills in an eerily beautiful light, and Guenloie basked in it, stretching slender arms to the sky, out and down again. When she saw them, the old playfulness in her welled over. Yelping with pure good spirits, Guenloie goaded the pony into a furious gallop straight at Dorelei in a mock pass, plunging by her only inches away and dashing on.

Dorelei wheeled about, yipping in chorus with her cousin. She gathered herself and bent low over the pony's mane to dash at Guenloie in return. Then Padrec saw her freeze the intent in midmotion. She reined the pony to a dead stop. She was not looking at Guenloie, but something beyond her, outlined in late sun and shadow amid the undulating rises they'd just left.

"Padrec! There!"

The pony shot forward. The whole action was so abrupt that Padrec just sat his horse watching as Guenloie dashed after her cousin, the sheep forgotten. They were barely within earshot when Dorelei's pony dug his hoofs into the last rise, drumming to the top. She leaped down, whirling and capering with Guenloie for pure excitement. Dorelei's voice floated back to Padrec, faint with distance:

"Rainbow!"

The two women spun about and fell in a laughing heap. Then Dorelei sprang up, waving to Padrec, jabbing her arm up and down again and again at the bump of ground she stood on. Pointing, shouting the word over and over, but after the first time, Padrec was galloping to join her.

"Barrow!"

*   *   *

There it was, and yet even Dorelei had been unaware that they'd walked their horses almost directly over it. A gentle, elongated swell parallel to the side of a small hill, more and more a part of it through the ages. The end facing west, when one really looked close, had a low but definable hump.

Watching the women caper in their excitement, Padrec felt a twinge of depression. A barrow, yes. Opening it could prove them as easily wrong as right, and the whole supposition that sustained them through winter an emptied hope.

Something else sobered Dorelei and Guenloie when they thought about it. Each barrow would hold the bones of at least one powerful gern whose magic might still guard the place.

"Will offer prayers to Mother, Padrec. And would much help to pray thyself."

She sent Guenloie to finish watering the sheep and led Padrec to the eastern end of the barrow mound. The spirit of the gern and her people had escaped through the hole left in the western end when the barrow was put up, but the holy place was always entered from the east. On a certain day of the year, perhaps the day of burial, the rising sun would shine directly down the central passage. At such solemn times, it was well to have all good magic working with one.

"Will all dig together," Dorelei ruled. "Give me thy sword."

Dorelei prowled back and forth in front of the low mound. Twice she raised the blade and touched the covering sod, then changed her mind. Suddenly she plunged the sword into the earth and cut a sod from it.

"Here. Will dig here."

The next day saw a break in custom, at least for the sheep. No one wanted to tend them today and miss the first sight of Rainbow-gift. Much to their confusion, the sheep were herded to water at first light by Malgon and Padrec, then back to byre and forgotten. All of fhain, including the children, rode to the barrow with tools and torches, then turned the animals loose to graze.

Digging implements were few, being rarely needed. There was an old bronze mattock, an antler pick, a small iron shovel made by Malgon last year at the forge, and another carved from the shoulder bone of an ox that served to shovel and scrape away loosened earth.

Dorelei's prayers were fervent but brief. Padrec muttered something invocative to Saint Alban, not sure of the potency, then drew his sword and cut a rectangle around the sod removed yesterday. The barrow was very old and the long deforested soil over it going to peat. The turf came away in neat strips, Padrec and the women pulling them back as Malgon chopped furiously at the underpart to free clinging roots. Dorelei was willing to inconvenience her ancestors but not offend them. The sods were stacked neatly to be replaced.

Judging from the character of the moor around them, there should have been an unbroken layer of peat under the turf, but the bare rectangle revealed a mixture of loose, darkish soil speckled white with bits of decayed granite. The women were eager to get their hands into it, but Padrec stayed them, scratching his shaggy head over the character of the earth and conferring with Malgon in terse monosyllables.

"What be amiss?" Dorelei asked. "Should dig now afore rain turns work hard."

Still, he and Malgon took some time to cut a square out of the side of the mound and squat over it before coming back to the mystified women. Whatever the delay taught them, it was eminently satisfying from Padrec's grin.

"Be nae the first to open this barrow," he told them.

If there was one thing he and Malgon saw more than enough of in the Coritani war, it was digging, ditches, and loose dirt. You could tell when earth had been turned before; it was looser than that around it, often of a different color as one layer sagged down into another. Old post holes were black against brown and clear as a footprint. The turf cut from the side of the mound revealed an under-layer of peat. The eastern end was a jumble of loose soil of varying textures. No peat had formed over it. At some point the tomb obviously had been reopened. They could very well be on the right scent, and Dorelei need not worry too much about profanation. The occupants were used to it.

And then, of course, at the height of expectant excitement, the inevitable distraction of children. Morgana Mary was damp and unpleasant, needing a change of swaddling no one had thought to bring. Bruidda was cutting teeth and not at all happy about it, and Crulegh howled when they took away the loose soil he wanted to taste.

"Ah, then." Neniane passed her pick to Guenloie, swooping down on the children like a harried hen to herd them all to the brook for washing. The rest of them worked on, swinging their tools with energetic purpose, not stopping when a brief rain shower passed over, dampening the earth and making the work more difficult.

They shouted with glee when the rainbow appeared to vindicate them: to the southwest of Cnoch-nan-ainneal, and from this point probably miles from any spot measured from the circle of stones.

Padrec crowed: "Be not where but only when!"

"Or from sea down to us," Dorelei answered. "Come, dig."

Gouging, shoveling, and scraping, they laid bare an inner covering of stones, not large but heavy enough when passed from hand to hand to be piled neatly by the strips of turf. Time passed, the pile grew higher. Then the mattock pried a stone aside and left empty dark under it, a ragged hole. Darkness and a sudden mustiness issuing from the gap, stale air undisturbed for years.

All of them worked together to clear it, joined by Neniane when she brought the cleaned children back. In a very short time the hole widened to a flat overhead lintel resting on two huge upright stones. To Padrec's Roman logic, recent disturbance or not, the barrow had to be of extreme age. When their tools scraped against the lintel stone, it was roughly at the level of Padrec's calf, and the excavation went far down. Either the heavy stones had sunk, or time raised the moor over it, or both.

They were all sweating and the children cantankerous when Guenloie unwrapped the cold porridge and sliced mutton for the midday meal. They sat in a circle near the turfs, feeding the children and themselves. After stretching lazily in the grass for a rest, Padrec flexed his whole body like a cat, got up, and wandered back to the lintel with his male fascination for a riddle with more to reveal.

The recumbent stone found yesterday tweaked his curiosity. The face of the lintel stone was partially smoothed but smeared with earth yet. He took a wadded handful of grass, wet it, and scrubbed over the stone's face until it was clean. Before Padrec finished, the others were close around him, peering at the stone. Dorelei brushed a hand over it like the blind feeling out unfamiliarity. The face had been roughly smoothed with a tool less durable than bronze, but now something more definite emerged from the clean, dry surface: two straight lines painted on the stone, a reddish double bar thinly bordered in blue woad that barely defined the ocher used to fill it in. To the right, even fainter, another double bar.

Dorelei wiped the shredded grass from her fingers. "Barrow be of Reindeer fhain."

Malgon appreciated her meaning, but many things were changed this year. He had a child and more of an interest in the future, a thought not so important before. "Would be shame to leave a now."

Neniane just said, "Will need the torches."

"Stay." Dorelei took up an antler pick. "Be a sacred place. Must show respect for presence."

If any spirits lingered, they might be alarmed and offended by intrusion. The spirit-hole at the western end must be cleared to allow them to escape. Fhain agreed with the wisdom, and the air would be fresher inside. They trooped around the barrow. Dorelei felt at the turf with the pick like a physician, then probed with Padrec's sword at various points. The blade struck rock at the same depth again and again. Then in one small area, so slightly depressed it might escape even her eyes, the sword went in to the hilt.

"Here. Dig."

The small but definite opening was quickly exposed.

"Light the torches," Dorelei ordered.

She felt a moment of apprehension. For such nearness to spirits, she was not properly prepared. Her body should be rubbed with nightshade and foxglove that would let her soul speak with them, fly with them. None of these she had, only a stubbornness born of hard lessons too well and suddenly known. She saw the same resolve in the others, especially Malgon. They would survive. Prydn could be as cruel and small-minded as any tallfolk when it came to that, and they would not share in this. Salmon alone would borrow from the borrowers; for the rest—in Padrec's tallfolk speaking—they could go to hell.

By the sundial stake near the entrance, it was two hours past noon. Padrec remembered that later. No more than two hours past noon on a day of bright sunlight and clear sky.

Malgon volunteered to lead the way, but Dorelei refused. If there was danger inside, she and Padrec would confront it first. She took the torch. They'd guessed the barrow was very old. The truth of that was the first thing to greet them. The huge supporting stones were not carved but painted with ocher as the entrance lintel. Even the hard-packed earthen floor was different from any soil they knew, not dark brown or black but of a reddish, sandy composition. Truly this was the threshold to Tir-Nan-Og.

They moved along the central passage, Padrec bending low under the overhead slabs. The light from the entrance spilled in only for a few yards; after that, gloom. Padrec, Malgon, and Dorelei moved ahead with torches, Neniane and Guenloie following with the wealth. On either side of the central passage, the barrow was divided by stone slabs into rows of cells or stalls. In each, stacked neat as the records in Marchudd's library, were innumerable human bones, all broken to some degree. Leg and arm bones, now and then a cell with nothing but skulls.

A little farther on they found the first whole skeleton.

Clearly a gern, the body faced them from its stone bench, legs crossed in formal position, although one arm had slipped down to dangle at her side. A few strands of hair hung from the parchment skull. The children whined, afraid of it. People should not look so. Draped about the body were the remains of an upper garment and a skirt of fringes. A heavy gold circlet rounded the skull, etched with Reindeer sign.

They moved on. The gloom closed in behind them as the passage angled slightly to the right, which disturbed Dorelei; there seemed no reason for it. More stacked bones, pile after pile; then they came upon the second gern.

By now the children vehemently wanted to be out of the dark, whimpering continually. Crulegh clung in fear to the nearest grown-up leg. They looked closer at this second honored remnant: subtly different from the first to Padrec's objective eye. The circlet about the skull and the heavy torc were of intricately etched but green-tarnished bronze. The tattered hide wrapping, now crumbling to dust, had been carefully painted with strange signs in woad.

"Do nae know such marks," Dorelei said. She reached out to part the rotted wrapping. A piece of it fell away. Malgon held his torch closer. The small ribs were smashed through over the heart.

"Spear or arrow," Malgon decided.

The woman died in fight, a braw gern of the first days. If she borrowed no gold or even saw it, she defended her fhain. Before passing on, Dorelei tried to rearrange the tatters about the broken ribs; the stuff simply came apart.

No real way to judge, but it seemed they'd come a long way under the hill to find one gold circlet that must be left inviolate. Still, the air was fresher now. The passage must turn again somewhere ahead. They couldn't see the spirit hole. The only light against the gloom flickered from their tallow-soaked pine torches.

More cells of stacked bones.

And a new sound.

It began as a whisper ... if it began at all; perhaps it had been just below the threshold of awareness all the time. A whisper that grew into a moan, rising and falling like the cry of the bean sidhe. Bruidda began to cry. Guenloie picked her up for her own comfort as much as the bairn's.

"Must be getting close to the hole," Padrec hoped aloud. "Just wind, like blowing through a pipe, that's all it is."

"Aye, the wind." Agreeing with him took much courage for Dorelei, and more not to drop her torch and flee back along the road of the dead. Determined she was, but that made this no less of a profanation. Padrec heard only the wind, but there was more than wind through the spirit hole. The pipe that blew was not of this world. Somewhere in that eerie wail, a voice knew her name.

Dorelei . . .

Her hand clenched tighter around the torch. *Who calls me? Who is't from the first days, Bruidda's blood or mine, who calls me so? Have I angered Mother, breaking her flesh this way?*

Come forward, Dorelei.

Padrec would not understand. These were things he would never hear. Firmly she stepped in front of him and moved ahead, blood pounding in her ears.

"Must be close to the end," Padrec said behind her.

No, she knew better. They were gone under the hill to world's-edge, to the very opening of Tir-Nan-Og, down and around forever. It could be that they were never to leave this place, the way back coiled in a circle like the stones. . . .

She felt a freshet of cooler air on her skin.

"Where's the hole?" Padrec fretted. "We cleaned the hole, can't be that far from it. Should be light."

Yet none beyond the flickering spill of their torches, smoke wraiths silhouetted against the brightness, and the wall of piled rock in front of them. Malgon thrust his torch to the left, exploring.

"Dost turn here."

The wind-whisper slid up a note in its mourning.

Malgon's torch revealed two heavy upright stones supporting another lintel, a doorway into darkness that threw back furtive gleams as it caught the light. Malgon made to move through the entrance, but Dorelei stayed him.

"Thy gern will lead."

Dorelei moved between the stones and held her torch high. Padrec and Malgon, then the others clustered about her. They were in a chamber the size of a small crannog. Just before them the floor was raised. Strewn in profusion over it were the objects that dully caught the light.

Rainbow-gift was real, and they had found it.

After a stunned moment, Dorelei whispered, "Be of Rome, Padrec?"

Of Rome and everywhere else, from what he could distinguish of the plethora. Roman work, Grecian, native British. Delicate Egyptian miniatures in fine gold, chain silver spilling like tears from Cretan jars painted with staring eyes that were troubling in their alien strength. Open chests spilling the tarnished silver, greenish bronze and dull gold coins about them over the packed earthen floor. Green and white jade and ivory cut into figures of impossible intricacy. Emeralds and rubies, uncut or set in elaborate filigreed pendants. Trading sticks of gold, easily two gradii in length. Obsidian statuary of an outlandish but energetic art that glowed queerly in the light. And more.

"Was a *great* borrowing," Malgon breathed. The rest of the thought he kept to himself. Bredei and Artcois should have shared this triumph, finest of borrowers that they were, and Cruaddan, to whom all horses cried their yearning for freedom.

They stared at Rainbow-gift, trying to stretch imagination around the reality while the wind sang softly through the passage behind them.

Padrec set one foot on the raised floor. "I've got to see—"

Dorelei held him back. "Stay. Be more. There."

The three torches were thrust forward as far as possible, throwing feeble light to the far rock wall. There was a more definite shape in the murk. Bruidda began to whine again. Bones in a pile were no more worry than those her mother cracked for soup; joined together was a different and terrifying thing.

"Ai, hush," Guenloie soothed her. "Nae fear. Be only a gern who did love wealth like thee."

They spoke no more as they moved forward to the skeleton. The wind keened yet higher in the passageway, and Dorelei heard the voice in it.

Gern-y-fhain . . .

There was an aura about the bones that compelled respectful silence. One did not approach her so much as come into her presence. Whoever she had been among Reindeer fhain, she was venerated as the later ones were not, for all their honors. The tiny figure sat upright on a backed chair of heavy ashwood, white and brittle with age, the thick timbers not sawn but rough-hewn and covered with the remains of a large single hide foreign to fhain, something like a hairy cow. Arranged about the chair and forming an arch over it were the huge antlers of a bog elk. A few lingered in the wild interior of Ireland, but their racks were nowhere near this size, Padrec knew. The head that bore them must have reared seven feet or more above ground.

In touching contrast to her cerements, the child-feet dangled from the chair, not even touching the floor. The fragile skeleton only added to the mystery for Padrec. He glanced at Dorelei rapt in her own thoughts, listening to the wind. *Here we are*, he thought, *just as we stand, the wealthiest family in Britain since the Caesars. And these bones have more of a tale to tell than any jewel I see.*

From a sampling of the coins, he knew his theory was correct: much of it was from the last undebased minting decades before his birth, when hard money was still common. The rest, the art and jewelry, from any time after his own ancestors went from thinking of themselves as Romans in Britain to Britons with Roman names.

The gern's bones were not so easily read, but he yearned to decipher them. She had been interred in nothing more than a kilt of some sort, from the few shreds not gone to dust around her loins. The gut waist-thong lay loose around the pelvic bones, dangling a fragment of hide sheath. On the covered seat where it dropped eons ago lay a small flint knife. The haft was painted in ocher with Rainbow sign.

Unlike the other gerns, she wore no metal at all. The thong about her throat, shriveled and dry, was strung with seashells, painted flints, polished bits of jet, and the elongated tusks of some predator Padrec couldn't begin to conceive. Nothing about this gern was of a past he could fit to a known world. She must have died long before the iron came or the need for a word like Blackbar, long before the Atecotti came with their bronze and stone molds. What mark she left on the land was cut with no more than courage and flint. She might have been the first to walk on Cnoch-nan-ainneal, skirted marshes that were now dry land, hunting the beast whose teeth hung about her neck, animals only vaguely remembered in stones that were themselves sinking into the past.

The temptation to name her was irresistible. Padrec's modern mind laughed at the presumption.

Then Dorelei moved, turned to him. "Dost hear?"

"What?"

"Dost *hear*?"

"The wind, no more."

"Nae. Under the wind."

Dorelei looked at the skeletal gern on the throne, her head canted queerly in that listening attitude. Then quickly: "Out, Padrec. Malgon, all of you, out. See to the wealth."

"What is't, wife?"

She turned on him. It was a command. "Thee dost nae hear? Go!"

"Not and leave thee here."

"Take him, Malgon."

"Nae," Padrec refused.

He might as well argue with the bones. "Have opened a door long shut, husband. Do wonder, then, who comes to greet us? Go."

She snatched his torch away as Malgon pulled him toward the chamber entrance after the women. Padrec's last glimpse of Dorelei: erect before the bones of the old gern, two torches held high.

The rising wind shrieked through the passageway now as they moved along it behind Malgon. To hurry them on, Padrec scooped up

Crulegh and Morgana Mary under each arm. They stumbled along expecting every moment to see the entrance and daylight, but the only illumination was the single torch in Malgon's grip. The light flooded over the stacked bones, winked lewdly from hollow eye sockets, gave a likeness of movement to the gerns, formidable in death as they were in life. Then Malgon cried out in fear, a sound Padrec never heard from him in war. They were at the entrance, moving into the open.

One by one they emerged from the barrow into starless, moonless night. The dark flowed over them, a black tide on the crying wind.

What the others might wonder at, Dorelei knew surely as her own face in the bronze mirror. She stood in the gateway between her own world and Tir-Nan-Og, so close she could hear the calling. Who but Mabh worthy to guard it? Who but she speaking to her sister gern on the wind? Dorelei was terrified, but she must answer like a gern. To name Mabh aloud, to invoke her in her very resting place was to bring her surely as naming the iron once summoned its evil. Yet Dorelei was called, and the thing was to be done. She wedged the torches into the earth and knelt before Mabh. With deep reverence she stretched her palms forward to touch the holy bones.

Ia! Great Mabh. Be Dorelei, first daughter to Gawse. Have taken thy name in honor to lead my folk. Great sister, my magic be small to yours, but do hear thy voice.

The wind howled through the barrow, moaning out through the spirit hole. The voice drew nearer on the wind that drove it as a sail.

Yah, Dorelei.

Great sister, give me your pardon for breaking this barrow. The tallfolk betray us, our own cast us out. Were much in need of magic.

I, too, had my war with tallfolk. I never called them brothers as you did. This strange hoard about me is not mine. Those who brought it did not even know me, only that I am Reindeer.

We try new ways as Mabh did. We try to find the mole on our back.

And found the world larger than you knew, as I did, and of a different shape. My war was as much with my own as tallfolk.

And mine, sister.

Those who were afraid to go and called it wisdom. Those afraid to lose what they had, calling it caution and me a moon-dreaming fool. The world does not change. Look on your sister, Dorelei.

The torches burned low, the shadow of the hide-covered chair dancing on the wall. The seated figure was dim but majestic, her black hair deep shadow about the strong face.

Be most fair, great sister.

306

I am of Tir-Nan-Og. I am young forever.

We would find it, Mabh. Show us the mole on our back beyond the tallfolk world.

The gray eyes looked through Dorelei to her soul, calmly merciless, as if to pin that quivering essence and hurl it through the spirit-hole on the singing wind.

For the few gerns who dare, there is always a place. My foot trod the wet earth at the very edge of the ice before Lugh melted it into river and sea. With this flint knife, my magic cut the sea between the lands. Have you not sung of it?

Many times. My mother to me, and I to my own wealth.

What magic have you made?

I put the good of fhain before all else, tried new ways, and found the truth and folly in them. I have born wealth, and here are the marks on my belly as yours. I have found the Fool of the World who wears my own face in my mirror, laughed at her, tamed her, and forgiven her. This I have done, my sister, and more beside. Lugh gave tallfolk a magic so strong we dared not name it but gave it a ward-name, Blackbar. For tens of seasons, no magic could stand against it.

It seemed the small figure bent forward slightly in curiosity.

What is this Blackbar that Prydn must hide from it?

Dorelei rose from her knees to stand straight before the ancient throne. Be called iron. I spoke its name aloud and defeated it. As Mabh led fhain where none dared go before, I found a new path. I tamed the iron into a good servant of many uses.

Dorelei held out the knife. See, sister. No edge will break it, yet it broke Prydn until I walked Mother's breast. Even Reindeer called me fool, but Salmon will always go where she must to make new life. This was my magic. Am I not a gern as Mabh?

In the flickering gloom, it might be thought the small head moved in assent, even admiration.

My sisters made a law out of fear, Mabh, but I was not afraid.

The smile was not Dorelei's imagination, a slight, hard curve. I *was*.

Ai—yes. I too.

But not so afraid I could not cross the salt marsh.

Nor I to dare the iron.

A braw knife, sister. Would dare for such myself.

Did cost us much. It is a thing hammered out of fire, yet we could not beat the whole evil from it. There was much death, much blood. There are those nights still, even in my husband's arms, when I am too much alone.

Does my sister think I came any surer to this land? I was young as you when we started, old as you when we reached world's-edge. There were many barrowed behind, many spirits who ride with me yet in my dreams that others never saw.

Aye, sister. That is the way of it.

The supple, delicate hand moved in the shadows, grasping the flint knife fallen from her side.

Will you dare Tir-Nan-Og?

I must, Mabh. There is no way but forward.

The knife stretched forward to her, its facets glinting red in the last of the light.

Will you rade with me to see what you have asked, the mole on your back?

What does Mabh ask of me?

Only what you asked of Mother. Does your courage fail?

Can I dare to let it fail, any more than Mabh could?

I see the end of Prydn coming sure as night. Do not say you have not seen it or that you are without fear.

But without hope if I yield to it. Who is not without fear? I have seen Bruidda, your own sacred blood, ask for truth and then run from it. I must dare. Show me Tir-Nan-Og.

Across world sea wider even than dream of it?

Show me.

Beyond world's-edge with no returning, east to west as the wind blows?

"Show me!"

Hold out the iron.

Dorelei stretched forward her hand with the knife. The flint blade dipped to touch it.

She had struck fire many times from flint and iron, but this light suffused the chamber, blinding her. She felt weightless, picked up by the wind like dust, sucked through the spirit hole, rising to lightness and freedom. Whirled like an autumn leaf, her hand in Mabh's, up through bright sunlight. The barrow receded below them, smaller and smaller, and wider the world in Dorelei's wondering sight.

"Come." Mabh veered gracefully as Hawk on the wind. "Will ride with Lugh."

They were of Lugh Sun himself, part of him in his radiant course over the earth, and there, impossibly far below them, was Mother, the full, true shape of the breast Dorelei was born in. Lowlands, mountains, loughs, glens, and rivers—all drew together into the whole, like wrinkles in a skin. She saw where and why they all joined, saw their common purpose, and cried out in her joy.

"Ia! Mother. Do see thy face!"

Clasped to Mabh's hand, Dorelei soared like a bird too long caged, looping, diving, hovering still in the warm wind but moving always westward with Lugh. There! Along the razor-backed high ridge, the forms so distant only their slant shadow betrayed them, a fhain on rade, the sheep swirled out behind like a brown cloud, herded by great dogs like Rof.

"And the dear wealth!" Dorelei laughed to see them skipping behind the ponies. "Mother bless thee, Lugh ride thy arrows. Mabh, our world be beautiful."

"And larger than thee knew," Mabh said. "Come."

Swooping down past the ridges to the lowlands: the folk who cut Mother more than they loved her. The plowed fields, straight tallfolk lines that no strength would stay in, an open thing from which the simplest magic could escape. Mabh pointed yet ahead to the ragged coastline and the sea pounding at it with a turbid white fringe. The claws of land splayed out into the water, tapered off, fell behind. The islands loomed up, sudden as shipwrecks upthrust from the sea. These, too, fell away as the horizon darkened, became a green shore spreading north and south.

"Tir-Nan-Og!" Dorelei cried. "Have I found it?"

"Not yet," Mabh said.

No, only a coast like the one fallen behind them, and the land stretched out before them much like Dorelei's own. Oxen scarred the land with tallfolk plows below hills mazed and ramparted with earthworks and centered with large thatched halls.

They flew on. Beyond the plowed fields, lonely in the mountains, Dorelei saw what she most sought, the familiar line of riders along a ridge.

"Prydn."

"Our brothers, the Sidhe," Mabh told her.

"And not yet Tir-Nan-Og?"

"No," Mabh whispered, the sound of her like the wind in Dorelei's ear. "Only a place of men."

"But most fair. Let us go down."

But Mabh bore her on toward the sea. "Nae fear, sister. Salmon will cut a new sign in this place, and a's name be sung as yours and mine."

"What gern will that be?"

"No gern but man." Mabh turned to smile at her sister. "Dost think we have the only knives to mark the land?"

The green hills sank behind them in gathering darkness. They flew on with the daylight, leaving night behind, over the last bleak rocks and scattered curraghs of the fishermen, on and on. The sea changed in hue and nature, a world in itself—slower, heavier in response to the deep beating of Mother's heart. Where the wind caught them, there were sudden whitecaps; in other places the same

309

wind caught up sprays of mist and carried them, as her own nipples stretched out rigid in loving Cru or Padrec, called forth by their urgent mouths on her breasts. And as the plow broke Mother's flesh, great black creatures rolled and slid over and through the moving surface. On and on they flew until Dorelei wondered if there *was* an edge to the world. Always before her the horizon fled as she raced after, like Rainbow. But this water, tens and tens and ten times again more sea beneath Dorelei than ever she imagined there was land to ride. Like the land there was sunlight here and storm there; storms to make those that whipped about their northern broch mere breezes for rage. The waves reared up tall as hills, white spray torn from them and sent hissing down the wind before the hills crashed into each other, broken yet again as slow, majestic creatures rolled through their chaos, serene as prayer. Tens of them, with blunt heads and giant flukes, each as long as two barrows dug end to end.

Gradually the heaving of the sea beneath Dorelei grew gentler, the air softer and scented with flowers. She smelled the green.

"Be sweet," Mabh murmured like the sea lulling below them. "Thee hast only a word for Dronnarron, but I remember it."

They glided lower, close over the subsiding waters gone greenish-blue now, the flower-scent mixed with the richer smell of moist earth somewhere. Dorelei couldn't see far ahead: a writhing fringe of surf, hints of a sandy shore under a low-lying blanket of white mist like clean-carded fleece. Then, just below her . . .

"Do see the Prydn, Mabh! The spirit folk of Tir-Nan-Og—oh, see!"

Mabh only guided her on toward the mist. "Dost think it so?"

"There in the long curraghs. Do laugh and call to one another. Have found Tir-Nan-Og!" Dorelei sang in exaltation. "*Found* it."

"A could be," Mabh answered like the wind on Dorelei's skin. "Be nae the first to find it or the last."

They soared on toward the fogbank, into it, through it into green splendor shimmering in the sunlight. Dorelei's eyes opened wide as her heart and imagination to see it all, to smell Dronnarron, and she was honored beyond Mary who bore Jesu, to see it all, to see the green stretch on to blue, distant hills and more land beyond that. The glory was endless, too large for the earth men knew. In her joy she broke free of Mabh, soaring high alone, hovering on the wind like a bird drunk with flight, rolled on her back to gaze unblinking and grateful at Lugh Sun over it all . . .

"Thank you, Lugh-Father. I have found it. I see it."

. . . While the golden light faded, darkened, and Mabh flew on

310

past Dorelei, too swift to catch again, and the scent of Dronnarron in Dorelei's nostrils went acrid with pine smoke and tallow.

"Dorelei!"

Padrec. She murmured his name in the dark. With the sleeper's sense, she knew he'd been calling for some time. She lay in almost total darkness, the torches only a blue sputter, the slight bones in the great chair only a pale blur against the dark.

I *have seen.*

"Dorelei! Answer me!"

No, not dream-journey. The memory didn't fade or mock in waking the truth found in sleep. She had flown with Mabh to world's-edge and found no end at all, only more world and more after that.

I *have seen.*

Tir-Nan-Og: huge, young and green, with her own copper-brown folk on the shore. It *was* there, waiting.

"Dorelei, call out!"

She heard Padrec in the passage now. She stretched her hands in respect to Mabh's bones. "Ia, Mabh."

"Do you hear me, Dorelei?"

"Here, husband."

He turned the sharp corner and stepped through the entrance onto the raised floor, reaching for her. "You've been hours. We heard your voice again and again."

"Hours...?"

"It's night outside. And there seemed to be ... no." His chest rose and fell against her as Padrec held her close. "No, just the wind. My God, this is not even time, but outside it. Be more wonder than I have ever seen."

Dorelei read the awe in his dim face. "Or I."

"Where *are* we, wife? God's world or Mother's, where are we? We came out of the barrow—not one hour were we underground, and yet be night outside. Ponies wandered off, and who can blame them, thee and the wind speaking to one another, the rest of us turned turvy, not knowing. Be all right?"

Dorelei nodded, rubbing her eyes. She took up the one torch still sputtering and moved past Padrec into the passage. The fresh morning wind blew a little renewed life into the pine nub. Together they moved back along the passage, which seemed shorter now. They easily marked the dim rectangle of light that was the entrance and passed through it. Dorelei held her light high, feebly illuminating her people, who squatted a little distance away. Dorelei drank the fresh air in long breaths and ground out the torch.

"No light at all, not even stars until a little while ago," Padrec mused. "Such dark is beyond the world, not of it."

"Bring my wealth to me," Dorelei commanded. She saw Neniane rise and lead the smaller shape to her in the gloom. Dorelei picked up her son, the small face close to hers. "Do have such gifts for thee, Crulegh. Be blessed; thy fhain marks will be cut in a new world."

Holding the child, Dorelei spoke to her people. "Do face the east for the last time. East to west, as the wind blew through the spirit-hole, as a carried me, my hand in Mabh's, Salmon will go. Thy gern has seen Tir-Nan-Og."

"Ai!"

Fhain listened in respect. No one broke the flow of it even to question the unimaginable.

"Be nae beyond world's-edge," she told them in a new, strong voice, "but in a place one can rade to. World sea be not forever. Dost end."

And yet, she tried to explain, the largeness was like Tir-Nan-Og itself, a reaching of mind as well as distance, a clearer sight of that truth known to them from birth. Salmon went where it must. If it spawned in familiar brooks, it knew world sea as well. Fhain would not be in a place so strange or far it could not speak in a tongue they knew.

"See thy gern: an I be despised, was nae Jesu? An Mabh spoke to me, did nae the bush speak as well to Mo-ses? Hebrew-fhain raded forty years to find the place a were promised. An I angered our Parents, did nae great Mabh as well? Will take the great curraghs that rade on world sea, snare the wind in a's sail, and go west."

Malgon could keep silent no longer; the thing was too big. "Off world's-edge."

"Be *nae* edge, man. None. World ... goes on. Will see Tir-Nan-Og long before. Oh, be braw, Malgon. Could drop Pictland and Britain into such a place and lose't whole. What says Padrec Raven?"

The audacity of the plan was staggering. Padrec could barely get his imagination round it, but of love he was sure. "Among Prydn, Salmon be the teacher of new ways and courage. Where Dorelei leads, Raven will follow."

"See!" Guenloie pointed suddenly, the relief bright in her voice. "Lugh rides."

"East to west as we must go," Dorelei said.

A thin line of gray broadening, lightening in the east. Whatever magic this night wrought, it was over. The dawn breeze had died down, and the air about them had a different smell. Malgon gazed about to see if the truant horses were anywhere in sight. Strange night, he thought with more than a little fear. They'd walked into

Mabh's barrow and far beyond any time or reality he knew. But ponies and horses thought of sensible things like water and graze. They'd wander toward the brook, and wasn't his good bow and quiver still tied to his saddle?

Neniane and Guenloie had felt the magic that touched their gern, but with the growing light there came back to them the realities of motherhood. All three children were exhausted from fitful, chilly sleep while they shivered outside the barrow and waited for Dorelei, wondering if they'd ever see her again or even a morning. They were all strained and hungry. They would follow Dorelei as they did in triumph and exile, do the impossible at her bidding—but first, the wealth. Breakfast to prepare, the flocks to be pastured. They were even glad for these homely truths in a torrent of magic.

Malgon cocked his ear, sifting sounds on the wind, and looked unsatisfied. With a word to Dorelei, he trotted away to hunt the strayed mounts.

The morning light spread over the east.

They decided to walk westward toward the rath, Malgon catching up with the ponies. They were barely started when he churned over a rise at a dead run toward them, jerking to a halt in front of Dorelei, one arm milling out behind him. Pointing.

"Reindeer."

Padrec's stomach sank. Perfect. *If Bruidda loved us before, she'll deify us now.* He loosened the sword in its scabbard as the first ponies crested the low rise from which Malgon had come, saw Salmon, and halted in a line of purpose all the colder for its silence. Dorelei, Padrec, the women—all of them realized Tir-Nan-Og could be much sooner than planned. The two groups faced each other in the gray morning light.

Bruidda and her shrunken fhain. Twelve in all, and three of those yearling children like their own, six women, three men too old for the holy war. Bruidda's eyes were fixed on Dorelei. The others barely existed for her.

That moment of preparate stillness, then the ponies began to file to the right and left, some of the riders leading a second mount behind them. Salmon recognized their own animals. They could do nothing. One sword and four knives against bows nocked and ready to bend at the word. The ponies stepped forward with delicate grace until Salmon fhain was framed in a deadly semicircle.

"Dorelei!"

"Need nae shout, Bruidda. Lugh's morning be still and dost favor Salmon yet."

Bruidda sat her pony, coiled like a snake already decided to

313

strike, only pondering where. "Dorelei who dared to take the name of Mabh."

"And more."

"Did see thy light from rath. Did hear tale-speaking that thee were gone in shame from Pictland."

Dorelei handed her son to Padrec and advanced toward Bruidda a few steps to stand apart from her people. "We go now."

The aging gern slumped a little, a furtive note of sadness in her hard voice. "Gawse kept the ways of Mother. A's daughter breaks every law that did make Prydn a chosen folk. A begged more favor of Mother than a had to give. See, Reindeer! In one season, with her Raven, did a nae send all the young men to death?"

Yah . . . truly. The mutter spread among Reindeer. One of the young mothers looked beyond Salmon toward the barrow. She spoke something to Bruidda and pointed. At a word from the gern, she trotted her pony wide around Dorelei toward the barrow. Padrec's stomach dropped even lower.

"They find the digging, that's our lot, Mal."

Malgon said nothing, eyes narrowed on the ready bowman. Would be a keening this day in Salmon if any of them saw the end of it.

Padrec turned his head slightly to follow the curious woman who'd seen the bare earth and sod at first. She was at the barrow entrance now, scanning the faint but readable signs on the lintel stone. A moment to wonder, another to grasp the enormous blasphemy. Then the small figure vaulted her pony and lashed it back toward them.

Padrec thought on the act of contrition in its briefer forms. He and Malgon had been closer than this to death. He wondered if he would look as surprised as Gallius did. Probably.

The crime was quickly told. Bruidda covered her face, her voice rising to a dolorous wail.

"Ai! Reindeer! The outcast Salmon did break a barrow of our fhain. There! Be still open to the wind that cries a's wrong through the spirit-hole."

The sound that rose from Reindeer fhain reminded Padrec of wolves hunting on a winter night: not stretched out, rising once and falling to silence again, as if there were more important things at hand.

"Did nae know this barrow of my blood," Bruidda said. "Should nae know't. Dorelei, have rightfully taken the rath from thee and hurled thy iron pots from the hill. In justice have stripped thee of ponies, horses, and sheep. Salmon be without presence. Thee dared take Mabh's name when Mabh would turn from thee—"

"Bruidda!" When Dorelei spoke, it stunned her own fhain. The voice that came out of their gern was even more powerful than Gawse's, born in a deep place. "Do lie, old woman."

The force of it as much as the insult stopped Bruidda dead in her vehemence. The voice was a curse itself, scathing, contemptuous, spoken to a child from the height of an adult.

"Fool, Bruidda. Some grow larger, some but old. Nae, thee prate of what Mabh would know and nae know. Thee would nae know Mabh did a sit to eat with thee. Mabh could change, thee cannot. Mabh did speak to *me*. An a thing be ended, Reindeer has ended. Because a runs back into the dark, not west with the light. I have *seen* Tir-Nan-Og and know the way."

Dorelei paused to let that work on them. The scorn died in her voice, leaving the sadness of waste and folly. "Thee's been an honored gern, Bruidda, a braw queen. Thee never feared to die, only to live. Take the rath, then, and the flocks, but leave our ponies. We rade to Tir-Nan-Og."

Bruidda's hand moved in a subtle sign, but even as the bows raised in answer, Dorelei's left arm shot out in a warding gesture. "Stay!"

She took a step toward the older gern, seeming the older now, patient wisdom reasoning with a stubborn child, almost pleading. "Hast nae been enough of dying and tears? Will Prydn tear at each other like Vaco's dogs? Hear the wonders of this barrow. Will leave thee most of them, but let it end here. Let us go."

Bruidda shook her head, implacable. "Salmon be poison on Mother's breast. Kill them."

Dorelei's right hand hooked back in a blur of speed and brandished the iron knife high. She hurled one word at Bruidda, more guttural sound than speech. Padrec had heard it once before. The bows hesitated; bowstrings in the motion of bending eased down again. Bruidda straightened as her folk looked to her, then leaped from the pony and hurled the same harsh sound back at Dorelei, as Bredei voiced it at Churnet Head before their lunatic charge.

"Gerns will answer for a's fhains," Malgon said. "Alone."

Not until Dorelei and Bruidda stripped off their upper garments and stood bare to the waist did Padrec believe it. "Be such things allowed?"

Malgon schooled him in few words. They were allowed but avoided. The thing had never happened in his sight or knowledge during his lifetime. Rare for men to fight, rarer still for gerns, and only in a matter grave as this. "Tens of seasons past," he remembered, "when Gawse's mother was Salmon gern, a woman of Marten fhain tried to draw a's first husband away. Not often, but so." Malgon nodded at the men of Reindeer. "A stay aside, so must we. Must nae touch thy sword."

Now the movements of the two gerns assumed the aspect of a ritual. Bruidda drew to her the young woman who had spied out the open barrow. Padrec remembered her, Bruidda's daughter Nebha. She put in the girl's hand the pendant ruby and received her daughter's reverence. Dorelei came to Padrec and kissed him. He tried to argue her out of it, but Dorelei paid no attention. The course was fixed.

"This?" She bobbed her head toward Bruidda. "Be a price, Padrec. All things change, nothing stays. Be a place I have seen and my folk will have't. An I be fool, then Mo-ses one as well."

She pressed her mouth to his one last time. "Thee was beauty in my arms. An I die, help Neniane to where a must rade."

Neniane knelt before her sister, hands to Dorelei's stomach.

"Have nae treasure to put about thy breast as our mother did, but Neniane second daughter will be Gern-y-fhain."

The small kitten face raised to hers. "Aye, sister."

Guenloie and Malgon came to pay their respects, as did those of Bruidda a little way from them. Malgon touched Dorelei's belly, frowning with concern.

"Have been in war, Gern-y-fhain."

And knowing that place, Malgon knew the eyes of those committed to kill and those not. Dorelei was not ready for it, would hesitate where Bruidda would not. "Kill a quick. Nae think, nae feel. Do't."

Dorelei embraced the children, her lips to their ears, a secret endearment for each. Last of all was Crulegh, who didn't understand any of it and squirmed in her arms, hungry for his breakfast. Dorelei brushed back the lengthening black hair, smoothing it down. Then she undid the thong that held her sheath, drew the iron knife from it, and strode forward.

"Reindeer, come."

She didn't want to kill Bruidda and wasn't sure she could. The older gern had fought more than once and bore the scars to prove it. Twice in Dorelei's life, one mad moment with Cru there was the vicious will to have blood, the stroke repented every day since. Again when the Taixali cut down so many of them—then she did it smiling, but not this. She would fight to stop Bruidda, render her helpless if possible. Only her vision Dorelei would not give up.

She crouched as Bruidda did, the two of them circling warily. Silent, no breath or concentration wasted on hatred now, only the act. The tense fhains ringed about them. Somewhere on the heath, a bird piped to morning.

Bruidda sprang. The wiry-muscled legs bunched and propelled

her forward, slashing up at Dorelei's throat. At the last instant the younger woman moved slightly. Her blade was not as long as Bruidda's, allowing her less reach. She must be careful, go for a wound that would stop Bruidda but not—

Guard!

Light as a dancer, Bruidda followed through the motion of her slash, whirling in a tight circle to cover herself again. Against Dorelei's defensive crouch, she darted in, slashing, whirling again as Dorelei faded aside like a shadow.

She moves to the right, Dorelei realized, *her strength and balance always to the right.*

They hovered like hunting birds on a lethal air, poised, coming together—*to the right*, but faster this time than Dorelei judged. Again she feinted aside from the slash, but Bruidda was too quick, not enough time before the line of fire burned across her upper arm.

She was bleeding, didn't know how deep it was—not too bad, not the dull shock that meant the deep muscles, but deep enough to stiffen the arm in a matter of moments. The pain lanced through her concentration. She wove, lowering her guard a little. The faltering did not escape Bruidda. Dorelei saw no hatred in her eyes now, only purpose. Bruidda feinted with a false step, swiveled sideways, and lashed out with her foot. The blow caught Dorelei in the stomach, tearing the breath from her lungs. She stumbled back, fought for balance, but her heel caught against a hummock, and she went down.

Even as she rolled aside to spring upright, Bruidda dove like Hawk, the long bronze blade streaking up to slash backhanded across Dorelei's throat. Dorelei's youth and desperation were quicker. Her own blade met it with a metallic sound loud in the deadly silence. Iron screamed at softer bronze, bit deep into it, snapped it short. Dorelei drove her fist into Bruidda's left eye, rolled away, and came up on guard.

Bruidda's eye was closing. She was shaken, crouching with the useless blade in her hand. Dorelei faced her, feeling the blood warm her skin as it flowed from the wound. The muscles were stiffening. She couldn't last much more, but Bruidda couldn't win. Her arms and legs trembled as she pointed the knife.

"Bruidda? Will say be over, done?"

The woman only shook her head, wasting no energy on talk.

"Need nae *be*, woman!"

"Thee's a shadow on Prydn," Bruidda panted. "A filth."

Dorelei lowered her knife. She felt suddenly ages beyond this woman, understanding her as a child. Not her crimes Bruidda wanted to expunge, not the loss of a generation, not even Dorelei's pride,

317

but the place she took and the name of Mabh, the presence usurped from Bruidda: more blows of the whip after the death of her son, a defeat never intended. Dorelei, who had no word for tragedy, found herself knowing it.

"Woman, enough," she said quietly. "Let us put it away. Salmon will go."

In Bruidda's voice there was still a rag-end of triumph. "Dost fear, Dorelei?"

"Do mourn thy death, old woman." Sadly, hating the words for their leaden truth. "Thee died so long ago."

An instant before she sprang, something flickered in Bruidda's eyes. Dorelei never knew why she did it; perhaps to deny the truth or because Bruidda knew it all too well. Dorelei melted away before the attack, sinking to one knee, catching Bruidda's wrist. The iron came up, driving home under the scarred ribs. Bruidda jerked, crumpled to one side, and lay still.

Only when she knelt beside the body did Dorelei realize the sun was shining bright and full on them. "Padrec," she piped weakly. "Pad . . ."

But she could make no sense of sound. The name blurred out to a wild keening. She drew her knife from the body and hurled it away in grief. The mourning was taken up by Reindeer and then Salmon. Far away, as the morning wind carried it, the Venicone heard the sound, misunderstood it as always, and never knew how much of an ending cried in it.

When the Picts took up Christianity in earnest, there was one story of native source of which only half ever appeared in any Church history: the surprisingly easy acceptance among Venicones of the Nativity as penned by Luke, for did they not know a story much like it?

Not in winter it was, when even sheep have the wit to stay inside, but nigh to the festival of Bel-tein fire, that certain Venicone shepherds abided in the fields with their flocks. And did they not hear the ghostly music as the priests described? Not angels but the bean sidhe, and one did not wander from the firelight in search of *those* singers.

On a night in spring, the shepherds heard the bean sidhe crying near and were sore afraid. And when the keening died away, there by the fire, half in light and the rest shadow, were three of the Faerie folk—a young queen, a man with a sword, another with a bow that bent on the shepherds. The Venicones did not ask why they came. When you have the ill luck to meet Faerie at night, you hear them out, praying it be good news and brief. The tidings were strange. Men argued their meaning for many years, and this was the way of it.

Seven statues—the four shepherds on one side of the fire, the three Faerie on the other, just within the spill of light. Weird they were, so still. The woman's lips hardly seemed to move when she spoke.

"Dost know me, Venicones?"

They did that, but none wanted to speak and be especially noticed by this creature. Her hands opened. Something jingled, glinting in the light, spilling to the earth at her feet, a shower of gold coins.

"Be gift from Rainbow's end. Be more, much more. Tell thy wealth that the tale-speaking of thy fathers be true. At Rainbow's end, nae where but when, Prydn hoard may be seen again."

At her sign the man with the great Michael-sword sprinkled rubies like dark blood over the gold.

"Gift be for a purpose," the woman said. "Tell thy wealth and let a tell theirs: let Prydn be nae forgot in Mabh's island. We were first to walk this land. Did greet thy kind in peace in the time of Dronnarron. Remember us."

Then one of the shepherds, bolder than the rest or perhaps encouraged by the gift, asked, "Great queen, it is our thanks you have, but where in this island does such a gift come from, that we may tell our elder?"

The poor shepherds and their bootless question; even as they asked it, were not the three fading into the dark, and only the woman's voice left to float on the wind?

"From Faerie-land, tallfolk. From Rainbow's end."

So the shepherds were left alone with large wealth and larger curiosity about the hoard it came from. They never found it, but all know it to be still there. Some of those red rubies can be seen yet in the crown Brude wore and that he passed to his son Erca as king of the Picts.

So where was the wonder in angels appearing to shepherds? In this island such magic was born and yet lived. The children were told and their children in turn. Different tales, to be sure, since there are as many stories as there are men to guess and lie about the matter, but it is a rare man and a fool who does not give careful respect in the matter of Faerie, scarce as they are now and always shy of human folk. But they are still there on the hilltops, although not many Venicones are that willing to go and prove it.

* * *

319

Some histories are never written, only remembered. On Bruidda's death, her daughter Nebha became Reindeer gern, a young woman with a yearling daughter of her own, named Cradda. The next year Nebha bore a second daughter. That was a year of more winter than warmth, when all Pictland came close to starvation. Nebha's second daughter was left in a tallfolk cradle that she might at least have a chance at life, a Roman woman whose husband was envoy to the Picts. Britons came to call such children changelings. Prydn mothers called it sacrifice when they spoke of it at all, but Prydn always know their own, and Nebha's grandson found his way home to wear the mark of Reindeer.

Cradda became Reindeer gern after her mother and bore two sturdy daughters. The elder, Dorelei—named for a gern of fabled if troublesome magic—was a gentle, playful woman. Her younger sister was anything but gentle, a passionate, moody girl named Morgana for no clearly remembered reason. Morgana had three husbands, and the third was Belrix, the son of Reindeer who found his way home by way of Cornwall, Severn, and VI Legio under Ambrosius. Britons remembered him as Arthur, a fact of no great interest to Prydn. They were not a people to write more of themselves than animal signs on stone, but, as in Genesis, someone begat someone. With Belrix, Morgana bore Modred. For a few years that flashed more than they shone, the Prydn moved closer into tallfolk light, where some image could be sketched from them. Like Dorelei, Morgana had her own vision of Tir-Nan-Og and tried to carve it out with Modred for a sword. Arthur broke them and died in the necessary act. After that, the Faerie were never seen again in any great numbers in Pictland, eventually not at all.

The storytellers forgot names like Dorelei, Cruaddan, and Malgon, while Morgana and Modred are clearly remembered among Britons. Their courage was the same and the desperation that bred it, but war leaves a more indelible impression than any peace. Still, Dorelei's fhain was remembered indirectly by men who never knew or spoke her name. Her first husband's name became one of those odd specks of fact that lodge forever under the eyelid of history; her second, that passionate man who lost his way so often, found he'd never left home at all.

Padrec didn't question Dorelei's decision any more than that of a man vowed to make pilgrimage to Jerusalem. It was a thing to be done. They would go to Tir-Nan-Og, and if they fell over the edge of the world, which she maintained was no edge at all, at least they would die determinate.

They sealed the barrow again with Reindeer, taking only as much treasure as would be needed, and one extra pony to carry it. The rest they left to Nebha for Reindeer. Dorelei invited and Dorelei reassured, but Reindeer would not join them. They would rade anywhere a pony could carry them, but world sea was a different matter and a dubious one. Would stay. And so the last great children of Reindeer—Morgana, Belrix, and Modred—were born in Mabh's island and not somewhere else. The underpinnings of history and legend alike are sometimes that slight.

Two days' journey to the sea, but fhain took four, traveling mostly at night. An easy rade without the flock, which Dorelei left to Nebha with the treasure. She held back only three rams and three young ewes to start over with in Tir-Nan-Og. Father-God and Noah might make do with one pair, but three allowed a better margin of husbandry. If she departed the tallfolk world, Dorelei would not leave her common sense behind.

They made southwest toward Cair Ligualid and beyond to the estuary that cut inland past the end of the Wall. There, at the mouths of Lyne and Esk, many boats could be had for hire; not large enough for their venture but, as Padrec reasoned, always bound out for the Isle of Arran. The island had been part of the main trade routes from the Middle Sea since time out of mind. In the looted tombs of Egypt, dropped or ignored by thieves in their haste to be off with more valuable booty, were necklaces of British jet that Phoenicians shipped from Arran while Moses still wandered in Sinai. To Arran came the oceangoing galleys and their mariners. It was the place to start.

The west was sparsely peopled, and those few they met spoke in Irish—tallish, handsome men and women, not timid but with no desire to linger in the path of a Faerie rade. Padrec explained it from some experience. The Sidhe of Ireland were even less predictable in their goodwill toward tallfolk than Prydn were, very like for familiar reasons. When one met them, one was polite and brief. To meet such nomads on a rade reminded Faerie and tallfolk alike of wrongs done, land usurped, and destinies cut off.

"Irish feel a guilt toward fhains, like Picts," Padrec told his folk. "Guilt be father to fear, and fear to hate."

Dorelei knew from her own pain that it could be that dismally simple. For all the sense it made, that was how they came by the slaves. They were well on their way after the third nightfall, moving out of a low gorge onto open heath, when they almost collided with the tallfolk party in the dark. Riding ahead, Malgon and Padrec heard something approach. Because the strangers were afoot, they were less detectable, but there was the distinct *chank-chank* of iron chain, then a growing mumble of voices. Then someone called out sharply.

Padrec and Malgon pulled up short, bow and sword ready as the first figures became visible in the moonless dark. The wind was at Salmon's back, carrying sound away from them; they would have heard the strangers far earlier otherwise. There was the tall figure looming up in front of them, not a dog's bark away, surprised and not at all happy about it.

"Who is it there? Speak out. Who's there?"

"Irish," Padrec muttered to Malgon. He let the wind work for him, thinned his voice to a plaintive buzz, and answered in the Gaelic. "Daone Sidhe. Make way . . ."

The words trailed off into a keening that floated on the wind to the startled Irish, who heard one voice, then two, half a dozen swelling on the black night air. They weren't warriors but slave traders bound for Esk themselves. They feared Sidhe but lost profits more, and there were ten of them, armed. Their leader decided to stiff it out.

"Merchants we are. Sidhe, creatures of the night, begone. We have no fear of you."

The moon slid out of the clouds then, and Padrec saw the mute, manacled stock-in-trade of these merchants.

"Slavers, Mal."

They both heard more than one sword hiss from a sheath. Malgon didn't hesitate an instant. His bowstring bent and hummed. The nearest Irishman went down with a choked-off grunt. In the moment of shock among the traders, the other-world wailing still chilling about them, Malgon sent another arrow for effect and shot his horse forward.

"We *go*, Padrec!"

It was like the day of the Coritani patrol in the fog. Howling like Malgon, Padrec kicked his mount after his brother, flailing about with his sword, scattering slavers in all directions from their merchandise. The tactic worked because Malgon didn't hesitate to kill, nor Padrec to follow him. They both remembered Churnet, where one man's hesitation cost so much. Screaming on the wind, counterpointed by the keening of the women, they wheeled their horses this way and that after the demoralized slavers until they were dead or in rapid flight, leaving a dozen terrified slaves all praying to different gods and not at all sure about the sword-bearing man who bore down on them out of the gloom.

"Now, then. Who's Brit here? Who's Pict or what? Speak up."

A moment of uncertainty among them, then the tentative voice of a man ready to drop for weariness. "I am Brigante."

"We are all British."

"Na, there's Crow the Halt. He's Picti like yourselves."

"Be nae Pict," Malgon asserted stiffly.

Then Dorelei was at their side. "Padrec, who be these folk that a be so bound?"

"Slaves for sale," he told her with a note in his voice she'd never heard before. "What's done is well done. Do have nae love for slavers."

Dorelei only shrugged; the men only did what was necessary then. She might have sickened at Bruidda's death, but she would not shrink from killing now any more than Padrec or Malgon. "Take the iron from them," she ordered. "Let a go free."

The decision was translated to the grateful British.

"God bless, lady ..."

"Jesu and Mary Virgin bless you."

"Where's Crow, then, poor little sot?"

"He won't last long, I'll be bound."

"Och, don't waste pity on that trash."

"Is he not crippled? He can't help it. Look where he just dropped down in his tracks."

"Dirty sot. Drunk when they took him, drunk when they caught him again and broke his legs—thank you, sir, thank you."

Two by two, with keys found on the dead traders, the iron dropped from the slaves until only one yoked pair remained, a wilted Brigante woman who sat patient as an old horse beside the inert body chained to her, neck and neck. The man looked frail and slight between the sprawled crutches.

"This is the one you call Crow?"

"Aye, sir, and a weary old woman would thank you to part us. Crow's a good soul but not much in the way of company."

Padrec sprang the well-greased padlocks on her neck and ankles. The woman stepped out of them, feeling gingerly at her chafed neck. "Bless you, sir."

"Yes, yes. Let me see to this sad little man."

Crippled as he was, they'd still put irons on him. Feeling at the twisted ankles, Padrec wondered why. The breaks hadn't healed that well, hands could feel out that much in the dark. Even unfettered, the little man would never run or even walk well again. Padrec unlocked the irons and tossed them aside.

"Right, then, Crow. You're free. D'you hear? Wake up."

"He's that ill," the woman sympathized. "Just dropped down there when we stopped, poor sod."

"Crow?" Padrec bent close over the starvling face under short-chopped black hair and a dirty smudge of beard. The head moved slightly. Even in the poor light, the fhain scars were clear.

"Dorelei!" Padrec's exultant shout rose like the trumpet of heaven, no doubt heard by the still-fleeing slavers and anyone else within a mile or two. "Dorelei, it's CRU!"

In a moment they were all about him, leaving the other slaves mystified as they were suddenly liberated. Guenloie, Malgon, Neniane, a shrieking knot of joy about the lost lamb found, and Dorelei tearing through them to dive at Cru like a hawk in love, squeezing him close, her lips against his mouth and bearded cheek.

"Husband . . . Cruaddan."

". . . Dorelei? Oh, wife, have been sick."

"But healed now, home."

"Nae, did break my legs as Padrec's."

"But healed and home, Cru. Oh, husband, have been so empty without you. Neniane, bring Crulegh. Oh, Cru." On her knees, his head in her lap. "Have been a gern, Cru. Have done such magic, but nae so great as this. See thy wealth, Cruaddan."

She gave him now the thing he'd once been jealous enough to ask. *Just as well*, Padrec thought. A man should know what was his and what not. He stepped quietly back from the circle of adoration. The fact didn't hurt; not a sadness but a stillness in joy. Cru was home; there was justice after all. Wherever Dorelei went, she'd be the more complete for Cru, halved without him, simple as that, and nothing to do with Padrec himself. When he could wedge a word between them, he pressed Cru's hand between his own.

"Greet thy brother husband. Hast been folly and war, much sadness, and now a joy with thee home. Be fhain again."

But Cru had no ear or eye for anyone but Dorelei and the sleepy, confused boy.

"Be a match for them an a come back."

Padrec peered down from the hill at the heath stretching away toward Esk, a blue line in the distance. "But keep watch, Mal."

They'd withdrawn into the hills as a precaution in case the slavers had any thought to repossess their goods. Once hidden, the lot of them slept a few hours. At daybreak a fire was made; since they were in sight of Esk, the rest of the tea and oatmeal was shared out to all, including the freed slaves. With Dorelei's permission, Padrec gave each a few coins and pointed them south the few miles toward the Wall and home.

"And you of Eburacum, if you go to hear Mass under Bishop Meganius, ask him to pray for me, Father Patricius."

Oh, then, they'd heard of him, right enough. He'd be the one called Raven, the Faerie priest. Och, the tales told about *him*—that he was dead, that he couldn't die ever, having gone under the hill with the little folk, slain a hundred at Churnet Head, turned water into wine. And here was the clout of him alive in front of them. *Dyw!*

"Actually, it was wine into water," Padrec informed them gravely. "There was a great deal of wine and no water, and we all needed a wash, but that's another story. Peace be with you. Go and pray for me."

That much was easy. Their problem, evident with the rising sun, was Cru. Fhain vied with each other to show him kindness and that his rightful place was restored. They brought his porridge first and hot, the children were pushed at him to be kissed and complimented for their beauty and resemblance to their mothers. The children squirmed to be away from him, and small wonder. Cru smelled foreign, even after a loving and meticulous shave by Guenloie to free his handsome face from the slothful tallfolk beard. Dorelei bathed him in a slow, sensual act of love just shy of copulation. She would have done that, right and proper as it was, if Cru were not so weak. He smelled like a man who'd drunk more than he'd eaten for months, the fine lines of his face blurred with uisge and defeat. More than his legs had been broken, but only they were healed. Dorelei was baffled.

"Padrec, help thy brother husband," she begged in private. "Be nae a cannot walk. A will not. Help me."

Help all of them. They shouldn't remain here in open, strange country. God knows what tales the slavers told when they stopped running. Fhain must be gone. But there Cruaddan sat. He could walk with the crutches alone, he said. A wonder the traders kept him, except that the slave market was never glutted.

Cru's quest was theirs in small. When Dorelei banished him, was he not gone off the edge of all the world he knew? No Tir-Nan-Og, only alien tallfolk places and open heath, hunting sometimes and borrowing others, even begging.

"Did cross the Wall. Nae dared go among Picts."

And sold his pony and then the rest of his few possessions, piece by piece. He was an oddity among the Brigantes. At first they were curious, having seen few Faerie so close. They gave him uisge to tell of himself. Funny in a sad way. What these folk took for magic was only Cru's sense of reality. Then they grew used to him and contemptuous, a monkey on a chain, a dancing bear, more annoyance than amusement with his begging. Sober he wouldn't clown for them, but drunk he was a lark, a sport. They fed him cheap uisge to see him whirl about, trying to sing in his heathen gibberish, fall over chairs. There was always a bruise or scab on his face from where someone cuffed him or he fell down drunk. Oh, it was fine to watch him. A body could die laughing. A man could die . . .

"Did live by making a laugh," Cru rasped in Dorelei's arms. "And did need the uisge."

Needed it to dull the fact that he was lost, gone from Dorelei, gone from fhain and no place in this loud, ugly tallfolk world still enough to hear Mother. Like Padrec's tale of Satan, he'd fallen out of heaven into hell, no fire but *noise*, empty laughter, meaningless cruelty.

Dorelei asked again and again through it, "Why did thee nae come home? Did forgive thee ten times over."

Cru only looked away then, and the sound he made was weak as the rest of him. "Forgive?"

He heard that the fhains were rading all together under Dorelei and Padrec. He was proud of them but would not stain their triumph with the shadow of Judas, as Dorelei named him. He drifted farther west. On a day when his head was aching but clear, he heard of the Coritani war and that the fine young men of Prydn rode ahead under Padrec and Malgon.

The hand on Malgon's trembled visibly. "Was a braw pride to hear of thee, Mal. My own fhain brother at the head of tallfolk. Did make to join thee."

Malgon's eyes brimmed with awkward pity. "Was nae pride, Cru. All gods did turn from it."

No matter, Cru was going to join Padrec's horse and redeem himself. After the next drink, just one or two, a few to stop the sickness. He was unconscious when the Irish slavers came into the village, and he woke up in chains.

Cru lifted his hands as if they still bore the obscene weight. "Chains. Such sweet sound for so evil a thing. Cha-ins."

Neither the slavers nor the other captives understood what chains did to one born to hilltops and far sight, never fettered. The first set of irons put on him were meant for tallfolk. Cru greased his ankles with the slop he was fed, slipped free, and ran. They rode him down. Once more he escaped, and once more they caught him through his own folly. He'd meant to keep running and got as far as the next village to Eburacum; didn't he need food, and the wine-seller's stall close by? He needed a drink first, just one. So they caught him again. This time the slavers weighed a bird in the hand against a gaggle in the bush. They were tired of this; they'd take a cut price on the little bastard. Sidhe or not, they broke his legs to slow him down. Some of them were against it. Faerie didn't forget a kindness and for sure not an injury. No good would come of it.

Padrec slapped his knee. "That's why they made off so neat. Because of thee, what fhain would do in vengeance."

Dorelei nodded grimly, knowing the value of reputation. "Would I not."

Then Cru said a strange thing none of them understood. "A did nae do this to me. Were only the hands. This . . ." He trailed off, busying himself with Crulegh, pretending to nuzzle the bairn to hide his eyes. "Did deserve it."

"Thy legs be nae well healed, but enough," Padrec said. "Why dost cling to these sticks?"

Cru looked away.

"Why?"

"I need them," he said. He didn't want to talk about it. He had the spirit of a whipped dog. Cru would not walk without the crutches and little with them. They weren't free of trouble yet. All of them knew where they went and what would be needed. A husband who had to be lifted to horse and down like a child?

They begged him by all he meant to them, all he loved. "Try," Malgon pleaded. "Try, Cruaddan. Nae, an thee will walk unaided to my braw army horse, a's thine. And I will walk until can borrow more."

"Try," Dorelei held him. "For me. For Crulegh, thy own wealth."

"What difference?" Cru was strangely remote. "Did say a was Padrec's."

"Never. Did never, Cru."

"Oh, nae word for word, but—"

"Husband, thee must walk."

"Nae, leave off," he lashed out suddenly. "Leave me be. Can*not*."

Dorelei looked up at the sun. So much time they could wait and no more. Two years ago she could not have left him. Now such a thing would be conceivable in her necessity, and more than that. "Think thyself the only fallen one? Thee dost nae know, Cru. I tell thee, try. Walk!"

Cru only rolled over on his side, sobbing with a greater loss than his legs. "Was so *proud* to be first husband to thee. And then Padrec came."

"Oh, Cru." There was pity in her voice, but it was thinning. "What it be that makes a man, thee's gone dry of't. A gern can nae ride with weak husband." Dorelei rose from his prostrate misery, calling to the others. "Better we never found Cru. Can nae weep with him. We go."

Cru turned to her, unbelieving. Go without him? "Wife. Please."

"Better we never found you." She tore Crulegh out of his arms

327

and left him lying in the pool of his midday shadow between the miserable crutches. "Come. Will leave him."

Malgon refused flatly. "Will not."

"Malgon, thy gern speaks."

"I know what Mal says," Padrec spoke up. "Have left too many."

Dorelei's expression was strange; looking at her, Padrec would call it terminal. "Be a's only chance, Padrec. Would speak to thee alone."

Apart from the others and the desolate Cru, Dorelei showed him her desperation. "Padrec, did never take thee into me once, love thee once that I did nae know I held a man of magic, a king. As Jesu. Do need thy magic again."

"You need Cru."

"Truly. From the first days." She touched his chest. "Here. As you need thy God, and neither of us will be filled without that."

"I know, Dorelei."

"Then let one love help another. I beg it, Padrec."

She spoke the truth. He felt less than whole away from God. He wasn't sure what he could do. There were feelings in his belly learned in war that had nothing to do with God. Once he was sure of his cosmos; now he knew more about men than gods, but that was a long way from miracles. "Will fhain do as I say in this?"

"Whatever, husband."

He searched her face. "It may be that we must leave him. Would truly go if thee must?"

Dorelei's gray eyes did not waver from his. "Aye. Have paid too much to get this far."

"Tell Malgon a must do everything I say. And the rest as well."

Padrec turned toward Cru with no clear idea of what to do, only what he felt in his belly. Cru mentioned Judas, the name Dorelei put to him on the day of his shame. Helpless and lost in a tallfolk world, Cru let that name burn into him, become part of him.

Sweet Jesu, tell me how to help him.

Not the image of Jesu came then, but Meganius, who would help a beaten priest to God only when and if he tried to reach himself. He refused then out of anger and hurt. He and Malgon knew where lost was; they'd been there. It was a long road back. He stood over Cru now and saw himself.

"Cru?"

The bleary, defeated eyes slid up to him. "Pray for me, Padrec."

"The hell I will." Padrec scooped up one crutch and broke it over his knee. "You did this for me once." He kicked the other crutch toward Malgon. "Break it."

Only a moment of hesitation, then Malgon splintered the second crutch. Padrec knelt by the stricken Cru, speaking softly.

"Mark me, you self-pitying little bastard. Like Moses to Pharaoh, you'll hear it only once before grief lights on thee. Salmon must be strong, must move or die, as Cruaddan said to me once. He was right, but Cru was a man then. Thee speaks of Judas? I failed my God as much as he. I looked at Drust hanging on the cross, and he believed more dying than I did alive. And Dorelei failed—*we* failed in so much, Cru, but we have done miracles just by staying alive and believing in each other. Be not easy, not cheap. Gern-y-fhain and I have more betrayal and death on our hands than thee could walk thy crutches over in a year."

Cru was weeping now. He stretched a hand to Padrec, who only struck it away. "Not yet; thee's nae my brother yet. Earn it. In my own pride I spoke of sin before I even knew the sight and smell of it. Do know it now. Sin is not forever, Cru. Good Christ, it *can't* be. If't were, why would we have a word like 'forgive'?"

"Be dead, Padrec. Dost hear me? *Dead.*"

"You want forgiveness? All right. For whatever Grace is left in my hands under the blood, I forgive you. Te absolvo ... and I ask your forgiveness for the pain I caused you. The next words are 'go and sin no more.' But for that, you've got to try."

Padrec rose, stretching his hands out to the broken man. "Be a fine wife, and thee can walk to her. A fine son, and thee can reach him. Will try, Cru? Or will lie there and let a better man take both from thee?"

Cru lowered under the pallor of his sickness. "Thee's cruel."

"That's a shame. But I took her from you once—"

"Tallfolk!"

"Wherefore?" Padrec slammed it back at him. "I rode with the fhains under Ambrose. I was with Dorelei every moment when she bore Crulegh into the world. I saw him come, still corded to her with the birthstring. And I have loved her better than thee ever could, scant man. Woman and wealth be mine. Have earned them."

Cru choked out something that deepened into a primal howl and propelled him awkwardly onto his knees. "Dorelei!"

Her only response was to gather up Crulegh and turn to her pony. "We go."

"Nae, wife. Wait."

"NO!" she screamed. "Be weak, Cru. Have paid too much. Do carry much. Cannot carry thee, too. Padrec will be father to Crulegh."

Cru's howl broke in a sob, but Padrec kept at him. "Fhain leaves thee."

"Thee will *not.*" Impossibly, Cru put one twisted ankle under him and wobbled up to stand half erect before them before collapsing again. Weeping, he tried to pull himself along on his elbows toward Dorelei. "Not my son. Not my wealth."

"Get up, Cru."

"Not my . . ."

"Get up."

Hopeless it was. Cru only snarled through his tears. "*Thee* lift me up, Jesu-man. Jesu cured the halt. 'Take up thy bed and walk,' was't?"

"That was a man who wanted to live, Cru. Could do nothing with thee who only want to die."

Agonized, Cru watched Dorelei fork Crulegh over the saddle and vault up behind him.

Now, Padrec prayed, *now if it's in him at all. Am I telling him to do his own miracle, or asking it of God?* And then Padrec had part of his answer, bursting out, "Cru, help Him to help thee!"

Cru tried. He struggled, desperate. Once more, gasping with the effort, he heaved up on the long-flaccid legs, got almost erect before they went out from under him. Defeat was too long a habit. He only covered his face.

"Leave him, Gern-y-fhain." Padrec waved her on. "Death is what a wants. Go."

Dorelei moved on without looking back, fhain after her. Only Padrec's horse was left, Padrec himself, and Cru weeping on his knees. Fhain was out of earshot now and Padrec despairing as much as Cru. So much for miracles. Padrec scanned the open sky.

"Ravens came for me once, Cru. Was nae dead yet, and a came. Ravens can wait. Can smell death coming. Here." Padrec dropped his knife beside Cru. "Should make an end before that."

Cru closed a grimy fist on the hilt. "Do hate thee, Padrec."

"Dorelei hated to kill Bruidda, but a did it. Jesu can nae help thee. Miracle will nae help. Thee will nae let it."

Padrec walked away to the horse. *God, Jesu, he did try, it's in him. Is it in You? Or me? Here, now, this is what faith reduces to. Let him try again.*

Then Cru's voice behind him, no longer weeping. "Will have thy horse, tallfolk."

When Padrec turned, Cru was heaving himself up, swaying for balance, the knife out in front of him, yearning for Padrec's flesh.

"Will have to come for it, Cru."

Cru lurched forward a step. "And kill thee."

"Will help." Padrec moved to a point halfway between Cru and the horse. "A little way, Cru, just a little. Here I am."

Cru swayed forward, wobbling precariously. Another step. Another.

"Come on, just a few more and you can reach me. A few more after that to the horse and all it can carry thee to. Come *on*, Cru."

The small man staggered forward, dragging each foot like the iron that fettered it so long. Only the knife never wavered. He was almost within reach when the legs buckled and tumbled him on the ground. When he raised his head, the hate was a pleading.

"Help me, Padrec. Help me reach you. Mother, Jesu, help me!"

"Help them, Cru. Dost nae understand? Be God that needs *you*. One more time, Cru. One more step."

Cru's shoulders bunched over the faltering legs. Another sob choked out of him. Then he saw Dorelei and fhain growing smaller in the distance, leaving his life and his miserable death. And somehow he stood up again, stumbled forward to lay the knife against Padrec's heart. But why should the great Raven be weeping like himself?

"Well, Cru. Can kill me now. Or I'll help you to horse."

Cru blinked through a mist over his soul as Padrec held out a hand. "Come, that's the style. One step, another. And another. Will help. Another."

"Miserable tallfolk filth—"

"Shut up," Padrec said, pulling him along tenderly. "I've seen God at work only once before—another step, that's it—and I think it's happening now, so be quiet and get on with it. Good, Cru, good. God needs you first, then He can help."

Cru pushed aside the supporting arm. "Will do't myself." He took the last slow but firming steps to grasp the saddle horn. "Nae, do nae help me."

The hands might tremble, but the shoulders were still powerful. With one heave, Cru pulled himself astride the horse and reached to gather the reins. "Have won thy horse, Padrec."

"And the rest." Padrec looked off after fhain. "If thee can do as much for thine, so can I. So must I."

The men looked at each other.

"Did hate thee," Cru confessed. "Could still, to think of thee with her." He turned the horse about, walked it a few paces. Padrec wasn't following. "Come up behind?"

"No, Cruaddan."

He'd said it to give Cru heart and only now realized the truth. Once before did he see God at work, not Jesu but Drust on the cross. All his faith, all his Christianity came down to that agonized but pure death and showed his own heart wanting. And now Cru did it by wrenching truth even farther into the light. God created men out of need, men like Cru and Drust and Meganius, women like Dorelei: far too noble to be called dust. That busy old Boyo working in his Six

331

Days, did He know all He took on? *Well, I do, and that makes me worth finishing what I started.* "Keep the knife, Cru. Let it be my gift."

"Thee do nae rade with us?"

"I can't go, I ..." How to say it? Could he ever? "Salmon goes where a must, remember? Cannae always be together. Tell Dorelei, a was beauty. Say I will be filled with her and empty." He reached for Cru's hand in farewell. "Between us, we found the road of the gods. I will always be her husband. We will meet again in Tir-Nan-Og." Padrec smacked the horse on the rump. "Till then, brother."

Cru turned once to raise a hand in farewell. "Lugh ride thy arrows, Padrec."

"Did always know Crulegh was thine. Kiss thy wealth for me." *And I will bless my own for thee and Drust.*

For a while he watched from the hill: Cru galloping after the others who stopped, expecting a different rider, but darting out to surround the one they got. It was far now; Padrec's eyes were not sharp as Malgon's. He saw the huddle of them paused together; then one who rode some way back toward his hill. *Don't, Dorelei. Understand it. We have had such beauty. Miracles. And this is one of them. I have found my own treasure.*

For all the distance between them, he felt her close and read the acceptance in her stillness. They watched each other for a long time, the spring wind blowing between them. Then Dorelei turned her pony and walked it back toward Cru and her people.

Padrec's pace south was half stride, half dogtrot, but he caught up with the freed slaves before long and slept that night in the house of Cair Ligualid's priest. Not too well; he wasn't used to beds anymore.

"Bless me, Father, for I have sinned."

Hearing confessions was one office Meganius usually left to the diocesan priests, but Father Colin was abed with a stomach disorder— not surprising the way he stuffed down pickled eel drowned in liquamen, and shellfish so far out of season. Someone else could be sent for, but the appointed hour was come and past, and the bishop happened to be in the church at the time. He couldn't honestly decline. Meganius settled himself in a cushioned chair behind the curtain and listened for the first of them.

"Bless me, Father."

Curious how rarely one heard anything new, although now and then on a warm spring day like this, the mind could wonder detachedly about the faces veiled by the confessional curtain. Over a lifetime, one could tell much just from sound. A swish of linen or samite, the delicate scrape of a sandal: a woman, probably young and well placed. The young ones hesitated, as if their sins were somehow novel. The older ones mucked on into it with the ease of habit.

Soft shoes, a heavy, clumping gait, the protesting creak of the kneeler: a merchant or farmer. Dull thud of bare feet, a peasant or scullery girl. The voice murmured through the curtain, soft or grating, plaintive, perfunctory, or greased with self-satisfaction. Meganius listened conscientiously and wished it done.

Soft shoes again, a light step but firm: a vital man in good condition. The creak and clink of a belt unbuckled, slight clatter of a sword laid aside. An officer from Ambrosius' legion?

"Forgive me, Father, for I have sinned."

Meganius raised his head, suddenly very still except for his pulse. The voice waited for his response. "Father?"

Meganius was glad for the curtain between them. "Yes, I am here."

"Forgive me, Father—"

And have you forgiven yourself, Sochet? Finally? "How have you sinned, my son?"

Meganius wondered if it was really chance that Father Colin was indisposed. It was a complex confession, more meditation than anything else, but sure and unhesitant.

"I thought I was lost and willingly so. I thought to turn my back on my Father's house but found in truth that neither He nor it would leave me; only that when I felt my soul move with His will, like His own shadow . . ."

Meganius waited. "That was well put. Go on."

"I—"

"In your own words." *You never lacked for them.*

"I am a priest like yourself."

God, was he not? Meganius felt like singing—dancing, even. "And?"

"My faith left me, but God would not. Does that seem strange?"

"Not for a priest."

"I once said that man was meaningless without God. That's not true, can't be true. Just turned around. God is meaningless without man. Please, Father, I am not a heretic. . . ."

Why not? Wasn't Christ so to the Pharisees?

"Or perhaps 'meaningless' is not the word I seek. 'Helpless.' What can God do unless we help? Without us, He's so lonely. I have nothing to repent, don't even know, beyond habit, why I'm making more devout folk wait like this. But I think—yes, I think I could do now what He set for me once, long ago. Not understanding, no." The voice had eased by habit into the gentle Prydn fall. "I'm not a scholar, I'll

333

never understand it all as scholars do. But if my Father will have a little patience, I might be easier now for Him to employ." Meganius could almost hear the rueful smile. "And perhaps to tolerate, if He won't mind an argument now and then."

That was all. Silence and the curtain between them. Meganius looked at his own hands lying in his lap, and for the first time in his life, and that quite happily, violated the rule of the confessional.

"If God has any patience at all, Sochet, you will be its measure. I'll expect you to supper tonight."

The soft laughter was barely audible. "I thought Your Grace would never ask."

The kneeler scraped, the sword belt rustled. The soft shoes moved away, overlapped by another nearing step.

"B-bless me, Father, f-for I have sinned."

Oh, Lord, the vintner's daughter again. The girl had a nervous stutter that made her seem always on the verge of tittering when actually she was painfully shy and withdrawn. She was fourteen, plain, and melancholic. She would tell him everything, and nothing ever happened to her. In spite of himself, Meganius' thoughts returned to Sochet.

Without us, He's so lonely.

That would include the vintner's girl. Meganius leaned closer to the veil. "In what way, child?"

TO HIS HOLINESS, CELESTINE, descendant of Peter, Vicar of Christ, Bishop of the Holy See of Rome. CAIUS MEG-ANIUS at Eburacum asks the papal blessing.

For that our mission to the Irish has long languished, we have this day received the pallium that we asked of Auxerre for consecration and have Germanus' personal blessing in the investiture of Father Magonus Succatus Patricius. We have appointed him to that See for which his aptness is exceeded only by his passion for that calling to which he was ordained. Father Patricius is an Augustinian long in my service. Through his efforts, the Word of God has spread north to the wild tribes of Pictland, even to the Faerie, an undertaking that would have been impossible to any other understanding of faith but that of the singular Patricius. We do not agree with those who say the Irish would make indifferent Christians. Being near to them in blood, we have never known them to be indifferent about anything. They are the tinder, needing only the spark that the Church this day sets to them. To His Holiness'

prayers we commend ourselves and Succatus Patricius, bishop to the Irish.

Like any powerful cleric and courtier, Meganius knew the higher forms of banditry and the uses of distance. He was at an *utter* loss (he later confessed to a peremptory Holiness) to understand why his earlier letters on Patricius had not been received. Had they been so, his actions would be completely clear. He apologized formally and promised to look into the discrepancy with a full report to follow.

Celestine was startled, displeased, and Auxerre heard of it forthwith. Who *was* this Briton? Why did Germanus send a pallium without informing Rome? Did he not know the See of Ireland was marked for as worthy and pious a man as Palladius, already about to embark?

Actually, it was the pallium for the new Coritani bishop that was sent, but Germanus even crowed over it a little. The Holy See could rest easy; Patricius was that same zealous enemy of the Pelagian blight, ever at Germanus' side in the recent and total victory over heresy in Britain.

Rejoice, O See of Peter, that thou hast a Joshua at the gates of Jericho. Glory to God, Alleluia.

If Meganius' reasons were dim to Celestine, at least one reference was totally incomprehensible. "Faerie?" he questioned his monk-scribe, a man of many travels and tongues. "What are Faerie?"

The scribe searched for simile. Ah, yes, Holiness. They were like the German trolls, little folk who lived under earthen mounds, or so it was said by Saxons. Many did not believe in them at all.

Like poor scholarship, the definition misted more than it illuminated and sent Celestine bemused to his next audience. "Trolls . . . mounds. This Briton is *digging* for converts?"

So Celestine—that is to say, Holy Church—gave it up for the moment. Palladius, who was to be bishop to the Christian Irish, quietly unpacked.

Waiting to say his farewell, Meganius fed bits of softened bread to his peacocks. The fat things hardly needed feeding, but it gave his hands something to do during this kind of prayer.

Lord, my God: this day he opens a new door in Your house. Though he goes to Ireland, he is not the man who came to me seething for it. Somehow he doesn't even look right in canonicals and tonsure anymore, yet men have attested miracles by his converts. Miracles are dubious expedients at best, the province of saints now and then. It is not a saint I send, nor even, perhaps, a cleric to Rome's cut, but my heart knows him the man for Ireland.

I commend into Your hands what may be my last significance. The sun takes longer to warm me now and leaves too soon. I ask Your blessing for my Sochet. If he chafes now and then, it is only because the Church must look with the eyes of men, more often shut tight than open, and Sochet's sight is painfully clear.

Did You worry when he left his vows? I did; I lost more sleep than a prelate should over one boiling young priest. But Sochet is one of those rare ones whose calling will always lie in the crucial gap between Your reach and human grasp. I understand his wife was much the same. Not surprising; I can't imagine him with the comfortable sort of woman—

"Your grace?"

"Oh. Sochet. And here am I, maundering over these silly pets of mine. Is it time, then?"

Padrec knelt to kiss the bishop's ring. "Up, Sochet." Meganius opened his arms to embrace his priest. "Godspeed."

"Pray for me, Cai."

"Of course I will, and you must write. Well, let me look at my investiture. My investment." Although Padrec's tonsure and new robes were carefully done, the canonicals did look strangely inappropriate to him now. Then Meganius frowned; over the priest's heart, instead of the Chi-Rho medallion, was hung a simple cross of cold-wrought iron. The bishop's frown deepened to distaste. "Really, Sochet."

"I know what your grace will say, but the cross has been used before."

"Not widely, I'm pleased to say, and not in civilized Britain." Meganius was genuinely put off by the notion. "The Chi-Rho is Christ's symbol."

"And the cross as well."

"Of a brutal death in a shameful manner. There are those cults who respond more to the death than the life. Clerics of taste do not dwell on it as a focus for prayer."

Padrec touched the cross. "Call it my last heresy. Rome need never know."

"Not from me at any rate," Meganius promised. "Why, Sochet?"

Padrec had settled unconsciously into that stillness never learned in Auxerre. "Do you think it is Christ's death I remember in this?"

Meganius remembered Malgon and eloquent pictures in the earth. "No, I suppose not."

"Chi-Rho is Christ in symbol. It was on that dirty cross that I saw the reality. What He tried to say and how well we are made to hear it. Some of us. Better men than me. From the cross it was that I was taught. It is not for other men but myself. And you know the kind of gauds Rome will be sending."

Meganius hid his private disappointment. He'd planned to send something himself, a Chi-Rho in enamel and gold or even a mosaic worker to adorn the first new chapel.

"Indulge me, your grace," Padrec smiled at him. "My sanctity is just out of the press and a bit stiff. Well, now: it's a fine day to start, isn't it?"

"Sochet, don't put me off, I'm serious. There is no bishop in Britain who wears such a sign or who would even consider it. You're not a hot young torch of a priest anymore, hooting after truant souls. You are a bishop. It is questionable taste—your grace."

A bishop with an odd, distant gaze, used to hills and horizons, never to be at home in anything like a house again. "You have my reasons."

"Reasons?" Meganius put an arm around Padrec's shoulder and led him to the open gateway and the waiting cart. "It's you will be wearing it, Sochet. If Christ were hanged, would you wear a noose about your neck?"

Padrec embraced him once more and sprang up onto the cart. "Why not? The Irish would."

He gathered up the traces, but paused before starting up the oxen. "There! Will you *look* at the dazzle of that sky, Caius Meganius? It almost puts your peacocks to shame."

VIII

The Last Rainbow

I n the ports of Arran where the galleys from the Middle Sea loaded and disgorged, there were many languages spoken, but the only universal tongue was money. The shipowners dealt in realities, the more so here in the decaying north, where hard cash was much scarcer.

Milius Apullo of Massilia owned not a galley but a ship of the newest kind, a covered afterdeck, ample cargo space, mainsail with intricate shrouding, and a new foresail that could half-reef quickly in a stiff gale or spread full and cut days off his time to landfall.

"No wallowing, not my ship. Turn her over, you'll not see the rot of some of these other seagoing sows. She's scraped regular as I pray. I know you've got gold, I see it. Do you people understand what I'm saying? What do you want of my ship?"

The ship itself they wanted, and that quickly. Milius had never seen Faerie before, though of course all seafaring men heard and traded fabulous stories. They didn't look fabulous, more . . . he couldn't quite find the word, but it wouldn't be 'warm.' They had a way of just standing there, looking dead at you as if they'd been sown, sprouted, and grown on the spot. It was better to talk business.

341

"Milius Apullo. My ship's for cargo hire. What do you transport?"

Themselves, they told him. A few ponies and sheep.

"Oh, well, you realize that's expensive. Have to take on supplies for passengers, ballast cargo. Very expensive."

The woman's hand passed over the rough table between them. Lying on the planks, lustrous and undeniable, was the fattest garnet Milius ever saw. Interesting, even of some value, but not near enough for . . .

Milius looked again and swallowed hard. The stone was not garnet but a ruby. His eyes widened as one of the little men, the one with the limp, solemnly laid a heavy gold trading stick between Milius and the ruby.

"Well." He cleared his throat. "Well, now."

The other man, the sleety-eyed one, put down a second bar to bracket the stone. Then another woman, the tastiest of the lot, reached into the bag, which must have come from Croesus' treasure-house, and drew out two more trading sticks. The woman who obviously led them completed the golden square and spoke to Milius.

"Be square, the tallfolk shape of things."

Milius thought nimbly. What he saw would pay for the voyage, but there must be more where that came from. None of them looked like they'd ever been near the sea.

"Enough." He clapped his hands together with a show of expansiveness and business well concluded. "That will do it. Now, where do I take you? Massilia? Antioch?"

More than a little disturbing, all of them, they were unearthly. The cold-eyed man with the bow leaned over the table toward him. "West."

"I see. Ireland. Leinster?"

A shaking of the dark head. "West."

"The western coast, then? Conaill? Shannon?"

"More west."

"West of Ireland?" Milius regarded the weird group and their round-eyed children, digesting the magnitude of their request. "There *is* nothing west of Ireland."

They didn't understand or didn't care. At the edge of the world sea the water boiled and whirled in a race that made the swiftest rapids look like a garden pool, didn't they under—

While Milius talked, the woman began to double the golden frame about the ruby.

—stand? Milius faltered. He hefted one of the bars. Full weight.

"West," said the woman, then whispered something to be translated by the man with the bow. "Gern-y-fhain says thee knows nae the

342

shape of the world. Water does nae boil at edge but turns calm."
Malgon hovered over the ship's master as if expecting him to rise and
be about it. "Can go now?"

Well, it was a hard world for sailing men, even harder for those
who didn't know fortune when it lay before them. Such people would
be no problem, not to the crew Milius was already recruiting in his
experienced calculation. He needed ten men; five had disappeared
the night they dropped anchor at Brodick. Nothing new there; men
were always to be had on Arran, especially for a very short voyage
like this.

"Gold!" he exhorted the new men, most of whom were known to him.
"Gold, feel it. Look at this stone. Here, give it back. We'll coast them
down the channel, then two nights out, three at most, when they're
bent over the rail and bringing up the bottom of their bellies ...
then."

Preposterous. Milius was more amazed than amused. The woman
said *he* didn't know the shape of the world? Due west, was it? Ah,
yes, of a certainty.

Intended or not, that was his course. A week later, whether the
edge of the world boiled or lay calm, Milius' ship was rolling through
open sea toward it.

Off the edge—she was off the edge of her own world when the
last hills she knew sank behind the unfamiliar ones. Cru was back,
and that a last true miracle from Padrec. If one barrow in her heart was
opened and its dead risen, another was sealed and must remain so.
Dorelei mourned his going, but nothing stayed. She accepted that. It
had to do with paying for what one got, and Cru need never know.

She didn't trust Milius or his tallfolk crew. The food was good,
the water still fresh, but all of fhain felt a sickness in their bellies. On
the second day out, making south along the Irish coast, one of the
sailors said it had to do with the motion of the ship. Salmon found this
dubious; they'd ridden all their lives without this nausea.

"Dost lie," Cru said, sick as the rest. "Have been on Mother's
breast two tens of Bel-teins and one. Did never feel so close to
death, even in uisge."

Something was amiss. They squatted about Dorelei among their
animals, the miserable, messy children patted and washed and re-
washed as they dampened the straw with clear fluid from their emptied,
agonized stomachs. Cru put the question for all of them.

"Gern-y-fhain, what shall fhain do against these tallfolk?"

Since that morning, when she found Milius snooping near their treasure-sack for no good reason, Dorelei needed no reflection on the matter. "Milyod be nae a heart to trust. None of them."

"Do mean to kill us with this unnatural sickness and take fhain treasure," Neniane worried. "Do nae go west. Dost Milyod think fhain ignorant of the sun? Sister hast flown with Mabh: tell us what to do."

That was already decided, Dorelei said, and waited only on the act that must be now, before they were too weak to move. The sickness was an evil magic, but Salmon had broken evil before, prevailed even over Bruidda (may she be young forever), and prospered even in Jesu. Clearly they were favored of all gods. This Milyod would quickly turn west. Dorelei described fhain's task in words they understood.

"This one or that among the tallfolk has the look of death about him. Just the look, mind, but must be ready."

Cru reached for his knife and honing stone, Malgon for his bow.

"Neniane and Guenloie will stay for now with the wealth." Dorelei beckoned the men to follow her up the ladder to the deck.

Milius himself was at the tiller aft. The three Prydn stood just outside the hatchway for a moment, a little clump of determination, their eyes summing the situation, spying out a coil of rope. Then they drifted toward Milius, Cru bending to pick up the coiled line, paying out the end of it into a loop. Malgon casually inspected an arrowhead, strung bow under one arm.

"Milius," Dorelei approached him, "thee will turn west now."

He barely glanced at her, busy at the tiller. "Be off, woman. It isn't time."

"Be time long since. Turn west, Milyod."

"I said—"

"Cru!"

Behind Milius, Cru flowed like a shadow. His knife flashed, then the loop jerked tight around Milius's neck as Malgon kicked his feet out from under him. Before Milius could choke out half a warning, he was lifted in arms too strong for such a small man and sent flying over the side, arms flailing. Cru secured the line to the rail. The gulls *squee-uked* their gratitude. The fish would come now. They might get a few.

The thing happened so quickly, most of the crew still didn't know what had occurred when they heard the strangled cry for help. Then Sejus the navigator felt the vibration of the arrow as it drove into the rail between his legs, just a hair below what he held most dear. The mean-eyed little woman didn't even change expression, only beckoned him to the yawing, abandoned tiller.

"West."

Quick as a Barbary ape, she leaped onto the aft rail, hanging out from the shroud, calling to Milius, who floundered, clinging to the rope. "Thee bleeds, tallfolk? Birds will smell it, and fish soon. Do go west with us, or east alone?"

He thrashed about. "Pu-pull me in." One of his arms was leaving a dangerous trail of blood in the water that sharks could trace from far away. "P-pull me in. Lay to!"

Dorelei looked back at the stunned crew and Malgon and Cru facing them with bow and sword. Once more she waved Sejus to the tiller. "West. Give the order, Milyod. West!"

Sputtering, hanging on to the line, Milius spat out salt water and cried his will to Sejus. Dorelei gripped the rigging tighter as the craft heeled over. "Pull up thy master."

A day later they were farther west than any man wanted to go. The first night after Milius' near-death, they planned to finish the Faerie for good and all and put about. Milius left one man at the tiller while they conferred on the foredeck in whispers: it's righted, we've come about. Aye, headed back for land. Right then, on my signal . . .

Yet someone thought they saw the shadows move on the aft deck. Milius called softly to the steersman. "Sejus? You hear me?"

Then he felt the craft heel sharply over, coming about yet again. "Come on."

They got no closer to the tiller than half a dozen yards before the shapes emerged from the shadows, the implacable woman and the limping man, and the archer to one side. Milius saw that the tiller was held firmly by the one called Guenloie while her absurdly small daughter clung to her leg.

"Where's Sejus? Where's my steersman?"

"There." Cru pointed to the form spread out in the rigging like a clumsy spider. A muffled, plaintive sound came from it. "Dost have the look of death."

"A's veins be opened," Dorelei informed them. "Must bind him up or lose him. West."

Milius thought on it. Next to himself, Sejus was the only other competent navigator, and none of them that good so far from land.

Dorelei spoke to them without raising her voice. "Mark me. Next hand to turn us back will nae be bound up."

Milius began to believe the stories about these creatures. They weren't human. *They'd like to kill us, they'd enjoy it.* "Woman, this is not reasonable. You need us."

"Then would do thee much profit to stay alive, Milyod."

No, she'd never heard of reason, none of them had. Insane. "You fool, do you know what you ask? Where you go? Two days, three at most. The edge. Nothing else."

"Lift the evil from our bellies."

"Nothing out there!" Milius screamed at her. "An edge. Frost, fire, serpents big as three ships like this."

"Lift the evil."

Quite mad. They were plain men against demons who would kill for no prize but the act. At a sign from Dorelei, Cru twisted Milius to his knees, the knife at his throat.

"Thee will look *up* to Gern-y-fhain. And mark."

"Did try to rob us. Did hear thee think to kill us," Dorelei accused. "Dost think a gern who raded with the gods will shrink from thee? Listen, then, and live to make braw tale-speaking for thy wealth. Mark, all of thee tallfolk: there *is* a land beyond. Have seen it. Be faithful, then, and keep the look of death from thee."

The knife at his throat improved Milius' hearing and did wonders for his common sense. Die now or later? He chose later and resigned himself to it in his meeting with the demoralized crew the next day.

"They'll kill us, and that easily. We can't frighten them." Milius explained as much as he understood of them. "They think they're dead already in a way. Don't laugh, I'm serious. Dead and bound for God knows where, something about being young forever. Mad, but there it is. I've done what I can, told the bitch the sickness is natural and to eat if they have to stuff it down."

His men ruminated in a growing terror on where they were bound. Absurd to think of an optimist in such a doomed company, but Sejus, rubbing his bandaged arm, conceived one small hope. "Could it be there *is* something out there?"

Milius gave him a weary smirk. "What do you think?"

The stubby little Manx sailmaker had a more practical question. "How long is it that they'll keep us alive?"

"As long as we hold due west."

"And how long would that be?"

"You ask me?" Milius shrugged, exasperated. "The damned woman says there is no edge. Well, we haven't seen it yet, and we're not dead yet."

Sejus still wouldn't leave the impossible alone. "But if there were something out there—we'd be the first to change all the maps, wouldn't we?"

If the crew was terrified of them now and didn't bother to hide it, fhain was paralyzed with fear and dared not show a jot of it; afraid not only of murder but of this heavy, changing, changeless monster sea that threw them high, over, and down, shuddering the planks, swallowing the prow only to spit up again. An endless world of sea, as Dorelei once dreamed in a safe crannog, with thunder for a voice.

They never slept all at once now. One was always awake close to the children, weapon in hand. They lost count of days since Bel-tein. Sometime after four tens of days, the drinking water turned so bad that the sailors rigged a spinnaker sail to catch the rain. It tasted flat to fhain, but they needed it to wash down the abominable dry ship's bread, the only solid food not turned moldy. When Malgon presented Milius with four large chunks of fresh, bloody meat, the master's stomach turned over at first, thinking them parts of his crew.

"Army horses," Malgon explained with considerable regret. They were not as tough or sure-footed as Prydn ponies. In the rolling of the ship during a high sea, they'd both broken a leg. The men could slice it thin and cook it. Not the best eating but not the worst, and the sailors were welcome.

"Milyod did nae think to come so far," Cru reasoned to Dorelei as they clung to the rail far forward on the pitching deck. The seas were running higher than ever, though the cold was days gone out of the wind. The horsemeat and the miserable bread kept their bellies too full to be sick, and sweet Milius had to eat it, too.

In the worst storms, sometimes Dorelei's faith deserted her. Not near the edge of the world they were, but at it, plunging through the last fringe of hissing spray, the long fall into limbo only heartbeats away, and only Cru's strong arms to keep her from screaming. Night was worst, and stormy nights beyond any word for horror. No light but dim stars here and there, the whole sky tilting this way and that over them, plunging down to black where it met the sea. They huddled below and prayed for Lugh to rise again. Starless nights when the world was nothing but dark, a pool of black and themselves drowning in it, no light but the small blue points of pale brightness shimmering below the boiling water: pallid light in the eyes of the drowned who failed too short of Tir-Nan-Og.

Then, new terrors. Dorelei and Cru stared, frozen. Not dream-flight now, but real. The monsters had found them. The ship had blundered into their wallowing, spouting midst—great black and white arcs of smooth-curving power. Huge, longer than the frail eggshell craft they clung to.

"Cru!"

Dorelei cried out in fright and wonder. Not a half-bowshot from the ship, one of the great creatures shot straight up from unimaginable depths—up, up, the impossible length of it aimed at Lugh himself, jewel-bright water streaming from its slick hide, writhing to steal one more foot of height from the air before it crashed back into the sea, rolled under, rolled on. Another leap, then two together. The moments passed; Cru and Dorelei remembered to breathe again. As the creatures veered away, Dorelei saw the majesty in the great rade. They had come to a place of magic. Where in the world of men were such creatures as these?

Is there an end, an edge? Did Mabh lie to me?

No, she told herself and the others. Beyond this nightmare was a white beach and long curraghs full of laughing fisherfolk, and beyond that the green went on forever into hills much like home. There would be hills. There must be.

Six tens of days, seven. Then the Morning of the Green.

"Salmon, come!"

All along the white-worn decks, the sailors were as intent on the wonder as fhain but none as jubilant.

"Dronnarron," Dorelei said fervently. "Did tell thee."

In the night the waters had calmed and turned from dark gray to green. And the gulls were back, no one knew from where. They'd not been astern for a month, but here were seabirds much like them. The sailors lured a few in with bread and ate them.

"Did tell thee, Milyod!" Dorelei wheeled a victorious arm at the green water. "Dronnarron. Be *close.*"

He only half understood, studying the rapidly changing sky. "Going to squall. Half-reef fore- and mainsails."

The storm came at sunset, driven by a strange warm wind that forced Milius to strike all sail before they foundered. At the tiller himself, he managed to keep them head on into the wind against the demon current. Never such a wind, like heated whips, not a hint of cold in it, and with an odd smell. The storm blew out by morning. When Dorelei climbed heavily on deck after a sleepless night on vigil, she stopped in the hatchway and gasped. The sky framed in the square of the hatch was ablaze with color. For a moment she stared, then, out of released tension and hopes strained to breaking, Dorelei began to cry.

"Cru . . ."

She stepped all the way onto the deck that no longer rolled or heaved under her. The sailors were about, some of them, yet blind or indifferent to the marvel.

"CruCru*Cru!*" And she went sprinting forward to the prow, singing in her joy. "CRU!"

"Ah, God," the wizened Manx sailmaker scowled, "and what's the weird sister on to now?"

Whatever, Dorelei danced with it, and the others, too, when they came on deck, herding the children like small, precious monkeys.

"With all of them up," the sailmaker notioned, "couldn't we be into that bag of theirs?"

Milius only barked a dry, pitying laugh for the retarded. "And do what with it, drown? Starve? Look at them up there. You'd think they never saw a stupid rainbow before."

And *such* a rainbow, closer, brighter than ever bent over the hills of home. The night's storm scrubbed the world clean and left clear blue above the green water of Dronnarron that lapped ever more gently against the salt-white planks. Gulls still screamed about them or hovered on the flower-scented breeze.

"Oh, could weep at it," Guenloie said. "See, Bruidda? Road of the gods to take us home."

Dorelei exulted, swinging on the rigging lines. "Did Mabh nae show't to me? Rainbow and the smell of flowers? All true."

"Yet Rainbow parts from Lugh," Cru observed.

So it did; not much, but a difference in what Padrec called the an-gle. Dorelei weighed the possibilities. Rainbow led them to Mabh. All they had seen, Mabh had showed her before. "Then will follow. Mily*od!*"

On the afterdeck, Milius saw the small, imperious figure pointing decisively to the southwest.

"Rainbow! Road of the gods."

Christ and saints, what now? "Yes, see them quite often after rain. Haven't you noticed?"

"Follow't!"

Follow a rainbow? Well, why not? What difference now? The edge couldn't be far past this sick, green, north-running current. Nothing was normal here, even his sea-sense was going, the smell of flowers in his nose when the closest blossom was that far behind in Ireland. Mad. He hadn't even bothered with a lookout this past week.

"Put her over," he called to the helm. "Where the rainbow goes down."

With the care of habit, he watched as they fell off onto the new heading. Then the one called Malgon bobbed his head to the hard little witch of a leader and swung up into the shrouds toward the lookout seat on the main spar.

Lugh was high overhead and still no cloud in the sky. Malgon knuckled his eyes that ached from staring into unrelieved bright green and blue, one arm wrapped about the spar, the horizon tilting to the right, level, left, level again. He was used to it now.

He could stare into the monotonous beauty ahead but not keep all his mind on it. Now and then when he rested his eyes, he thought of Padrec. They shared something apart from the rest of fhain, wove a new design into the fabric of Malgon's life. Two tens of Bel-teins this past spring made for him. Not young anymore, and so much seen. Even before Churnet Head, he and Padrec would never have been quite the same again, or the rest of fhain, for that matter. A war and a rade to the end of the world, old ways broken, new ones forged. Malgon saw it as a picture like that he scratched in Meganius' garden: not the hard line of reality but its spirit, one ray for Lugh, one sweeping curve for all the waves that ever were.

And what for the horizon? One sharp line where sea met sky, curving about him in a circle to keep the magic in. He peered ahead, imagining. The sea rolled away, changing color imperceptibly as it receded toward that knife-edge.

No, not a sharp edge now, but blunted somehow. Low, colorless, and vague, but something was there between sea and sky.

He'd been staring for time without end; he shut his eyes against the hard sunlight to rest them for the space of ten breaths, then shaded his brow and looked again.

There—a smudgy line like his own first, unsure thoughts of a picture before he scratched it out. He stared a long time as the smudge thickened, became a reality between sea and sky.

So it was that Malgon was the first of Prydn to see the mole on his back. Lugh's redeemed promise, which later and duller men called Virginia with no sense of the miracle impaled forever on Malgon's forward-thrusting arm—

"TIR-NAN-OG!"

What? What did a say high in the ropes? Slow as a dreamer, Dorelei looked up to Malgon, then followed the motion of his rigid arm. Then she was running forward to the prow, calling to the others. Fhain pressed close around Dorelei to watch Tir-Nan-Og rise up out of the west, the dream broken free of sleep into day. Guenloie scampered for the rigging to kiss her sharp-eyed husband and share it with him, while Neniane hugged her sister, crying a little, and Cru held his son high to see, hardly believing it himself.

"Ai, my bairn, now may thee sing of thy mother and father. Be the Land of the Young. Will never grow old now." *Nor would I be here without Padrec,* he confessed in his heart. *He put in me a wolf's rage, cursed me, made me hate him enough to walk. I will tell my wealth of Raven someday.*

Dorelei's prayer was as secret and personal as she held onto Cru. *Sweet Padrec, dear love. What we have done, have dared between us, I do not yet dare imagine.* "Milyod!" She spun about, racing down the deck past the sailors stunned with the fabulous as she, and halted before the master, a small study in triumph. "Make thy ark swim faster!"

Milius would do that. He could believe anything now, even Atlantis, that barnacled old Greek folly. God alone knew what a man could find in such a place. The thing took time just to imagine. They were the first. They could go home rich.

"Riggers up!" he bellowed. "Crowd her, crowd her!"

The smudge on the horizon became a long, low sandspit with a narrow inlet where the sea had beaten through. Milius put into the shallow channel to keep the spit between his battered ship and the tide. Once through into calm water with sandy bottom, there was a large landmass dead ahead and a thickly wooded island off to starboard.

"There," Dorelei pointed to it. For her, the island would be a wise beginning. There was much here as ordinary as home; still, like Mabh, she preferred water between herself and strangers, real or spirit.

First over the side was Malgon. He splashed only a few yards in the shallows before his feet touched bottom. "Be warm! Jump the ponies, then the sheep."

The ponies were unloaded by a direct if dangerous process in keeping with Salmon fhain. Cru strung them in a line with a long leader and jumped, swimming to join Malgon. Between the men pulling and the women lashing from behind, the ponies went over the side like their masters, to survive or not.

They neighed in protest, balked and wallowed about, but eventually followed the men up onto the white sand beach. Then the starved, rib-showing sheep, and at last the women and children in the ship's boat, Neniane and Guenloie singing to the wealth, Dorelei with the treasure bag, one eye on a new world and the other on the untrusted rowers.

Milius watched from the deck, half his mind agog at miracle, the rest on the treasure bag as the boat scraped bottom and swung about. Women and children scrambled out, Crulegh splashing at Morgana Mary to make her squeal. So they gradually came together on the white strip of beach: two men, three women, the children, scraggly sheep and ponies—all miserable in Milius' grudged admiration, but tough as cured gut.

Suddenly his boatmen jerked their heads toward the edge of the woods and hastily pushed the boat out of the shallows, pulling hard for the ship to make fast and scramble up the ladder. Miracle had turned to terror.

"Jesu, there's more like *them* in there."

351

*   *   *

Malgon stood beside Cru, the bow strung and ready, looking at the men who had materialized out of the wood very silently. His mouth twisted with a grimace of disgust to hide the fear. "Would thee nae know it? Tallfolk."

But were they? Under their Pict-paint, the men's skins were coppery as Prydn, and their long hair, worn in fantastic conceits, quite as glossy black. Their scanty dress was not that different, nor were the men much bigger. See? Some even with feathers as Padrec wore.

"Be Prydn." Dorelei swept up Crulegh, hesitated, then set him down to manage for himself. She raised her arm high in greeting to the wary strangers.

"Dorelei," she called, pointing to herself. "Gern-y-fhain."

There were no women in the tense group of warriors watching them, nor did the men respond to Dorelei. Among their kind, women did not speak first. They waited, still as the newcomers. Only when the small man spoke did one of them move.

"Cruaddan." Cru tapped his chest. "Cruaddan."

The most elaborately feathered and painted among the dark strangers stalked toward them, stiff-legged as Rof circling another strange hound. Dorelei started forward to meet him, but the painted man walked by her with barely a glance.

"Dorelei," Cru advised gently, "this day let first husband do't." He felt Mother's soft breast under his feet and Lugh overhead, praying to both as he moved to meet the man, trying not to limp too noticeably. They stopped a pace apart, the garish leader peering at Cru with pride and suspicion. He touched his decorated chest. "Masoit."

"Cru-a-ddan."

To Dorelei, the Ma-so-it man looked terribly stern, very like Vaco trying to brazen it out when he wasn't that sure of himself. So even in Tir-Nan-Og, some things didn't change. Neither would she.

"Would best learn to smile at us," she advised the stranger, giving him her brightest. "Be nae going back."

True enough. Milius never saw them again. For that matter, neither Milius nor his ship were ever seen again in any known port of call. The mystery and the wealth behind the white sand beach were left undisturbed for a thousand years, to be discovered again by men who wrote of it in English before they disappeared themselves in another mystery never solved to anyone's satisfaction. A very strange island.

*   *   *

From a letter to the Virginia Company, London, on the vanishment of the Roanoke Colony, September 1592—

... We met many savages with skins of a hue like to copper and of a goodly stature. However, on the north of the island and on the main land, there are others like unto children but for their broad and powerful shoulders. These were not so quick to trade or, in truth, even to parlay with us. They were not as friendly as the Roanokes, that being a pity, for they are bedight in such goldwork as Raleigh and Smith did write of, the which they regard as sacred and will not trade. They live in peace with the villages about them who, nonetheless, can report little of them. They are here, there, and silently gone, most commonly with our own valuables, particularly iron. They are accomplished thieves.

Thus far I digress only to return the surer to my argument, that the vanished company most certainly met them and knew their name which falleth on the ear as CRUATHAN and is writ in English as CROATAN. . . .

Author's Afterword:
What's in a Name?

T he name *Prydn* for Dorelei's people is my own derivation from *Pre* tanic or *Prettanic*, the earliest designation for the British Isles. Personal names—Dorelei, Neniane, Guenloie, Cruaddan, etc.—are taken directly or in slightly altered form from the cornerstone compilation of monographs, *The Problem of the Picts*, edited by F.T. Wainwright. I used the term *Faerie* for easy identification, although it is a much later term. Surely these people had their own name, pride, and concept of creation.

Before men put a seed in the ground and stayed to harvest it, they were nomadic hunters, then herders. The moving herd became a way of life. Nomads even today live by their own sense of time and in their own relationship to nature, unwilling to quicken their step as history moves ever faster. Some of them could change, others could not. If they seemed backward, remember that "progress" is always measured in terms of the winners.

Thousands of years before the first word of Celtic was heard in Britain, the Mesolithic hunters were inching north after the retreating glaciers of the last Ice Age. Some went east across the land bridge from Siberia to North America, others north and west across Europe, finally to Britain. We have labeled them *proto-Celts* or Iberians, small, dark people whose physical type still exists in the northern and western fringes of the British Isles. In the extreme north, there was at least one historical people, the Atecotti, who spoke a language with no Celtic root at all. There are fragments carved on stone in readable Greco-Roman letters that do not translate into any known Indo-European tongue.

Since *Picti* meant only "the painted ones" north of Hadrian's Wall, the term is about as accurate as calling an oriental a "gook." Undoubtedly some of the Pictish language and ancestry was Gaelic/Brythonic. Some must have been considerably older, from a time far before ca. 1500 BC when the name "Celt" began to have specific meaning. I've imagined the Prydn as one of these dawn-folk like the Atecotti, still nomad herders in a land putting names and fences to itself and about to become Scotland, people already an anachronism in Patricius' day. Their ancient language, like Basque or Lapp, would contain much the rest of the world had forgotten. Their gods, pushed into the remote hills with them, would become the demons of the stronger people, haunting the night about their walls.

Forget the names, forget the time. For a moment imagine two pictures without dates.

The Indian warrior sits his pony on a hilltop, watching the white man's wagon train/railroad bite deep into his older truth with a blade of iron. He wonders how the spirits can allow this. He has done the ghost dance to bring back the buffalo and the Green Time That Was, but the buffalo will not return.

Dorelei sits her pony on a hilltop, looking at a tallfolk village with its timber walls and planted fields. Their queer, straight lines are an alien geometry to her. She prays in the ring of stones and wonders why these tallfolk thrive where her own decline.

Where is the essential difference? Both were a people, both wanted to survive on their own terms but failed to keep up with the quickening dance of the world. Both had a concept of existence and man's place *in* nature before Christianity placed the human soul apart from it. Both were called devils by the people who pushed them out of the good lands. The Indians were overrun in a time of cameras and the written word. The Faerie/proto-Celts/Iberians were engulfed in a time of illiteracy and superstition. For this reason alone, Indians are a recorded fact while Faerie retreat into distorted legend.

Take them both without tears. Remember them watching from a very real hill, and that both had a truth quite different from our own, but one that worked for them for thousands of years before their time ran out. The same has happened to more than one people who considered themselves chosen of their gods, and perhaps it will again.

Acknowledgments

THE LAST RAINBOW is a work of fiction and fantasy, but for the framework of fact to reconstruct the Britain of the years 429–432, I found the following works of the most help to me:

In the Steps of St. Patrick by Brian De Breffny © 1982, Thames and Hudson Ltd., New York.

The Battle for Gaul, Julius Caesar, tr. by Anne and Peter Wiseman, David R. Godine, Boston, 1980.

The Problem of the Picts, ed. by F. T. Wainwright, Greenwood Press, Westport, Connecticut, repr. 1970.

The Bible As History, Werner Keller. Newly revised English translation © 1980, Hodder & Stoughton Ltd, G.B. Printed in the U.S. by William Morrow, New York, 1984.

The Christians as the Romans Saw Them by Robert L. Wilken, Yale University Press, 1984.

A History of Christianity, Paul Johnson, Atheneum Press, New York, 1970.

The Age of Arthur, John Morris, Scribners, New York, 1973.

There were also the standard works; the *Anglo-Saxon Chronicle* records burial of treasure by Roman Britons under the entry for the year 418, with the caveat that datings for that period may not be absolutely accurate. There was as well *The Gospel of St. Luke* and *Psalms*, re-read with total delight in their pure poetry; and, for as much fun as enlightenment, *The Encyclopedia of Faeries* by Katherine Briggs, Pantheon Books, New York, 1976.

Finally, to Professor Aubrey Burl, John Rowley and Roger Martlew of the 1979 Earthwatch expedition to Machrie Moor, Arran, Scotland, who taught me, through three weeks in the field, more of the common-sense nuts and bolts of Scottish prehistory than I could ever have learned from the best reference books. My heartfelt thanks.

ABOUT THE AUTHOR

With *The Last Rainbow*, Parke Godwin concludes his triptych on Roman Britain begun with *Firelord* and *Beloved Exile*. While not a minimalist, Godwin was an early student of Parker and Lardner and firmly believes in shutting up when it's been said once—an unpopular approach to genre writing, but typical of the boy teachers called "untalented, unmotivated, unwashed ... disturbed."

Through the tireless scholarship of Marvin Kaye, Godwin's early works are now in some readable chronology; hence *The Lady of Finnegan's Hearth* and *Darker Places*, hitherto numbered K.1 and K.2 respectively, must now be considered ca. K.14 and K.15. Godwin wrote his first short story at the age of eight, the year he also set fire to the family piano in a fine spirit of adventure. That he coolly denied guilt in the face of evidence also displayed what Hemingway called "grace under pressure." Somewhere among the earliest Kaye-numbers must be placed Godwin's immature appearances in *Stag* and *Male* (1952–54) and the contributions to short-lived but now legendary periodicals like *Popular Embalming* and *The American Pederast*.

Thanks to Kaye's unpublished memoir *The Giant Rat of Chelsea*, much light can now be shed on the lost or "Mississippi" period of Godwin's life, particularly his rumored contribution to the privately printed *Donner Pass Cookbook* (referring, of course, to the attributed recipe for *filet d'enfant Chretien* in which internal evidence is rather convincing, particularly in the use of basil, ginger, and pressed garlic juice). Despite these unresolved issues, Godwin is best known to gourmets for his ringing denunciation of catsup.

His award-winning novella, *The Fire When It Comes* has recently been optioned for a major motion picture. In 1984 Godwin turned to writing contemporary comedy, feeling that a script as bad as this world could only be dignified by playing it for laughs.